The Reactivation of Albert Doyle

A Novel

Author of NAKED BRUNETTE

H.J. WALKINS

Order this book online at www.trafford.com
or email orders@trafford.com

Most Trafford titles are also available at major online book retailers.

Printed in Victoria, BC, Canada.

ISBN: 978-1-4269-0409-7 (Soft)
ISBN: 978-1-4269-0410-3 (e-book)

*Our mission is to efficiently provide the world's finest, most comprehensive
book publishing service, enabling every author to experience success.
To find out how to publish your book, your way, and have it available
worldwide, visit us online at www.trafford.com*

Trafford rev: 5/5/2010

 www.trafford.com

North America & international
toll-free: 1 888 232 4444 (USA & Canada)
phone: 250 383 6864 ♦ fax: 812 355 4082

Foreword

I CAN STILL REMEMBER RIDING into Logan International Airport in Boston as a youth, with my mother and father, when my maternal grandparents departed for their native Ireland, and how I marveled at the enormous jetliners through the window a few feet away. When my grandparents returned, weeks later, we'd again travel to the airport to receive them and then drive to their home, where we were often bestowed generous gifts like Irish knit sweaters, Waterford crystal, Belleek ware, Claddagh rings, Irish linens, blackthorn walking sticks, and shillelaghs. Still being a child, though, I was more enthralled with the funny-looking money that my grandfather gave me, and the savory country sausage that my grandmother brought back in her suitcase, some of which she immediately fried-up in a pan to our delight. Meanwhile, my grandfather stood in the living room, impishly holding a bottle of clear liquid, musing over how he had again persuaded Customs Inspectors that it was Holy Water he was bringing into the country; when, in fact, it was *potcheen*, the ubiquitous grain alcohol in Ireland – moonshine, if you prefer. Times have changed.

When I made my first trip to Ireland in 1998, I traveled extensively throughout the country but stayed primarily in the seaside village of Kinvara, County Galway, where my grandfather had lived and grown up until immigrating to the United States at age nineteen. There, I was taken in by cousins I had never met, as if I were one of their own, and sampled some of the renowned Irish hospitality, for which I'm forever grateful. Shortly after returning to the U.S., I acquired dual citizenship with Ireland, which I learned I was entitled to based on my heritage. Before I visited Ireland a second time, my grandfather returned on, what would prove to be, his final trip to Kinvara, and he brought me a wooden model of an Irish sailboat, black with maroon sails, most commonly known as a *hooker* in Ireland. That sailboat, which sits on a shelf in my home, coupled with the experiences and personalities encountered during my two visits, served as the basis for the short story, "Beware Father Time," which appears in my first book, *Naked Brunette*. Due to the responses I received to several stories and novellas in the book, among them "Beware Father Time," I decided to expand the story into a novel, which constitutes the book currently resting in your hands.

Also woven, henceforth, into this story is an homage, of sorts, to the Sisters of Mercy, with whom my late grandfather and I shared a mutual association. He had been taught by the Sisters of Mercy at Seamount in Kinvara, and some of those same nuns immigrated to the United States to start a religious community outside Atlanta, Georgia. Shortly after, several Sisters moved north to found my alma mater, Saint Joseph's College of Maine, in 1912, where their successors and the college still thrive a century later.

For those who have already read *Naked Brunette*, you'll soon discover that I've incorporated a negligibly modified second edition of "Beware Father Time" into this current novel, because it serves as a necessary component of the story. For those who feel cheated due to this inclusion, I've inserted a bonus feature, "Sad Maddie Weller," which follows the novel and is a sample story of a future fiction series to be released.

May the measure of your redemption exceed the weight of your injustice.

1

Always the skeptic, I can't recall a time when I wasn't wary of fortunetellers, prophets, psychics, and the like, especially when they attributed the faculty of their clairvoyance to communications from spirit world entities or in dreams. For me, they were always swindlers and hucksters preying on the hopeless in order to turn a Euro. And then there are those con men and women who are not motivated by money but, instead, seek to bask in the public limelight while assisting investigators solve high-profile crimes. For them, the payoff is attention, which feeds their self-importance – their ego, if you will. You could've lumped them all together and tossed them into the middle of the Atlantic Ocean, for all I cared. That is, until I became one of them.

My payoff was a bit different, though, you see, which left me open to the idea that all psychics are not frauds. I'm now convinced that there are legitimate people circumambulating among us who are *activated* to serve as mediums. The implication here, of course, is that a supreme being is responsible for engaging such human hosts, ostensibly to channel details of evil deeds. And when we consider the variety of crimes that have taken decades, sometimes even centuries, for mankind to solve, one wonders what it is about a particular misdeed that impels the Omniscient One to put a "rush order" on its discovery and resolution. Surely there have been worse crimes than the one I'm about to impart to you. After ruminating considerably on this matter, I, first, determined that it wasn't so much the crime that was paramount here, as horrific as it was, but, more so, a decision by the Omniscient One to provide me with a more intimate revelation of Himself. Over time, this rationale caused my head to swell, because I regarded myself as so important that the Omniscient One had chosen *me* to stir. However, after many years passed, without any subsequent reactivation, I became convinced that the sinful pride and arrogance borne from my initial selection had dissuaded the Omniscient One from utilizing me for future service. But who can say, really. During that lull, I continued to look for hints of new engagement, and, despite my lack of service, maintained my newfound belief in the abilities of mediums, particularly those men and women roused in the same manner as me. That said, the most significant aspect of my clairvoyant experience was the bolstering of my faith in a life beyond the debauched, perishable world in which we live. For me, this was *my* payoff.

I'm convinced that in order for me to have realized full activation, it was essential to act on my obsessive notions, which differed distinctly from everyday intuitions and, I believe, were transmitted supernaturally and embedded into my being. Had I not acted, I would've continued to traipse the Earth a cursed man until disseminating details of the abomination. Upon proper utterance, the troublesome notions would then be purged from my being – this I knew, but not before townsfolk and friends had deemed me "certifiable."

It was a raw, drizzly, mid-November afternoon, and I was sipping a pint of Guinness stout at the Pierpoint, a dining establishment nestled in the seaside village of Kinvara, Galway when, across the way, I saw Gerry McBrine and Tom Casey making their approach. As I reflect back, this was an oddity in itself because, in spite of the Pierpoint's superior waterfront location with panoramic views, Gerry and Tom favored the quaint Sexton's Pub, where they were regulars. To the west, I looked out onto Kinvara harbor; to the north, just in front of the Pierpoint's main entrance, I espied a hooker. And for you Yanks studying this conveyance, I'm not alluding to a lady of the evening. There are no such adulterers adulterating this idyllic spot. A hooker is a small sailing vessel, generally one-masted, used for fishing here in Ireland.

Gerry was the postmaster in Kinvara, his brother-in-law, Tom, drove truck, and I was a geologist who had been living in the area for several years, after being assigned by the Irish government to survey and study the west central coast of Ireland, with particular focus on the Cliffs of Moher and The Burren, a rising, rocky, botanical landmass that also features caves.

"How's the business of rocks," asked a straight-faced Gerry McBrine in a playful but jeering manner as he and Tom bellied up to the bar.

"Well, there's a little more to it than that, Gerry," I responded with a chuckle and a wink.

"I'm sure there is, Albert."

"How are ya, Mr. Doyle," asked Tom Casey, waving from two stools down.

"Fine, Tom. How's yer wife, Angela? She teaches my great-niece over to the school, you know."

"I didn't know that, Albert. Angela's fine. She's very happy now that our daughter Jacqueline has moved back from Dublin. Jackie just got married last spring to a lad named Phil who also works with computers."

"Good...good. They'll do well in that field. What about yer son, Padraic...is he still up in Galway City?"

"That he is."

Turning my attention back to Gerry, I looked to return the favor of a verbal poke. "And what about *your* bride, Carolyn, Mr. McBrine? Has she put her black belt in karate to use in order to keep you in line?"

"I'm wise enough not to provoke her, Albert."

"Barkeep, these two look a bit parched. Set them up with imperial pints of Guinness, would you."

"That's very kind of you, Albert," responded Tom.

The round of stouts was not unmotivated on my part, though, you see, because I had questions for Gerry and Tom, and I needed answers. Last night, I had dreamt vividly of a poker game that took place at the home of Angus Wilde, who went missing more than two weeks earlier on All Hallows Eve. Angus, a single fisherman, was also a regular at Sexton's and often could be seen lodged between Gerry and Tom at the bar. Some people called him by his proper name, Angus, as did I, but others in Kinvara derisively called him "Oscie," a reference to Oscar Wilde, the famous writer. For Angus' fellow fishermen, though, and others who knew him well, as Gerry and Tom did, they referred to him as "Wildman."

"Gerry, it seems ironic that you and Tom would walk in here today, because I had a dream with you two in it last night."

"Is that a fact?"

"There are many curious aspects to the dream, the foremost being that I rarely recall any of my dreams at all. However, in this dream, I can recollect the most specific of details…as if it were no dream at all but a day in my life."

"We're all ears," replied Gerry as he licked some tan Guinness foam from his upper lip.

"In the dream, I'm sitting at the kitchen table in the home of Angus Wilde, but none of you are aware of my presence. Also seated at the table are you two gents, plus Angus and Haimish Devlin…and the four of you are playing that card game called poker."

"What is this, a joke?" Gerry put his pint down and looked sternly at me. Tom Casey actually got off his stool and stood there waiting for my response.

"It's not a joke at all. Why would you both react so adversely over such a trivial matter?"

"Nobody knew about those poker games except the four of us. We were playing for money and didn't want word getting back to our wives, and we certainly didn't want to attract the attention of the Garda."

"I doubt if police would bother with the arrest and prosecution of four men playing a friendly game of poker in someone's home, Gerry."

"That's beside the point. How did you find out about the games, Albert," demanded Gerry.

"I'm telling you like it is, friend. I had a dream and nothing more. But, I would like to ask *you* something. How is it that the four of you became so interested in poker? It's not something that's commonplace here… in our culture."

"I was over to America last year to tour some of the East Coast and to visit with relatives near Boston. When Carolyn and I had some down time in the hotel room, I got to watching poker tournaments on television featuring that game *Texas Hold'em*. I took a liking to the game so assembled a group to play when returning home to Ireland. We had to play at Angus' home, though, because he's a bachelor. Haimish isn't married either, but you're aware of his living arrangements up there at Seamount House – he only has a room that the Sisters of Mercy provide him with as part of his compensation."

"Well, this is quite odd, isn't it?" I then set down my pint. "I swear to you that neither Haimish Devlin nor Angus ever whispered a word to me about those games."

"Yes, it's a little too peculiar." Gerry continued to study me with cynicism.

"And so nobody's heard a word from Angus Wilde over the last two weeks. It's not like him to vanish the way he did. Angus was a dependable man."

"And you think that Tom and I might be involved in his disappearance? Mind your manners, man!"

I had neither suspected Gerry or Tom, nor was I suggesting that they were implicated, but now Gerry's defensive posture was causing me to wonder about the two of them.

Gerry had more to say on the matter. "The Garda has already been through Kinvara to question everyone, Albert. They've got a handle on the situation. Thanks for the pint."

Tom took Gerry's cue and quickly gulped down last of the Guiness in his glass. I remained at the Pierpoint for another pint and avoided chatting up other locals that dropped in, now preferring to sit alone and to reflect on that which had just transpired. Unbeknownst to me at the time, my dream last night, pertaining to the four men playing poker, had been the seed of my activation as a medium. Tomorrow, I would pay a visit to Haimish Devlin up at Seamount House.

2

THE CONVERSATION I HAD over pints with Gerry McBrine and Tom Casey the day before had left me particularly troubled because I had always known the men to be forthright. Their abrupt departure from the Pierpoint, however, now signaled to me that something was amiss. With Haimish Devlin, on the other hand, people expected deception and controversy. Life hadn't started out that way for young Haimish. He was a clever lad who had grown up in the Salthill section of Galway City, and graduated with a degree in mechanical engineering from the University College of Galway. But then, curiously, after four years of study, he never put the degree to use and immediately entered the seminary. Before Haimish could observe even his first anniversary as a priest at St. Joseph's Catholic Parish, in Kinvara, though, he managed to impregnate a woman, from nearby Gort, who he had deceived by failing to inform her that he was a priest. Poor girl and her family all nearly died of cardiac arrest after learning that the father of the child was already a father – Father Devlin. And, to add fuel to the fire, Father Devlin was shortly after accused by fellow priests of embezzling Church funds. After the accusations were proven by Church accountants brought down from Galway City, young Father Devlin was kindly asked to unfrock and depart from St. Joe's, else be defrocked, to which he swiftly complied.

After such a disgraceful public sacking from a revered institution in Ireland, the Catholic Church, most men would've fled to some quiet, remote part of the country and attempted to blend in with folk. Haimish, in contrast, it seems, had no shame. Kinvara had charmed him sufficiently, and here he would stay, taking a position as a custodian up to Seamount House, a secondary school run by the Sisters of Mercy, after coaxing the nuns into hiring him. Haimish had evidently heard about the exorbitant funds being spent on the maintenance and accuracy of the large clock located in the antiquated tower that abutted the school. Previous to Haimish's employment there, the nuns regularly had to dip into coffers and pay an outfit from Galway City to come down and maintain the clock, which many locals relied on to tell time as they passed by and looked up on the hill. When applying for the job, Haimish touted his mechanical engineering degree, and he subsequently negotiated a deal in which he would maintain the clock, in addition to his custodial duties, if the school also provided him with room and board. The nuns crunched the numbers and accordingly tendered Haimish a job offer.

It was a Saturday morning, a gray day, and a storm was in conspicuous formation off to the west. En route to Seamount House, I made a short detour over to Dunguaire Castle in order to take some pictures using the new digital camera I had received for my birthday. It's a six-day work week for most full-time workers in Ireland, so I expected Haimish to be doing something constructive as I pulled up to the boarding school.

Once passing through the main entrance doors, I was approached by Sister Mary Jude Murray, who was headed over to her room in an adjacent dormitory.

"Sister, how are ya? I'm Albert Doyle. You'll recall my youngest daughter Tessie went through Seamount."

"Ah, yes, Mr. Doyle. How've you been? How's Ms. Tessie doing these days?"

"Tessie's fine. She's running a tourist home down on Great Blasket Island... off the coast of Dingle. She found it a bit creepy at first, though, because the inn's only source of electricity is wind power, which causes the lights to dim constantly. She's accustomed to it now, though."

Sister Mary Jude chortled. "Sounds creepy, indeed. What brings you up to Seamount, Mr. Doyle?"

"Actually, Sister, I was searching for Haimish Devlin. Is he about?"

"I'm afraid Haimish is up to Galway City this morning. He claims that the statues up on the clock tower would fare better with a coat of a marine specialty paint, which is only available at a store there."

"Is that so? How's Haimish working out for you, Sister... you know, in light of his recent travails."

"Actually, pretty good...better than we had hoped for. He is, of course, working in a trade that's far beneath his skill set. But, all things considered, it's a good fit for both of us. He's been able to resolve any and all mechanical issues arising within the clock tower, and that has saved us many Euros. The savings, in turn, have benefited our students greatly here at Seamount. We've bought new computers, added some items to the cafeteria menu, and taken class trips to the Aran Islands."

"Brilliant. Well, I'll be on my way, Sister."

"Okay, Mr. Doyle. God Bless. Shall I tell Haimish that you were calling on him?"

"It's not necessary, Sister. I'll just catch up with him in town."

"Fine."

"Bye, Sister."

"Bye, now."

As I backed out of the gravel parking lot at Seamount, I peered upward at the larger than life statues, situated on the platform halfway up the old clock tower, to which Sister had alluded; the same four statues that Haimish Devlin would soon be painting. Suddenly, a single, hurricane-like gust of wind, thrown off the Atlantic Ocean, caused most of the heavy, cemented casts to rock. As I looked away, the wind died. Once more, I glanced up to the statues, and a second stalwart wind staggered some of the sturdy statues. 'Twas an eerie feeling indeed, and I dared not rest my eyes upon the statues a third time this day. This line of thinking had certainly seemed ridiculous at the time, that there was some connection between my looking up to the statues and the subsequent winds delivered. But, then again, in retrospect, I had not yet realized my recent activation as a medium. The statues, by the way, represented vocations in Irish culture, more so from the past than the present, it would seem – a farmer, a fisherman, a priest, and a nun.

Haimish had eluded me this day, and, while I believed my visit to Seamount to have been meaningful, I curiously felt satisfied that I was not intended to immediately find him. For the remainder of the daylight hours, I hiked about the Burren and took pictures with my new camera until tuckered out. On the drive home, I weighed stopping in at Sexton's for a pint, to see whether Gerry or Tom might be about, but the exertion of hiking and fighting off winds all afternoon had left me feeling battered and weary. Instead, I retreated home for a hot meal, a cup of tea, and my bed.

When awakening Sunday morning, I sat up in bed realizing that I had experienced another round of vivid dreams involving the lads playing poker. There were new revelations in this dream sequence, and I would need to search out Gerry and Tom, this day, to get answers to my questions. Angus Wilde was still missing, and I believed that I was on to something, but, moreover, I felt this visceral need to purge the notions from my being. I was confident that I'd eventually be able to find the men, but, getting them to talk, in view of their less than amicable departure from me at the Pierpoint, on Friday afternoon, might be another thing altogether.

If I knew Tom Casey well, and I think I did, I'd find him at Sexton's after Mass. Tom liked his Sunday afternoon pints, and then he'd go home to eat dinner and retire early in order to rest himself for the workweek ahead. With Gerry, however, it was hit or miss on Sundays. He had a chum up in Galway City, and sometimes the two would venture over to a rustic pub, the Quays, after Mass. In hindsight, though, I'm certain that the Omniscient One had intervened this Sunday, as I walked into Sexton's to see them both seated at the bar. Gerry greeted me with a slap of contempt upon entering.

"Well, look who's here! Tom, you don't suppose we're obliged to buy the *professor* a pint, do you...especially after his rude innuendo on Friday."

Gerry was being flippant with me, but I understood his reason. After my second dream sequence, though, I was now doubtful that he and Tom were involved in Angus Wilde's disappearance. However, one hundred percent certain, I was not.

"Nevermind, Gerry. You and Tom escaped before I could buy you another round on Friday. Allow me, please."

"And what do we get with the pints, *professor*...another round of accusations?"

"Not at all. Gerry, I know you and Tom were interested to know of my dream the other day, so I thought you'd want to know of my latest dream in which you fellows were again playing poker."

"Oh, here we go, Tom. Alright, let's have it, Albert. Out with it."

"Before I describe to you what I saw in the dream, allow me to ask you a question. In the poker games which you gents played, over the last several months, was Angus far and away the biggest winner among you?"

"Yes, as a matter of fact, he was... especially most recently," replied Gerry, now with a glum look on his face.

"He certainly took plenty of *my* family's grocery money," added Tom.

"And you were witness to that in your latest dream?" Gerry asked.

"Actually, I only observed him winning a couple of pots in the dream. But it was his behavior that clued me in that he was probably winning more than his share. As you gents were studying your cards, Angus was not looking down at his own. He had cleverly positioned several reflective objects around the kitchen...some of them everyday appliances that would go unnoticed...in such a way that he was able to view everyone's cards."

"How is that so? We were sitting in front of our cards as we looked at them. Surely we were blocking any vantage point," said Tom.

"Did Angus always sit in the same seat when you played at his home," I asked.

"Yes," replied Tom. "In fact, he regularly left the back door open and was already sitting when we arrived. I found that peculiar...that he never got up to receive us."

"That's because if one of you men had slipped into his chair and unwittingly denied Angus his seat, he would've, in turn, been deprived his winnings that evening."

"That rotten bastard," shouted Gerry out loud but to nobody in particular.

"Careful what you say now, Gerry," I said. "Remember, Angus is still missing."

"I need to know if Wildman was doing that for sure. I'm going to call his sister down in Lisdoonvarna and then drive down to get the keys to his place. She trusts me. I'll tell her that Angus has some of my fishing gear, which he does, and that I need it. When we get in there, I want to reconstruct what you've just described. Come along to Angus' if you like, Albert," said Gerry.

"I'll do just that. I'm sure it will be helpful."

Gerry tossed down the remainder of his pint and scampered out the door like a man on a mission. Once obtaining the keys to Angus' home, he'd stop back at Sexton's to collect Tom Casey and myself. In the meantime, Tom and I sat there nursing our pints while chatting with proprietor Estie Sexton. Tom had already called his wife, Angela, to inform her that he would be late for Sunday dinner.

Gerry had returned from Lisdoonvarna in less than two hours, and he, Tom, and I subsequently proceeded out to the home of Angus Wilde. Precisely as I had envisioned the kitchen setting in my dream, Angus had cunningly situated several shiny, mirrored objects about the room. Gerry strode over and removed a deck of playing cards from a junk drawer, where he knew Angus to keep them, and took Angus' seat. Tom Casey and I sat in two other chairs at the kitchen table. Gerry then dealt the cards as if we were playing. Angus was a tad shorter than Gerry, who stood 6'2", so he needed to slouch slightly in the chair in order to realize Angus' perspective.

"I would've been so pissed that I would've knocked him around..." announced Gerry as he read off the playing cards in my hand as well as Tom's, "...but I wouldn't have killed him for cheating, Albert...and neither would Tom."

"I believe you. And I'm doubtful that Haimish Devlin knew about the cheating either, because he probably would've alerted the two of you. But I still think the Garda needs to talk further with Haimish."

"Won't you be able to discover what really happened to Angus through your dreams?" Tom asked.

"I immediately told you both the details of my previous dreams because I felt compelled to do so... bound by a force I've never experienced before in life. But I have no idea if I'll continue to dream in the same manner in the future."

Gerry drove me back to Sexton's, so I could collect my car, and the three of us split up that day. During the drive, I had encouraged him to contact the Garda, to apprise them of the cheating that had been going on and that Haimish Devlin should be sought out for additional questioning. For now, though, I asked that Gerry not reveal, to the Garda, the psychic phenomenon, namely me, who was advising he and Tom, because I had a sense of the lack of credibility in which mediums are held by some police agencies. At this point, the mere mention of

my declarations could hinder more than help the effort to solve Angus'
case. For police agencies that have allowed psychic contributions, and
that advice has led to solved crimes, the agencies have sworn by their
sources; for other law enforcement entities, allowing such collaboration
has resulted in departmental embarrassments, which, in turn, has led
the tax paying public to question the credibility of the police force
working on their behalf.

Gerry contacted the Garda that evening, and they paid a visit out to
Seamount House in an attempt to question Haimish Devlin, however,
the deposed priest had been gallivanting somewhere up in Salthill,
and they failed to reach him. The Garda then requested that the nuns
call the department when Haimish returned that night, but he didn't
straggle in until the wee hours of the morning while the nuns slept in a
nearby dormitory. As for me, I was in a deep sleep also, on the opposite
side of town, and again dreaming.

3

The moment my feet hit the floor on Monday morning, I felt certain I knew what had happened to Angus Wilde. The poor fellow had surely been murdered, and I was now convinced of his killer's identity. The potent forces again inciting me to act on this enlightenment were such that I called over to my administrative office in Dublin and put in for a personal day off.

Tom Casey would be on the road early this morning, but I was confident that postmaster Gerry McBrine would be at his office in downtown Kinvara – he was. I provided few details over the telephone and told Gerry that I would fetch him at his workplace. When I arrived, Gerry's wife, Carolyn, grabbed his attention, and I gestured for him to join me outside. Although it was mid-November, and only 8:45 a.m., it was an unusually warm morning, so we'd talk outside on the sidewalk. Gerry leaned back against his vehicle and crossed his arms while I described my latest dream.

If my dream proved accurate, Angus Wilde had sadly met his demise two and a half weeks earlier on October 31st, All Hallows Eve. Every year on this night, upon the fall of darkness, Kinvara residents dim the lights in their homes, crack their windows and doors, and commence to bellowing sporadic cries, screams, and howls in a ritual, thought since so long ago, to scare the evil spirits away. The array of frightening, disturbing noises provide for an ominous ambiance in the seaside village, especially as pubs begin closing and patrons scurry in

13

the black of night to their homes, some on foot, others double-timing to their cars, trying to escape the eeriness.

Haimish Devlin didn't possess the amenities or space to entertain guests at Seamount; his accommodations were meager but free. So, after purposefully intercepting Angus Wilde, who had just disembarked from his hooker down at Kinvara Harbor, following a normal day of fishing, Haimish enticed his fellow bachelor to follow him up to Seamount that All Hallows Eve. There, within the clock tower, below the large clock gears and creaky ironwork, Haimish had arranged a makeshift lounge by procuring some ragged, albeit comfortable furniture. The two men relaxed while feasting on a smorgasbord of good grub that Haimish had copped from the school cafeteria; they sipped Jameson's Irish Whiskey, gossiped about townsfolk, and listened to the screams emanating from down in the village. After tackling half the jug of Jameson's, they jocularly began mimicking the cries, and provided a few screams of their own from inside the clock tower.

I suppose that, considering the harrowing disposition Angus Wilde would face, it was generous of Haimish to provide him with a last meal and a drink. And, given the physical requirements of their recent occupations, one would think that the sinewy, stronger fisherman could've overtaken, or at least adequately defended himself against, the less taut, former clergyman. However, factor in Haimish's methodical planning, the element of surprise, and his angry, adrenaline-charged assault, and suddenly Angus was under Haimish's submissive control. Haimish had swiftly bound Angus' wrists together using duct tape, and now he was wrapping his ankles with the same. Recklessly drunk, Angus wrangled about in resistance and confusion.

"What the hell're you doin', man! Why?" Angus shouted.

"Because you're a *feckin'* cheat, brother."

"Cheat? What! No!"

"I'm an engineer, you *arse*! You don't think that I couldn't perceive what you designed in yer kitchen...that one-hundred-eighty degree arc of mirrors behind us? You're a feckin' cheat, I tell you!"

"You're right, Haimish. I am...I'm sorry. Now cut me loose...please, I beg of you!"

"It's not going to happen, man."

If this had this been any other night of the year, Haimish would've also taped Angus' mouth, in order to muffle his cries and screams, but he had planned meticulously for this night and, in a sick and twisted way, allowed Angus' screams to blend with those already pervading the night air in Kinvara. It was now 10 p.m. After Angus' hands and feet were securely bound, Haimish removed a twenty-foot section of medium-sized rope, with a noose tied at one end, which he had concealed in a toolbox. Angus screamed wildly at the sight of it. He slipped the noose over Angus' head while Angus hopped about trying to escape. Haimish promptly punched him in the gut, and Angus doubled over, falling to the floor. Haimish then quickly climbed the ladder that led up to the large clock gears while holding the opposite end of the rope. He fed the rope in between two slow moving gears, and with each passing minute the slack in the rope lessened. In Haimish's practice run of the hanging, a week earlier, the mechanical engineer was able to calculate that Angus' body would be entirely suspended just minutes before midnight, and he would likely be dead as the minute hand reached twelve.

For the next two hours, Haimish Devlin sat in a comfortable chair and drank whiskey while occasionally standing up to knock Angus Wilde down, as the cheat fought to break himself free. Haimish verbally taunted Angus, and Angus desperately appealed to Haimish to spare his life.

"That's where my dream ended, Gerry. I woke up with the image of Angus still standing, because the slack in the rope had reduced so. He was then only waiting to be gently hoisted to his gradual death."

"We've *got* to go talk to the Garda, Albert. It's time you came clean about your psychic abilities but, more importantly, we've *got* to get into that clock tower. You're confident that Wildman is dead, but there's a chance he may still be alive. Based on where your dream ended, Haimish may have only been trying to teach Angus a valuable lesson. But, if Haimish really is dangerous, we're going to need the Garda at our side."

"Agreed." I had much trepidation about disclosing the details of my dreams to the Garda, because I had a reputation to protect. But, then again, there was this force compelling me to see the matter through.

The Garda Homicide Unit for County Galway was presently operating out of a small installation up off of College Road in Galway City. It would take Gerry and me about thirty minutes to reach there, so I asked if he might drive, because I needed to focus on how I wanted to present my revelations to police.

Gerry and I entered the facility and requested to speak with a detective. We waited less than five minutes and were called into the office of Inspector Pearse McElwee. My palms were sweating and my voice trembled as I began to tell my story. I wasn't so much nervous about the content of my account, as I was the source, because to sit down and ask police to look into a matter because of some unusual dreams I'd been experiencing was no less than mortifying.

"If you turn out to be truly psychic, Mr. Doyle, I want you to know that you're not a phenomenon...you're not unique in these parts is what I'm trying to say," said Inspector McElwee. "There's a young woman named Trish Jennings, from Castlebar, who has assisted us with several murders over the years. Trish has never provided us with a bad lead."

"Well, I have to tell you, Inspector, that I feel relieved to hear that."

"But, let's not get ahead of ourselves. We must, first, prove your allegations and assertions. And, for Angus Wilde's sake, I hope that you're wrong."

"My friend Gerry and I would like to tag along when you go up to Seamount in Kinvara, if that's permissible, Inspector. We're interested to look inside the clock tower."

"I think we can allow that...although I would ask that you keep your distance as we confront Haimish Devlin...if he's there at all."

Inspector McElwee summoned a uniformed officer to join him, and the two drove to Kinvara as Gerry and I trailed close behind.

As we accelerated up the drive, leading to Seamount, I noticed that, finally, progress was in sight. There, on the platform level, half-way up the old clock tower, stood a shabbily dressed Haimish Devlin. It was a clear, dry autumn morning, and Haimish was painting the first of four statues. As our two cars pulled into the parking area, Haimish discontinued painting and stood there with the paintbrush raised in his hand. He had clearly made out the police car and now studied Gerry and me as we climbed out of Gerry's car.

"Any word on Angus Wilde?" Haimish yelled down to our group.

"Actually, we *are* here concerning Angus. Would you mind coming down, Mr. Devlin," requested the Inspector.

Haimish laid his paintbrush down on the paint can and wiped his hands clean on a rag hanging from his belt. He walked through a door on the platform level, into the interior of the clock tower, and down a narrow set of wooden stairs to the ground level. He then emerged from a door that led out to the gravel parking lot.

"Mr. Devlin, I'm Inspector McElwee of the Garda out of Galway City. You don't mind, do you?" McElwee's latter remark signaled for the uniformed officer to pat Haimish down for any weapons.

"What the hell's this?" Haimish objected.

"Just police procedure. Mr. Devlin, our investigation concerning the disappearance of Angus Wilde is ongoing, and, in order to narrow the field of suspects, we're re-interviewing those people that were closest to him."

"I wasn't close to him! I was a friend from town who played cards with him from time to time and saw him in the pubs. It's not like we were best friends!"

"Be that as it may, Mr. Devlin, where were you on All Hallows Eve?"

"I was right here…in this very clock tower…eating a dinner I brought in from the cafeteria, and wetting my whistle with some Jameson's."

"And you didn't see Angus Wilde at any time during that evening?"

"No, sir, I did *not*."

"Take us inside the clock tower, if you would, Mr. Devlin."

The four of us followed Haimish a few yards to the clock tower but not before the uniformed officer hustled in front to open the door and enter first. "Allow me," he said. The officer then strode about scanning and probing for weapons while our group filed in behind. Suddenly, I experienced a rush of anxiety as we stepped into the clock tower and stood below the guts of the great clock. Anxiety, because I was certain that Angus Wilde had died here, and that his killer now stood among us. As I gazed up to study the inner workings of the clock, I recognized that the features matched perfectly with those of my dream the night before. I had never had reason to enter this space, but the familiar setting now added a cold chill to my nervous sweat.

"This is quite a retreat you've arranged for yourself, Mr. Devlin. You could even entertain here if you wanted to," prodded the Inspector.

"It's just a place to relax. My living quarters are scant."

"Are the nuns aware of your little haven?"

"The sisters are a sharp bunch, Inspector. There's not much that escapes them here at Seamount."

Recalling my description of the purported method in which Angus Wilde was hanged, Inspector McElwee climbed the ladder leading up to the gear works. Upon reaching the top, he immediately pulled a thick, residual strand of hemp that the gear teeth had evidently chewed off as the rope gradually passed through the gears.

"You maintain this clock…isn't that so, Mr. Devlin?" The Inspector had turned and shouted down to Haimish.

"Aye. That I do, Inspector."

"What would a piece of rope be doing up here in the gears?"

"I haven't the foggiest, Inspector. It could've come from most anywhere."

Inspector McElwee clasped the strand of rope in one hand and made his way back down the ladder. He then proceeded directly over to the toolbox, where Haimish had concealed the noose, according to my dream. I glanced over to Haimish, who now plainly looked uneasy. The Inspector opened the lid of the toolbox and removed the top tray to examine the contents underneath. The metal box contained tools only.

"You're certain that you know nothing about the disappearance of Angus Wilde…is that your position, Mr. Devlin?" The Inspector was now up in Haimish's face, invading his personal space and attempting to make him feel uncomfortable.

"That's right, Inspector. I hold no grudge against Angus."

"I hope for your sake that you're telling the truth, Haimish, because my department will be inclined to come down on you very hard should we develop information to the contrary."

"I understand perfectly, sir."

"Now, let's have a look at your dormitory room."

"Aye, whatever you say, Inspector."

The subsequent search of Haimish's personal quarters rendered no incriminating evidence, however, the uniformed officer accessed a fingerprint kit and proceeded to dust the room, as well as the clock tower lounge. Meanwhile, Inspector McElwee asked that Gerry and I leave Seamount, and the Inspector took Haimish to a school conference room, where he interrogated him for more than an hour. He also interviewed some of the nuns. After departing Seamount, the Inspector telephoned Gerry McBrine to ask him a few questions, unfortunately about me, with particular focus on my state of mind. The Inspector inquired if I had experienced any trauma or stressful events in life that Gerry thought might be affecting my mental health. The Inspector neglected to call me that day, nor would he at any time in the near future.

I used the remainder of that day-off to return to the Burren. It was a beautiful day not to be wasted. I didn't really need to clear my head; my purpose was merely to engage in sufficient strenuous activity so that I slept well enough for my mind to again be fertile ground for dreaming. This haunting ordeal concerning Haimish Devlin and Angus Wilde needed to come to an end, now as much for me as for them.

Regrettably, my efforts at facilitating new dreams had been unsuccessful overnight. While I was certain I had dreamt, my inability to recall anything remarkable left me feeling distressed, and I lingered in bed the following morning. I had dreamt vividly for three consecutive nights of Angus, Haimish, Gerry, and Tom, and their goings-on, however, had now come up empty. Eventually, I rolled out of bed, fixed myself some fried eggs, ham, and black coffee. I started to feel better, so decided to drive down to the Cliffs of Moher to resume a surveying project I had been working on, related to the erosion of the Cliffs. I had some latitude in my work and definitely needed a change of scenery.

4

THREE DAYS LATER, ON a Friday, I was finishing up the week's work down at the Cliffs and decided to stop in for a pint at McDermott's Pub in the town of Doolin, County Clare, on the way home to Kinvara. Two things I'm sure of in life are that word travels fast and that people can be cruel. I had been sitting at the bar and scarcely got the first mouthful of Guinness into me when this old timer, older than myself, leaned over and asked, "Did you hear about the *nut job* up in Galway who claims he's psychic? He's had the Garda runnin' all over the county trying to solve a crime because of some dreams he had."

"Do tell," was my only response. I let the man go on with himself, as he described what he thought he knew. I had finally heard enough from this fellow, who knew a lot about nothing, and I essentially guzzled the remaining half-pint of stout. "Gotta run," I told him.

I'd be back home in Kinvara in thirty-five minutes, but, as I drove along, an immense feeling of humiliation pulsed through me. If word about my self-professed supernatural abilities had already reached County Clare to the south, then it had surely spread in other directions as well. I nearly veered off the road when imagining the scale of gossip that had evolved in the pubs of Kinvara, where this ordeal had all began. (I had been commuting back and forth each day to the Cliffs, over the past week, but chose not to stop in for a refreshment once reaching Kinvara, instead opting for the comfort of my home). Would I ever be able to venture into town again without subjecting myself to the mocks and glares of townsfolk? I refused to subject myself this night, anyway. I drove directly home, prepared a hot bath, and cracked open a bottle of Jameson's that had been sitting on a shelf in the pantry for nearly five years. I ate leftovers.

Providence. Sweet, sweet providence – unfortunately, not for Angus Wilde or Haimish Devlin but for me. I had suffered much over the past week and even prayed for a miracle. When awakening on Saturday morning, I realized I had experienced a whole new series of revelations. Now I had to persuade Inspector McElwee to again act on the lead I would provide him. I decided to call Gerry McBrine first, however, with news of the dream that manifested overnight.

"Gerry, Albert Doyle here. Have you heard from Inspector McElwee this past week?"

Gerry had not, and I later learned that the reason the Inspector had not been in contact with any of us in Kinvara, over the last several days, was that Gerry, Tom, and myself, in addition to Haimish Devlin, were *all* being investigated in connection with Angus Wilde's disappearance, because there had been suspicions in the Garda Homicide Unit that my presentation, with psychic overtones, may have been a smoke screen designed to shroud our entanglement.

"No, Albert, I haven't heard from the Inspector or anyone else at the Garda. Where are you?"

"I'm at home. Gerry, I hadn't dreamt about Angus, Haimish, or you fellows, or the clock tower all week long…but, then, last night, I began dreaming again. As I awoke this morning, I came to realize what Haimish had done with Angus Wilde's dead body."

"Albert, are you sure you want to carry on with this? Most of the people between here and Galway City, who have heard about all this psychic business, think that you've flipped your wig. And despite the accuracy of your accounts at the home of Angus and the clock tower, I'm inclined to think the same."

"I'm sorry to hear you speak that way, Gerry… but I could only operate with the information as it was being imparted to me by the Omniscient One. Things are different now. I'm going to be able to give the Garda the location of the body. This should bring closure to this ordeal for all of us, and then we can get on with our lives. I imagine this has been quite a distraction for your family…and for Tom's."

"Indeed it has. It's been very stressful. Where is it that you're contending Angus' body to be located?"

"It's up to Seamount. Gerry, I'd like you to do a favor. I'm going to ask you to go out on a limb for me. Even though I haven't seen the body yet, I want you to call Inspector McElwee, to inform him that I was dreaming again, and this time I know where Angus is, and that he's dead."

"Albert, you're putting us all in a precarious situation here."

"I know it, Gerry…but you must admit that I've been correct about everything, so far. All we were missing was a body. I promise you that Angus is up there. Please call Inspector McElwee. I'm going to drive up to Seamount ahead of ye. I'll be waiting."

"All right, Albert, I'll call the Inspector."

"Thank you, Gerry. Bye."

"Bye."

After my wife died, and my second daughter, Tessie, moved away, I converted a spare bedroom in my home into an office. Aside from the standard office equipment, I stored the tools of my geology profession in a trunk in the room, to include a mini-jackhammer used for taking samples from rocky outcrops. I removed the jackhammer, placed it in the boot of my car, and made the short drive to Seamount.

I now stood in the gravel parking lot at Seamount, again having encountered Sister Mary Jude, this time, headed to her car.

"Mr. Doyle, you're back for *another* visit? "What's cookin' *this time*," she queried me with a contemptuous intonation and corresponding countenance. Sister Mary Jude and the other nuns had been, needless to say, inconvenienced by all the ruckus I had caused earlier in the week with my allegations about Haimish Devlin.

"The Garda will be joining me here shortly, Sister. I'm afraid we're going to have to continue our search."

"Well, I hope your search doesn't have anything to do with Haimish. He apparently left us yesterday afternoon. Nobody's seen him since. He slipped a letter of resignation under Mother Superior's office door, which she didn't discover until this morning. Haimish wasn't supposed to go anywhere while the Angus Wilde investigation is being conducted, without first informing the Garda. I called up to Galway City this morning, and they said they received no such call from Haimish."

"Such an abrupt departure. That is troubling. What did he state as his reason for resigning, Sister?"

"He was seeking a position with more 'intellectual stimulation,' it seems."

"But he loved Kinvara...I would imagine he'd be staying."

"I don't know. I truly don't. I think that for those of us in Kinvara, who have come to know Haimish, he has proven himself to be a bit of an enigma...not unlike *yerself*, Mr. Doyle."

This Sister of Mercy was being uncharacteristically merciless and unfair with me, and I was about to provide her with a retort not to her liking when, suddenly, up the Seamount drive, arrived Inspector McElwee. As he parked in the lot, Gerry McBrine and Tom Casey were thirty seconds behind in Gerry's car. The two had undoubtedly been surveying the entrance to Seamount, to see if, and when, Inspector McElwee was going to act on the information that a body would be found. Sister Mary Jude delayed in anticipation that we might need her assistance, while I opened the boot of my car to remove the small jackhammer.

Inspector McElwee studied the tool in my right hand.

"Whaddya have planned for us, Mr. Doyle?"

"I've got a dead body to show you, Inspector, but first we need to access it. If you men would follow me, please."

Inspector Pearse McElwee, Gerry McBrine, Tom Casey, and myself entered the clock tower from the ground level. We then climbed the narrow set of wooden stairs to the door that led to the platform level, where the four statues stood. It was fortuitous that Tom Casey had joined us that morning, seeing that he normally worked Saturdays, but he had taken the day off to help his daughter and son-in-law move into their new home. We would need his muscle. I led the men over to the statues and stood before the fisherman.

"We need to tip this statue, men."

"What the hell's this all about, Doyle," demanded the Inspector.

"Angus Wilde's body is inside the statue of the fisherman, Inspector. These statues are made from concrete casts and are heavy, but they're also hollow. In my dream last night, I was able to perceive Angus' dead body inside one of the statues, and I believe Haimish stuffed him up inside *this* statue because Angus was a fisherman. Over a week ago, I came out here to attempt to speak with Haimish, and some tremendous wind gusts were blowing in off the ocean, winds so strong that they caused the statues to rock back and forth...all except the fisherman. I think that the added weight of Angus' body stabilized the statue of the fisherman, and I believe that I was intended to see it...by the Omniscient One."

"Oh, is that so? Well, you're really living in a fantasy-world up inside that head of yours, aren't you, Mr. Doyle? As big and heavy as these statues are...how is it that one man with the scrawny, priestly arms of Haimish Devlin could manage to tip this statue without assistance and without scathing the platform? And, how did he break the concrete base of the statue without alarming the good sisters, drag a dead body out onto the platform, and stuff it up inside... without the nuns or the student population taking notice, re-seal the base of the statue, and then stand it back up by himself. Explain to us all how this miracle occurred, would you, please, Mr. Doyle?"

"You're overlooking the most important attribute of the killer, Inspector. He approached the process with the mindset and skills of an engineer. First, he did all his handiwork during the Devil's hour, at 3 a.m., when everyone was fast asleep. He had hanged Angus by midnight and only needed to wait three hours before beginning his work, which was well planned out. Apparently, he fashioned some kind of fulcrum to aid him in the raising and lowering of the statue, which, as a mechanical engineer, he easily could've rigged using the gears and cables inside the clock tower. He only had to run the cables through this doorway to harness the statue. Upon prostrating the statue, he needed to perform probably the trickiest part of the operation – he had to breach the bottom and make the opening wide enough so that he could push Angus' body through the hole, and he had to accomplish it without the use of noisy power tools. He used a mason's chisel, I suspect. Once stuffing Angus' body inside, he sealed the bottom using quick-drying cement. Then, it was only a matter of raising the statue, with the same fulcrum system he had devised, to its normal position."

I thought that my explanation had sounded reasonable and logical, and as I glanced over to Gerry and Tom they didn't seem to take exception to anything I had said. They only continued to stand stoically, like the statues in our midst, waiting to hear the Inspector's response.

"Well, that's a nifty *theory*, isn't it? But what are the chances that anything like that actually happened here? None, I say. Haimish Devlin is a fornicator and a thief, but you'll have to show me a body before I believe he's a killer, too. But, I'll tell you what, Doyle…you took the trouble to haul that tool up here, so we're going to put it to use. And after you destroy the bottom of *that* statue, and find nothing, and then decide to tip and open up the remaining statues, which I'm sure you'll want to do, I'm goin' fishin', and I'm gonna let the good sisters have at ye."

Inspector McElwee *was* correct about one thing. If we didn't find Angus Wilde's corpse up inside the statue of the fisherman, I would want to view the innards of the other three.

I was the eldest and slightest among us four men so stood off to one side and pushed on the statue while the three younger, stronger men eased it down. I sweated in nervous anticipation, to see the bottom of the statue, because, if Haimish Devlin had breached the original base and sealed it with quick-drying cement, there would be evidence of such.

With the statue now fully prostrated, I stooped over to examine the bottom. The cement was dark and fresh looking and didn't match up with the surrounding concrete.

"Take a look, Inspector."

McElwee's face quickly transformed.

"Let's open it up," he said.

The mini-jackhammer, I used, contained a sizeable battery and was rechargeable so that it could be deployed and used remotely. If I ran out of juice, I could always plug its cord into a power outlet, but I expected this to be light work. It was, as I concentrated on the area where the dark, less resistant cement prevailed.

After I cleared roughly a fifteen-inch diameter area, we glimpsed an object that didn't belong within the statue: the bottom of a shoe, a generic workman's boot worn in any number of trades. Inspector McElwee reached inside and pulled the boot through the jagged hole.

"I recognize that boot," said Tom Casey. "It belongs to Wildman. I've sat with him enough times at Sexton's to know that it's his."

The boot was also still attached to Wildman's foot. I continued to chip, grind, and drill away, using my tool, until I had cleared away much of the base of the statue. In the interest of evidence that might proceed from inside the hollowed cast, Inspector McElwee then leaned over the railing and asked Sister Mary Jude to kindly fetch a broom, so that we could sweep away the cement chips and other debris before extracting the body. Tom Casey took the broom from the nun, at the top of the stairs, to spare her from viewing what would follow. After the clean-up, Inspector McElwee and Gerry McBrine each grabbed onto a boot and pulled the foul, decaying corpse of Angus Wilde from inside the statue. Taped to Angus' shirt was a piece of paper with the words, "Here lies the stinking body of a stinking, cheat fisherman." The handwriting would later be matched up with that of Haimish Devlin's.

Consistent with police procedure, the Garda had already been attempting to locate Devlin both up in Salthill and Kinvara, following the earlier call by Sister Mary Jude to inquire if Haimish had informed the Garda of his intended departure. Now a regional manhunt for the murdering, deposed priest had ensued.

5

THE TRAIL FOR HAIMISH Devlin remained cold for three days, following the discovery of Angus Wilde's body inside the fisherman statue at the Seamount clock tower, until Angus' sister from Lisdoonvarna provided police with a curious lead. She and her husband had driven up to Kinvara to arrange for the disposition of some of Angus' personal belongings and, upon riding down to the harbor, to access her brother's hooker, they discovered the small sailing vessel to be missing.

The Garda had not been able to prove that Haimish Devlin stole the hooker belonging to Angus Wilde, but he did, and I knew it, albeit at a much later date. In their search for the hooker, possibly being navigated by Haimish, the Garda deployed air and watercraft in order to scour the west coast of Ireland and beyond. Authorities calculated how far he could've traveled, according to estimates of when the boat had gone missing, and searched as far north as Malin Head and as far south as Cork Harbor, but to no avail. The Garda subsequently speculated that virtually anyone with knowledge of the fisherman's demise could've stolen the boat.

Before Haimish fled in the hooker, he broke into Wildman's home, I would also later learn, and located and removed the cheat's stash of winnings totaling almost three thousand Euros, a crime also committed at the Devil's Hour.

Almost a year to the day after Angus Wilde's body was discovered, and Haimish Devlin had gone missing, I experienced two more meaningful

27

revelations, both of which were communicated to me in vivid dreams by the Omniscient One. I considered His points of advice, to me, to be post-resolution, though, for reasons I will divulge momentarily. The first revelation I was able to verify through the assistance of my *friend*, Sister Mary Jude Murray, who I had gained the newfound respect of following my psychic contributions, which led to the crime solving up at Seamount. It seems that, long ago, back in 1878, four Sisters of Mercy had secured some donated land in Kinvara and opened a primary school. In 1921, they subsequently acquired Seamount House and started a secondary boarding school. The nun that led the effort was Sister Aloysius Doyle, who I learned was my great, great, aunt on my father's side. I also gathered from the dream that it was Sister Doyle's "nudge" to the Omniscient One that had put the rush order on the discovery of the crime, and, that I, her far removed nephew, was the instrument chosen to facilitate such.

Ironically, the family that had petitioned a wealthy landowner to donate the land to the Sisters, long ago, had been the Murrays, from whom Sister Mary Jude was descended.

Sister Aloysius Doyle's spirit no doubt dwells at Seamount, probably in a protective way, and perhaps she couldn't bear the idea of poor Angus Wilde decaying up inside the statue. Other times, I think that she was able to foresee, from her eternal perspective, additional horrific misdeeds that would proceed from Haimish Devlin's retention at her beloved Seamount, and that she wouldn't allow them.

In my second revelation, which, to date, I've yet chosen to verify, because attempting to do so might put me at a variety of risks, I'm certain that I know of Haimish Devlin's whereabouts, what his current occupations are, and how he escaped from Kinvara one year ago. The difference between *this* vivid dream and all the others is that I presently feel no compulsion to act on it in order to purge it from my being. It's almost as if the Omniscient One provided me this latter revelation for informational purposes, so that I could get some closure on the matter. If He's testing me, however, to see what I'll do with the knowledge, I've done nothing with it at the time of this writing.

I gathered from my dream that, anticipating his departure from Kinvara, Haimish had been keeping a close eye on the weather. Specifically, he was waiting for stronger than average winds to help drive his hooker swiftly to the south. The Devil, no doubt, aided in providing the ideal conditions for Mr. Devlin to take sail at the Devil's Hour, which he did, promptly at 3 a.m.

By the time Irish authorities had been searching as far away as Cork Harbor, Haimish was already braving the open-sea waters, far south of there, in the Bay of Biscay, and hadn't slept for nearly forty-eight hours. He remained in open waters until eventually reaching the northern coast of Spain, where he moored in a small seaside fishing village, ironically, not too unlike Kinvara. He only stayed long enough, though, to replenish himself and his supplies and to apply some of the marine specialty paint he had purchased in Galway City the morning I first went up to Seamount. The hooker formerly belonging to Angus Wilde now looked nothing like the vessel it had once been.

Haimish then departed northern Spain, safely hugging the Iberian Peninsula, and continued to guide the small sailing vessel southward. With fantasies of life on the French Riviera, he contemplated steering east through the Strait of Gibraltar, into the Mediterranean Sea, but, later, settled on a place more subdued and tropical. He remained on a southerly course until, at long last, reaching the Canary Islands, an autonomous territory of Spain, located off the northwest coast of Africa. Once there, he hopped from island to island, sampling local culture, food, and women. Initially, he spread himself between, La Palma, La Gomera, and Tenerife to the west; later, preferring Fuerteventura to the east. And it was on the island of Fuerteventura, which he had yet to defile through any means, that Haimish Devlin began to call home. Whenever feeling the urge to sow his wild oats, he launched his hooker and sailed to one of the western islands. Otherwise, he based himself in Fuerteventura, where he befriended a lone pastor with a small, remote parish, and, first, as a substitute, and, then, later, on a full-time basis, a fully-frocked, Father Devlin, was again saying Mass.

6

CURSES! BLOODY FREAKING CURSES!

It's been seven long years since we discovered Angus Wilde's foul, decaying corpse up inside the hollow fisherman statue at the Seamount clock tower, and just when I was certain the Omniscient One would no longer summon me for future service, he proceeds to embed a seedling into my being that compels me to again act on the information.

Despite the tragic events that came to pass in Kinvara, and anxieties caused to all in the process, there was a time when I yearned to be returned to service as a medium, because of an innate desire to know more about who and what lurks "on the other side." However, in the seven years that passed, I had retired and grown content to live as a simple pensioner. The Omniscient One knows that I now possess the freedom and means to act on any imperatives that arise in life, self-initiated or otherwise, and I thought, perhaps, *that* had been the reason for my reactivation. But, once realizing the Omniscient One's true objectives, I comprehended precisely why He had chosen *me* to rouse:

It was an early Saturday morning in the month of March, and I sat sideways on my bed, having risen and swung my legs onto the floor. I rested the heels of my palms on my knees and, not one to dilly-dally, pondered what I wanted to do with the day ahead of me. There were definitely days since my early retirement when I had felt lonely and sorry for myself, and this day started out as one of them. My wife had long been dead – fourteen years, in fact; with one daughter Tessie living far away on an island down off the coast of the Dingle peninsula, and the other daughter Jodie engaged to be married in Dublin. What in the dickens was I dreaming about overnight that made me feel as though I had run a marathon? I certainly didn't *feel* well-rested, in spite of having slept straight through for seven and a half hours. Unfortunately, the revelations of that dream came to me as I stood before the mirror with a razor up against my chin. *Holy Mother of God, not Haimish Devlin!* I shouted out in the empty house, save for myself, while blood trickled down my neck.

Readers will recall me recounting having received a professedly final "transmission" from the Omniscient One that provided details of Haimish Devlin's means of escape from Ireland, as well as his destination, following his heinous crime. As aforementioned, I elected not to act on the information, because I incongruously felt no compulsion to do so, relative to previous communiqués; but, moreover, I felt satisfied that we had solved the Angus Wilde murder case, and, after putting many in our seaside village through hell, people needed a respite. The foremost issue that continued simmering on my mind, however, was that Haimish Devlin would ultimately learn, through any number of modern resources, that his crimes had been discovered, and that I was the chief protagonist responsible for bringing him to light. And, given his vengeful history, and ability to slither away like a slippery eel, in that vein, I deemed the fugitive a threat to my family and friends, not to mention myself.

Well, it soon became clear that the Omniscient One would employ the same methodology, used seven years earlier, by leaving breadcrumbs as a means to direct me, with those breadcrumbs largely taking on the form of embedded dreams. Speaking from personal experience, this approach causes real trepidation when one is dealing with life and death situations and being led blindly through the process and not always knowing how and when to act. So, I suppose that's where faith comes in. Whether He utilizes this same method with other mediums remains a matter of some curiosity to me.

Anyhow, you'll recall that Haimish Devlin sailed his hooker swiftly to the south, bypassing the Iberian Peninsula, and eventually settled in the Canary Islands off the northwest coast of Africa. According to my latest dream that materialized overnight, I deduced that Haimish was again in the thick of things, and there were implications of murder. In that respect, time was of the essence, and the Omniscient One was inducing me to travel to the Canary Islands to search out the killer.

At first, I considered just notifying authorities of Devlin's whereabouts, according to my perceptive faculties, in order to rid myself of the ordeal. Surely Inspector Pearse McElwee would be interested to hear of my recent insights; that is, if he hadn't moved on from the Garda. I soon realized, however, that each time I seriously contemplated telephoning Inspector McElwee, the Omniscient One sent my mind reeling in some fashion, seemingly to deter me from informing him. Part of me enjoyed volleying back and forth with a supreme being in this manner, but, once reminding myself of the time-sensitive nature of the crisis set before me, I prayerfully beseeched the Omniscient One, "Why not just let police handle the matter now? They're young, energetic men and women skilled in their professions. Why must a lone, aging, retired geologist travel a thousand miles or more and jeopardize himself with a known killer? I may not even reach there in time to prevent the victim's demise. Angus Wilde surely wasn't spared due to my initial activation. In fact, I wasn't activated until *after* his murder."

The Omniscient One's rejoinder was curious, indeed. *Sometimes when you're cutting the grass, Albert, you chop up a few crickets, buttercups, and toads along the way. You can't be constantly pulling up the lawnmower, and even when you do it may not be in time.* I assumed my interpretation about His reply to be accurate, or else the Omniscient One would've set me straight: the conclusion being that, in the execution of His master plan, beautiful innocents sometimes fall victim.

As stated, having been through a similar process seven years earlier, I remained optimistic that I'd be presented with recurrent allusions to the murderer's behavior and activities, so that I could calculate how to proceed. I also expected the Omniscient One to provide some means of protection, because, I was, after all, an agent working on his behalf. Or would my fate be like that of the cricket beneath the lawn mower? And, given the Omniscient One's palpable resistance to the idea of notifying law enforcement authorities in advance of my journey, I wondered what His reaction might be to me informing my former collaborators, Gerry McBrine and Tom Casey, of the same.

7

'Twas a beautiful day, and, after booking a flight over the Internet, for Monday, from Dublin to Grand Canary Island by way of Rabat, Morocco, I decided to venture out and enjoy the weather. I considered driving up to Galway City to catch a day-ferry over to the Aran Islands, but, after passing by Seamount and viewing the time up on the clock tower, I knew I should've gotten an earlier start. So, I doubled back. Instead, I'd stay more local this day and visit an old haunt, The Burren, where I'd hike and snap some pictures – that way I'd have a better chance of catching Gerry and Tom at Sexton's in the afternoon.

I left The Burren after five hours and made a quick stop at home to shovel a salmon-salad sandwich into me so that I wouldn't be drinking on an empty stomach. I didn't dawdle while there and otherwise only checked my answering machine for messages. Several minutes later, I had already parked in front of the Kinvara Post Office, just steps away from Sexton's, and I was confident that Gerry and Tom were inside before opening the door. And I say that because, although I had willfully chosen the time to enter the pub, in search of the men, I was certain that divine intervention was again working in my life.

"Hello, boys," I said to Gerry and Tom, placing my hands on their shoulders. Both men had been caught up in conversation and lurched around in their seats.

"Albert!" Gerry said, smiling. "It's been ages..."

"How are ya, Mr. Doyle," asked Tom Casey, raising his foamy glass of stout in my direction.

"I'm well, gents. Mind if I join ye?"

"Not at all. Please, have a seat." Gerry then summoned Estie Sexton. "Estie, give our friend, Albert, whatever he wants."

"That's awfully nice of you, Gerry," I said. "I think I'll have a Jameson's, Estie. Neat, please."

Estie returned with a glass of whiskey before I could even properly situate my aging frame on the stool.

"Where've you been off to, Albert? I can't remember the last time we saw you in here," said Gerry.

"Well, you know how I prefer the Pierpoint... but, you're right, I *have* taken small trips here and there." I then sipped some Jameson's and welcomed the warm sensation of the whiskey going down, after being exposed to the elements all day. "I also retired a while back."

"Oh, did you now?" Gerry said.

"What are *yer* plans?" Tom Casey asked, from two stools down.

"It's funny you should ask," I replied, and swelled my mouth with more whiskey before gulping it down. "It seems that the Omniscient One has seen fit to stir me again."

"Oh no, Albert."

Gerry didn't really know what to say beyond that, and I could sense him pondering the implications of me making a rare appearance at Sexton's this afternoon with such news. Both he and Tom remember, well, the stresses and difficulties caused by the Angus Wilde murder case, seven years earlier, when I was first activated as a medium and consequently sought their cooperation. Tom Casey said nothing and merely stared across the bar until eventually taking a substantial mouthful of stout, as if to brace himself for the news to follow, which he suspected would embroil he and Gerry.

"Gerry... I know where... " I then began gagging. Believing that some whiskey had gone down the wrong pipe, Gerry patted me on the middle of my back. But after I persisted to forcefully cough and retch, Estie Sexton came shuffling across the floor with a glass of water, in hand, to assess my condition. I couldn't yet talk but waved to let Estie know that I'd be fine. Fifteen seconds later, I had recovered.

"We thought we were going to lose you there for a moment, Albert," Gerry said playfully, still lightly tapping between my shoulder blades.

Tom Casey continued gazing across the bar, as if he had never heard me fighting for air.

"I'll be fine, Gerry," I said, and finished the last of the whiskey.

"You were about to say something, Albert. You know where... what is?"

I attempted, a second time, to tell Gerry and Tom that I knew where Haimish Devlin was holed up. "I know where..." I gagged again lightly. "I know where..." I then stood up from the bar after deciding that a change in position might help me speak.

"What is it, Albert? You know where *what*... is? Gerry's curiosity was now building, despite the awkward spell I was fighting through.

"I know where..." My coughing and gagging had now become severe enough that everyone in Sexton's gawked in our direction. I motioned to Gerry that I should leave and then waved over to Tom, who still hadn't broken his gaze: Tom wanted no part of me or my news, I could tell.

I finally recovered during the short drive home. Once inside, I hung up my coat, and telephoned Sexton's to see if Gerry was still there. He was.

"Gerry, Albert Doyle here."

"Hi, Albert. That was quite an episode you had. You alright now?"

"Yes, I am. I'm not sure what came over me. Once I got in the car I was fine. Anyway, Gerry, what I was attempting to tell you when I was in Sexton's was that I know where..." I then began with the gagging again.

"Yes, Albert... you know where... *what* is? Out with it, man!" Gerry was growing impatient.

"I know where..." Again with the coughing and gagging. "Gotta go," I only managed. Before hanging up the telephone, I heard Gerry shout, "See a doctor, for Christ's sake, man!"

Over the succeeding twenty-four hours, I repeatedly attempted to write Gerry McBrine a note in order to communicate Haimish Devlin's whereabouts; however, each time I picked up a pen, my hand cramped intensely, and I was unable perform the simple task. Oddly, I was easily able to compose a "to-do list" for my impending trip to the Canary Islands, and it was now clear that the Omniscient One, for whatever sagely reason, did not want to involve the third parties that had assisted me during the Angus Wilde murder case.

On Sunday morning, I asked old chum and Kinvara shop owner, Tom Leech, to drop me at the Galway City train station near Eyre Square. The trip from Galway to Dublin would take almost three hours and was always a pleasant one, but this journey was especially sweet because I knew that daughter Jodie waited for me at Heuston Station.

As a former geologist, I wondered if other travelers noticed the same land attributes, as me, as we progressed; in particular, the abundance of hard rock, such as granite, that prevails in the west of Ireland, which farmers use to construct stone walls and contain sheep and cows in pastures. As one advances toward the central part of the country, the presence of stone walls diminishes, and barbed wire is instead used, in conjunction with the natural boundaries of tree lines and brush, to enclose pastures.

I hadn't disclosed my recent reactivation when informing daughters Jodie and Tessie of my planned trip to the Canary Islands – reason being that I had yet to receive a second communiqué from the Omniscient One, foreshadowing how to proceed; and, while I was confident that that would occur, I didn't want my daughters worrying with concerns for my safety.

It was grand to lay eyes once more on Jodie at Heuston Station, because, in her, I could see my late wife at a young age, the similarities being so great. Jodie's fiancé, Terrence, who I had met on one previous occasion, joined her and politely carried my small travel bag. Jodie had mentioned the day before, over the telephone, that she recently purchased a foldout couch and that she would sleep there, allowing me to use her bed. I wouldn't have any of that, though. Jodie's flat in the city was expensive but small, and I didn't want to put her out, so I'd stay the night in the Temple Bar Hotel. But, first, the three of us rode back to her flat, where she had been simmering a sumptuous brisket with all the trimmings. I stayed with Jodie and Terrence three hours more that night, chatting and reminiscing, until growing sleepy, and I asked Terrence to drop me back at the hotel, where I slept like a top.

Upon rising the following morning, I realized the Omniscient One still hadn't deposited the next breadcrumb. Would my journey to the Canary Islands be in vain? I wondered.

My flight from Dublin International Airport didn't depart until 2:45 p.m., so I arranged a short field trip and early lunch for Jodie and me, after she had been kind enough to take the day off from school.

Jodie was a teacher. She hopped a double-decker bus down to Temple Bar that morning where I met her outside the hotel, and we made the short walk over to Trinity College. There, I finally laid eyes upon something that had eluded me all my years in Ireland: the Book of Kells. Interestingly, the ancient illuminated manuscript of the four gospels, styled by monks, had only recently been returned to the college, as it had been on extended loan to Australia's National Gallery in Canberra, so I nearly missed seeing it again. Jodie and I also learned while viewing the fragile book, in which only one page per day is turned, that it had sustained damage it while in Australia's possession, which explained why the curator had been storming around the display case that day. After also viewing a copy of the Gutenberg Bible, located in the Long Room on the top floor of the same Old Library building, (which, unexpectedly, I found more fascinating than the Book of Kells), we departed for lunch at a favorite Dublin haunt, Leo Burdock's Fish & Chips on Werberg Street. Following the meal, Jodie cared to ride with me in a taxi to the airport, to see me off, but, preferring not to inconvenience her, I hugged her good-bye in Temple Bar, collected my bag from storage in the hotel lobby, and departed.

Fifty minutes later, I had checked through Dublin airport, and was waiting patiently to board a RyanAir flight to Rabat, Morocco, when I experienced a star sighting. It was Tyne Daly of that former television program, *Cagney and Lacey*, in which she played a detective. Ms. Daly was joined by her two daughters. Not that any of this relates to my implicit pursuit of Haimish Devlin – just a point of interest.

8

Not even the fair beauty of the flight attendants sashaying the aisle of the DC-10 could keep me awake that afternoon. Once the jetliner reached cruising altitude, I dropped off to sleep and was disturbed one time only by a four year-old, sitting between me and his mother, who apparently marveled at the variety of subtle noises and tics emanating from the stranger next to him. During that nap, the Omniscient One didn't delay in providing me with a plethora of mostly unambiguous information. (Some details I would need to sort out and verify for myself once arriving in the Canary Islands).

I finally emerged from my slumber as we descended into Rabat, and soon felt distraught once realizing that a victim had recently fallen prey to Haimish Devlin, his kill being the same kind priest who had taken him in seven years earlier. And, as with the Angus Wilde case, the Omniscient One again illustrated to me the meaningful episodes that transpired before and during this latest murder, as though I had stood there inconspicuously amidst it all:

It seems that from his very inception as a substitute priest at Iglesia del San Miguel, in the town of Puerto Del Rosario, on the island of Fuerteventura, Father Devlin had been keeping one eye glued to the collection basket. But this isn't difficult to imagine, really, considering his earlier embezzlements at St. Joseph's in Kinvara, which contributed to him being persuaded to unfrock. You'll also recall that Haimish had managed to locate Angus Wilde's stash of winnings before fleeing Kinvara in the hooker. Thus, after arriving in the Canary Islands with a sack full of Euros, he barely skimmed the collection proceeds at Masses he officiated over. However, once Father Devlin began serving as a full-time priest, the access he enjoyed prompted him to increase his withdrawal amounts, and, over time, with the breadth of his greed getting the best of him, he conspired to rid San Miguel's parish of the aging Father Serna, in order to gain full autonomy over parish monies.

Although Haimish had largely settled on a convoluted scheme to murder Father Serna, his eyes were opened to a novel, less complicated ploy one Sunday morning as he administered the sacrament of communion. With San Miguel's being a relatively small parish, each priest served communion by himself and did not utilize the services of a civilian Eucharistic minister to assist in the distribution of communion. And for those parishioners choosing to receive the host directly into their mouths, altar boys stood off to one side while holding brass communion plates under communicants' chins, to prevent the wafer from falling to the floor, in case a fumble were to occur.

Well, it seems that, like Father Devlin, the two altar boys serving alongside that morning had a bit of the devil in them. With two lines of communicants filing up to the altar, Father Devlin typically alternated between lines, as the two servers suspended the wooden handled, brass plates. Father Devlin soon noticed that both altar boys, Eduardo Sessler and Juan MacKenzie, were engaging in a brand of mischief that evidenced their collaboration before ever stepping out to the altar, and, as a result, the boys were barely able to contain themselves:

As a matter of convention, the moment each parishioner stepped up to receive the host, Father Devlin pronounced, "The Body of Christ," prompting the communicant to respond with "Amen," and then open his or her mouth; at which point, Sessler or MacKenzie, in the respective line each was serving, prankishly rubbed the sole of his shoe against the carpeted runner and purposefully touched the brass communion plate to the neck of the communicant. The static electricity produced by this rubbing action, of course, shocked the communicant into having a religious experience for which he or she wasn't, otherwise, prepared.

Now, this is a rather superfluous way of describing the circumstances that led to Haimish Devlin's "Eureka moment," when deciding to use electrocution as a means to snuff out Father Serna, but I'm only presenting the situation as the Omniscient One did with me, in my dream, so that one can gain insight into the evil mindset of Haimish Devlin. Once settling on electrocution, Haimish merely had to engineer the rest of his plan.

After living in the same two-floor, cottage-style rectory with Father Serna for nearly seven years, Haimish had come to know his fellow priest rather well. The two men predictably went out socially from time to time, but it wasn't until Haimish invited Father Serna out for a day of fishing on his hooker that he learned of the rector's extreme hydrophobia. Haimish thought it a pity that, here, Father Serna was dwelling on this beautiful tropical isle yet didn't dare to even dip his toes at the beach. His abnormal fear of water was also sufficient that he never showered when bathing, because he dreaded the thought of water running over his face. Instead, Father Serna took tub baths, and he explained to Haimish how he let the water drain from the tub before kneeling under the faucet, and then wet his hair, to shampoo, while careful not to let water near his face; he was equally cautious when rinsing his hair. In spite of his abnormal fear of water, Father Serna did enjoy the therapeutic effects of a good soak, and, as a rule, listened to a favorite evening radio program to further distract him from the reality that most of his body was submerged in water.

On the few occasions, over the years, that Haimish had found it necessary to enter Father Serna's personal bathroom, he took notice of the antiquated radio nearby to the bathtub. His scheme now in formation, Haimish entered the bathroom, alone, at an opportune time, opened up the radio using a small screwdriver, and snipped a tiny wire to render it inoperable.

Two nights later, at supper, Haimish mentioned news he had heard over the radio about the world's largest marlin being caught off the coast of Grand Canary. He did so in order to prod Father Serna into talking about *his* radio, because Haimish knew that the rector had taken a bath the night before. When Father Serna began venting about the apparent malfunction of his old radio, Haimish described the clock-radios he had recently seen on-sale at a retail shop in downtown Puerto Del Rosario that were designed for bathroom use. Haimish extolled the modern digital clock feature, which Father Serna's old radio certainly lacked, but the feature he found most appealing was the suction cups that enabled the radio to be mounted on bathroom tiles, so that music or news could be listened to while showering or bathing. Haimish subsequently related that he thought he might like to buy one for himself and, if Father Serna also desired one, he'd be glad to purchase two. Resolved that it would likely cost more to repair the old radio than replace it, Father Serna agreed.

Haimish purchased two clock-radios the following day. After taking one out of the box, he stuck it to the bathroom tiles in his shower and plugged it into an outlet, doing so to demonstrate to Father Serna how he might set up his own radio, when the rector later passed by.

The following afternoon, Haimish obtrusively entered Father Serna's upstairs bedroom while the rector sat reading a newspaper on the first floor of the home; he glanced into the bathroom to see if the clock-radio had been removed from the box. It had, but Father Serna had elected not affix it to the tiles using the suction cups. Instead, he simply placed the radio on the same small table situated between the tub and toilet, where he had kept his former radio.

Haimish had read the warning label thoroughly before making the purchases and took notice that, while the clock radio was designed to safely withstand the kind of splashing water that normally occurs during a shower, it was not intended to be submerged. Moreover, the instructions clearly specified that direct current (DC) power, i.e. batteries, only be used while operating it near water. Hence, the consumer was strictly warned against the dangers of using alternating current (AC) to power the radio near water.

Father Serna had officiated over a funeral Mass early that Wednesday morning but, otherwise, it was ordinary day in which he only walked leisurely before the heat became too oppressive. He ate lunch prepared by Senorita Alvaro, who lived away from the rectory but came in to clean and cook six days weekly; soon after, Father Serna read a book out on the veranda, until succumbing to an urge to nap. Meanwhile, Father Devlin had returned from fishing out on his hooker, and, presently, sat alone in an air-conditioned pub in the lower level of a popular restaurant, near the marina, while refreshing himself with a glass of ale and mulling over his scheme. The day, so far, had been uneventful for both priests; the night, however, would not.

Following their evening meal, the men adjourned to the den, where they typically watched the news and discussed the seemingly sad state of the world. Once the broadcast concluded, Father Serna stood and announced that it was "bath night" and that he would retire with a book thereafter, thusly saying good night. But before Father Serna left the room, Haimish spoke up:

"Have you had occasion to try out your new radio, Ruben?"

"Yes, I have... only once. I turned it on this morning while sitting on the *throne*. I was impressed with the quality of the sound."

"It does seem to be a fine product. I'm afraid I'm having a bit of a problem with the digital clock in mine, though. I'm still trying to rectify it... hope I don't have to drive back and exchange it for another."

"Yes, well... I'm sure you'll work it out. Good night, Haimish," Ruben said and walked over to climb the short, winding staircase leading to the second floor of the rectory.

Senorita Alvaro had been predictably efficient in her post-dinner clean-up and didn't delay in departing the rectory. Twenty-five minutes later, when Haimish was sure Father Serna had finished drawing his bath, he made his way upstairs to his own bathroom, where he pulled on his radio until the four suction cups broke free from the tiles. He carried his radio with him and strolled presumptuously into Father Serna's bedroom, where he noticed the bathroom door slightly ajar. Once hearing the swish of water and music playing, Haimish, with radio in hand, rapped gently on the door.

"Ruben, I don't mean to disturb you..."

"Yes, what is it, Haimish?"

"I'm trying to pinpoint the problem with my digital clock. I wonder if I could take a quick look at yours."

"This is highly irregular. Can't it wait... until later or tomorrow?"

"I'm really very sorry for the intrusion, but I need to use the alarm feature to wake me for an appointment in the morning. Couldn't you just cover yourself for a moment... or pull the shower curtain across."

"I suppose." Father Serna reluctantly acquiesced. Now, not wishing to painfully contort his aged body while reaching for the shower curtain, Ruben merely cupped his hands over his private parts. "Alright, Haimish... take care of your business... quickly, please. I quite enjoy the radio program that's playing, and I don't want to miss any more than's necessary."

Haimish nudged the door open and shuffled into the bathroom without glancing at Father Serna in his naked state. "This won't take but a minute, Ruben," he reiterated.

Haimish placed his own radio down on the closed toilet lid, the radio only being a prop, really, to further convince Father Serna. He then reached over to stabilize the plug in the wall with his left hand, doing so to ensure that Ruben's radio stayed in place for what he would next do, which was to pick up the radio off the small table, with his right hand, and toss it cavalierly into the deep end of the bathtub.

Father Serna now instinctively forgot about his fear of water and began thrashing about the bathtub in an effort to climb out. Meanwhile, Haimish panicked because, despite the radio being submerged in water, and operating on alternating current, the small appliance just sat at the bottom of the tub. Suddenly, Haimish realized that he had foolishly neglected to develop a back-up plan, and envisioned himself bludgeoning the priest to death. But with what? A radio?

Father Serna soon lifted himself out, so Haimish reached over with his free hand and shoved the elderly priest back into the tub, all the while scanning the bathroom for potential murder weapons. Much to Devlin's relief, water finally seeped inside the radio and made contact with powered components. Ruben wasn't so much flailing now as he was reacting to the conductivity of electricity in water, as his body violently quaked and jerked. At one point, Haimish perceived an eerie green aura enveloping the priest's exposed body. The murderer had witnessed a similar phenomenon, once as a youth, when a lightning bolt hit nearby to his family's house, and the wavering "green ghost" lingered for three seconds in an area where several cords, cables, and wires converged inside the home to service a television and stereo system. This similar, gaseous-looking, electrically charged, green field eventually dispersed after a prolonged crackling noise, followed by intermittent sparks firing from the rector's eyeballs and right ear. Father Serna's body now only lay vibrating in the bathtub, and when Haimish was certain the priest was dead, he pulled the plug from the outlet.

Haimish returned with his radio to his own bathroom, and bunched up the cord before inserting it in a small compartment in the back of the radio. He again mounted the appliance on the bathroom tiles, using the suction cups, and threw a switch so that the radio operated on battery power; he made sure the time was correct. Father Devlin then called police to report his shocking discovery. Once officers arrived, he explained that it appeared the suction cups had given way on Father Serna's radio, causing it to slip from the tiles down into the tub. Haimish further opined that his "old friend probably didn't realize he wasn't supposed to operate the radio using alternating current near water." After Father Devlin showed police the instructions that came with the radio, and demonstrated the manner in which his own bathroom radio was correctly installed, officers found the theory plausible. For the time being, Haimish was not suspected in connection with the rector's death.

9

I HAD AN OPPORTUNITY TO consider my dream, of a short while ago, as our RyanAir jet taxied across the flight line at Rabat International Airport, and the foremost matter beleaguering me with curiosity was: what *is* it with Haimish and the clocks? Murder *again* using a clock? Granted, it was electrocution that ultimately caused Father Serna's demise, and, in Kinvara, Angus Wilde suffered death by hanging, but both instances involved the element of time. Perhaps it was a fascination with mechanisms or gadgets, because Haimish had been trained as a mechanical engineer. Whichever the case, I hoped the Omniscient One might, one day, provide me with some insight on the matter, because this common denominator in both murders frankly intrigued me.

After collecting my carry-on bag from an overhead storage bin, I disembarked the plane and took an intra-airport shuttle to the gate where my Iberia Airlines flight to the Canary Islands soon departed. Two hours later, I had already arrived in the capital, La Palma, and was riding in a small bus provided to guests by the Santa Catalina Hotel. Sunset fast approached, and I imagined I'd be staying a minimum of one night in the hotel, during which time I expected to receive the next transmission from the Omniscient One. The island of Fuerteventura, where Haimish Devlin ostensibly dwelled, was accessible by small plane or watercraft, but I was a little fatigued from air travel, at this point, so planned to ride on a public hydrofoil the next day.

Once checking in, I spent a short while exploring the hotel and took in views of the picturesque Ciudad Jardin and the Atlantic Ocean from my balcony, before the skies darkened. Within the charming hotel, which was built in 1890 for British employees of the Grand Canary Island Company, sat a very worthwhile pub. Famished for a proper meal, though, I'd first venture into town, on foot, for a light supper. Once emerging outside, I noticed that the area was well lighted, especially the promenade leading to the nearby marina, where two fishermen had just moored and were busy pouring crushed ice over a large container of fish, to better preserve their catch. I thusly paused to watch the men in their work. Standing unassumingly with my elbows resting on the blue metal railing, my eyes naturally wandered to survey other boats in the marina; in one respect, the boats were ordinary fishing and recreational vessels, most having been hewn by local craftsmen and featured designs specific to that region. I easily recognized one boat that distinctly stood out from the rest, however – that of an Irish hooker.

My French language skills are better than Spanish but, both being among the romance languages, I was able to make out from a sign adjacent to a wooden gate, "Boat owners and their guests only beyond this point." The two fishermen still shoveling ice were the only others in the area, so I boldly pushed the gate open and walked down a ramp to take a closer look at the Irish sailing vessel. Angus Wilde's boat had once been black with maroon sails; this boat was light gray, like that of the statues up on the Seamount clock tower, but also featured maroon sails. There was one aspect of the boat that would be a giveaway, though, if I could only maneuver close enough to examine the stern. Angus Wilde had been a fisherman but also used the boat recreationally, so, in order to give the boat a more leisurely appearance, he named his boat, "Wildman." One advantage to me taking my pints down at the Pierpoint in Kinvara, vis-à-vis Sexton's Pub or The Old Black Shawl, was that I regularly enjoyed an unobstructed view out onto Kinvara Harbor, and I recalled that the lettering on Angus Wilde's hooker had a stenciled look to it. I was also confident that, despite the boat being painted over by Haimish, unless he had painstakingly painted over the lettering numerous times, there should be evidence of such.

After moving to within about five feet from the stern of the boat, I squatted down to study the area in question. A few fluorescent tubes illuminated the marina, and some boat owners had hung solar-powered lanterns near their watercraft for security, and, presently, I didn't have the benefit of a full moon working for me, or even a crescent moon, but, through it all, I was able to make out the formations of "W", "L", and "D" on the stern. Therefore, although Haimish Devlin apparently resided on the island of Fuerteventura, the killer currently visited the capital of La Palma on Grand Canary.

Certain that the Irish sailing vessel belonged to Haimish, I scurried up the ramp and through the gate, eventually situating myself on a bench in a more dimly lit area. There, I remained an hour longer just in case the murderer returned. What I would do beyond confronting him about his slayings of Angus Wilde and Father Ruben Serna, at that point, I didn't yet know, because it appeared I was working ahead of the Omniscient One's schedule. But after an hour passed, with no sign of Haimish, now weakened by hunger, I continued into town on foot.

Making my way through the maze of small streets, I peered randomly into some of the establishments in hope of espying the fugitive priest. With no such luck, I settled in at a restaurant called The Asturias, where I ordered a piece of swordfish that came with couscous and a green salad, and the waiter coaxed me into trying one of the dark rums for which the Canary Islands are renowned. I soon grew eager to spend more time surveying the marina, however, in the chance I might still behold Haimish this night, and left out of The Asturias without taking dessert or coffee. I returned to the bench, where I had sat two hours earlier, and remained until about 11 p.m. Once satisfied that Devlin would not be coming back to the marina for any reason, I retired to my bed at the Santa Catalina Hotel.

I awoke minutes after dawn and scarcely lingered in bed, instead rising to open the doors leading to the balcony, where I gained a different perspective of the locale in daylight. I looked in the direction of the marina, but a corner of the hotel largely obstructed the view, so I knew that in order to continue scrutinizing the activities there, to include Devlin's inevitable attendance, I would need to assume my familiar position on the bench. Oddly, it didn't occur to me until standing in the shower, minutes later, with water pounding down on my head, that I had dreamt overnight, and revelations of that dream quickly pulsed through me:

First, The Omniscient One conveyed that I should relax and slow down because, while I had risen early to return to the marina, I hadn't awoken early enough. Haimish had a long day of sailing set before him, to reach Fuerteventura, and had gotten up with the birds; in the process, he upset his slumbering female companion, who he hadn't informed of his planned departure until that morning. I thusly took my time eating breakfast and decided to better explore the quaint maze of streets, boasting shops and cafés, where I had dined the night before, because the next hydrofoil didn't depart until 1 p.m. While strolling and browsing, the Omniscient One imparted yet more information pertinent to Haimish's visit to Grand Canary, which was streamlined to me in a daydream-like entrancement, and I was compelled to sit and fathom it all:

It seems that Haimish had underestimated the scale of Father Serna's popularity in the town of Puerto Del Rosario, as the rector had engendered many friendships over the years. As a result, Haimish's suppressed moral conscience unexpectedly resurrected, and he found himself overwhelmed by the emotional outpouring from grieving parishioners and friends while officiating over Father Serna's funeral Mass. Consequently, after enduring a stressful initial police investigation, followed by a two-day viewing of Father Serna's body (for which "Father Devlin" needed to be present), and subsequent funeral Mass, then a tension-filled follow-up police inquiry, Haimish naturally felt frazzled. Recognizing his need for diversion before he was to next conduct Mass, Haimish had sailed for Grand Canary to rendezvous with an old flame, who he had met three years earlier on the island of La Gomera and had since moved to the capital, La Palma. "Gloria," it was no surprise to learn, had never known that Haimish was operating as a Catholic priest.

One thing that Father Devlin had been clever enough to do, before embarking on his sailing trip, was to notify local authorities of his intended journey, but did so only because he believed he was not considered a suspect and that they believed Father Serna's death was the result of a tragic accident. And, in case incriminating evidence was developed while he was away, Devlin did not sail to Isla Graciosa, as reported, but in the opposite direction to Grand Canary; whenever opportune, he monitored local news reports.

After drinking more than his share of rum, and lecherously working over Gloria in the hotel room during those two days, Haimish left La Palma and sailed for Puerto Del Rosario (and I narrowly missed him that morning). And, according to the Omniscient One's illustrations, once safely back at Iglesia del San Miguel, Father Devlin intended to increase his withdrawals from church collections.

10

Having belted myself in on the hydrofoil alongside other passengers, I gazed back at Grand Canary and wondered if I'd ever set foot on the island again. From my perspective as a former geologist, the volcano-formed islands feature many physical attributes that interest me. *Perhaps there will be greater opportunity to explore Fuerteventura*, I thought.

The sizeable hydrofoil skimmed effortlessly over the ubiquitous ocean whitecaps that afternoon, and, once land was in sight, an announcement was made in multiple languages advising of our imminent arrival in the town of Puerto Del Rosario. I studied the island during our approach and was curious to know what appeal Fuerteventura had had for Haimish, and why he preferred it over islands like El Hierro, La Gomera, or Tenerife. Interestingly, everywhere I looked I saw large herds of wild goats, seemingly flowing up the side of barren hills; in the foreground, near a beach, goats grazed on dune grass. Minutes later, when the hydrofoil eased in to its docking station, yet more goats hovered fearlessly, as if waiting for loved ones to disembark.

Once unbuckling my restraint, I collected my travel bag and filed off the watercraft. I had every good intention of seeking out a hotel, but, first, cared to accomplish a couple of things: I fought my way through the throng of ambitious vendors, fellow travelers, their greeters, and a few inquisitive goats, to a less touristy section of the harbor, where one can better view the boats. Just as I suspected, Haimish's light gray Irish hooker, with maroon sails furled around its mast, gently rocked in the harbor waters – he was back in town.

The next item on my agenda involved scouting out Father Devlin's parish, Iglesia del San Miguel, to familiarize myself with the surroundings before returning to confront the murderer. I thusly strolled back to the disembarkation point, where drivers waited for fares, and climbed into a taxi. "Iglesia del San Miguel," I instructed the driver.

Much to my surprise, when arriving at San Miguel's parish, I noticed people trickling into the compact church. It was late Tuesday afternoon, and it didn't make sense that Mass was being held, so I inquired through an usher in the vestibule as to the reason for the congregation. From the conversation we managed in my broken Spanish and his broken English, I learned that a Mass was always said on the Tuesday eve before Ash Wednesday, to commemorate the hundreds of lives lost on Fuertaventura during a category-4 hurricane, some thirty years earlier. "I'll stay and pray for their souls," I told the kind man.

Mass was well under way, and I took a seat in a pew half way down the church on the left. Father Devlin and his two altar boys, Eduardo Sessler and Juan MacKenzie, sat to the right of the altar, facing the lector, who read the first of two scripture readings. Father Devlin apparently hadn't noticed my conspicuous late arrival, or at least he chose not to turn and look; nevertheless, once settled in, a feeling of eeriness inundated my being. (It was the same chilling feeling I experienced when entering the Seamount clock tower for the first time with Gerry, Tom, Inspector McElwee, and the killer now sitting up by the altar, to prophetically view the interior clock setting, after perceiving it the night before in an embedded dream). I had similarly foreseen how this church backdrop should appear before ever entering San Miguel's, in addition to the faces of altar boys Eduardo and Juan as they currently flanked Father Devlin.

During that moment of reckoning in the pew, I appeared calm, but my heart thumped and my hands sweated as the verification process again played out in my mind. The moment turned extraordinary for me when realizing that I sat ostensibly in the house of the Omniscient One and, among those present, I was the instrument chosen by Him to operate on his behalf.

Father Devlin's homily following the gospel was brief, which was understandable given his long, demanding day of sailing, but I must admit how impressed I was with his articulation, composure, and overall effectiveness as he spoke to his flock, and I thought it all to be a great shame, given the hypocrisy of his true life.

Once Father Devlin performed the consecration of the bread and wine, my heart again raced, because I had now resolved to take communion, and wondered if Haimish would recognize me. My hair was more silvery than when he had last seen me in Kinvara, seven years earlier, and I currently wore thick, black-rimmed glasses. Perhaps the considerable sunburn I had collected on my face, during the hydrofoil ride from Grand Canary, would further throw him; sunburn which he noticeably shared.

I continued to study Haimish's countenance as the line of parishioners, in which I ambled, gradually made its way toward the priest to receive communion. From afar, I could discern from the jerking heads of communicants, and smirking faces of altar boys Eduardo and Juan, that the juveniles were up to their old tricks with the brass communion plates. I was now just a few feet from the murderer and began to tense up, again wondering if Haimish would recognize me. Father Devlin, strangely, glanced up at that precise moment, to survey the remaining communicants, and looked directly at me, so I tried not to react in a perceptible manner.

It was now my turn for communion, and I stepped before my fellow Irishman.

"The Body of Christ," he said.

"Amen," I responded and leaned backward before Eduardo Sessler could rub his shoe on the carpeted runner and touch the brass communion plate to my neck. "No electricidad, por favor," I said, looking at the adolescent, which astonished both Eduardo and Haimish. Eduardo then drew back the plate, and Father Devlin placed the Eucharist on my tongue while looking intensely at my face.

Following communion, Haimish performed his routine housekeeping up on the altar, but he was clearly distracted and seemed more interested in remotely perusing the church pews, in a patent attempt to locate me, as his eyes shifted and darted. Once spotting me, he further dissected my appearance and, due to the distance, I wasn't sure if he was merely trying to put a name with the face or if he had already identified me, and his glares were intended as threats. Subsequently, Father Devlin was expeditious, if not blatantly hasty, in bringing Mass to a conclusion, and I remained seated as other parishioners filed out from San Miguel's.

Feeling emboldened that this was as good a time as any to confront the killer, I strode up the nave of the church and across the right transept to the sacristy. Outside the sacristy, a narrow hallway with closets served as the vestry where altar boys hung their vestments, and, there, stood youngsters Eduardo Sessler and Juan MacKenzie shedding their surplices and cassocks. Eduardo was visibly nervous, because he probably thought I was about scold him for his antics using static electricity, but then he seemed to relax some after I requested, in my best broken Spanish, that he summon Father Devlin. The altar boy again grew anxious when suspecting I might reveal his shenanigans to the rector. Unbeknownst to both Eduardo and Juan, however, Father Devlin had been aware of their foolery all along and sadistically allowed them to carry on, even to that day.

Eduardo tapped on the sacristy door, turned the knob, and entered. The lad returned a moment later, peering out the cracked door to query me in Spanish, "Who would like to see Father?"

"An old friend from Ireland," I said slowly.

Eduardo left to convey the message and returned seconds later to advise that Father Devlin would be able to see me in twenty minutes. Agreeing to wait, I emerged from the vestry and walked back across the transept to take a seat in the first pew, just in front of the shrine to St. Joseph.

Twenty minutes came and went, and the altar boys were long gone, so I again entered the vestry adjacent to the sacristy. After receiving no response to my persistent knocks on the sacristy door, I turned the unlocked knob and stepped inside; the small rectangular room was empty and the lights were off. The late afternoon sun provided ample light through a lone window, which revealed a second door that didn't appear to be a closet, so I shuffled across to open it and stepped out onto a concrete walkway that abutted a courtyard with a prayer garden to Our Lady. It would've been nice to pause and reflect and say a prayer, however, the murdering priest I pursued was obviously trying to elude me.

Reaching the end of the walkway, I gazed across the parking lot and recognized the white, cottage-style rectory from my dream, and strode across the lot and lawn directly to it, paying no due regard to a designated footpath. Senorita Alvaro observed me through the kitchen window, and walked to the rear door to receive me. Again speaking in my best broken Spanish, I inquired if Father Devlin was available. This time, I was told the priest had departed without eating the dinner she had prepared. When I asked if he carried any possessions, she responded affirmatively. Haimish was now in flight, I was sure of it, so I thanked the kind lady and left. Within minutes, I had flagged down a taxi, and asked the driver to take me to nearby Puerto Del Rosario harbor, where I cleared a few inquisitive goats and marched over to inventory the boats.

Haimish's hooker was missing.

Suddenly, in the same manner the Omniscient One had sent my mind reeling when I intended to telephone Inspector Pearse McElwee about Haimish's location in the Canary Islands, this time He was bombarding me with thoughts of a thing or place of which I had never heard. *Corralejo... Corralejo*, I kept hearing, as if hallucinating.

An ice-cream vendor, operating a large tricycle, happened by, so I grabbed his attention and asked him about Corralejo, which, he informed me, was a town up north. I thanked the man but he persisted with me until I bought a sorbet. Unsure of how long it would take to reach Corralejo, I returned to the station where the hydrofoil had docked earlier, and I asked an attendant about the town and how to reach there. No commercial boat service existed between Puerto Del Rosario and Corralejo, but buses ran several times daily along an eastern scenic route to the northern tip of Fuerteventura. Twenty-five minutes later, I was riding on a bus to Corralejo.

11

DESPITE THE STRESSFUL EFFECTS of the cat and mouse game in progress, I managed to relax somewhat en route to Corralejo that late Tuesday afternoon; nonetheless, I couldn't help wondering about the reactions of parishioners who would show up at Iglesia del San Miguel for Ash Wednesday services, the following day, only to learn that their priest had vanished. This, on the heels of losing their long time pastor, Father Serna, to a bathtub accident, in which he was electrocuted. I was also astute enough to realize that once an investigation was underway concerning Father Devlin's disappearance, that altar boys Eduardo and Juan, the church usher, and housekeeper Senorita Alvaro each would describe, to police, their encounters with the unknown, silver-haired visitor with marginal Spanish language skills.

As with La Palma in Grand Canary, I arrived in Corralejo, northern Fuerteventura, with limited daylight remaining. After receiving a lodging recommendation from a fellow bus passenger, I took a taxi to the Dunapark, another hotel with a colorful garden, which I wouldn't appreciate until morning. Once checking in, I washed up and immediately departed for the local marina to search for the familiar Irish hooker. The marina was compact due to the sparse local population, and, once certain that I hadn't overlooked the light gray sailing vessel, I resolved that my bus had arrived first. I thusly walked into town for dinner, finally settling in at a restaurant called La Marquesina, where I devoured a magnificent, thick piece of local white fish that I couldn't pronounce but which the chef had skillfully flavored with herbs, spices, and olive oil. I again left without taking dessert or coffee, nervous that the indulgence might cause me to miss Haimish.

Back at the marina, there was still no sign of Haimish's sailboat, so I walked about, inspecting the area, thinking he might've moored covertly in a nearby inlet. Finally satisfied that he hadn't yet arrived, I hiked back to the Dunapark, set my alarm, and hit the sack.

When the alarm sounded at 6 a.m., my embedded dream unraveled almost immediately. Light winds had delayed his arrival, and Haimish sailed into Corralejo about midnight, opting not to draw from his sack of cash to pay for a comfortable hotel room, instead sleeping in the hooker under the stars; he had re-launched at 5 a.m. Again, the Omniscient One was advising me not to fret but to take my time: the next leg of my journey, in pursuit of the murderer, would be to Playa Blanca on the southern tip of Lanzarote, a short boat ride which could be accomplished even faster using the inter-island hydrofoil service.

I ate a hearty breakfast in the hotel, not knowing when I might take my next meal, and checked out. It was a half-mile walk to the hydrofoil dock, and during that stroll I curiously felt like I was enjoying all this business with Haimish. It was exciting.

As the hydrofoil edged away at 10:15 a.m., I turned around to glimpse, once more, the island of Fuerteventura, and jocularly waved to a small herd of goats, in attendance, chewing on some sundry vegetation.

Time passed quickly on the ride from Corralejo to Playa Blanca, after I got caught up in conversation with the young lady seated beside me. "Mimi" resided on Lanzarote, and was an invaluable resource, filling me in on the best way to get around the island, as well as hotels and restaurants. Analyzing her saintly face as she talked, I was certain the Omniscient One had placed her with me.

I routinely surveyed the boats in Playa Blanca harbor during our approach, and, there, as plain as the tattoo on the deckhand's forearm, Haimish Devlin's sailboat bobbed about in the water. The hooker was moored remotely, relative to the nearest dock, so evidently Haimish had needed to navigate over to a dock when arriving, attach a dingy, drive his boat back out, anchor it, climb into the dingy, and paddle back to the dock.

I thanked Mimi for her advice and fellowship and bid the kind woman farewell. I then wrote a note and paid a local boy, loitering at the harbor, to paddle out in the dingy and deposit the piece of paper in Haimish's hooker, ensuring to affix so that it wouldn't blow away into the water. The note read, "*It's time to come in from the cold, Haimish. Stop running and return to Ireland and turn yourself in. Most sincerely, Albert Doyle.* " I then hired a tricycle operator, with passenger compartment, to transport me and my bag to Hotel Hesperia Playa Dorada, and I enjoyed the sun and breeze on the way.

It was mid-afternoon before I pried myself away from the scenic balcony that overlooks the beach. In one respect, I hoped that Haimish would see the note in his boat and comply; in another, as aforementioned, I was deriving satisfaction from this cat and mouse game. I hadn't yet tired of eating fish so decided to try out the inexpensive seafood restaurant Mimi had enthusiastically described. I asked my taxi driver to pause at the harbor first, though, while I confirmed the presence of Haimish's hooker – it was still there. We then proceeded to El Marisco Casa Brigida restaurant, where I tried the sea bass and ate a salad with warm goat's cheese wrapped in grape leaves (the cheese product being from my horned friends in nearby Fuerteventura, no doubt). But the highlight of the meal was a local white wine called Malvasia that Mimi insisted I try before leaving Lanzarote, and which enhanced an already outstanding meal. While polishing off the half-bottle of Malvasia, I wondered where Haimish lurked in Playa Blanca and how he would react upon discovering the note in his sailboat. The answer to that question was answered when returning to the harbor after lunch: the hooker was no more.

Just when I was feeling a little full of myself, this little crisis was set before me. It was late afternoon, and I was standing on the southern tip of Lanzarote, cogitating on how to proceed. The Omniscient One wasn't currently streamlining any critical nuggets, as he had done with echoes of "Corralejo" when Haimish had fled Puerto Del Rosario, so I decided to return to the hotel and force a nap, in the chance He may embed a dream. An hour passed before I dozed off, but, once awakening, I staggered out to the balcony realizing I had come up empty, failing to quarry anything useful. I thusly splashed cold water on my face and walked down to purchase a map of the Canary Islands, in a shop within the hotel. During that jaunt, I considered that the Omniscient

One had Haimish's *will* to contend with and, while He knew the instant Haimish had decided to travel to Corralejo, hence conveying the information without delay during my consciousness, perhaps the murderer hadn't yet settled on where to go.

Studying the map in my room, I plotted Haimish's recent stops and noted that he appeared to be heading north – that's not to say he couldn't change course at any time. I also imagined how difficult things might become for me, if Haimish were to start island-hopping among the small northern islands, such as Isla Graciosa, Isla de Montana Clara, and Isla de Alegranza, because no hydrofoil service exists between those islands. Presently without a clue of what to do, I donned some walking shoes and strolled to the harbor and beyond. When finally tuckered out, I returned to the hotel and ate a late dinner in my room, while watching local news. I failed to understand much of the Spanish broadcast but easily surmised the subject matter of the top story when Haimish's picture appeared with the subtitle, "Desaparecido: Padre Devlin" *(Missing: Father Devlin)*. The story naturally riveted me, especially considering that there may have been mention of a silver-haired stranger in his pursuit, but, eventually, I dropped off to sleep.

Once awakening in the morning, I was confident the Omniscient One would direct me this day, because sufficient time had passed for Haimish's plan to go into operation. I hoped that he had sailed only to the port of Arrecife, on the northeast coast of Lanzarote, so that I could take a bus there. As it turned out, I would indeed travel to Arrecife, but not because Haimish had anchored there: the Omniscient One was now conveying that the killer was sailing in more open waters, toward the African mainland, to the coast of Morocco. Consequently, after making calls to local airlines, I discovered that I wouldn't be able to fly direct from Arrecife to a major Moroccan city like Rabat or Casablanca, but, instead, needed to fly from Arrecife to Grand Canary, and then Grand Canary to Morocco. I also had no clue of Haimish's destination in Morocco, and neither did the Omniscient One, apparently, so I settled on Casablanca, when making reservations, because of its more central location on the coast.

Well, Murphy's Law, after an arduous day of hopping on and off buses and airplanes, I deduced from the Omniscient One's illustrations, during the last leg of my journey from Grand Canary to Casablanca, that Haimish had abandoned his hooker in the port of Safi, well south of Casablanca, but that his eventual destination was Marrakesh. Had I known this, of course, I would've flown directly from Grand Canary to Marrakesh.

Haimish would be riding a train from Safi to Benguerir, and change trains to get to Marrakesh. And, while air service certainly exists between Casablanca and Marrakesh, I soon discovered that I could reach Marrakesh faster by train because of the lengthy layover in Casablanca. The curious aspect of the Omniscient One's disclosures, this time, was that He knew precisely how Haimish would proceed once arriving in Safi. I drew two conclusions after receiving this prophetic advice: either Haimish possessed some kind of information resources about Morocco in the boat, or he had traveled to Morocco previously.

So, now the race was on. It didn't matter much who arrived first in Marrakesh, although if the Omniscient One was to learn where Haimish intended to stay in the city, I would revel at the opportunity to stand there waiting for him as he arrived.

12

From the moment I disembarked onto Moroccan soil, I found myself utterly mesmerized. The Canary Islands had emanated shades of a familiar European culture, albeit tropical with pockets of North African influence; conversely, the bustling Moroccan multitudes engaging in commercial activities yet unfamiliar to me, amidst a backdrop of ancient architecture, were all very exotic. And the smells of Casablanca accentuated things even more so: wafts of grilled lamb kebab, a medley of spices and herbs, and the essence of new fabrics and handmade rugs, all proceeding from a nearby *souk* or open-air market. Before climbing into a taxi, which I made sure contained a working meter, and again when stepping out from the vehicle, I was converged on by several shifty men, each operating independently and eager to serve as my guide. "Let me show you the way," I heard repeatedly as they motioned with their hands. "*Non, Merci*," I responded, fully aware that many of these Berber Arabs speak French as a second tongue. In doing so, I was planting the idea that I wasn't a newcomer to Morocco, which had largely been under French rule during the early 20th century. During the short ride to the Casablanca train station, vendors recurrently rushed my taxi, whenever it stopped or slowed, in attempts to sell to me and the driver various foodstuffs, trinkets, and small rugs. I felt relieved once arriving at the station and, although I was unsure if it was customary in Morocco to pay a gratuity in excess of the fare, I included a few extra *dirhams* in my payment, which demonstrably pleased the driver. After collecting my small travel bag from the back seat, I scurried into the train station while discouraging more would-be guides.

Perhaps I was swayed with lingering concerns of harassing opportunists who might also appear on the train, but I decided to splurge and secure a first class seat on the journey from Casablanca to Marrakesh. Once settling in, and the train proceeded, I sauntered back through the adjacent cars and noticed no such pests. Later, we first-class passengers were served a snack of garlic-flavored hummus and wheat crackers, which I washed down with a glass of chilled, white Bordeaux. Shortly after the attendant cleared my glass and plate, I dropped off to sleep. I was still unclear, when finally awakening, if there had been a meal service following the snack, because it took the jerking movement of the train entering Marrakesh station to rouse me. One thing I *was* certain of was that the Omniscient One had been industrious with my mind during the trip.

According to the Omniscient One's advice, Haimish Devlin arrived first in Marrakesh and had set up at the Ibis Moussafir Hotel, near the train station, an ideal location if a fast getaway was necessitated. Armed with this information, I chose to save a few dirhams in taxi fare by braving my way, on foot, through the sea of vendors, hustlers, pick-pockets, and yet more guides, who insisted on "showing me the way."

I attempted to check-in at the Moussafir Hotel, but, apparently, a group of students with reservations, who had been aboard the same train as Haimish from Benguerir, had taken up the last of the rooms. When I inquired about Haimish's room number, so that I could pay "my friend" a visit, I was denied the information due to hotel security policy. I easily discerned the great feeling of temptation the clerk fought through, when offering him a cash incentive to disclose such information, but he tactfully declined the offer. During the failed negotiation, however, I determined that Haimish still brazenly used his real name, which I found inconceivable, given his unlawfulness and status.

A moment later, I used the house phone and requested to be connected to his room: no answer, so I remained in the lobby thirty minutes and tried a second time. I doubted that Haimish had been so tired that he failed to hear the telephone ringing a few feet away, and resolved that he had likely walked to the *medina* to eat or, otherwise, depravedly amuse himself, which he was so adept at doing.

Eventually, I, too, would venture out to the medina this evening, but, first, needed someplace to stay, so I approached the same clerk I earlier attempted to bribe, and asked his assistance. After making a couple of calls, he located a room for me at the Hotel Farouk, also in the Gueliz section of Marrakesh.

During the taxi ride to the Hotel Farouk, I noticed a place called the Chesterfield Pub, which had a rather British sounding name, so I questioned the driver, in French, about the establishment. The driver confirmed my belief that the bar was a draw for tourists from the United Kingdom and elsewhere who desired a British Pub ambiance, not to mention a short selection of fine British ales. On a hunch that Haimish may have moseyed in there, I asked the driver to pull over and wait while I searched for a friend. Unfortunately, Haimish was not in attendance, and, according to the bartender, who had worked all afternoon, no patron matching the fugitive priest's description had entered the bar.

The Omniscient One presently wasn't streamlining any information to me, so I could only guess that Haimish was browsing the medina, which was normal in this tourist infested section of Marrakesh. After checking into the Hotel Farouk, I washed up, unpacked a bit, and walked toward *Djemaa el Fna*, the popular square in the heart of the medina. I was quite hungry and, at some point, needed to stop and eat but thought I'd search out a café in or around the touristy area.

Naturally, the moment I exited the hotel, I was again inundated with offers to "show me the way," but discouraged these new petitioners with a few stern French phrases, which, after recognizing their effectiveness, I reemployed throughout the evening, as more prospective guides inevitably emerged from the shadows. I had paid strict attention to the concierge's directions to Djemaa el Fna but, given the variety of distractions in the ever-bustling *kasbah*, I apparently took a wrong turn, here and there, and only managed a considerable tour of the city.

Some tourists find the circuit of walls running throughout Marrakesh uniquely interesting and charming, but I derived an unnerving feeling from them, especially as the Sun started to set. The ancient walls made of *tabia*, I later learned it's called, which is red mud from the plains mixed with lime, are too high to see over, and I often felt lost, as if navigating a byzantine maze. Before finally getting back on track toward Djemaa el Fna, I had meandered by the scenic Agdal and Menara Gardens, the intricately carved Saadian Tombs, and caught a glimpse of the famous Koutoubia Minaret. I even inadvertently wandered into a *hammam*, a Turkish-style steam bath, at first mistaking it for a café.

Finally succumbing to weariness and hunger, I hired a petit-taxi to get to Djemaa el Fna. The square being the big tourist draw in Marrakesh, I figured I had a good chance of spotting Haimish there, in addition to grabbing a worthwhile bite to eat. Readers will recall the culture shock I experienced when first arriving in downtown Casablanca. That shock had tempered somewhat during my many hours in-country – that is, until ambling into Djemaa el Fna at dusk. I now experienced new awe while beholding snake charmers, sword swallowers, human flame throwers, monkey handlers, acrobats, child boxers, storytellers, pipe musicians, drummers, dancers, and comedians – all while the smell of whole lambs, roasting on rotisseries, and other exotic, hot foodstuffs, permeated the evening air. The activities in the square easily spellbound me and, despite my hunger, I couldn't imagine removing myself anytime soon from this quasi-circus to search out a restaurant. I thusly maneuvered through several pockets of small crowds, to a stand where meat was being sliced, and I haggled with a vendor in French until comfortable I wasn't being overcharged for a plate of lamb au-jus, chickpeas, and a chopped green vegetable that the man persuaded me to try. Following the meal, which was perfectly satisfying, even though I would've preferred to sit while eating, I prowled about the square, now, not so much paying attention to the hodgepodge of entertainers, but, instead, intensifying the search for my elusive fellow Irishman, Haimish Devlin.

Suddenly, as I paused to purchase an ice-cream product from a vendor, the Omniscient One began streamlining information to me: Haimish had been dawdling nearby and, while I failed to notice him, he had glimpsed me and was in flight. "Khettara... Khettara," I kept hearing in my head. After urgently completing the transaction for the ice cream, I asked the demure-looking Moroccan where I might find Khettara. I soon discovered that Khettara wasn't a place, per se, but a network of archaic, underground channels, like an aqueduct, in the kasbah. How would Haimish ever know about the Khettara, or to go there, I wondered, which reinforced my belief that he had traveled to Morocco previously. Upon receiving directions to the nearest entry point, I scampered toward the Khettara while chomping on the frozen treat I refused to toss away despite the consumption hindering my progress.

Once back outside Djemaa el Fna, I paused unexpectedly and sat on a bench, mulling over the risky scenarios that might play out within the obscured channels, realizing that Haimish had endured immensely stressful conditions in recent days, with me showing up virtually everywhere in his path, and to corner a desperate fugitive wouldn't be prudent on my part. I, therefore, aborted my pursuit. Finding my way through an ancient, walled maze, at dusk, had been sufficiently challenging; however, to endeavor into a murky, outmoded labyrinth, in search of a fugitive killer, was definitely out of this retired geologist's league, I decided.

I must admit to feeling a little disappointed that the Omniscient One hadn't dissuaded me from venturing into the Khettara and, in the end, felt pleased about my own good judgment. Instead, I wrote a note similar to the one I asked the lad to insert into Haimish's hooker, at Playa Blanca, urging him to "Come in from the cold and turn himself in." I then took a petit-taxi to the Moussafir Hotel, where Haimish would still ostensibly sleep this night, and, after loitering in the lobby more than an hour, with hopes of intercepting him, I paid a front desk clerk a handsome gratuity to ensure that Haimish received the note, personally. I hired another petit-taxi to the Hotel Farouk, where I tottered exhaustedly through the lobby and was barely able to stand while unlocking the door to my antiquated accommodations, eventually collapsing onto the bed.

13

THROUGH THE OMNISCIENT ONE's intervention, I immediately came to recognize the events that transpired overnight, when awakening with an urge to urinate at 5:10 a.m. I wouldn't be returning to bed this morning, despite my stubborn fatigue, because Haimish had departed Marrakesh ten minutes earlier on the 5 o'clock train to Fez.

As I scrambled about in a half-stupor, dressing and packing, my unraveling dream revealed that Haimish had stayed out most of the night on fears that authorities lied in wait for him at the Moussafir Hotel. To pass the time, he drank at an Algerian dance club called Diamant Noir and became recklessly drunk. But eventually he risked returning to the hotel, because, there, he had stashed his sack of cash, deep within a bathroom vent; he never received the note I asked the clerk to deliver, because he didn't dare pass through the lobby to get to his room. Instead, at 3:45 a.m., he daringly broke a window to a nearby suite that he perceived to be unoccupied, and unlocked the window before crawling through. Once inside, he exited the suite into the hallway, and entered his room when satisfied that no police lurked. He then grabbed his belongings and cash and climbed through a window and fell to the ground, head first, knocking himself out for more than five minutes in the process. Still drunk, he had no idea what had happened, when regaining consciousness, and later reflected on how lucky he was that nobody wandered by to scoop up his bag containing several thousand Euros.

The next train to Fez didn't depart until 6:45 a.m., so Haimish would benefit from a two hour head start on me. During the trip, I enjoyed excellent views of the Atlas Mountains, which had escaped me during the leg from Casablanca to Marrakesh after falling asleep. If traveling by automobile, as a geologist, I certainly would've had cause to stop and hike about the mountains, which feature a variety of spectacular reddish hues, suggesting that the soil in this arid region vastly contains iron.

Although I rested my eyes during the journey to Fez, I failed to nap. In the late morning, a savory meal, slow-cooked in a *tajine*, was served and included chicken, green olives, and lemon. Using thin bread, to scoop up the food, my server demonstrated how it's customary to, first, eat the vegetables at the edges of the cooking vessel and eventually work toward the middle, where the meat is situated. A middle-aged Moroccan businessman looked amused while watching me eat his native food, so I spoke to him. "Hashem," it seems, owned the Hotel Lamrani in Fez and was just returning from Marrakesh after two days of negotiating to acquire a hotel there. According to Hashem, there remained a few details to work out, but he was confident the deal would go through. An hour before our train reached Fez, Hashem moved over to sit in the vacant seat beside me, and we chatted about Morocco but, also, unexpectedly, about Cork, Ireland, where he had visited during his college years. Once arriving at the Fez train station, located in the French-built Ville Nouvelle section, and confident that I wasn't about to be swindled in some fashion, I rode with Hashem in a petit-taxi to the Hotel Lamrani.

While Fez certainly boasts its share of sightseers, the city didn't appear overrun with tourists, as was the case with Marrakesh, and it radiated an "old world" charm. The Hotel Lamrani, where I stayed, is located near Bab Boujeloud, which is the gateway to the Fez el Bali district, the extraordinary old medina. Bab Boujeloud also gives easy pedestrian access to Fez el Djedid, the massive Royal city district, where I would ultimately discover Haimish staying in the Hotel du Commerce, an old, comfortable hotel, with a lively café frequented by prostitutes.

When Hashem and I entered the Hotel Lamrani, employees immediately "snapped to," which validated to me that the boss had returned. Hashem then rattled off a few words in a Berber Arabic dialect, and the head clerk removed some registration papers straight away for me to fill out. A bellhop subsequently marched across the lobby and hovered, ready to snatch my small travel bag, but I informed him alternatively in French that his help wasn't necessary.

I must say that Hashem proved to be an exceptional host and ambassador, for his country, during my time in Fez. First, he invited me to experience a traditional steam bath at the nearby Hammam Sidi Azouz; later, I enjoyed another meal simmered in a tajine, this one prepared by his lovely wife, which contained lamb, prunes, and almonds, and accompanied by thin bread, as always. Fortunately, I received no untimely communiqués from the Omniscient One during those enjoyable hours, and it wasn't until I returned to the hotel and sat down to watch television that the Omniscient One began infiltrating my thinking in a manner, now, all too familiar. That had been the moment I first learned Haimish was holed up at the Hotel du Commerce, and was again operating a hooker. However, on this occasion, Haimish was situated some hundred miles from shore, so this hooker sported maroon panties not sails.

Perhaps the Omniscient One was prompting me to take a petit-taxi to the Hotel du Commerce, in Fez el Djedid, to confront Haimish, but, instead, I picked up the telephone and called the hotel and asked to be connected. The fugitive had again daringly registered under his real name. The telephone rang several times before he picked up.

"Haimish, don't hang up. It's Albert Doyle."

"I'm gonna slit yer *fookin'* throat, Doyle. You're a royal pain in *me arse*."

"Everyone knows that you killed Angus Wilde, Haimish. Why not just come home to Ireland and turn yerself in?"

"Why? So I can rot in prison the rest of *me* days? No thanks, Buster."

"It's better that you return to Ireland, Haimish. The world will soon learn that you also murdered Father Serna in Fuerteventura."

"Prove it. Ruben Serna died in a bathtub accident."

I quickly sensed that Haimish was liquored-up and that I might engage him a while, to persuade him to travel with me to Ireland. Whether he would actually follow through, once sobered up, was another matter.

"Haimish, I know that you tossed that clock-radio into Father Serna's bathwater, and I've become a credible source to police since the Angus Wilde case. They're gonna listen to me."

"You still can't prove it. Nobody can."

"You had the means, opportunity, and most importantly the motive, Haimish. I know you were skimming the collection proceeds at San Miguel's Church over the past several years, and that you wanted Father

Serna out of the picture so that you could become rector and gain control over parish monies."

"How do you know all this shit, Doyle?"

"I didn't ask to receive the extraordinary insights into your life... but I do and, apparently, will continue to do so until the Omniscient One deems otherwise."

"The Omniscient One? Who the *hell'sssss* this*ss* Omniscient One?" Haimish asked slurringly and hiccupped. I subsequently heard a door slam in the background. "There, ya happy, Doyle? My date just up and left, and I had only *done* her once. That really pisses me off, and I hardly need any more reasons to *ice* you. Who's this*ss* Omniscient One again?"

"The One who knows all and sees all. You were a Catholic priest, for crying out loud. I assume that you believe in God and all His powers?"

"Oh, I believe in God, alright," responded Haimish, "but my belief system is *prawbly* different than yours."

Haimish was about to digress, but that was okay. As long as he continued talking, I had a chance to peacefully bring this ordeal to a close. I thusly prodded him on.

"Oh, really. Well, I'm interested to hear your beliefs, friend."

"Yeah? Don't call me friend, you pain in the arse." I then heard Haimish swilling a drink. "I believe in God, but I don't believe that Jesus Christ was any more divine than you or I. And I certainly don't believe that he rose from the dead after three days, rolled back a heavy boulder under the watch of soldiers, and ascended to the Father in a reconstituted form. No, Jesus Christ was a good and wise man who suffered and perished under some very unjust circumstances. The rest is all *friggin'* mythology, I tell *ye*. I think that Christianity is the greatest mass-delusion in the history of mankind."

"You don't believe that Jesus Christ is the Messiah? You stood up at the altar at St. Joe's in Kinvara with the Holy Eucharist in your hands, after consecrating it... and did likewise, as recently as a week ago, at San Miguel's in Fuerteventura!"

"Those were magic shows, nothing more... nothing less... just a way to make a living.

"*Aw*, Haimish, you're disappointing me, friend. Tell me what it is that you *do* believe, then."

"I'll do *that*, but I told you *not* to call me 'friend,' you geezer." Haimish took another drink and continued: "I believe that 'God' is the natural essence of all universal matter... and whenever elements of the universe get out of balance, both physical and the intangibles... like injustice... that natural corrections or re-balancing occurs. Call it karma if you like. Oh, I definitely believe in karma."

"You're getting profound on me now, Haimish. And, so do you believe that the abilities and insights of the man dispatched to pursue you is part of a natural correction process playing out? Am I an agent of karma, so to speak?"

"Yes and yes."

"Then, if you sense things unfolding before you, why not just succumb to the inevitable? Come home to Ireland with me tomorrow, Haimish. Turning yourself in voluntarily has got to count for something... both in Irish justice and in the universal elements which you believe."

"But if I ultimately evade apprehension, and all its consequences, then it was the conditions I was forced to endure as a fugitive that was the *intended* dispensation of justice. So, I must soldier on..."

"Or it could be just luck so far... or skill... or a little bit of both. Look, Haimish, I'll tell you what I'm gonna do. You're probably thinking about yer next move right now, and I doubt you intend on remaining at the Hotel du Commerce, for fear of being arrested, but I'm gonna do you a favor, and I give you my word. I'm not going to call the police tonight... and I won't go near your hotel either. I'm goin' to remain here, across town, and get a good night's sleep, and I want you to do the same. I'd also like you to think about what we talked about, and to consider flying back with me to Ireland tomorrow. Just sleep on it. Would you do that?"

"Yes, I'll do *that*, but I'm not thankin' *you* fer nuthin'. You've done *me* no favors. Yer still a pain in me arse, and I'd still cut yer throat if given the chance."

Haimish slammed down the telephone. I hung up the phone in my room at the Hotel Lamrani, turned off the television, and sat in the dark, reflecting on our exchange. I couldn't help but dwell on Haimish's last remark that he would "cut my throat if given the chance," and was grateful I had chosen not to follow him into the ancient Khettara aqueduct system in Marrakesh. The following morning, I awoke at 6:45, telephoned the Hotel du Commerce, and asked again to be connected with Haimish Devlin's room. Haimish had checked out at 5:30 a.m.

14

THE OMNISCIENT ONE HADN'T steeped my mind with any dreams overnight so, despite Haimish apparently fleeing, I chose not to pack, because I had no idea of his whereabouts or destination. I took a quick shower, dressed myself, and walked down to a café off the hotel lobby, where I ate a fried duck egg, a croissant, and drank a cup of strong Moroccan coffee that left me jittery for hours. I had just received the check and was finishing the last bit of coffee when the Omniscient One finally chimed in.

From what I was able to deduce from the illustration of Haimish's morning activities, and whispers of his intentions, the fugitive had crossed over Bab Boujeloud, from Fez el Djedid into Fez el Bali, and was presently trolling the souks in the medina. The Omniscient One further hinted that Haimish wasn't shopping but merely killing time before he could gain access to a place, ironically, known as "The House of the Magician," where a one of a kind Water Clock exists. After examining the archaic clock, he intended to travel by bus to Tangier in northern Morocco. How Haimish actually became aware of the Water Clock was unclear to me at the time, but, after learning more about it, and, given his obvious fascination for such mechanisms, I understood the trained engineer's motivation for wanting to visit there.

Opposite the Medersa Bou Inania, the most beautiful, elaborate, and extravagant medersa (old college) in all of Morocco, Bou Inania's property carries over to the extraordinary clock that was built above some

vendor stalls in the road at The House of the Magician. The clock itself
had been removed several decades earlier for research and restoration –
research because, to this day, nobody has been able to figure out how it
actually works. Still a curiosity to locals and tourists, the Water Clock
consists of a row of thirteen windows and platforms, seven of which
retain their original brass bowls. A contemporary account details how,
at precisely every hour, a window would open and drop a weight down
into a corresponding bowl.

Many years after the Water Clock was damaged, a copper trough,
with spigot, was installed beneath the clock as part of a rudimentary
gutter system, to catch and prevent displaced water from splashing
below onto merchants, customers, and passers-by on Talaa Kebira.
The intention had been for the trough to remain in place only until
restoration again rendered the clock operational; however, in the early
years following the clock's destruction, those repairs never took place,
and even after modern restoration was carried out, the trough remained,
now part of its history.

I didn't discover until exiting the Hotel Lamrani how hard it had
rained overnight. Rain is often considered an omen in this arid region of
the world, but whether the omen is bad or good depends on one's acuities
and beliefs, I suppose. Across the street, near the cinema, the closest sewer
drain had not diverted the fallen rain as designed, or perhaps there had
been an obstruction, like trash, and water pooled in front. I presently
stood under an awning, outside the hotel, and pondered my next move.
Given the Omniscient One's advice that the killer was determined to
examine the Water Clock before fleeing to Tangier, I decided to try to
intercept a now, hopefully, sober Haimish, at the House of the Magician,
to make one final appeal for him to return to Ireland.

Drizzle persisted, and I was fickle whether to walk and search out the
clock or just hail a petit-taxi. About that same time, a casually dressed
Moroccan in quasi-western attire, toting an antique bumbershoot,
emerged from a narrow alley between the hotel and a neighboring
commercial building. The 40-something man, whose bushy, black
eyebrows and thick moustache gave him a sinister look, appeared to be
yet another ambitious guide, and he gestured for me to follow. At first,
I didn't dare and simply looked away, but, after glancing at a familiar
hotel porter, with whom I had exchanged pleasantries with on several

occasions during my stay, he sensed my need for direction and nodded approvingly that the guide was trustworthy.

"What your name," the guide asked in broken English.

"Peter Frampton... and I want *you* to show me the way," I replied, doubting he'd understand the humorous reference.

"Yes, let me show you the way, Mr. Frampton," he said seriously, gesturing with his hand.

Following that brief dialogue in English, I switched over to French, and we haggled on a price for him to escort me to the House of the Magician. Once agreeing on an amount, we departed on foot, and he politely sheltered me from the drizzle using his bumbershoot. As we progressed toward the House, unbeknownst to me at the time, Haimish had already joined a small tourist group and was currently up inside the structure, looking down through a window at the one-of-a-kind clock. A few feet away, an English- speaking guide elaborated on the history of the House and clock, the group gradually filtering downstairs to the main floor, save for an intrigued Haimish, who lingered furtively and without authorization, studying the clock.

It would be senseless, at this time, to point out that Haimish was one to flout conventions, so I suppose it's no surprise to learn that viewing the Water Clock from afar failed to satisfy his curiosity. And, once confident that nobody was within earshot, he forced open an upstairs window, climbed out onto the roof, and slid down until his feet made contact with the Water Clock, preventing him from sliding further. He then maneuvered fearlessly about its appendages, so that he could enhance his analytical vantage point and attempt to accomplish what nobody in modern times has yet been able to do: comprehend how the clock once worked, which has long remained the obstacle preventing its complete restoration.

I'm not certain how long Haimish had been up on the roof, shifting and clutching like a cat, when I arrived at the House of the Magician, but I could never forget, for the rest of my earthly days, the events that ultimately came to pass that morning.

Convinced that I'd later be able to find my way back to the Hotel Lamrani, I paid my guide and thanked him for his services. Subsequently, the tourist group exited the House of the Magician, so I waited for Haimish to emerge but saw no sign of him. Having resolved that he was probably still inside engaging an employee about the unique clock, I paced intently toward the House's main entrance. At that moment, I heard a grunt from above, and then a second louder grunt, so I peered up innocently to notice the familiar fugitive priest stretched out across the clock. Haimish was struggling to reposition himself.

"*Jaysus*, man," I shouted. "What is it that you've involved yerself in *now*, Mr. Devlin?"

Haimish was sufficiently alarmed that his concentration was broken, and he lost his grip. As he began slipping, he glanced down and, in that instant, I deciphered a micro-expression of deep-rooted resentment in his aspect; his mind had clearly registered the identity of the person uttering the distracting words. His face transformed into an angry scowl, and he was about to yell at me, I gathered, just as his head bashed against one of the clock's brass bowls. His eyes closed, and his whole body went limp as he slipped into the copper trough that filled with rainwater overnight.

It soon became apparent that Haimish's plunge into the water had failed to bring him to his senses, so I darted inside the House of the Magician and described succinctly, in French, to the tour guide, what had just transpired up on the roof. I then scuttled back outside to see if Haimish had yet awakened, while the guide raced up to the second floor to climb through a window and rescue him. Suddenly, as the rescuer extended a leg out onto the roof, a violent rumble sounded from above, followed by a lightning strike that crashed down onto the roof of the House. I watched with paralyzing awe as the tour guide reflexively retracted his leg inside the window, and the lightning bolt deflected down the grade of the roof, skipping from the Water Clock, which it momentarily danced around, and jumped to the trough containing the unconscious, drowning Haimish Devlin. The rainwater-inundated copper tub, tinted green after hundreds of years of oxidation, served as an attractive electrical conductor, as witnessed by a corresponding green field, now vacillating overtop the trough, which emitted crackles and sparks from within.

After the tour guide refused to venture out onto the roof a second time, due the hazardous conditions, the city's fire and rescue department was summoned. Fifty minutes elapsed before Haimish was finally pulled from the copper trough, but it was too late to resuscitate him; soon his body was transferred to a city morgue. Meanwhile, I conferred, at the scene, with police, who had found my account of recent events all a little too spectacular, and they detained and transported me to district headquarters, for further questioning, where it was necessary to contact Garda Inspector Pearse McElwee, in Ireland, for purposes of corroboration, which turned out to be a difficult task in itself: McElwee currently worked as a regional supervisor and had been out in the field, overseeing a case in which medium Trish Jennings provided leads.

Once Inspector McElwee satisfied Moroccan authorities, I requested that he also contact local police in the Canary Islands, to attribute Father Ruben Serna's death to Devlin, which prompted the chief homicide detective in the Canary Islands to board the next flight to Fez, Morocco, in order to interview me over the following two days.

Between the events that came to pass in both countries, I had a mountain of paperwork to accomplish before I'd be permitted to leave Morocco, and the city of Fez kindly saw to it that my accommodations at the Hotel Lamrani, as well as meals and incidentals, were taken care of. And, over time, I had developed such good rapport with police in Fez that the department assisted me in taking care of a personal item before I departed – one that had been nagging me guiltily:

The thought of Angus Wilde's hooker being left behind at some Moroccan port didn't sit well with me, despite him being dead for more than seven years. I felt as though Angus' spirit dwelled on the small sailing vessel and that he wouldn't rest peacefully until the hooker was returned home to Ireland. Thus, using a little persuasion, I coaxed a police official in Fez to call his counterpart in the port city of Safi who, in turn, dispatched marine officers in search of the distinctive-looking sailboat.

More than two weeks had passed since Haimish arrived in Morocco, so I wasn't surprised to learn that the hooker went missing from the Safi dock where he abandoned it. In the end, Angus' boat was located in a small seaside village south of Safi. Amusingly, the thief who made off with it had painted the boat black, hence, returning it to its original color. The one aspect he wasn't able to disguise, however, was the hooker's characteristic shape and design, which was not common to Morocco.

After my interviews and statements were completed, I traveled by train from Fez to Benguerir, changed trains and took another to Safi. From Safi, I rode a bus to the seaside village, eventually searching out a waterfront fishmonger's shop, where a guard was posted to keep an eye on the boat. From there, I embarked on what would become a thrilling, sometimes treacherous, and memorable journey. I wasn't a skilled sailor by any stretch, but had spent enough time on hookers as a youth that I felt perfectly comfortable navigating the watercraft. Thus, after purchasing adequate supplies and sustenance for the first leg of my voyage, I launched Angus Wilde's hooker on the long journey home to Ireland.

15

THE WEATHER HAD BEEN cooperative early on, but, feeling the trepidation of a novice, I continued to hug the Moroccan coast while sailing northward. Curiously, I hadn't received any communiqués from the Omniscient One concerning Haimish Devlin's death, (nor is He obliged to do so), since His advice of a few weeks earlier, which pointed me to the Water Clock. During lonely hours out at sea, I often thought back to the uncanny, ironic circumstances of Haimish's death, relative to his victims. Haimish had electrocuted Father Serna in a bathtub using a clock radio and, in the end, also perished in a tub of water adjacent to the Water Clock, after the timely introduction of electricity. And, like Angus Wilde, who met his demise high up in a clock tower, Haimish also departed this life at an elevated location, juxtaposed with a clock. I felt convinced then, as I do now, that the Omniscient One was responsible for shaping the events that unforgettable morning, to include delivering the lone, powerful lightning strike on the House of the Magician, which, by the way, avoided sustaining an iota of structural damage in the process.

The first place I moored, to rest properly and replenish supplies, was the port city of Tangier where, naturally, I again thought to Haimish and what he might've done there (besides trying to elude me) and where he would've stayed. While in Tangier, I called home to Kinvara and managed to reach Gerry McBrine at the post office, and finally succeeded in telling him what I attempted several weeks earlier at

Sexton's Pub: that I knew of Haimish Devlin's whereabouts. Gerry was, of course, astonished to learn the recent events in the Canary Islands and Morocco, and he insisted that I deserved to receive an award of some sort, especially when returning Angus' hooker to Ireland.

From Tangier, I sailed past the Strait of Gibraltar, which leads into the Mediterranean Sea, and I wondered how Haimish's life would've turned out if he had, instead, settled in the French Riviera, as he once contemplated when passing by the Strait from the north – similar, I intuited; different venue and circumstances but same outcome.

I never drifted more than a mile off shore while sailing along the Iberian Peninsula, and made an overnight stop in the port of Aveiro, Portugal, where I anchored and slept in the hooker, under the stars, taking the idea from Haimish who had done so in Corralejo. From Aveiro, I sailed to the northern tip of the peninsula and moored in El Ferrol, Spain, where I again stocked up and ate well at a seaside café.

The most treacherous part of my journey occurred after leaving El Ferrol for Pointe de Penmarch, France, because I had resolved to traverse the open-sea waters of the Bay of Biscay, doing so because the weather was forecasted to remain placid, and to continue safely hugging the coast would've added a week or more to my trip. Once finding myself several hundred miles off shore in the black of night, however, blindly rocking about in the unsuitable sailing vessel, and being pelted by rain, I wished I *had* taken the coastal route. Feeling much despair, I beseeched the Omniscient One to tame the waters and ensure my safety; but, despite my cumulative service to Him, my pleas went unanswered, and conditions actually worsened. Perhaps His rejoinder had come in the form of instilling me with more courage, as I managed to weather the storm, as it were.

I persevered that night, and the next, and if I had managed any sleep while crossing the Bay of Biscay, it was by accident; for to have allowed any appreciable lapse or distraction, during that stretch, surely would've yielded my demise. More than forty-eight hours passed before I reached Pointe de Penmarch, France, where I anchored in a tranquil cove, two miles from harbor, and collapsed in the boat. After sleeping six hours, I re-launched, navigated into the nearby port, and docked at a slip, eventually checking into a tourist home and spending the next fourteen hours recovering.

From Point de Penmarch, I sailed for St. Agnes Island in the Isles of Scilly, off the southwest coast of England, and grew giddy with pride and excitement that I was drawing close to Ireland and that my journey would be a success. It then commenced raining so hard that it was necessary to suspend my pilotage, more than an hour, while I bailed out the rainwater that pooled-up in the hooker – a gift of humility from the Omniscient One, no doubt. Still fatigued from the trip across the Bay of Biscay, I moored at St. Agnes that night and again secured accommodations and supplies.

Despite my desire to reach Kinvara expeditiously and bring this arduous voyage to a conclusion, it was necessary to pass between the Dingle peninsula and Great Blasket Island, en route to the central west coast of Ireland, so I decided to surprise daughter Tessie with a visit. I rose early in St. Agnes and sailed most of the day, reaching Great Blasket in late afternoon. Tessie had once pointed out the location of the tourist home on a map, before moving there, so I had a good idea of where to secure the boat when approaching the island.

Once disembarking onto Irish soil, I had every good intention of bending over to kiss the ground, but the toll of my journey prevented me from doing so. Instead, I sluggishly dropped to one knee and patted the ground affectionately with my hand. Standing again, I espied a small cluster of homes with thatched roofs, save for one larger structure that featured a slate roof. Situated on a rise, behind the dwelling, stood a windmill twirling efficiently. I had previously envisioned the inn when Tessie described how wind was used to power it, so I hiked up and knocked on the main door. Nobody answered, and I was just about to wander around and search out an alternate entrance when an attractive young woman, collecting laundry from a clothesline, emerged.

"Hello. Is Tessie Doyle about," I inquired.

"Tessie's up in her room, napping, I suspect. Who shall I tell her is calling?"

"How do you do? I'm her father, Albert. I'd really like to surprise her, though."

"Oh, goodness. How are you, Mr. Doyle? I'm Patricia Reilly. My mother owns the inn. Tessie will be surprised, indeed. I'll go fetch her... but not to worry, I won't say a whisper."

Ms. Reilly invited me inside, and I sat in the front room, beside an elaborate reception desk, while she buzzed my daughter on an intercom.

Tessie soon emerged, sleepy-eyed, and paused at the top of the stairs to gaze down while leaning on a handrail.

"I'm Tessie. Can I help you?"

"You could provide some dinner company for an old man," I responded, smirking affectionately.

"I beg your pardon, sir?" Tessie still had no idea who I was.

"You need to take a closer look down here, little lady," I said, now smiling. The moment Tessie heard the words "little lady," she reacted, because I had often addressed her that way during her teen years, when she rebelliously strove for independence from her mother and me.

"Daddy, is that you?! Saints alive, I never would've recognized you! You look awful... are you alright?" Barely awake, Tessie slowly made her way down the distressed, creaking staircase, and I stood to receive her. Finally embracing me, she said, "Not even a call to let me know you were coming, Daddy. That's not like you. You really look horrible, you know. Are you sure you're okay?" She then pecked my cheek.

"As far as I know, I'm well... just dog-tired." I then lightly clasped her arm to direct her. "Step outside for a moment," I said. "I want to show you something." The two of us shuffled through the front door onto the sturdy granite landing outside, where I pointed down and across to the dock. "See that black sailboat down there... with furled maroon sails? That's Angus Wilde's hooker. I just sailed it back from Morocco... that's the reason I look so tired.

"Sacred heart! Is that why you traveled down off the coast of Africa? You're no sailor! How did you manage that? And how did you ever locate Angus' boat?"

"It's a long story, the details of which I'll explain over dinner. For now, suffice it to say that the Omniscient One chose to engage me again. I didn't want to worry you or your sister, so I simply told you that I had always wanted to visit the Canary Islands... which was true."

I had imagined Tessie and me breaking away to some quaint little pub where I would treat her to dinner, but the reality was that the inn where she worked boasted the best grub on this sparsely populated island. Tessie was a jack of all trades – handling the books, ordering food and essentials, even getting involved in meal preparations during peak tourist season – but was spared any duties this night, as we dined at the inn and were served by her peers. Over dinner, I described to my daughter the details of my reactivation as a medium in Kinvara, to include the gagging episode at Sexton's, and ensuing adventurous pursuit of Haimish Devlin in the Canary Islands and Morocco. Throughout my recitation, the lights dimmed and flickered, due to power fluctuations, and eerily wavered longer, it seemed, whenever evoking the name of Haimish Devlin. I was afforded a room at the inn *gratis* that night and thought I might like to stay a second night, not knowing when I might see my daughter next, but, after Tessie assured me that she'd return home soon for a visit, I sailed for Kinvara the following morning.

16

THIRTEEN HOURS AFTER DEPARTING Great Blasket Island, I sailed into Kinvara Harbor. Nobody had known when I would arrive, so no fanfare awaited, although I must admit that I secretly desired some form of reception by friends. Once securing the hooker at a vacant slip, I glanced over to the Pierpoint and perceived some revelry going on inside, and contemplated entering the pub to see whether any familiar patrons might be willing to further transport this weary, retired geologist, who had no business carrying on the way he did, over the last several weeks, if not for the Omniscient One's inducements. I soon reckoned, however, that if I *were* to presently enter the Pierpoint, it would be several hours before I'd be permitted to leave, considering the requisite recounting of events to curious townsfolk; accounts that would inevitably be slowed by several rounds of Guinness. No, I would *not* enter the Pierpoint this night, I decided, but, instead, dragged myself and travel bag around the switch and up the modest hill to my home in the Dungora section of Kinvara.

After convalescing for two days, I finally ventured out in the afternoon, intending to collect my mail at the post office. I also needed to do some food shopping at the Londis market, because I could no longer bear eating canned goods. I soon found myself daydreaming, though, and coasted past the post office, to the switch that leads to the harbor and Pierpoint. I thought about the stack of mail that awaited me, and knew I should turn around, but something was compelling me to continue on, and I never made that U-turn. With the Pierpoint in sight, it now felt as though a potent force was guiding me, and that I didn't have a choice in the matter. *To hell with it*, I thought. *I'll get to the mail and shopping... when I get to it. 'Tis time for a bit of the "craic."* Only one parking space was vacant near the Pierpoint, so I didn't delay in taking it.

There was something mysterious in the air at the Pierpoint that Friday afternoon. In one sense, it was similar to the feeling one experiences when returning to a familiar place after being away a long time. Yet there was something else to it, and I couldn't quite put my finger on it. It *was no accident that I was induced to bypass the post office*, I thought – *the Omniscient One surely has his hand in this one.*

The first observable anomaly, that afternoon, was that 80-something spinster Francie O'Rourke had just collected a ladies pint of Harp beer from the bar and was making her way to a booth near a window overlooking the Atlantic Ocean. Everybody in Kinvara knew Francie well. She had been the postmistress before Gerry McBrine assumed postal operations, and was recently placed in a nursing home; yet, presently, she maneuvered spryly about the lounge. The sultry conditions outside the pub notwithstanding, Francie was prepared for the Pierpoint's efficient air-conditioning system and was attired in a violet raincoat that extended below her knees.

"Francie, what are *you* doing here?" I asked sincerely.

"I'm flashin' the lads. What in the dickens do you suppose I'm doin', Doyle? I'm enjoying a pint like the rest of ye," Francie retorted while situating herself at the booth.

"I don't mean to meddle, Francie, but you were infirm. I mean *really* ill... even in a nursing home for a while."

"That's right, but I'm better now, and it's a good day for a cold drink, don't you think? You don't mind, do you?"

Francie was acting her feisty self. Good for her.

"Any news from your brother Michael John and his wife Helen in America?" Michael John O'Rourke and Helen were old friends, and I inquired of their well-being just to be polite before stepping over to the bar.

"That's the other reason I'm here. They flew into Shannon two hours ago, and I'm to meet them here. Michael John told me he dropped you a postcard to inform you of the same... that they'd be arriving today. Don't you read your mail?"

"Like you, I've also been out of circulation a while, Francie. I need to stop by the Post and collect my mail. But, you know, after being away from Ireland, there's nothing more that I'd like than to sit and listen to Michael John sing an Irish lullaby."

Francie sipped her pint and didn't respond. She didn't seem interested in where I'd been off to, so I motioned that I was going to the bar.

The Guinness tasted like nectar that afternoon, and I had just ordered a second pint when a young lady, apparently in her mid to late 30's, entered the bar and sat beside me. I nodded hello and she smiled. The attractive, dark blonde woman looked a bit disoriented, as if it was her first visit to the Pierpoint, but I was still another pint away from prying, so let her be. Minutes later, a young fellow of like age, who I also failed to recognize, entered the bar and took a seat on the opposite side of me. I greeted him also, but our dialogue didn't extend beyond salutations. Both young people ordered pints, and, during the several minutes I sat between them, they never made an effort to speak to one another, so I decided that they weren't acquainted. Hence, I never made an offer to change seats so that they could sit together. Finally, the man spoke up, but not to me – to the bartender, wiping up nearby:

"Would you happen to know Albert Doyle, sir?"

"It's yer lucky day. He *settin'* right beside you," the barkeep said.

I raised my hand. "Guilty as charged," I said in jest while studying this unfamiliar lad who had me at a disadvantage.

He then extended his hand and introduced himself. "How do you do? My name's Liam McCool."

"I'll bet you're from Antrim," I said, associating his last name with the place.

"I am, indeed," he said.

During our brief exchange, the woman on the other side of me had been squirming to get a better look at Liam, and now clearly wished to interrupt. I was still curious to know how this lad knew me and why he had sought me out at the Pierpoint, but, sensing the woman's eagerness, I leaned back and allowed her to join in the conversation.

"*You're* Liam McCool?" The woman verified, as if she had known him. "*I'm* Trish Jennings," she said, expecting that he should know her.

The young fellow had had no idea who Trish was, but I knew *of* her due to references made by Inspector Pearse McElwee, first more than seven years ago, and as recently as three and a half weeks ago, when I telephoned the Inspector from Fez, Morocco. I spoke up as the two sat bewildered:

"So *you're* the famous medium, Trish Jennings, from Castlebar," I said, giving her the once-over. "And if *I* know about you, Trish, and *you* know about Liam, who's no doubt a medium... 'Am I right, Liam?'... and *Liam* knows about me... then I'll tell you what's going on here. The Omniscient One has seen fit that the three of us should meet and get acquainted."

"The Omniscient One?" Liam reacted dumbfounded. "I can't believe I'm hearing those words from someone else. I thought *I* was the one who originated that terminology."

"Oh, no, Liam," Trish butted in. "You don't have exclusivity on calling Him that. I've been calling Him *that* for years."

"Well then, it's simple," I interjected. "It's the Omniscient One who desires to be referred to as such, so He must be responsible for our utterances. And, while we're on the topic of the Omniscient One, I'd like to thank Him, personally, for arranging our little meeting in Kinvara today, instead of making this old-timer drive all the way up to Antrim or Castlebar, seeing that he just dragged my *behind* all across the Canary Islands, Morocco, and elsewhere over the past few weeks."

Liam and Trish laughed out loud.

"You're hardly an old-timer, Albert," said Trish. "And you don't *even* want to get me started about all the tiresome travel. I've got more complaints than you, I'm sure. But it's made for an interesting life." Trish hoisted her pint and swelled her mouth with stout.

"I actually knew about your exploits to the Canary Islands and Morocco," said Liam. "Marrakesh and Fez, right?" he verified.

Initially, I was bowled over by Liam's remark because, except for the telephone call I had made to Gerry McBrine from Tangier, I had yet to disseminate details of my odyssey to my chums in Kinvara. But then I thought about Inspector Pearse McElwee, and my call to him from Fez, and I reckoned that Liam had learned of my journey through him.

"Oh, Inspector McElwee filled you in on my recent experiences, did he?" I asked Liam.

"I don't know Pearse McElwee. I gather from your earlier comments, though, that both you and Trish know, and have worked with, the Inspector. Trish must be doing good work – that's probably why I haven't had cause to interact with him. The reason I know about your challenges in Morocco and the Canary Islands... and the Bay of Biscay, I might add, when you were being tossed about in the boat that night, is that the Omniscient One often sends me 'visual packets' of people from across the globe. Usually the packets are for informational purposes... to acquaint me with a case before dispatching me. But, oftentimes, cases are resolved of their own doing and it's not necessary for me to act. I was sent visual packets of you and Haimish Devlin throughout your pursuit, but I never came close to traveling to Africa. The closest I came to assisting was when you thought you might die in the Bay of Biscay. The Omniscient One was preparing me to get involved with a prospective rescue effort."

"My prayers really *were* being heard," I muttered.

Having survived that ordeal, I was presently *more* awestruck to hear the nature of activities in which Liam McCool was regularly involved. Over the succeeding two hours, Trish and I learned what an extraordinary human being Liam McCool was, operating as what can best be described as a "true channel of supernatural knowledge." Liam not only functioned as an individual medium but simultaneously monitored the activities of numerous mediums, worldwide, by way of the so-called "visual packets," a communication method the Omniscient One had yet to bestow upon Trish or me. And, when I think back to the way my head swelled with pride after the Omniscient One first activated me for service in the Angus Wilde case: I certainly had no justification – not compared with the man sitting beside me, or even Trish Jennings, who had been working nonstop in recent years, while I experienced a seven year lull.

Given his capabilities, I had plenty of questions for Liam, the foremost being, "Why was I not activated in time to save Angus Wilde or Father Ruben Serna?" And, "Considering the coincidental circumstances at the Water Clock, did the Omniscient One produce the converging elements that brought about Haimish Devlin's death? Did the Omniscient One smite Haimish?" But as desperately as I yearned to hear the answers to those questions, I desired, more so, for things to remain light-hearted this day and decided to wait before asking.

Liam had been looking pensive and spoke up:

"I believe we've been brought together for a good reason, Albert... Trish. Life's gonna get *more* interesting, I can sense it."

"I agree," responded Trish.

That said, the main door opened, and Gerry McBrine and Tom Casey strutted into the Pierpoint.

I threw my hands up to greet the men. "Gerry, Tom... it's ironic that you would walk in here today, because I had a dream with *you two* in it last night."

"Oh, Albert," Gerry said with a ghastly look. Tom Casey stopped dead in his tracks and deliberated over whether to sit at the bar.

"Joking, boys," I said and then laughed. "Barkeep, these two look a bit parched. Set them up with imperial pints of Guinness, would you.

"That's very kind of you, Albert," said Tom.

The whole scenario had an eerie, deja-vu feeling to it, and I related it to that day, seven years earlier, when Gerry and Tom made that similarly irregular appearance at the Pierpoint, which was my inception, really, into the Angus Wilde murder case.

Gerry and Tom situated themselves at the bar, adjacent to Liam McCool, and I introduced everyone (without getting into the forces that had assembled us, or else it surely would've scared Gerry and Tom off). Subsequently, old friends Michael John O'Rourke and wife Helen entered the Pierpoint. It had been many years since our last meeting, and, after they hugged Francie, I greeted them warmly.

Liam, Trish, and I enjoyed one more round of pints that afternoon and, considering their respective journeys back to Antrim and Castlebar, I suggested we eat dinner at the Pierpoint. The restaurant had been especially busy that evening, though, and, once it was clear that their departures would be delayed, I offered my home as accommodations, which they gratefully accepted.

I enjoyed an unobstructed view to the lounge from my seat and, just as we were being served coffee and dessert, I noticed a Pierpoint regular, Frank Hanley, running a bow across his fiddle. I then heard the familiar wheeze of Michael Dolan's accordion. The two men were ready to play, so Michael John O'Rourke stepped up on a chair and commenced singing *Galway Bay*. I thusly excused myself to go and listen to my friends perform. But before I edged away, Liam McCool clutched my right arm while emanating a look of pre-eminence.

"Enjoy this night, Albert. For surely there's work to be done tomorrow."

17

WITH DAUGHTERS JODIE AND Tessie having moved away long ago, I had grown accustomed to living alone and didn't sleep well the night Liam and Trish stayed as guests in my home. And I think it's fair to say that, despite our common bond as mediums, we were, after all, still strangers to one another.

I arose shortly after 6 a.m. and immediately brewed a pot of fresh coffee, imagining that the aroma would rouse my new friends, because they still had long journeys ahead of them. I then preheated the oven and broke open a tube of Pillsbury cinnamon swirls, that had been sitting in the fridge since Hitler was a Corporal, and arranged them on a cookie sheet. When baked, I hoped they would serve as acceptable fare for Liam and Trish, because I didn't have the ingredients to prepare a full Irish breakfast.

After sliding the cookie sheet into the oven, I poured myself a cup of coffee and heated it further in the microwave while stepping out to collect the *The Irish Independent*, which sat in a receptacle near the front steps. I wasn't wearing eyeglasses, and the Sun had yet to peek over the eastern landscape, but the dawn light shone sufficiently that I was able to make out the headline on the newspaper, "British Prime Minister to Visit Dublin." Once back inside, I put on my glasses and read the subtitle, "Sir Nigel Etherington has a friend in Irish President Fitzgerald." Now sensing my guests stirring, I placed the newspaper on the kitchen table and removed my boiling coffee from the microwave. A sleepy-eyed Trish shuffled into the kitchen first while half-yawning.

"How'd you sleep, Trish?"

"Morning, Albert. Surprisingly well, considering the big dinner last night... and that I didn't sleep in my own bed."

Trish had also dreamt but was presently reluctant to share the details, I would later learn.

Liam entered the kitchen and arched his feet, stretching toward the ceiling. "Morning everyone," he said.

"G'morning," Trish and I said in unison.

"Sleep well?" I asked Liam.

"Yes, very well," Liam said, his eyes now fixed on the newspaper on the table. He then rotated the paper to read it more closely. "Etherington dares to travel to the south, eh?"

I found Liam's remark a bit troubling. I inferred some antagonism from his words but, after recalling that he hailed from Antrim in Northern Ireland, which is part of the United Kingdom, I suppose I shouldn't have been surprised, because British rule there remains a source of dissension not only for many residents of Northern Ireland but the Republic as well. His words did, however, reveal where he stood on the matter.

"Let me pour you both some coffee," I said. "The cinnamon swirls will be ready shortly."

"Oh, you shouldn't have, really, Albert," said Trish. We weren't expecting anything this morning. We didn't want to put you out." Trish had expected Liam to echo her remarks, but he was plainly engrossed in the article about the British Prime Minister's planned visit to Dublin.

I dug out two mugs from a kitchen cabinet, rinsed them, and placed them on the table.

"How do you take your coffee," I asked them.

"If you have a bit of cream or milk that would be *grand*," said Trish.

Liam remained focused like a laser beam on the news article but finally muttered, "Black."

I retrieved some half and half from the fridge, for Trish, and then donned a protective mitt to remove the hot tray of cinnamon swirls from the oven. Meanwhile, Liam garnered a sip of coffee but never took his eyes off the newspaper. I wondered what enthralled him so much about the news of the British Prime Minister's intended visit, and asked him casually about it while knocking the swirls from the cookie sheet into a small wicker basket I had lined with a paper napkin.

"What's the reason for Etherington's visit? You follow politics, do you?"

Liam broke his attention to check my expression, before responding.

"He and Fitzgerald are buddies. Fitzgerald is only the second modern President of Ireland to hail from Northern Ireland, you know. He was born in Belfast. He's a barrister and former Professor of Law. Fitzgerald grew up during 'The Troubles'," Liam went on, referring to the height of violent times in Northern Ireland, "but the thing that seems to have brought he and Etherington together, oddly, is the printing industry," he proclaimed authoritatively while looking back and forth between Trish and me. "Fitzgerald worked in his father's printing business while growing up, and again when attending Queen's University in Belfast. As for Etherington, he's a former printing mogul... that's where he made his millions before entering politics."

"I see," I only managed while distributing plates and napkins to Trish and Liam. Trish had already snatched a steaming cinnamon swirl from the basket and taken a nibble, and apparently didn't care to talk with food in her mouth. She did, however, keep her eyes fixed on Liam and studied him, now not so much because of the information he had imparted, I decided, but due to his features, which she now deemed strangely familiar.

"Surely you both knew that Fitzgerald is only the second person from Northern Ireland to be elected President of Ireland," Liam said interrogatively, again panning back and forth between Trish and me.

"Yes, of course," I said.

"Mary McAleese being the first," said Trish, demonstrating her knowledge. She then took a long draw of coffee.

I noticed that Trish's scrutiny of Liam McCool's face finally seemed to register some recognition on her part, despite having sat with Liam for several hours at the Pierpoint last evening; Trish was as focused on Liam as he was on the newspaper. *Surely Liam felt Trish's eyes on him from across the table,* I thought. *Why didn't he look up?* I now only waited for Trish to ask Liam something revealing – anything – that would clue me in to what she was thinking. She remained silent.

I removed a cinnamon swirl from the basket and took a bite while Trish sipped more coffee and reached nervously for second swirl. Liam didn't eat a stitch that morning and, somewhat rudely, continued concentrating all his attention on the article pertaining to Prime Minister Etherington's forthcoming visit. On a different subject, I felt compelled to finally question Liam about a remark he had made to me last evening.

"Liam, take the newspaper with you, if you like, but, for now, I'd like to continue our chat from the Pierpoint."

Liam politely folded the newspaper and placed it in front of him on the kitchen table.

"When I stood up from the dinner table last night, to mosey in and listen to my friends perform, you clasped my arm and admonished insightfully, 'Enjoy this night, Albert, for surely there's work to be done tomorrow.' We'll, it's tomorrow now. Did you receive any transmissions from the Omniscient One overnight? I surely don't recall any dreams, or at least they haven't occurred to me yet. And Trish isn't talking much, so I have to figure she's come up empty. So... what about you?"

"Negative," replied Liam, almost curtly.

"Well then, what's the plan?"

"Like you, Albert... and Trish, I figured that if the Omniscient One had brought us together, it was for a good reason and that we would be put into service almost immediately. But, frankly, I'm a bit mystified, not only because we've yet to receive any direction but, ever since we met yesterday afternoon, I've discontinued receiving any visual packets concerning the lives of victims and other mediums."

Trish still sat without offering a word.

"You've been at this *medium thing* longer than both of us. What do you recommend we do?" I asked Liam.

"I suggest we exchange telephone numbers and e-mail addresses and go about our lives. When the Omniscient One is ready to engage us, individually or collectively, He will do so."

18

THE DRIVE FROM THE Pierpoint to my home takes all of five minutes, and I figured that the reason Trish Jennings had ridden with me the night before was that she didn't want to risk driving in unfamiliar territory after drinking a few pints. But once she asked about the bus schedule from Kinvara, the following morning, I realized she had used public transportation to reach our seaside village.

The next bus bound for Galway City wouldn't stop in Kinvara until mid-afternoon, so I offered to drive her to the station there so that she could catch an earlier bus to Westport and connect to Castlebar. Standing and listening to us, Liam felt obliged to mention that he wasn't immediately returning to Antrim, or else he would've dropped Trish someplace convenient. Sensing something suspicious from Liam's aspect, Trish and I looked to each other as he clutched the newspaper and took flight out the door without bidding us proper farewell. In truth, Liam *was* headed in a different direction – east toward Dublin, I would soon learn.

After perfunctorily cleaning up the kitchen and turning off the coffee pot, I directed Trish through the rear door and down the steps to my car. The Sun was fully visible now, its rays kissing the frothy ocean whitecaps to the west, just beyond scenic Kinvara Harbor. 'Twould be a beautiful day to do just about anything outside.

As we drove past the Kinvara Post Office, I observed old friend Gerry McBrine inserting his key in the front door, to open up for the day, his wife Carolyn standing behind him, waiting to enter. Carolyn recognized my car and waved before noticing the attractive young woman, sitting abreast, whom she failed to identify as either of my daughters. I sensed Carolyn's curious reaction and only tooted my horn while snickering and imagining her imminent speculation to Gerry. Carolyn and Gerry were early to work, this day, because pensioners like myself received their checks, and the volume of foot traffic through the post office would be heavy. I intended to pick up my check on the return trip from Galway, and expected to be probed, thereafter, concerning my mysterious female companion.

Passing by Seamount House, I pointed up on the hill to the now infamous clock tower and described, to Trish, the school there as it related to my initial activation as a medium. Trish behaved perceptibly intrigued once learning about the hollow fisherman cast, where I predicted Angus Wilde's corpse would be found, and she hinted that she wished to visit the tower. Knowing how infrequently buses ran to Westport, however, I persuaded my new friend that I'd arrange for such a tour, through the nuns, sometime in the future.

Trish and I had been chatting about this, that, and the other until passing beyond Kinvara's town limits, and the stillness along a woodsy, scarcely populated stretch of the Galway Road prompted a momentary silence between us. It was then I decided to question Trish on her persistent scrutinizing of Liam McCool's face, across my breakfast table this morning, which elicited discernible recognition in her face.

"Oh you picked up on that?" Trish responded. "You don't miss a trick."

"Well, I've been around enough years that I'm good at reading expressions. What about it? Do you think you know Liam from somewhere?"

"When we sat at the bar, getting acquainted yesterday, Liam was just another *Paddy* to me. Same thing at dinner – nothing occurred. But then at breakfast, when he began discussing 'The Troubles' in Northern Ireland, he seemed vaguely familiar. For a moment, I just dismissed it, after resolving that he simply possessed some characteristic ethnic features – it was Liam the Irishman, looking Irish, is what I decided I saw. However, I continued to study his face and mannerisms up until his rather abrupt departure from us this morning, and now I think Liam might be related to a man I once dated from Antrim. And I say 'related' because the fellow has a different last name, 'Tierney.' Logan Tierney was his name.

"I see. Well that's always a possibility. How did you meet Logan?"

"We met in a pub in Belfast. I was working on a case. The Omniscient One had guided me there." Trish then returned to the topic of Liam. "I want to reiterate, though, that the thing that got my mind working was all the talk by Liam about Northern Ireland. Did you see the passion in his face when he spoke, and the intense way he gripped the newspaper while reading the article about the British Prime Minister's visit to Dublin?"

"Yes, I did notice. And, as I mentioned, I also watched the manner in which you dissected his aspect. By the way, Trish, who broke things off between you and Logan Tierney, and why? When was your last contact?"

While riding along, Trish had been responding as if she was talking through the windshield, but now she snapped her head around to look at me in the driver's seat. My question had clearly struck a nerve.

"Well, if you must know... and I don't know why the information could possibly be useful to you... *I* broke it off. It's been more than a year since I've seen Logan."

"You didn't say the reason. Are you sure that *Logan* didn't break things off?"

"No! For Christ's sake, Albert, *I* broke it off! Because I discovered the bastard was a member of the Irish Republican Army, that's why! Okay?! Is that what you wanted to hear?" Trish's face became flush with anger, but she also clearly felt remorse over her outburst and now sat quietly while facing front again.

"Sorry to upset you, Trish, but my experience with the Omniscient One has taught me that most everything revealed to us mediums is connected. And, unless we have the benefit of having received information through embedded dreams, or being streamlined information, as if daydreaming... or in the case of Liam, receiving those 'visual packets,' then we have to try to figure out how things are related. I only asked you to elaborate because, like you and Liam, I think we were brought together for a reason. Once you described the similarities between Liam and Logan, I felt compelled to press on with it."

"I'm sorry, too, Albert. I didn't mean to respond so harshly. It's just that *Logan* is a sensitive topic with me – sensitive because he duped me.

If I had known that he was wrapped up with the IRA, I never would've carried on with him."

"One can understand his reasons for not wanting to readily divulge that kind of information, though. How did you eventually learn of his involvement with the IRA?"

"He kept insisting that we meet in pubs where IRA members were known to congregate. And once he and the other Paddies got a few pints into them, they often dropped their reserves and spoke explicitly. It only took a few visits to Belfast before I saw the writing on the wall. And when I finally confronted him on the matter, over the telephone, he never denied it. That was the end of it. I changed my telephone number and never called him back."

Despite the generation gap between Trish and me, I felt we had really clicked as friends – friends with a powerful common bond. We were as comfortable as new socks. I appreciated her frankness, and she didn't brood over the little outburst I had provoked. A moment later, we pointed simultaneously to the small Homicide Unit building, up off College Road, where we had respectively spent time with Inspector Pearse McElwee. The coincidence made for a humorous exchange and helped smooth over any lingering resentment she felt due to my meddlesome questions.

There was still something Trish was keeping from me, though. I could sense it. The details of that secret, and its implications, soon came to light after I dropped her at Eyre Square, just across from the Galway station.

19

TRISH HAD DREAMT OF Logan Tierney overnight in my Kinvara home, and I discovered the revelation in a very unexpected way. After dropping her at Eyre Square, I turned around and drove back up College Road. It was necessary to pause while a municipal construction crew lowered a culvert-pipe into an excavated area, so, meanwhile, I fiddled with the radio tuner to try to find some news. Nearly ten minutes elapsed before I resumed driving, and fifty vehicles, it seemed, had amassed behind me during the delay. As the stream of cars gradually followed, I had just finished passing a long stretch of tourist homes, and was about to negotiate a turn on a roundabout, when I experienced my first-ever visual packet.

I suppose it's worth mentioning that I didn't immediately recognize the manifestation, as such, until recalling Liam McCool's description of a visual packet, as he, Trish, and I shared medium experiences over dinner at the Pierpoint the night before. By the time I realized it was a visual packet, I was well into the traffic circle, and my fascination over the unusual display caused me to almost veer off the road and crash. Thankfully, I was able to turn off into a convenience store parking lot, while huffing and puffing, I might add, due to the trauma of it all, and I quickly shut down the engine. By now, the packet had vanished, and I didn't have chance, really, to consider the contents. Meanwhile, drivers, speeding past, leaned on their horns to object to my erratic driving.

Interestingly, once I collected myself in the parking lot, and was distraction-free, the visual packet reappeared. And I think it would be helpful at this time if I described the display so one can better understand my experience:

This first visual packet materialized over the hood of my car like a floating, four feet by five feet television screen, without any of the related television hardware – just an oscillating screen. I soon noticed that any time my eyes were diverted from the screen, by choice or due to distraction, the packet immediately diffused, as if vaporizing. When returning my attention to the area, the screen reappeared and resumed its presentation.

After determining that the phenomenon was, indeed, a visual packet, the first thing that occurred to me, in that parking lot, was: *I just sat idling at a road construction site for ten minutes – why couldn't the Omniscient One have indoctrinated me there, instead of introducing the device as I drove around a traffic circle, thereby endangering me? I may be in good enough shape to hike about the Burren, but I don't need any unnecessary jolts to the ticker.* Once again, it caused me to me wonder how the Omniscient One operates.

As for the subject matter of this first visual packet, it played out in three parts. First, I perceived Trish Jennings sleeping at my home the night before, dreaming of Logan Tierney, and, fantastically, it was as if I was able to tap in to those dreams. And, while Trish had quite evidently dreamt of Logan, (and she and I had just talked about the lad's physical resemblance to Liam McCool, during the drive from Kinvara to Galway City), she had chosen not to divulge the dream.

Did the Omniscient One provide me this first visual packet because Trish was opposed to alerting Liam and me of her dream? I wondered. In the dream, which, again, I was strangely able to view all contents, Trish watched Logan scaling Switzerland's Matterhorn, once regarded among the world's most dangerous mountains to climb. She subsequently observed him sitting at an outdoor café along Bahnhofstrasse, a main drag in nearby Zermatt, Switzerland, where he drank a hot beverage with a man he had hired as a climbing guide. Logan appeared demonstrably satisfied, after conquering the Matterhorn the day before, and chatted away with his guide-friend – that is, until noticing the headline on a *Financial Times* newspaper being sold by an adolescent along Bahnhofstrasse. Logan quickly paid the youngster and seized the newspaper in order to read the article about British Prime Minister Nigel Etherington's impending visit to Dublin. He soon became so immersed in the article that his guide-friend strayed into a nearby shop without Logan noticing.

In her next dream stage, Trish perceived Logan sitting in an aisle seat of an Aer Lingus jetliner in Zurich, the day after he left Zermatt. The aircraft had yet to taxi out to the runway, and Logan eagerly searched that day's *Financial Times*, which he purchased minutes earlier at an airport kiosk, for updates of Etherington's visit. The *Times* featured no headline-worthy news subsequent to the previous day's reporting, however, on page 15, he noticed a piece under "Education News" that he deemed infinitely valuable, relative to his own evolving plans. Some primary school children were to put on a play about the life of Johann Gutenberg, the notable 15th century printer, who was the first to use moveable type, and Irish President Fitzgerald and British Prime Minister Etherington, both veterans of the printing industry, topped the list of guests scheduled to attend a private showing. Fittingly, the play venue was listed as the Long Room of the Old Library at Trinity College, where a copy of the famous Gutenberg Bible resides. For security reasons, the date and time of the play was not published.

Trish Jennings may have considered her dream ordinary at the time, but if she had revealed it to Liam and me over breakfast, Liam would have spoken up immediately, because his brother, Logan, was just returning from a mountain-climbing expedition to Switzerland. Logan, you see, was Liam's fraternal, not identical, twin, who had commenced using the last name 'Tierney,' in recent years, on the streets of Northern Ireland, due to allegations of collusion in IRA bombings, which were true but not yet proven.

Having never laid eyes on Logan, I didn't actually know the individual to be Liam's brother, in the visual packet, until the second part of the presentation, which played out like a narrated documentary. And through it all, I wondered if the narrator's voice was that of the Omniscient One. During this stage, I, too, observed the person I'd eventually come to know as Logan McCool, climbing the treacherous Matterhorn and, later, browsing the shops along Bahnhofstrasse, in neighboring Zermatt, in tandem with his guide.

In the third part of the presentation, I watched as Liam McCool presently drove from Kinvara to Dublin, to pick up his brother Logan at the airport, which caused me to think: *What if the Omniscient One had chosen to engage Liam, Trish, and me in Kinvara? Would Liam have still proceeded to Dublin, regardless, to pick up his twin?* Then again, The Omniscient One *had* attempted to engage us, I decided. Trish Jennings merely failed to report her dream, which would permanently alter the lives of countless people.

During his drive to Dublin International Airport, Liam finally resumed receiving visual packets, after an eighteen-hour dry spell, but one packet only: of his brother sitting on the tarmac in Zurich, reading the newspaper article about the play Etherington and Fitzgerald would attend at Trinity College.

Thus, in this first dazzling visual packet I experienced, in addition to tapping into Trish's dreams, and viewing a presentation intended exclusively for me, I observed Liam McCool studying his own packet, so that I was aware of the information conveyed to him. I must admit to being impressed that Liam was able to continue driving while watching the contents of his own packet, without having to pull off the side of the road, as I did. But, then again, he had encountered thousands of packets over the years, according to him, and had developed a knack.

After my visual packet diffused, I started my car but idled in the convenience store parking lot, while reflecting. I shuddered when considering the coincidence of my own recent visit to the Old Library at Trinity College, to examine the Book of Kells, which, also, unexpectedly, led to a viewing of the Gutenberg Bible upstairs in the Long Room. It also prompted recollection that I had curiously found the Gutenberg Bible more intriguing than the Book of Kells, despite the Book's status as an international art treasure. So, one can imagine that, given the timeliness of my own first visit to the Old Library, my longstanding desire to view the Book notwithstanding, with this ordeal concerning Logan (and Liam) McCool shaking out the way it was, and the Omniscient One upgrading my communication system, to facilitate more timely, less ambiguous transmissions, I hardly deemed my visit to the Long Room to be happenstance. I was also forced to consider how Trish Jennings' life, by way of her brief relationship with Logan McCool, was intricately woven into this increasingly complicated affair. As Trish presently napped on a bus traveling from Westport to Castlebar, she was blissfully ignorant of the extent of her connections to Logan and Liam, or me, for that matter, but soon I would edify her, and, in the process, confront her on the omission of reporting her important dream.

One thing that *was* growing clearer, after viewing the contents of my visual packet over the last thirty minutes, was the reason Trish, Liam, and I had been drawn together, and that the Omniscient One unquestionably had His hand in it all.

20

CONFRONTING TRISH JENNINGS ABOUT the implications of her unreported dream would likely produce anxiety for us both, so I decided to wait until sitting comfortably at home in Kinvara. En route, I stopped in at the post office to collect my mail and was greeted by Carolyn McBrine, who, at first, made no mention of my mysterious female passenger from this morning, but I quickly deduced that that was the foremost subject on Carolyn's mind, once perceiving her devilish grin and exploring eyes, as she handed me my stack of mail. I simply greeted Carolyn and thanked her for her service, but, when it appeared I would get away without satisfying her curiosity, she cunningly extracted Trish's identity.

"Your daughter Tessie looked so grown up when I saw her riding with you this morning, Albert. How long has Tessie been away now?"

"Oh, that wasn't Tessie, Carolyn. Tessie's still living and working down on Great Blasket Island."

That's all I had intended to say, but Carolyn persisted with me.

"Oh, really. Well, *who* then was the attractive woman riding with you, Albert? Do tell."

I chuckled before responding, which caused Carolyn to laugh also. I knew that Carolyn wasn't snooping as much as she was trying to discover if I was finally taking up with another woman, since the death of my wife so many years ago.

"The young lady is from Castlebar, County Mayo. It seems that she and I possess the same insightful faculties."

Being married to Gerry McBrine, who was integrally involved with me on the Haimish Devlin case, Carolyn was well acquainted with my so-called "insightful faculties" and didn't probe further. I smiled and waved good-bye before reaching for the door.

"Take care, Albert," said Carolyn. "All the same, you two look good together," she half-whispered while cupping her hand around her mouth.

I laughed again and eased out the door.

After fixing myself an early, light lunch, I nestled into a wing chair with a cup of tea and my cellular phone, and switched on the lamp to better see the numbers pad on the miniature phone. I felt ill-at-ease about the call I was about to make to Trish Jennings; nevertheless, it was a call that needed to be made.

If my calculations were correct, Trish was likely on the final leg of her trip to Castlebar. I considered that she might not want to "get into it" while riding on a public bus and that I would need to call her back when she arrived home. However, as it turned out, she had switched her cellphone to the vibrate mode, and instead of situating the phone against her person, where she could feel the vibration, she had placed it in her handbag; Trish presently napped, and the vibration failed to wake her. How did I come to discover this? When repeated calls to Trish went unanswered, the Omniscient One provided a second visual packet, the first such I had enjoyed in the comfort of my home. Suddenly, His provision made me feel important again.

Faced with the fact that it might be several hours before I connected with Trish, I decided to call Liam McCool, who was nearing his destination, Dublin International Airport:

"Liam, Albert Doyle here."

"Hi, Albert."

Out of the blue, a visual packet materialized in my living room so that I was able to view Liam talking to me, on a real-time basis, as he drove on the outskirts of Dublin.

"Liam, I was interested to know if you had resumed receiving visual packets since departing Kinvara. I know you were a little concerned about the lapse you encountered."

"No, Albert. Still no packets, but I'm enjoying the respite, really. Being bombarded with packets every day can be de-energizing, at times... as you might imagine."

Liam, of course, had just lied, because I observed him, earlier, viewing the packet informing him of his brother Logan's status and activities in Switzerland, through my own packet, which I watched in the convenience store parking lot in Galway City.

"It's funny you put it that way, Liam, because I no longer have to *imagine* what it's like to experience a visual packet. That's the other reason I'm calling. I wanted to tell you that I viewed my first packet this morning."

"Oh, did you, now? Well, I can recall how excited I was when first making the transition from dreams to packets. The novelty wears off some, though. Everything's relative. What was the subject matter of your packet?"

"Actually, Liam, it was of you... and your brother, Logan. You're driving to Dublin International, now, to pick him up, right?"

"Oh, you know what, Albert... I've got an incoming call... a very important one that I've been waiting on. I'm afraid I'm going to have to take it. Sorry.

"Okay, friend," I barely managed, before Liam said, "Bye" and disconnected.

Liam had lied a second time when saying that he needed to answer an incoming call. I knew this because I watched him all along by way of the suspended visual packet still playing out in my living room, which just showed him folding up his cellular phone and tossing it cavalierly on the empty passenger seat.

Liam had had few misgivings about being deceptive when it came to protecting his fraternal twin brother, because, while he didn't entirely agree with Logan's deep-rooted convictions about the use of violence to affect England's occupation of northern Ireland, he certainly empathized. And after watching the *final* visual packet he would ever experience in life, it turned out, which foreshadowed the evil he knew Logan to be capable of, Liam decided not warn authorities, because he believed doing so would lead to his brother's arrest and prosecution for conspiracy to assassinate the British Prime Minister – a prosecution that would've been successful, it's fair to say, given the precedence of allegations of Logan's complicity in IRA bombings in Belfast and

Londonderry. Hence, Logan McCool would likely go away to prison for many years.

Once picking up Logan at the airport, Liam's plan, instead, was merely to remove his brother as quickly as possible from Dublin, where Sir Nigel Etherington and Irish President James Fitzgerald would soon meet and, among other ceremonies and activities, attend a play to be put on by some primary school children.

I stayed close to home that beautiful day and repeatedly tried reaching Trish Jennings, but to no avail, as she had been outdoors lungeing a horse, in-training, at a riding ring on her family's Castlebar equestrian property. Meanwhile, her cellphone vibrated intermittently inside her handbag, which sat on a dresser in the thatched-roof cottage she occupied, a quarter mile from her parents' residence. When failing to connect with Trish, I tried a few follow-up calls to Liam McCool, but he wasn't picking up either, and I had to figure that he had identified me through the Caller I.D. feature and had chosen not to answer. What's more, his cell wasn't set up to receive voice-mail, which I found peculiar, given his longstanding, critical role as a conciliator.

I stayed busy by straightening up my home that afternoon while waiting for another packet from the Omniscient One that would hopefully illustrate that Liam had successfully transported Logan far away from Dublin. But when that packet never materialized, given the potential perils at hand, I weighed calling Garda Inspector Pearse McElwee. Knowing McElwee, I expected him to remind me, from his professional law enforcement perspective, of the competence and thoroughness of the British agents assigned to protect their Prime Minister, all the while, fastidiously recording details of my insights, which he would surely act on. But before calling the Inspector, I'd first watch the evening news for word of Sir Nigel's arrival, and hope that I'd be able to reach both Trish and Liam, who I still believed were brought into my life for a reason, and me into theirs.

21

Unsurprisingly, the top news story being reported that evening pertained to British Prime Minister Etherington and wife Meg's earlier arrival in Ireland. Not wanting to miss a moment, I set up a dinner tray in my living room, to watch. The first segment showed the Etheringtons waving as they disembarked their plane at Dublin International Airport. They were subsequently received by Irish President James Fitzgerald and wife Robin, and upon observing the foursome embrace familiarly, I imagined how Logan McCool would feel about the public display of affection, wherever he currently idled.

After the correspondent concluded her airport piece, coverage switched to a live shot of the President's home in Phoenix Park, where the Fitzgeralds and Etheringtons reportedly enjoyed a casual dinner together. In the foreground, on the drive in front of the residence, a small army of civilian security agents conspicuously hovered. The reporter lastly speculated about the Prime Minister's itinerary while in Ireland, but, due to real security concerns, that schedule remained strictly confidential.

Following the news, I washed my dishes and returned to my chair with a cup of tea and cellular phone. I now only waited for the dinner hour to expire, so that I could again attempt to reach Trish Jennings. While perusing the channels, I couldn't resist pausing to watch a re-run of that old *Cagney and Lacey* program, largely because the improbable airing of the long gone-by series sparked recollection of spotting Tyne

Daly at Dublin Airport on the day I departed in pursuit of Haimish Devlin. Was it only coincidence that I presently viewed this program? I had quickly grown accustomed to the Omniscient One utilizing visual packets as a means to communicate with me, but now I suspected there might be some cryptic message I was supposed to decipher from this episode. Predictably, I fell asleep while watching the show, and, by the time I awoke, I knew it would be impolite to call Trish at such a late hour. The program that was running when I awoke, by the way, was *Judging Amy*, and Ms. Tyne Daly was, mysteriously, again front and center on the television screen. My mind naturally wandered.

I had been sitting in my kitchen, the following morning, eating a buttery scone and drinking the last of some Moroccan coffee I had brought back in the hooker, when I received my next visual packet, and I must say that it was as enjoyable as watching a nature program. As the packet unraveled, I first recognized Trish Jennings emerging from the quaint, white cottage, with thatched roof, she occupied, at her parents' sprawling Jennings Equestrian Centre property. Trish wore beige, slim-fitting riding pants, a white, long-sleeve top, and black riding boots that came up to just below the knee. Her shoulder-length, dirty-blonde locks played marvelously off her outfit and accentuated her undeniable feminine allure.

Most of the twenty-odd horses at the Centre were already out on pasture that morning, and I soon perceived Trish enticing them back to the stables with a flake of alfalfa-hay, so that she could halter a favorite Morgan for riding; however, the horses had plenty of rich pasture to graze on this early spring, and snubbed the offering. Trish countered by throwing some sweet-feed into a bucket and shaking it, signaling that a treat was being provided, and the herd galloped thunderously toward her. She subsequently warded off the powerful, bobbing heads of a few horses competing for the feed, and allowed her chosen Morgan to garner some mash. Next, she haltered the horse and led it a short distance to a stable overhang, where she cross-tied and groomed it. It was then I noticed Trish's cellular phone clipped to her riding pants, and I considered calling her but recognized the potentially hazardous situation at-hand, with a potentially skittish, thousand pound beast standing beside her; I didn't want to put her at risk by calling and alarming the animal, so waited for a more opportune moment.

Having groomed the Morgan, she strode back and forth between the horse and a nearby tack room, collecting an English-style saddle, a bridle, and protective riding hat. Once saddling and bridling the horse, she donned her hat, untied the horse, and mounted it. She then prodded the handsome Morgan forward, and as the horse pranced energetically away, I made out a sign posted on an exterior stable wall, "Jennings Equestrian Centre, AIRE Approved, Indoor and Outdoor Schools, Trail Riding, Trekking, 18 Horses, 11 Ponies."

Trish eventually planned to access a familiar trail system located at the base of an adjacent short hill, but, first, followed the wide, gravelly path leading to her parents' stately residence: a fieldstone-constructed, north-facing, two-story manor that was in harmony with the rest of the charmingly mature, rustic property, and featured a durable slate roof, suitable to withstand harsh maritime conditions, as well as a more modern conservatory on the west side of the home.

The horse that Trish rode frolicked some, and perhaps that's the reason she preferred him, but I easily discerned the bond between the two and that the creature was clearly under her docile control. I thusly decided it timely to call Trish, who I observed accessing her cellular phone without incident.

"Hello, Trish. It's Albert Doyle."

"Albert. How've you been? You know, it occurred to me last evening that if you or Liam had been trying to reach me, you wouldn't have been able. I had unwittingly left my cellphone on the vibrate mode, inside my handbag. We're you trying to reach me?"

"Yes, Trish. As a matter of fact, I was. Listen, I won't beat around the bush, because a lot has transpired since I dropped you at Eyre Square."

"Really? What is it?" Her voice inflection suggested genuine concern.

"But before I describe the state of affairs, I need to ask you some questions, and I want you to be forthcoming."

"Naturally, Albert. I have no reason *not* to be."

"Why didn't you inform me or Liam about the dream you experienced overnight at my home? I know you dreamt about Logan in Switzerland. You also had ample opportunity to reveal the dream as we discussed Logan during the ride to Galway City."

A conspicuous lull suggested real deliberation at Trish's end. She dismounted her horse and was now leading him on foot. If Trish didn't know me to possess the same clairvoyant capabilities, she might've tried to deceive me because, frankly, "Logan" was none of my business. But I think she sensed she was about to discover some unfavorable implications due to her omission, and grew visibly nervous.

"True enough, Albert. I did, indeed, dream about Logan Tierney while sleeping at your home... and the reason I didn't tell you or Liam was that I determined that Liam's resemblance to Logan had subconsciously triggered the dream. And I say 'subconsciously' because I had spent the previous afternoon and evening across from Liam at the Pierpoint without knowingly drawing any similarities between them. Obviously, my *mind* was working in that direction, though. As I described to you during the ride from Kinvara to Galway City, it wasn't until Liam talked passionately about 'The Troubles' in Northern Ireland, at your breakfast table the following morning, that I consciously recognized his likeness. So, once attributing the reason for the dream, I decided not to raise the topic of my relationship with Logan, which, was, and still is, a source of embarrassment and aggravation for me."

"That's all well and good, Trish, but you need to know what's developed in the aftermath. First of all, I received my first visual packet just minutes after dropping you at Eyre Square..."

Trish interrupted. "Oh, did you now? "I've been at this medium thing longer than you, and the Omniscient One still uses dreams to transmit His communiqués to me. I'm envious."

"Nevermind that. Your time will come. Time is now of the essence. The foremost thing you need to know is that Logan's last name is *not* 'Tierney.' Tierney is an alias. His real last name is *McCool*, and Logan is Liam's fraternal twin brother..."

"Oh my God!" Trish reacted by gasping and momentarily letting go of the horse's bridle, to place both hands over her mouth. She then grabbed the bridle again and efficiently pivoted the horse about face, to walk him back to the stable. Trish had yet to hear the more critical elements of my exposé but intuited that she wouldn't be riding this morning; after serving as a medium for more than a decade, she knew, well, that everything was subject to change.

"... And, not only did I perceive you dreaming about Logan, but I was able to tap into those dreams. In part, that's how I know about

Logan's mountain-climbing excursion to Switzerland. Through my visual packet, I also observed Liam McCool driving to Dublin en route to the airport, yesterday, to pick up Logan. Plus, I viewed Liam watching his own packet, the contents of which I analyzed. But when I telephoned Liam to inform him that I received my first packet, and that it concerned he and Logan, he abruptly terminated the conversation. He cut me off is what he did. Trish, I'll confirm to you now what you might have suspected when pondering your own dream about Logan McCool, and what his brother Liam already knows to be true: Logan is considering assassinating British Prime Minister Etherington."

Trish was bowled over and distraught.

"Sacred Heart! Albert, I really had no idea, when perceiving Logan poring over that *Financial Times* newspaper in my dream, that he was thinking about murder! I never made the connection, or else I would've spoken up."

"Trish, do you know that I'm currently observing you, through a packet, walking your horse back to the stable?"

"I believe you, Albert."

"The point is... the Omniscient One is clearly initiating a process that will put us into action. I must have your cooperation, and you *must* be available to travel at the drop of a hat. I think that Liam tried to usher Logan from Dublin before he could harm anyone, but I also believe that Liam will try to protect his brother at any cost... even if he's not successful at removing him. The problem is that I have yet to receive a packet updating me of Logan's or Liam's statuses."

22

AFTER TRISH AND I got off the line, I took care of some household matters, because I assumed I'd be traveling to Dublin to intercede, in some manner, the impending perilous situation that could irreparably impair Irish-English relations and claim the life of one or more people. I happened to know that old friend Tom Casey was on vacation this week and, after convincing him that I wouldn't enlist him in any affairs that might cause anguish for him or his family, Tom agreed to drive me, when requested, to the train station in Galway City. He would be remunerated for his services.

The telephone rang while I paid a few bills, so I picked up. It was daughter Jodie calling from Dublin. Jodie kindly inquired of her aging father's well-being, and, after informing her that I was fine, I alluded to the possibility of me soon traveling to Dublin on a "consulting matter." I didn't like being evasive with Jodie, or her sister Tessie, but knew the two would sleep better if remaining oblivious to the nature of their old dad's recurrent dealings. The call from Jodie prompted me to, in turn, call her sister, Tessie, down on Great Blasket Island: Tessie was well and happy but hinted that, due to the isolation she once found appealing, she was presently considering a move back to the mainland. I encouraged the move and assured her that she was welcome to return to live in the Kinvara home where she had grown up. Tessie thanked me but suggested she was thinking more along the lines of a move to Cork

City. She was a young woman enjoying her independence, I could tell; nevertheless, I felt obliged to make the offer.

I had been sitting at my kitchen table, and was half-way through a tuna-salad sandwich, when a long awaited visual packet appeared, updating me of events from late yesterday. The first segment showed Liam McCool, leaning against his illegally parked car at Dublin International Airport, waiting for his fraternal twin brother, Logan, to arrive through the automatic glass doors. Logan soon emerged, and the two shook hands and embraced. Logan then tossed his gear into the back seat of Liam's car, and they sped off.

In a conversation that rapidly escalated into heated argument, Logan informed Liam that he didn't care to immediately return to Antrim and, instead, intended to spend the rest of the week unwinding in Dublin; specifically, he wanted to hit the pubs in the Temple Bar district.

Logan was well aware of Liam's service to the Omniscient One over the preceding fifteen years; he often begrudged Liam, in fact, because of his powers, and felt excluded. Logan reckoned that, as a twin, he should've been endowed equally by the Omniscient One, and, as the years passed without any similar bestowal of extraordinary faculties upon him, Logan increasingly gravitated to the darker side of things in life, in rebellion.

At first, Liam refused to drop Logan in Temple Bar, and referenced the visual packet he recently received in which the Omniscient One proposed that Logan was scheming to assassinate the British Prime Minister. Logan responded by laughing at the absurdity of it all, and contended, "Your (Liam's) god has faults, after all... because I planned no such thing! I was merely fantasizing while reading those newspapers in Switzerland."

Liam's current dilemma was that the Omniscient One had discontinued providing him visual packets, and he wasn't able to discover if Logan was lying to him or not. (In retrospect, as I recount the events that have already transpired, I believe that Liam was, ironically, shut off from receiving additional packets due to elements of his own dishonesty related to Logan, which the Omniscient One deemed intolerable. That's my opinion, I welcome yours).

Once Liam ceased receiving packets, and was put in the precarious position of not being able to verify the truthfulness of Logan's declarations, he made the critical mistake of allowing Logan to persuade him to stop for "two pints only" at a former favorite watering hole, The Foggy Dew, in Temple Bar, before proceeding home to Antrim.

Logan slyly excused himself to go to the men's room after finishing his first pint at The Foggy Dew. Next, he crawled out a window, scampered through an alleyway, and, when unable to retrieve his bags from his brother's locked car, barefacedly broke a rear window, unlocked the door, and fled with his belongings. In doing so, Logan indifferently left his brother with the bar tab, a broken car window, and the burden of a potentially disastrous situation, should he decide to act out his assassination fantasies.

Liam soon discovered Logan's antics and, rather than return to Antrim, chose to remain in Temple Bar to scour the district for his wayward brother. He checked into a well-appointed tourist home up off Grafton Street, while Logan had already set up at a seedy rooming house down near the intersection of Gardiner and Railway Streets, using a new alias, "Joe O'Malley." Logan was now also on the prowl to acquire an illegal firearm.

This had all occurred the day before, of course, after Liam left my home to pick up Logan at the airport, and the Omniscient One was now inducing me to travel to Dublin. Consequently, the instant this latest visual packet diffused, I telephoned Tom Casey over in Parkroe, Kinvara, and asked him to drive me to the Galway train station. While waiting for Tom, I heedlessly packed enough clothes for three days, into the tattered travel bag I had toted all over the Canary Islands and Morocco. I locked my home, and, as I stood on the back landing waiting for Tom to arrive, I called Trish Jennings in Castlebar, on my cellular phone, to inform her of the revelations contained in my packet of a few moments ago.

Trish had earlier indicated she would meet me at the train station in Galway, and we would make the three-hour journey together. Due to the urgency of the situation, however, I informed her that I wasn't waiting around and would board the first available train. Trish thusly decided, at the last moment, to drive to Dublin.

23

BEFORE LEAVING HOME, TOM Casey had telephoned his son Padraic in Galway to arrange a visit with him while in the city. After purchasing my ticket, I realized I had an hour and fifteen minutes to kill before the train departed, so decided to join Tom and Padraic at the nearby rustic pub, The Quays. Tom was naturally curious to hear more about the Haimish Devlin case, of which he had once been involved, that eventually propelled me beyond Ireland, to Africa, in pursuit of the deposed, murdering priest. I was glad to oblige with the particulars. Tom and Padraic especially enjoyed the recounting of Haimish's final moments in Fez, Morocco, when the fugitive slipped from the unusual Water Clock, knocking himself unconscious in the process, and slid into the copper trough that had filled overnight, after an uncharacteristic heavy rainfall; with Haimish only to be electrocuted, an instant later, by a crashing lightning strike that deflected down the grade of the metal roof, to seemingly find him. I then described my return sailing trip from Africa to Ireland in Angus Wilde's hooker, which prompted Tom to inform me that the now-legendary hooker had recently been sold at auction, after Angus' surviving sister, from Lisdoonvarna, elected to liquidate his remaining property. Tom and his wife, Angela, had attended the auction, and Tom recalled that a young chap from Westport, County Mayo, who had settled on fishing for a livelihood, paid a handsome premium to acquire the infamous boat. Once the fellow remitted payment, he sailed the hooker from Kinvara harbor, northwest to Westport.

Tom and I had strayed from the topic of my sailing trip from Africa to Ireland, and now he began pressing me on "what (I) was currently working on with *that* blonde lass." Given the uncertainty of a still unfolding situation, however, I looked at my watch, gulped down the last of the Guinness in my glass, and politely bid the Caseys farewell.

On the hike back through Eyre Square to the train station, I wondered how Tom had known about Trish Jennings, or "*that* blonde lass," as he referred to her, but soon remembered that Carolyn McBrine was Tom Casey's sister-in-law, and I deduced that he had heard about Trish and I riding together, in my car, through the family grapevine.

Unlike my most recent train trip across Ireland, when I knew that sweet Jodie waited for me on the other side, this journey had a palpably ominous feel to it. The visual picket I received from the Omniscient One, over lunch in Kinvara, had been timely and detailed; nonetheless, a fear of the unknown pervaded my being.

After disembarking in Dublin, I stopped at a retail eatery inside Heuston Station to purchase a beverage and call Trish Jennings, to check her progress. Trish was still on the road, with another hour to go, according to her, because she had punctured a tire and needed to get it plugged at a station in Athlone. I told Trish to ring me up after checking in at the Temple Bar Hotel, where I recommended we stay.

I boarded a taxi curbside at Heuston Station, with instructions for the driver to take me to the Temple Bar Hotel. I was hopeful I'd receive another visual packet en route to the hotel, but, when that packet failed to materialize, I determined that the Omniscient One had deemed it not yet necessary. But that's just speculation. Once checking in, I called my daughter Jodie to notify her that I had arrived in Dublin. I would've been remiss, otherwise, because to have bumped into her while in the city would've proven awkward. Then again, Jodie was generally in school with the children during the day. When she questioned me, in more detail, about the "consulting matter" that had brought me to Dublin, I regrettably uttered a white lie. "Boring geology stuff," I told her. "A bunch of old men sitting around talking about rocks."

I fell asleep while resting at the hotel and waiting for Trish Jennings to arrive, and the Omniscient One chose to communicate to me in a dream during that nap. When awakening, I first fretted that He had downgraded my means of receiving communications, but, then, rationalized that I wasn't awake to receive His visual packet, so He must've resorted to embedding a dream.

As for the contents of the dream, I perceived Logan McCool exiting a medical supply store off O'Connell Street, Dublin's main thoroughfare, where he had just purchased a small trash container, white in color, typically found in any hospital room, clinic, or doctor's office. The cylindrically-shaped waste receptacle featured a removable, sturdy, plastic liner and a pedal at the base, so that when the pedal was depressed, the lid opened. Logan then tramped down a side street, perpendicular to O'Connell Street, and entered a neighborhood store, where he purchased some non-perishable food and bottled water, finally sauntering several blocks to the rooming house and emptying the contents onto his bed. The last item he removed was a long-barrel, .44 magnum pistol, which was tucked away in the small of his back, covered by the windbreaker he wore. He pushed a release on the side of the revolver, to open the loaded cylinder, and twirled it like a cowboy from a bad B-movie. Suddenly, I experienced real dread.

That aspect of the dream had faded, and I next perceived his fraternal twin brother, Liam, trolling the streets of Temple Bar in search of Logan. Liam entered the larger bars in the district and audited the clientele until satisfied that Logan wasn't present; for the smaller pubs, he simply opened the main door, to peek inside, which, more often than not, drew unpleasant reactions from rankled patrons and employees.

Knowing, intimately, his forgiving twin's inclinations, Logan had predicted that Liam would remain in Temple Bar to search for him. So, when it was time for his next pint, he unearthed an obscure, alleyway dive in the bowels of Railway Street and, there, he drank, far removed from Temple Bar.

Once resolving that there was nothing further to quarry from my dream, I again attempted to connect with Liam McCool, by way of his cellphone, but he still wouldn't take my call, which rolled over to a familiar automated message, "the wireless customer you're trying to reach is not currently available," which I knew to mean that he had neglected to set up his voicemail. If Liam had only known that I was able to provide him with the information he needed to intercept his brother, and, therefore, prevent Logan from carrying out his malevolent imperative, Liam, in retrospect, most certainly would've taken the call, and, in the end, spared us all the eternal grief that would follow.

Given the Omniscient One's explicit advice, in terms of the twins' whereabouts and activities, I considered just going out on my own and intervening in Logan's affairs before Trish arrived. First, I thought about confronting the hooligan down at that squalid barroom off Railway Street, and wondered if Logan was again packing the piece in the small of his back. Interestingly, I related the situation to when Haimish Devlin had desperately fled into the ancient Khettara aqueduct system, in the old, walled fortress of Marrakesh, Morocco, and I quickly ruled out braving the likes of Logan over on Railway Street. Instead, I ventured out into Temple Bar, in the chance I might stumble into Liam, who, according to my dream of a short while ago, still searched for his brother.

After almost an hour of hunting for Liam, I finally recognized him from afar as he exited a café near the intersection of Great Strand and Jervis Streets. Liam had on the same jacket and trousers he had worn to Kinvara. I reacted by leaping joyously and waving while shouting his name. Liam lurched around because he thought it had been his brother, Logan, calling, but, the instant he recognized it was me, Albert Doyle, scurrying toward him, he melded into the dense city foot traffic to elude me.

Liam's flight on foot prompted me to again consider my call to him, the day before, as he drove to Dublin to pick up Logan, and how he reacted upon learning that my first visual packet pertained to him and his black-sheep brother. *Liam had too much experience with the Omniscient One*, I thought. Despite being deprived his packets, I was certain Liam had accurately intuited not only what I was about to confirm to him about Logan's visit to Switzerland, but everything that had occurred in the twins' lives over the succeeding thirty hours in Dublin. Moreover, when Liam McCool had just fled from me, it reinforced my belief that he intended to protect his brother at any cost.

24

I WASN'T ABOUT TO CHASE an agile 40-year old through the streets of Dublin that night, so I returned to the Temple Bar Hotel, hoping that the Omniscient One would eventually chime in with further guidance. When I strolled into the lobby, Trish Jennings was just checking in, so I smiled thinly and nodded, and then walked up to hug her, which caught her off guard but did not entirely displease her. She and I subsequently engaged in small talk at the desk as the clerk processed her registration, during which time Trish vented over her cross-country travails, which were not limited to the punctured tire near Athlone. Before departing registration, I asked Trish if she had been clever enough to request a room nearby to mine, or at least on the same floor, in case elements of our collaboration required frequent face to face contact. She had. I then carried her meager luggage to the elevator and, during our ride to the fourth floor, updated my attractive friend on matters pertaining to Logan and Liam.

Trish was expectedly horrified to learn that Logan had procured an illegal firearm, a powerful one at that, during the short time he had been in Dublin. She also felt guilty, after speculating that she'd be of little help to me on this case, because, while I was regularly receiving critical communiqués from the Omniscient One, she had failed to recall even one dream since the one of Logan, in Switzerland, that she experienced at my home. I consoled Trish by reassuring her that even if the Omniscient One had chosen not to utilize her as clairvoyant instrument in this case, she would be invaluable to me in matters requiring legwork and human interaction.

Trish was frazzled, following her demanding journey, and didn't care to step out to Temple Bar for a hot meal, so, instead, we ordered room service and dined together in her room while continuing to discuss the "The McCool case," as we now referred to it. Our discussion soon led to a joint decision to contact Inspector Pearse McElwee, with whom we had both been accustomed to dealing, and who was well-acquainted with our extrasensory gifts. Trish and I were especially concerned about Logan McCool's possession of a handgun, which had been the driving factor in the call.

Upon telephoning McElwee's Garda district office, and explaining myself to an underling working the evening shift, I was patched through to the Inspector's home in County Mayo, and I recounted my recent paranormal experiences, detailing the looming perils relative to the British Prime Minister. The Inspector recorded my number and assured me he'd call back that evening.

Trish ate cheesecake and I ate carrot cake, and we drank tea and watched television for news updates of Prime Minister Etherington's visit, while waiting for the Inspector's call. McElwee telephoned about forty-five minutes later to inform me that a Garda representative from Dublin, accompanied by one or more British security agents, would visit Trish and me at the Temple Bar Hotel, to interview us.

At half past eight that evening, the telephone rang in Trish's room. It was Inspector Chaz Murphy, of the Garda-Dublin, calling, who asked that Trish and I come down to the lobby. Even though the referral had come from his colleague, Pearse McElwee, it was Murphy's first experience with the likes of Trish and me, so, in the interest of security, introductions would take place in the more public lobby. Inspector Murphy was joined by a fellow Garda Inspector, Patrick Kerrey, and two senior British agents assigned to protect Prime Minister Etherington. The Brits identified themselves as Edmund Rathbone and Michael Lyons. After introductions were made, the six of us made an uncomfortably quiet elevator ride up to the fourth floor, where it was predetermined, I surmised, that Trish and I be split up during interviews. Garda Inspector Murphy and British agent Lyons interviewed Trish in her room, and I was interviewed by Kerrey and Rathbone in mine.

Trish and I compared notes after the interviews concluded, and humorously discussed the unmistakable, dubious attitudes of the four law enforcement officials, because, unlike Inspector McElwee, clearly none of these men had had previous "medium experience." And, while they dutifully notated, carefully explored, and would imminently attempt to corroborate our assertions, for purposes of ensuring the protection of the British Prime Minister (and Irish President), Trish and I were not convinced that the men would approach the agenda, derived from our interviews, with the same zeal they ordinarily applied to their work. Simply put, they questioned our credibility. That, my friends, would prove a fatal mistake.

Before departing, the four men recorded our cellular phone numbers and, similarly, we were provided primary and secondary telephone numbers for them, in case a subsequent consult was necessary. Despite the discernible "attitude" we received from the men, I will admit that all parties were, at least, thorough and professional in their work. Lastly, Trish and I were asked to remain in Dublin at the Temple Bar Hotel until Prime Minister Etherington left Ireland, although we were never told when that would be, and that arrangements would be made by the Irish and/or British governments to pay for our accommodations and meals. Trish and I hardly resisted the offering. Once the men left, Trish reiterated how drained she felt, after her taxing day, and decided to hit the sack. I drank a second cup of tea in my room and watched television until about midnight, when experiencing my next visual packet.

25

MEMBERS OF THE GARDA, accompanied by agents of the British security service, scarcely delayed in acting on the information Trish Jennings and I had provided during our interviews that night. As the visual packet unraveled in my room, I quickly turned off the television to view the contents without distraction, so that the packet would play through without stoppage. In the first stage, I perceived both uniformed and plainclothes officers pounding determinedly on the front door of the seedy rooming house where Logan McCool purportedly stayed. An aging woman, with moisturizing cream applied liberally about her face, came to the door and frightfully peered out an abutting window to behold the uniformed callers. The woman unlocked the door and self-effacingly bunched her nightie up around her neck, to prevent her cleavage from being ogled. The lead officer immediately showed the woman an enlarged picture, produced from Logan McCool's driver's license, and asked to be directed to the room of "Joe O'Malley," the alias I alleged Logan to be using. O'Malley had serendipitously checked out earlier in the evening and, after the proprietor related such, the officer demanded to inspect the room. Several officers proceeded to turn the room upside down, for evidence possibly left behind by Logan, and the raucous activity caused several sleep-eyed tenants to emerge. The lady of the home and occupants were subsequently interviewed concerning their contacts with Joe O'Malley, as trivial as his comings and goings might have seemed at the time, and were also queried about his destination. None of those questioned had known where Joe intended to go, however, one tenant did observe him carrying a backpack, fully stuffed.

In the next stage of the visual packet, I watched as a second group of police officers arrived at the comfortable tourist home on Grafton Street, in search of Logan's fraternal twin brother, Liam. This raid had actually occurred simultaneous to the search for Logan at the rooming house; different venue, albeit same outcome – Liam had fortuitously checked out. At first, I felt relieved when processing this coincidence in my mind, because I determined that Liam had managed to track down his brother, after all. *Did Logan agree to return to Antrim with Liam willingly, or was it necessary for Liam to seize Logan off the streets and manhandle him, to the extent that he forced his brother into the vehicle?* I wondered. The answer to that question came later – too late, it's sad to say.

In retrospect, I came to recognize the period following the apparent vacation of the McCool brothers, from Dublin, as one of the most mystifying of all the Omniscient One's dealings with me over the years. The reasons are twofold: due to the suspension of my (and Trish Jennings') insightful gifts during the succeeding days, the Omniscient One allowed me to unsuspectingly ebb into a state of appeasement. I thought that all was well; hence, He was not impelled to apprise me of Liam and Logan's statuses. All was *not* well. The second, more devastating reason was who the Omniscient One allowed to die as a result of the disastrous events that day.

The next visual packet I received didn't materialize for two plus days, when Trish and I had just returned to the hotel after a late lunch at Leo Burdock's Fish & Chips. Once in my room, I prepared a cup of tea and sat down, intending to read the newspaper, when, suddenly, the packet appeared and played out like a horror movie. So late was this packet to arrive that, as with the cases of Angus Wilde and Father Ruben Serna, there was nothing, really, Trish or I could do to mitigate the situation. The following is an account of the contents of that packet, the revelations of some corroborating investigative work, and my personal experiences and observations in the aftermath:

Logan McCool had not left the city of Dublin and neither had his fraternal twin, Liam. It seems that while Liam had been poking around the Temple Bar district in search of his brother, he happened upon a tourist home every bit as nice as the one on Grafton Street but much less expensive. Accordingly, he left Grafton Street and checked into a home on Essex Street. Had I been aware, of course, I would've shared this information with the Garda.

In my opinion, after members of the Garda and British security service had corroborated my critical assertions about Logan and Liam's respective stays at the rooming house and tourist home, it would've been prudent, on their part, to swiftly issue an all-points-bulletin, notifying the public of the McCool brothers, to increase the likelihood that they be picked up. This would've been especially timely in the matter of Logan, who had been slinking doorway to doorway along Dublin's main thoroughfare, O'Connell Street, making his way toward Trinity College, where he would soon prowl about trying to engineer an after hours break-in at the Old Library. When Logan couldn't manage a way into the historic building, he broke open a door on a large utility shed that houses landscaping implements, and, there, he slept overnight. The moment the doors were opened to the public, the following morning, Logan intended to be first in to the Old Library.

After officers had failed to locate the brothers on the night of the raids, copies of Logan's picture *only* were issued to officers at roll calls, and additional manpower was put out on the streets. Lateral notifications were also made to authorities throughout the Republic of Ireland and Northern Ireland, in the event the brothers had already departed Dublin. But after diligent searches and vigilance failed to turn up either McCool over the succeeding forty-eight hours, the primary source in this case, namely me, again came into question, and skepticism of my perceptive faculties rapidly infiltrated the ranks, which, in turn, deteriorated efforts being made out on the street.

During the preceding day and a half, Logan McCool had tried desperately to discover Prime Minister Etherington's itinerary while in Ireland. He combed through newspapers, and called the British Embassy, posing, first, as a 10 Downing Street staffer and, later, as a journalist, doing so, because he knew it would be, otherwise, near impossible to get close to Etherington, as he sought to identify the site where he imagined the Prime Minister to be most vulnerable to assassination. If successful, Logan also, naturally, preferred to escape apprehension and to continue living as a free man, but those aspirations were now secondary to his deadly political objective.

In the end, Logan had to settle for relying on the condensed news article he noticed, several days earlier, in the *Financial Times*, while sitting on the tarmac in Zurich. As aforementioned, the article disclosed that the British Prime Minister would attend a theatrical production to be put on by some primary school children at the Long Room of the Old Library at Trinity College. Logan had now resigned to assassinating Etherington at the play venue even though he fully comprehended that disrupting the presentation in this violent manner would traumatize the children for years to come.

Posing as the parent of a child who he claimed would appear in the play, Logan telephoned the local school district and gained the confidence of a respondent by telling the woman that he knew his child's play would be held at the Old Library, but didn't know the date and time. When the respondent refused to divulge the information, and reminded him that even parents were prohibited from attending this private showing, Logan accomplished a little playacting of his own, and took the woman to task by telling her, "I *know* that the play at Trinity is exclusively for President Fitzgerald, Prime Minister Etherington and their guests! But if I don't know when to deliver my child's costume, which is still with the tailor, he'll have to wear civilian attire! And just think how foolish my Timothy will look if he's the only student without a costume. The poor boy will be crushed!"

The respondent excused herself to seek guidance from a higher-up and returned a short while later. She then unwittingly informed the assassin-hopeful that the play was scheduled for 9 a.m., Thursday, and curtly said goodbye.

Presently, it was Tuesday morning of the same week, and Logan had emerged from the equipment shed shortly after dawn. He brushed himself off, combed his hair with his fingers, and followed the signs to the school cafeteria, where he bought a bran muffin and an orange juice. Although the cafeteria opened at 6 a.m. on weekdays, most students slept in as late as possible and rushed through breakfast just before first class. Logan was currently joined by one "other" student, who sat at an adjacent table.

At forty years old, Logan was passable as either a graduate student or young professor, but the backpack he toted suggested he was a student. He'd need to wait more than two hours before the Old Library was opened to the public, so he ambled outside to purchase *The Irish Independent* from a nearby vending machine, all the while glancing repeatedly at his backpack, resting against the base of his chair, to ensure that nobody walked off with it.

He wolfed down his bran muffin but scarcely sipped the orange juice so that it stayed half-full, seemingly to justify his loitering, as he read the newspaper to whittle away time. The articles and commentaries pertaining to the British Prime Minister were all recent history, and still neglected to disclose where Etherington would visit next in Dublin, or beyond, which continued to frustrate Logan, despite having resolved to kill his victim there, on campus.

Logan had read the newspaper practically front to back, including the comic strips, before finally departing the cafeteria; he lingered across from the entrance to the Old Library to observe any comings and goings.

At precisely 9:30 a.m., he heard the door being unlocked from the inside, and shuffled over to open it. The attendant winced as Logan yanked on the door and entered abruptly, but then quickly focused on the visitor's backpack:

"Traveling from afar?" the man inquired.

Logan smiled as if satisfied with himself. "Switzerland," he said, and slithered on by to pay his nine Euro entrance fee.

Logan had been the first visitor into the Old Library, as planned, that Tuesday morning, and, like any other fair-weather day in Dublin, soon the institution would be teeming with tourists. He had arrived early because he was eager to conceal himself before a worker or tourist could discover his antics. Upon locating a hiding place, he wondered if he'd be able to remain there or need to furtively search out a more suitable location. He did, after all, still have two days to wait before the play was to commence.

Once inside the Old Library, he saw a sign pointing to the Book of Kells, and paced in that direction, slowing negligibly to peer in the gift shop. The Book was the main attraction at the Old Library, so he was obliged to delay and examine the literary art treasure in the presence of an individual superintending the station, so that he could pass himself off as a legitimate tourist. In reality, Logan didn't give two shits about the Book; his primary goal remained to reach the Long Room as expeditiously as possible. Logan spent about five minutes inspecting the ancient illuminated manuscript from different angles, and pretended to marvel while shifting about the protective case containing it.

Having noticed a sign, posted on a bordering wall, that indicated the Long Room library was located upstairs, he eventually said to the monitor, "Long Room up this way, is it?"

The monitor nodded affirmatively, and Logan adjusted his backpack and trudged upstairs. Once out of the monitor's sight, he quickened his gait, only to encounter a second monitor, beyond the top of the stairs, now standing between him and a copy of the famous Gutenberg Bible. The good news, for Logan, was that this man would serve as the lone monitor in the enormous chamber during the first hour, until a second monitor arrived; and, because the monitor was alone, the man was required to stay close by to the Bible.

Logan smiled to greet the monitor, and paused briefly to study the Bible, which had been the first book printed using moveable type, a technology developed by Johann Gutenberg in the 15th century. Like his first floor co-worker, the monitor eyeballed the bulky backpack worn by Logan, but chose not to comment because he had seen many tourists routinely lug packs through the building over the years.

Logan soon recalled the newspaper article he had read while sitting on the plane in Zurich, reporting that the play, to be attended by Prime Minister Etherington and President Fitzgerald, pertained to the life of Johann Gutenberg, and he hadn't considered, until that moment, that the reason the Long Room was selected as the play venue was that a copy of the famous bible resided there. Moreover, Fitzgerald and Etherington were, as previously stated, both veterans of the printing industry, and when Fitzgerald had learned about the play from a female staff member, whose eleven year old son had a lead role in "Das Drucker" (The Printer), the President requested that the teacher and her students provide a private showing at the Long Room. That same staff member, who had brimmed with pride that the Irish President and British Prime Minister would attend her son's play, was nearly fired after it was discovered that she had been the one to leak the news to the press.

His glimpse of the Gutenberg Bible completed, Logan sauntered unassumingly into the Long Room chamber, which extends 65 meters, while passing by marble busts of historic figures lining both sides of the expansive central aisle. He paused to pore over an impressive bust of writer Jonathan Swift, but his eyes were soon drawn upward to consider the dramatic, barrel-vaulted ceiling and gallery bookcases.

The church-like solemnity commanded by the Long Room failed to dissuade brusque Logan from courteously returning to the monitor's station before asking a question, as he turned and shouted, "How many books contained in this library?" His words resounded within the chamber.

With his hands interlocked behind him, the monitor reacted by creeping to Logan's location, and leaned toward him while replying in a hushed tone, "Two hundred thousand." The man's actions had mocked Logan's impolite demeanor.

Logan merely nodded to acknowledge the man's assistance. He then noticed a middle-aged couple emerging at the top of the stairs, behind the monitor, and the scuffle of footsteps prompted the monitor to turn about face. Logan perceived the opportunity at hand and slinked past an irreplaceable fifteenth-century harp on display, scarcely paying it due regard; he passed between bookcases and stepped over a velour tubular divider intended to block unescorted persons from currently accessing a stairway leading to the gallery level. He subsequently spent several minutes brazenly opening doors, about the gallery level, to appraise prospective hiding places; he had an excuse prepared if noticed or caught. The custodial closets were generally too small and crammed with cleaning paraphernalia, not to mention reeked of solvents. He was tempted to hide and wait in an empty closet of a small, unoccupied office, but feared the monitor might remember him and become suspicious, and that a search effort would easily ferret him out.

He sneaked between two gallery bookcases, toward the middle of the chamber, and peered down guardedly to again observe the monitor. Several tourists had now filtered up to the Long Room and were engaging the employee near the Gutenberg Bible. At that moment, Logan impulsively decided that he would rummage about the gallery level more scrupulously during the evening, when alone, in order to locate a prime hiding place – a place where he could safely conceal himself over the following two days. For now, the anxiety building inside him was such that he'd settle for a temporary hideaway.

Minutes earlier, he had noticed three gallery bookcases that didn't rise up to interconnect with the barrel-vaulted ceiling. He crept over to one that overlooked the monitor's station and, swiftly, using cat-like agility, the sizeable backpack he towed notwithstanding, efficiently scaled the side of the bookcase; his years of mountain climbing had forged strong toes and fingers, sensitive to the objects he negotiated, as he leveraged himself on shelf edges to make progress. He soon hoisted himself on top of the bookcase, and lay on his stomach while reaching back to slide off his pack.

Climbing a gallery bookcase was hardly as challenging as scaling Switzerland's Matterhorn but, once perching himself safely and realizing there was little chance of anyone finding him, he derived similar satisfaction. Meanwhile, the volume of tourists filing up to the Long Room had plainly increased over the last several minutes, as their energetic prattling deflected off the ceiling into his ears.

Logan literally kept a low profile all morning and afternoon, and, once sensing that the Old Library had finally closed for business, he sat up for the first time; he naturally twisted, turned, and stretched after laying on the hard surface for a prolonged period.

His plan to leave the backpack on top of the bookcase, and venture down to familiarize himself with the gallery's features, was soon thwarted upon noticing the first of several security personnel making their rounds that evening. But, once recalling the Old Library's treasures: the Book of Kells, Books of Durrow and Meath, the Gutenberg Bible, the ancient harp made from oak, willow, and brass, the sculptured marble busts, not to mention the valuable 200,000 books contained in the Long Room, it had been foolish not to allow for staff working after hours, when devising his stratagem.

After repositioning himself, which caused the top of the wooden bookcase to creak discordantly, he resolved that, unless he was willing to risk climbing down the bookcase, he'd have to remain there until the play commenced two days later. Under such a scenario, his emergence from the shadows as an unfamiliar, uninvited guest would likely prove an even riskier undertaking, he thought. Consequently, he decided to descend the following morning when lively tourists again rambled about the Long Room and provided ample distraction. Logan was confident that if his climb down went undetected, he'd inevitably locate a safe haven.

Still evening, the main chamber of the Long Room had presently grown tranquil, save for the occasional shuffle of a passing security officer or custodian, so Logan carefully removed the contents of his backpack. The largest item in the pack was the compact, cylindrical, medical waste receptacle; when concealed, it was suggestive of a bedroll or lightweight sleeping bag. After placing the white receptacle down, he pushed on the pedal, at the base, to force open the lid. He reached inside to remove the contents: three bottles of water, a roll of toilet paper he had copped from the rooming house, a paperback book about the life and times of Irish revolutionary leader Michael Collins, and a long barrel .44 magnum revolver. He then gingerly placed the objects away from his person, lest he turn and inadvertently knock an object off the bookcase onto the floor below, consequently drawing the attention of a security officer. He did likewise with the remaining contents of the backpack, which primarily consisted of food items to sustain him over the succeeding forty or so hours. Logan then proceeded to use the waste receptacle for the reason he had purchased it. (When imagining himself lying in wait, to assassinate Sir Nigel Etherington at the Old Library, he had pictured himself holed up in a crawl space or other secluded location for an extended period where he wouldn't have access to a toilet). He couldn't have foreseen *that* place to be atop a gallery bookcase, but, presently, nature urgently called, so he rose to his knees and urinated into the receptacle, closing the lid when finished.

Logan remained watchful for opportunities to descend the bookcase that evening, but such an advance couldn't be managed without risking everything. The frequency of security tours in the Old Library had decreased overnight, but only because a slacking security officer napped off and on in a chair on the gallery level, where he occasionally woke to gaze down and account for the Library's treasures. The same officer had set the alarm on his digital watch, and, four hours later, he changed places with his wide-awake co-worker assigned to watch the Book of Kells on the lower level.

To further complicate matters, the following morning, Logan discovered that the Old Library would be closed all day to prepare for the private play showing for the President, Prime Minister, and their guests the next day. Logan made the discovery when overhearing two monitors squabbling over "having to watch a bunch of snot-nosed kids set up (for a play)," in addition to a crew arranging seating for an audience.

After the staging and other components were in place, and supplementary workers had vacated, Logan peered down stealthily to regard the play venue, and was delighted to notice that the stage set was fittingly juxtaposed with the Gutenberg Bible. Thus, among the three bookcases in the gallery that didn't extend to interconnect with the ceiling, he had fortuitously situated himself on one with an excellent vantage point and line of fire, despite him needing to remain there, uncomfortable, one more day.

The monitors demonstrably behaved more engrossed during the afternoon hours, when a team of British security agents arrived to perform advance site work, their discernible accents and occupational jargon tipping Logan off. At first, Logan trembled as he lay flat, fearful that some persnickety, method-driven agent would ascend the mammoth bookcase on a ladder to inspect the ideal perch.

He soon sensed doors opening and closing at the perimeter of the chamber below, as agents inspected the contents of anything featuring a door, i.e. rooms, cabinets, credenzas. Following a physical inspection, the distinct utterances of additional officers, coupled with the pattering of feet and chain-like jingles, now signaled the arrival of bomb-detecting dogs. Logan's trembles soon transformed into quakes when realizing that the canine teams had just climbed to the gallery level. He then perceived sniffs and subtle, animalistic grunts emanating nearby, which triggered ideations of dogs looking up while sniffing, and he feared that the smell of his urine in the waste receptacle might attract one, to the extent that the dog's handler would feel compelled to inspect. Logan cursed himself due to his flawed plan and for failing to factor in such variables, because he had naively only envisioned the British Prime Minister entering the Old Library under close escort and sitting and enjoying a play with his friend and contemporary.

Logan finally managed to relax some, once determining that the dogs and their handlers had moved on and it was apparent that nobody would discover him – at least yet. But, despite his poor planning, he was more resolute than ever about seeing his objectives through.

Following the security sweep that afternoon, two British agents were assigned to remain in the Old Library overnight, or else a subsequent comprehensive inspection would be necessitated the following morning, prior to the Prime Minister's arrival. The Trinity College security guards arriving for the graveyard shift were expectedly perturbed to learn from their evening counterparts that British agents would remain with them; perturbed, because it disrupted the routine that conveniently allowed them a little shut-eye. Similarly, the British agents would've preferred a quiet night by themselves and were equally irked because they needed to shadow the officers on their rounds and account for every activity, because security policy dictated that they not trust anyone outside agency circles. Hence, the Trinity officers were responsible for the Old Library's treasures, and British agents had to remain due to the unfamiliar natives.

During those evening and overnight hours in the Long Room, Logan predictably spent most time reading, resting, and sleeping on his back. When hungry, he rolled onto his side and used a pair of grooming scissors to cut into cellophane wrappers that contained snacks, because he feared that tearing the wrappers would produce a crinkling noise that would ultimately draw attention. The only time he rose to his knees or feet was to urinate or defecate into the waste receptacle, and he always waited until a security round had recently been made, before rising, which, unfailingly caused the bookcase to creak as his body weight shifted.

At daybreak, on the morning of the play, a team of British security technicians arrived at the Old Library and was provided access by a Trinity security officer accompanied by a British agent. The technicians hauled a thin metal crate and two smaller crates, the contents of which comprised a magnetometer. The technicians swiftly dismantled the crates, removed the various components, and assembled the magnetometer just inside the main entrance, where the device would integrally assist British agents check guests and unfamiliar essential workers for potential weapons. Once an individual passed through the magnetometer, he or she was scanned manually, at close range, with a wand-like instrument, also designed to detect metal objects.

Individuals clearing both the magnetometer and manual scans were accordingly issued color-coded, laminated badges, and allowed to circulate unfettered, albeit the building would soon be swarming with alert security professionals.

Minutes later, the canine team returned to make an unscheduled second sweep through the building, in the event an evildoer had compromised security overnight. When Logan heard the now familiar noises of paw patters and chain-jingles in the chamber below, he again experienced immense trepidation, because he was certain the volume of urine and feces that had accumulated in the receptacle, during the preceding hours, would unquestionably attract the dogs. His fear soon abated, however, once convincing himself that the canines were probably trained only to react to the smell of incendiary devices, and that the dogs were no more likely to pause below his bookcase than a gallery restroom. But a feeling of terror once again came over him, when recalling that each of the bullets loaded in his .44 magnum contained gunpowder in their cartridges. Nonetheless, he was powerless to do anything, and could only lay there hoping to escape detection.

The canine teams conducted their gallery-level check, last, and departed the building without cause for further inspection.

By 8:15 a.m., all children appearing in the play, their teacher, headmaster, and administrators (who would not have attended if not for the prominent guest list), had passed through security and were busy making last minute preparations in the Long Room. Only the costumed children were exempted from wearing laminated security badges.

Presently, all guests except Irish President James Fitzgerald, his wife Robin, and British Prime Minister Sir Nigel Etherington and wife Meg had arrived and taken their seats. And like the first day Logan had lain up on the bookcase, the chamber again buzzed with nervous chatter and nondescript babble that reverberated off the barrel-vaulted ceiling into his ears. Soon the students were directed to take their places so that they would be ready to commence the play at President Fitzgerald's whim.

By 9:20 a.m., the prattling in the Long Room had amplified, as people began speculating why the Irish President and British Prime Minister were late to arrive. But the two men were, after all, important dignitaries, and perhaps a matter of grave importance had developed, which required their attention.

At 9:47 a.m., the arrival of the diplomats and their parties was foreshadowed by the first of several energetic security agents emerging at the top of the stairs. Three minutes more elapsed, however, before the distinguished guests entered the grand chamber, because, in spite of the motorcade accident that caused their delay, Prime Minister and Mrs. Etherington had paused to examine the Book of Kells, after President Fitzgerald pointed out the literary art treasure during their ascent.

Once the two diplomats, their spouses, and remaining entourage arrived in the Long Room, President Fitzgerald smiled and addressed the audience, while others were shown to their front row seats.

"Ladies and gentlemen, boys and girls, I'd like to apologize for keeping you waiting... but the motorcade, in which Prime Minister Etherington and I were riding, was involved in an accident, not far from here. Due to the dangers in our complex world, we statesmen are taught that an initial accident, sustained in a motorcade, is often only a diversion to a secondary assault... and security guidelines prescribe that the dignitary be whisked away immediately to safety. But when we observed the unfortunate pedestrian suffering the way he was, the Right Honorable Prime Minister insisted that we stop to inquire of the man's well-being. We hope and pray that the man... a fellow from Antrim, Northern Ireland, it seems... will survive his ordeal."

Logan had heard every word and reacted by sitting up. He was in shock because he reckoned that the victim must've been his fraternal twin, Liam. How many men from Antrim were coincidentally walking the streets near Trinity College, he thought. Suddenly, when realizing that his profile up on the bookcase might get him noticed, he laid back down.

President Fitgerald went on. "That said, Prime Minister and Mrs. Etherington, and Mrs. Fitzgerald and I, now look forward to the presentation by Ms. Jodie Doyle's fifth grade class, about the life of legendary printer, Johann Gutenberg." The President then looked over to an astonished Jodie and said, "My staff member informed me of all the hard work by you and your students." Jodie smiled and said, "Thank you, Mr. President."

My Jodie was shocked to hear the President of the Republic of Ireland acknowledge her in this manner. That's right, Jodie! Unbeknownst to me at the time, as I sat in my room at the Temple Bar Hotel, my daughter had been standing in the main chamber of the Long Room as Logan McCool lay high up on a gallery bookcase, now clasping a .44 magnum revolver with his sweaty hand!

I suppose it would helpful if I recounted the succession of events that occurred on the streets of Temple Bar, that morning, which resulted in the diplomatic motorcade coming to a halt, because the accident ultimately shaped Logan McCool's actions up on the bookcase.

The driver of a red double-decker bus had routinely stopped to pick up three passengers along Fleet Street, and had just resumed operation when he thought he recognized one of the boarding passengers. He consequently gazed into his rear view mirror to behold the American actress, one Tyne Daly, taking a seat with her two daughters. (Ms.

Daly reportedly found the double-deckers charming and often rode them while in Dublin). And as the driver got caught up scrutinizing the celebrity in his mirror, he failed to notice the Garda officer standing in the street, seventy-five feet in front, temporarily blocking traffic at the Westmoreland Street intersection. The reason traffic had been stopped was to allow Prime Minister Etherington's motorcade to pass unimpeded. (The Fitzgeralds had been riding in a separate limousine in the same motorcade). Meanwhile, on the far side of Westmoreland, an elderly lady, pulling a wheeled-basket used to transport groceries, had entered a pedestrian crosswalk and was either oblivious to the motorcade, or flat-out refused to be hindered in her progress. The lead motorcade car accordingly slowed to allow the senior citizen to pass, which caused the trailing limousines to stop suddenly.

Now perceiving an opportunity to cross the intersection, a harried middle-aged man, headed for Trinity College, took advantage of the delay and marched across the same crosswalk. By now, the Garda officer standing before the leviathan double-decker sensed that the distracted bus driver failed to notice the motorcade hung up in the intersection, and that the bus was bearing down, about to broadside a limousine. Therefore, the Garda officer lurched around to alert the agent sitting in the right front seat of a limousine, who immediately radioed the lead car to clear the intersection. The driver of the lead car reacted by gunning the accelerator, and he ran into the pedestrian, Liam McCool. It was at that point Prime Minister Etherington insisted that the motorcade be halted to look after Liam's welfare. In the end, both limousines escaped being hit by the bus, but a motorcade trail car was impacted in its right front quarter.

As Logan lay high up on the gallery bookcase, listening to President Fitzgerald's words, he knew, viscerally, that his fraternal twin brother had been the accident victim, and he was barely able to repress his emotions. Initially, Logan feared that Liam had died, and blamed himself, because if he had only agreed to return to Antrim, the accident never would have occurred. But then he blamed "the *fookin'* Brits," who didn't belong in Ireland anyhow, and he became even more enraged, now placing the pistol down and turning on his side, intending to stand.

All spectators had presently taken their seats, and Jodie stood obliquely to the makeshift stage, holding a copy of the screenplay, ready to prompt a student if he or she forgot a line. The play was set to commence. Once Logan sensed that all attention was on the children, he rose to his knees but maintained a low profile, again worried that the creaky noise resulting from his shift in weight might attract eyes. He picked up the sizeable revolver and inserted it into the small of his back. He thought of his brother, Liam, lying somewhere in a hospital or, worse, a morgue, and his blood boiled. He then used his hand to push down the pedal of the white receptacle, to force open the lid, and removed the plastic bucket-liner containing two days of waste matter. The stench immediately elicited his revulsion, and he dry-heaved upon viewing the fecal matter floating in urine.

Fifty-two hours after first climbing up on the gallery bookcase, Logan McCool stood upright for the first time. Once resolving that no spectators noticed him surfacing, he strained to identify the British Prime Minister sitting in the first row, and, without delay, yelled, "ENGLAND OUT OF IRELAND, you *fookin'* poms!" He then hurled the putrid contents of the waste receptacle down on Sir Nigel Etherington, which, needless to say, also befouled guests in the periphery.

Spectators naturally shrieked and gasped upon observing the frenzied, unkempt man high up on the gallery bookcase, and most scrambled to get away, as Logan reached behind his back and drew the .44 magnum revolver, pointing it downward. British agents similarly drew their weapons, but not before Logan squeezed off the first of two rounds, causing children and adults to scream, once hearing the powerful blast; some guests dove for cover under metal folding chairs, others sought refuge between nearby bookcases.

Despite the difficulty in concealing a long-barrel pistol, Logan had recognized, when acquiring it, that if the urgency of the situation prevented him from aiming, he could merely point the weapon and, in all likelihood, hit his target. The first bullet pierced Sir Nigel on his upper right side, just as security agents clutched him and tried to remove him to safety. The high-velocity bullet broke a rib, ripped through his torso, and severed the Prime Minister's spine just below the neck. Logan couldn't have known the damage his first shot had caused, and again prepared to fire, this time aiming his revolver. The instant he squeezed the trigger, he was hit by gunfire, which staggered him atop the bookcase. Meanwhile, he succeeded in discharging a second round of ammunition, but the bullet strayed far from its target and hit the sunshine of my life, daughter Jodie Doyle, in the upper right thigh near the groin. When Logan finally collapsed on top of the gallery bookcase, the impact of his fall caused the heavy .44 magnum pistol to break loose from his hand and drop to the gallery floor.

By now, all guests had cleared out of the seating area, some hunkering protectively over children in between bookcases while reassuring the youths. Sufficient time had passed that it appeared the gunfire had stopped; nevertheless, many children still cried hysterically.

Sir Nigel had since been evacuated downstairs by his security agents, to an ambulance that had been the last vehicle in the motorcade. The agents didn't know the extent of Etherington's injuries, and he would've been better served if allowed to remain motionless while medical professionals removed him methodically, but the agents refused to allow the Prime Minister to lay there vulnerable.

My daughter, Jodie, still lay on the Long Room chamber floor, in a massive pool of blood, while a Trinity security officer applied pressure to her wound, to try to stop the bleeding. Jodie had been hit in the femoral artery. Soon, a second ambulance would arrive, and emergency medical personnel would ascend to the Long Room and briefly treat her before removing her to St. James Hospital.

Once recognizing that the assassin's revolver had fallen to the floor, and Logan evidently lacked other firearms, two British agents sprinted up to the gallery level, with weapons drawn, and quickly scaled the bookcase from opposite sides. The first agent, reaching the top, peered over the edge to observe the assailant dazed and approaching unconsciousness, lying in his own pool of blood. Logan had weakened considerably due to blood loss, but it had been the blow to his head, when falling backwards on the bookcase, that rendered him senseless. He was handcuffed, eventually placed in a rescue-basket, and lowered to the gallery-level floor by emergency workers. And, like his brother Liam, the British Prime Minister, and my daughter Jodie, Logan McCool was transported to nearby St. James Hospital for treatment.

26

I ASSUMED I HAD *NOT* been watching the contents of my visual packet on a real-time basis, while sitting in my room at the Temple Bar Hotel, and that events were recent history, so I immediately grabbed my jacket and headed for the door. The phone rang as I turned the knob, and I only hoped that it was Jodie calling from her hospital bed to inform me of what had happened and that she was okay. Instead, it was Trish Jennings, who described the special news report she currently watched:

"*Atrocity At Trinity College* is the banner running across the bottom of the television screen," she said.

"My Jodie's been shot!" I shouted. "I just watched the whole thing play out in a visual packet! Meet me in the lobby! Now, Trish!"

Trish reached the lobby first, after accessing a nearby stairwell, while I took the elevator down, and she held the main door open to hasten our departure. The siren sounds pervading the Temple Bar streets blared into the hotel, and a sickened feeling swiftly overtook me, causing my legs to buckle as we exited.

Once outside, we naturally looked in the direction of Trinity College, and noticed several Garda officers, whose sober aspects aptly reflected the grave matters at hand. Most officers diverted foot traffic away from the college while lights flashed atop their idling vehicles – it was apparent to anyone who hadn't heard the news that something serious had happened.

Trish and I soon collected a taxi, and I instructed the driver to take us to St. James Hospital. During the ride, I described to Trish, in more detail, the gruesome tragedy that had taken place up in the Long Room of the Old Library, according to the contents of my recent visual packet. She sobbed when hearing the news, especially when realizing that disclosing her dream about Logan, to Liam and me in Kinvara, might have prevented the tragedy. The driver slowed as if intending to drop us at the hospital's main entrance, but I urged him to follow the signs to the emergency room, located around the side of the building. I'm not sure how many quid I tossed onto the front passenger seat when we arrived, but apparently it was sufficient payment because the driver chose not to speak as we climbed from the vehicle.

We scurried through the automatic doors, where emergency patients are ushered through on gurneys, and were challenged, first, by a hospital employee, who noticed our abrupt entry, and, secondarily, by a British security agent posted there due to the Prime Minister's occupancy. After announcing that I was the father of Jodie Doyle, shooting victim at Trinity College, Trish and I were escorted down a hallway leading to the emergency room reception desk. There, I was asked to provide identification before I'd be allowed to see Jodie. While frantically digging out my driver's license, I inquired about Jodie's condition, and the nurse-receptionist exuded a daunting look, before responding, "I should let the attending physician speak with you, Mr. Doyle." Like me, Trish sensed the worst, and held my arm to brace me, fearing I might collapse to the floor.

I was encouraged to sit in the waiting room, so Trish and I did so. My mind was so active during that period that I was unaware of how much time had elapsed when a nurse finally summoned me. Initially, Trish wasn't permitted to accompany me into the recovery area, but, after a gentle plea to the nurse, that Trish was a close family friend whose support was invaluable to me at this time, she was allowed to pass.

Trish and I followed the nurse up a short corridor, and we had just turned right, up a longer corridor, when a patient being wheeled from surgery, to a recovery room, delayed our progress. What's more, the patient was under escort by the Garda and a British security agent. At first, I failed to recognize the individual because I had only perceived him through visual packets on previous occasions. Trish, however, identified him immediately, and, in spite of his diluted state, he recognized her.

"What in the *Christ* is the 'Witch of Castlebar' doing in a Dublin hospital the same day as me?! That's what I want to know!" Logan McCool shouted at Trish while shifting up onto his elbows. He grimaced in pain from the ill-advised movement, and his eyes bulged and ears seemingly pricked, awaiting her response.

"Being the pompous ass that you are, I could never convince you otherwise," Trish retorted.

"Witch!" Logan yelled, as loudly as his weakened condition allowed, and coughed severely as medical personnel wheeled him off.

Logan's time in surgery had actually been brief; he had emerged from anesthesia just minutes earlier. Despite losing significant blood, the bullet that hit him nicked but failed to break his clavicle and passed through his shoulder to lodge in the barrel-vaulted ceiling in the Long Room.

Once settled in a recovery room, Logan attempted to pick up a telephone adjacent to his bed so that he could inquire if his brother Liam had been admitted, because he still suspected that Liam was the accident victim in the Prime Minister's motorcade. However, a British agent, posted in the room, observed him reach for the phone, and moved it out of range and yanked the cord out of the jack. Logan cursed at the man. "Fookin' pommie!"

The agent tried not to react in a discernible manner that would give Logan satisfaction, but couldn't avoid becoming flush with anger. Logan subsequently activated a bedside mechanism to summon a nurse. When the nurse arrived, he explained that he thought his brother, Liam McCool, had also been admitted to the hospital, due to an auto accident, and he asked the kind nurse to find out on his behalf. The nurse returned five minutes later to confirm Liam's admittance and reported that he had sustained a fractured hip and some internal contusions but was in "Very Good to Excellent condition." Logan felt relieved, and after the nurse departed he looked to the British agent and said animatedly, "Ya see? Ya can't keep us Irish down, you prick." He then spat in the agent's direction.

Trish and I were led into Jodie's room, and I immediately noticed that the curtain was drawn around her bed, causing me to again falter, because I believed that Jodie would only be shrouded in such a manner if deceased; Trish sensed me going down and again steadied me. My heart soon leapt, though, when perceiving a doctor behind the curtain.

"Doctor Finnerty," announced the nurse as we neared, "Mr. Doyle has arrived."

Doctor Finnerty pulled the curtain back, but I failed to acknowledge him because I wanted to lay eyes, first, upon my daughter, whose color was ashen but breathed of her own accord. The myriad tubes and wires, leading from Jodie's body to medical devices, spoke to her serious condition, and I naturally welled up.

"Mr. Doyle, I'm not going to sugar-coat this for you. Jodie lost considerable blood and has been lapsing in and out of consciousness. I did speak to her once, though. Her femoral artery was severed by the bullet that hit her. It's fortunate that she arrived at the hospital in a timely manner so that we could transfuse new blood... but the next twenty-four hours are critical. We've done all that we can. Now it's up to her body. Does Jodie have a husband?"

"No, she's engaged."

"If you'd like to call her fiancée to come and visit, that's fine. But no attempts should me made to wake the patient. I'll inform reception about her fiancée. Any other family members?"

"Just her sister. I'll be calling Tessie soon."

Before the doctor left, he turned and said, "Mr. Doyle, my experience, in cases like these, is that expectations should be kept low."

I felt like giving Dr. Finnerty a piece of my mind, because of his directness and for dashing my hopes about Jodie's chances for recovery, but, after he had been gone a few minutes, I recognized that he dealt with the reality of life and death matters on a daily basis.

27

TRISH REMAINED WITH JODIE while I slogged down the corridor, away from the recovery room, where I might disturb Jodie, to call my other daughter with the heartrending news. Tessie wept when hearing what had happened to her big sister and informed me that she would depart Great Blasket Island immediately.

Given the variety of modes of transportation she would need to utilize to reach Dublin, I didn't realistically expect Tessie to arrive until the following day. First, she needed to take the Peig Sayers Ferry to Dingle Harbor, then a bus to Tralee; from Tralee she'd ride the train northeast to Dublin but have to change trains twice, en route, at Mallow and Portarlington, before finally arriving at Heuston Station. From there she'd catch a taxicab to St. James Hospital.

After Tessie and I got off the line, my attention was drawn to a small crowd, standing inside the visitors waiting area, watching a flat-screen television mounted on a wall; I stepped inside to inquire if news was being aired about the Trinity College tragedy. It was, and a correspondent was coincidentally reporting from outside the nearby emergency room. The correspondent reported that Prime Minister Etherington had survived his ordeal and was stabilized but would soon be airlifted to Queen's Hospital in London. The reporter never alluded to the Prime Minister's paralysis, because she hadn't been aware, but I knew, due to the visual packet in my hotel room an hour earlier.

Just as I turned to go back to Jodie's room, a nurse rushed up to meet me. "Mr. Doyle, your daughter appears to be regaining consciousness." I thusly dashed down the corridor to Jodie's room.

Trish was standing at Jodie's bedside; the two had apparently gotten acquainted. Meanwhile, Doctor Finnerty had been summoned and was allegedly on his way. Jodie managed a thin smile but waited until I was close enough before speaking, after recognizing her own weakened state. I leaned over the bed to kiss my daughter lightly on the forehead and clasped her shoulders affectionately. She was clearly too feeble to hug.

"I don't want you talking too much, Jodie," I told her. "Save your strength. I want you to rest."

Jodie had heard me but had some things she wanted to communicate and was impelled to speak.

"You're probably disappointed that I didn't invite you to watch the play in the Long Room, Daddy... but there's a good reason."

"No, I'm not. What ever do you mean?"

"Well, it was the fieldtrip you took me on to the Old Library, the day you were flying out to the Canary Islands, that inspired me to have the children develop a play about the life of Johann Gutenberg. When you and I viewed the Book of Kells and Gutenberg Bible, I saw how enthused you were... so, after the children and I put the play together, I planned to surprise you by inviting you to the school to watch the production. However, once President Fitzgerald caught wind of the play from an aide, whose son has the lead role, he requested that the children present it for he and the British Prime Minister and their guests."

Jodie was expending far too much energy on her story, as intrigued as I was to hear the conclusion, so I interrupted.

"Nevermind that now, Jodie. You must conserve yourself, please."

"I'm almost finished, Daddy. Anyway, I postponed the play to be presented at the school, because the children and I had to continue rehearsing... because I wanted the presentation that was to be attended by the President and Prime Minister to be perfect. Plus, we had to work on designing a stage set and make costumes."

"Yes, yes," I said as if prompting her to just rest.

"But when we were finally ready to present the play, British agents got involved and requested that, due to security concerns, we provide a *private* showing. We were also instructed not to inform any public citizens of the location of the play, after President Fitzgerald decided to change the venue to the Long Room. Oh, Daddy, when I learned that we were going to put the play on at the Long Room, right there beside the Gutenberg Bible, I was so excited and proud. I wanted so badly to tell you... and for you to be there! So many important people were there because of *two* persons, Daddy! Johann Gutenberg and you!"

Jodie had tried to make me feel proud with her words, but when fathoming the slaughterous consequences eventually arising from our innocent little trip to the Old Library, the guilt I experienced felt more like culpability. To compound matters, the exertion of relating her story had just caused Jodie to seemingly lapse back into unconsciousness. I immediately buzzed for a nurse and, after the longest fifteen seconds of my life, a nurse, followed by Doctor Finnerty, scurried through the door to Jodie's bedside; Doctor Finnerty checked Jodie's vital signs while the nurse audited the medical devices hooked up to her. In the meantime, I described Jodie's noteworthy resurgence to the doctor, and he responded by abruptly asking Trish and me to leave the room and wait in the visitors lounge.

Almost an hour later, Doctor Finnerty finally sought out Trish and me in the waiting area. I gnashed my teeth as the doctor informed us that Jodie was still breathing on her own but was not responding to attempts at waking her. Doctor Finnerty asked if we had said anything to excite or agitate my daughter, to which I could only truthfully recount the story Jodie had enthusiastically insisted on telling. Doctor Finnerty subsequently requested that Jodie be left alone overnight, because he feared that, upon recognizing a guest in her room, she might feel compelled to speak and, therefore, exert herself further. Hence, Trish and I were encouraged to return to the hotel.

As we stood in the hospital waiting area, about to depart, Jodie's fiancé, Terrence, entered the space looking distraught. Terrence had seen the news on television and sensed it was Jodie who had been shot because she had purportedly been the lone teacher at the scene. Doctor Finnerty updated Terrence on her condition, and he was allowed to look in on her from the doorway only. Terrence was then escorted back to the visitors lounge, and we rode with him to the Temple Bar Hotel, where Trish and I changed into more comfortable clothing, and the three of us stepped out for a light dinner. It was then I informed Terrence, more thoroughly, of what had come to pass at the Old Library. I'm not sure if Jodie had ever referenced my capacity as a medium to Terrence –

perhaps he would've been scared off if hearing her talk that way – but I edified him about myself (and Trish) that evening. After dinner, the three of us rode back to the hospital to inquire of Jodie's condition. Sadly, she had not regained consciousness, so we remained another hour before Terrence dropped Trish and me back at the hotel.

The following morning, my cellular phone rang at 8:15 a.m. while I readied to return to St. James Hospital. It was daughter Tessie calling, who had just arrived at Heuston Station. I briefly filled Tessie in on her sister's condition, and asked her to meet us at the Temple Bar Hotel so that the three of us could ride to the hospital together.

Despite the tragic events that had reunited us, it was naturally wonderful to see Tessie. She had rung me up when arriving in the lobby, and I came down to receive her and help with her luggage; my room featured twin beds so Tessie would stay with me. Tessie and I embraced warmly and wept over Jodie's ordeal while I tried to console her. During the elevator ride to the fourth floor, Tessie informed me that, under the circumstances, she had decided to quit her job at the tourist home and leave Great Blasket Island for good. The family employing her, over the last several years, was expectedly disappointed to learn that she wouldn't be returning, but they certainly sympathized with our circumstances. Tessie related that she still wasn't sure where she'd ultimately settle, or what she would do, but that her new life would be "somewhere on the mainland."

After placing Tessie's things in my room, I telephoned Trish, and the three of us met in the lobby, where introductions were made. We soon collected a taxi outside the hotel, and during the ride to St. James Hospital my cellular phone rang. It was a nurse from Jodie's section calling, who urged us to come to the hospital right away. While I had the kind nurse on the line, I took the opportunity to ask her of Jodie's condition, but was advised in a transparently ambiguous manner that (I) "should ask for Doctor Finnerty, upon arriving, so that (I) can receive the most accurate information." The lack of encouraging words from the nurse, coupled with her discernible poignant voice inflection, elicited a dreadful feeling, but I forced myself to remain positive, especially considering that daughter Tessie sat beside me. Once we arrived at the hospital, I perceived several familiar faces among the medical staff congregated near the visitors reception desk, and I wondered why they weren't busy with patients.

Like a big, black, sooty cloud, the Omniscient One stole the sunshine from my life that morning when allowing sweet Jodie to die. The initial excessive blood loss, associated with the severing of Jodie's femoral artery, was ultimately attributed to her cause of death. Tessie dropped to her knees when hearing the devastating news from Dr. Finnerty, and I would've collapsed if not for the stalwart support of friend Trish Jennings.

Jodie had made many friends while living and teaching in Dublin, so, while I planned to have her funeral Mass said at St. Joseph's in Kinvara, where she had grown up, I arranged for a memorial service, also, at St. Mary's Pro-Cathedral in Dublin before her body would be transported.

After making the Dublin memorial service arrangements, Tessie and I expectedly sulked in our room at the Temple Bar Hotel for the remainder of the day. The next morning, however, Trish persuaded us that we would feel better if getting out and about, rather than sitting and waiting for the service to take place the following day. I then let Trish talk me into returning to the hospital, despite the sick feeling I knew I'd derive from the visit, to look in on Liam McCool, who sustained a fractured hip in the motorcade accident. Meanwhile, Tessie contacted a former Seamount classmate currently residing in Dublin.

Trish was skeptical that Liam had received any visitors since being admitted to St. James and, with everything that had happened, suspected he was unfairly blaming himself for the tragedy at Trinity College. He had been watching television when Trish and I arrived but, upon noticing us, closed his eyes and pretended to nap. Like myself, Trish picked up on this, so she wasn't apprehensive about touching his arm, to insist on his attention, when sidling up to his hospital bed.

"Liam, how are ya? It's Trish and Albert," she said in a kind voice. "We just wanna make sure you're on the mend."

Liam feigned his awakening and spoke:

"Oh, goodness. It's so nice to see you both again. This is very unexpected."

"Liam, all of Dublin is dealing with the blow... and nobody's feeling it worse than me after my daughter Jodie died yesterday. But you mustn't blame yourself," I told him.

"I *do* feel horrible. I'm so sorry for your loss, Albert... and to think that my brother caused such destruction."

"Liam, do you know that when I was tracking you through the streets of Temple Bar, I was attempting to tell you where you could find Logan?"

"If I had only known, Albert, I would've acted appropriately. You must believe me when I tell you that. It was Logan I was trying to protect... because of his history... I knew he'd go to jail for a long time. I thought that if I could only get him away from Dublin... back to Antrim... that everything would be okay, and that he'd carry on as normal. But, in the end, he's going to go away for a long time anyhow."

Trish wanted to get Liam off the topic, and inquired of his condition.

"I don't see any cast on you, Liam. How's the hip?"

"I took quite a jolt but then bounced and rolled onto the street, so it wasn't a complete break. Doctor said I'll have to walk with a cane for a month or so when checking out in a few days."

"Have you been allowed to communicate with Logan since he was admitted?" Trish asked.

"No, I haven't. But I'm so angry, and he can be so volatile, that I'm bound to agitate his condition, so it's best we don't talk right now."

"Liam, you should be aware of something," said Trish, "and it's probably best that you hear it from me, because it makes the recent tragic events even more baffling. Your brother Logan and I used to date."

"What?!"

"It's true. Over a year ago, the Omniscient One induced me to travel up to Belfast to work on a case, and I met Logan in a publick house there. He didn't exhibit any anti-social behavior that day... quite the contrary, he was a real charmer. We dated a short while, until it became apparent that he was wrapped up with the IRA. I also, frankly, didn't care for the way he started behaving. He was a bit full of himself, I decided, so I broke things off. But... in hindsight... considering everything that's recently transpired, I believe that our encounter was no coincidence. The Omniscient One surely intended for me to meet Logan."

"When you put things in that context, it certainly appears that way."

Trish anticipated that I wanted to ask Liam something and looked at me.

"Liam, have you resumed receiving visual packets?" I asked.

"No. It's been many days now."

"The last one being the one you received while driving from Kinvara to Dublin?"

"Yes. Why? You observed me viewing that packet through your own packet?"

"Exactly."

"Those are always interesting, aren't they? Sure makes it easy to verify if someone's telling the truth."

"Indeed, it does. Liam, between the doctor and yourself, if you decide that you're ambulatory enough to get around on your own tomorrow, I'd love for you to attend my daughter Jodie's memorial service at St. Mary's Pro-Cathedral."

Trish reacted as if she thought it was a bad idea. Liam, at first, seemed grateful for the invitation but then seemed reticent.

"I hope that I *can* make it, Albert. I really do."

I decided to change the subject.

"Liam, after you're discharged, I hope we have the opportunity to sit and talk about the Omniscient One... seeing that you've been dealing with Him much longer than Trish or I. I particularly want to know why He insists on stirring me to act on His behalf but, lately, seems to be getting the information to me too late to help the victims. Here, I've been assisting Him for several years now and He even allows my daughter to become a fatality."

"It does cause one to wonder about His master plan, doesn't it? Yes, we should meet and talk about such... the three of us. However, I can tell you that many people would've lost their lives, over the years, if it hadn't been for His intervention... and my actions. But, yes... we'll talk."

Trish warmly laid her hand on Liam's arm. She sensed our visit had done some good. "We'll let you rest now, Liam," she said. "I'll come see you again."

28

THE FOLLOWING MORNING LIAM McCool was persuaded by medical staff to get out of bed for the first time since his accident, and he hobbled down a hallway at St. James Hospital with the aid of an aluminum walker. Several blocks away, St. Mary's Pro-Cathedral was filled to capacity for Jodie's memorial service, as the school district had given teachers and students the day off to pay tribute; people stood nearby in the streets, listening to the service being broadcast on speakers, while journalists and camera crews covered the event. Inside the church, the school headmaster and some of Jodie's fellow teachers each took turns extolling my daughter as a natural born teacher, who consistently inspired her students by encouraging them to always wonder and to strive to do better. Jodie's fiancé, Terrence, followed with a eulogy in which he sobbingly pledged to never remove the ring Jodie had given him after they were engaged, which brought the church to tears. I didn't expect that I would be in any condition to speak publicly that day but, after Terrence returned to the pew, the priest looked in my direction, and I pulled myself together and stepped up to the lectern. During my brief oration, I, first, shared with my fellow mourners the highlights of Jodie's childhood while growing up in Kinvara, and I told them how proud her mother would've been of the woman she had grown to be. Before stepping down, I fought through the temptation to publicly invoke the Omniscient One to provide me with an acceptable answer as to why a loving god would allow an angel on Earth, like Jodie, to fall victim the way she did. Such a plea, however, would've been self-indulgent and futile, I suspect.

At the conclusion of the service, we, bereaved, exited the cathedral, and a local undertaker and his pallbearers took custody of Jodie's body for further transport to County Galway. Jodie's official funeral service would take place in two days at St. Joe's in Kinvara, where old friend Father Jack McLaughlin would preside. Tessie and I had planned on checking out of the hotel and riding with Trish to Kinvara this day, but Trish surprised me when informing me that she regretfully wouldn't be making the trip to Kinvara; instead, she'd remain in Dublin until Liam McCool was discharged. I suppose it was unreasonable to expect Trish to attend two services; nonetheless, she had been at my side for every other aspect of this ordeal and caught me off guard with her decision. Alternatively, Tessie and I would ride in the hearse from Dublin to Kinvara, and, in the end, I felt good about the way things worked out, because Jodie returned home with her father and sister at her side.

Before Tessie and I checked out of the Temple Bar Hotel, I conscientiously took the time to contact Garda Inspector Patrick Kerrey, who had interviewed me along with British agent Edmund Rathbone in my room before setting off in search of the McCool brothers that night. The purpose of my call had been to inquire if police might have any follow-up questions before I departed Dublin. Kerrey speculated that someone from the Garda and/or the British security service would likely want to speak further with me but, in respect to my family during this trying time, he and his colleagues certainly could wait.

Tessie and I, and the undertaker, had covered about two-thirds of the westward journey across Ireland, and had just stopped for petrol in the town of Ballinasloe, when I received my next visual packet. Considering everything I had recently been through, I swiftly grew nauseated once beholding the now familiar conveyance, especially after anticipating that the Omniscient One might compel to me to act on an unrelated case at this very inopportune time. Presently, the undertaker conveniently pumped petrol, and Tessie still napped, so at least I wasn't distracted as the packet unraveled:

I perceived Trish Jennings at St. James Hospital walking alongside Liam McCool, who trod gingerly with the aid of his aluminum walker. Trish smiled while chatting with Liam, and, despite experiencing discomfort, he managed to radiate happiness. Upon reaching the end of a corridor, Liam suggested that he needed a change of scenery, or perhaps he cared to prolong his promenade with attractive Trish, and decided to turn right, up a longer corridor, where the two noticed a Garda officer sitting outside a patient's room, which roused their curiosities. Once reaching the officer's station, they greeted him and peered inside the room at a man in a business suit seated across from Logan, who lay secured in bed, staring at the ceiling. Liam and Trish paused at the doorway to study Logan, and, when Logan sensed his onlookers, he snapped to.

"Oh, Mother of Mercy, who do we have *here*?" Logan then laughed in a manner that implied disgust. "Is that why I keep seeing you at the hospital, Ms. Jennings? Because you've taken up with *me* brother, now? Perhaps you'll wanna do our daddy next."

"Shut your mouth, brother," Liam shouted into the room while stooping over his walker. The Garda officer stood, and the British agent ambled toward the door as if to usher Liam and Trish onward.

"How is it that you became acquainted with the *Witch of Castlebar*, Liam? This is no bloody coincidence." Logan asked in a sarcastic, raised tone.

"Mind your manners, brother. If you must know, Trish is a friend who possesses the same gift. We're a small network, we are."

The Garda officer and British agent had now recognized that Liam and Logan were related but still requested that Liam and Trish move along, to avoid any escalation in the situation. Liam complied and slowly pivoted with the aluminum walker, to turn about face.

"Same gift, eh?" Logan replied. "Seems more like a curse, than a gift, to me. Now, what you'll be receiving from Ms. Jennings back in your room... that's the real gift, brother." Logan then laughed.

"I told you to shut your mouth, brother!" Liam again shouted, this time as if to defend Trish's honor.

"Any man who takes up with the *Witch of Castlebar* is no brother of mine," said Logan, looking at the British agent.

Liam had resumed inching forward while searching his mind for a rejoinder, and finally looked around the Garda officer before shouting, "And any man who does what you did to decent people trying to do good in the world... like you did in the library... is no brother of mine."

"England out of Ireland!" Logan only responded and winked at the British agent.

Liam labored back toward his room, half-trembling, with Trish resting her hand on the middle of his back. My visual packet then diffused.

After sleeping in my own bed in Kinvara, I woke up feeling remarkably refreshed the morning of Jodie's funeral. If I had dreamt, and I'm sure I did, I had no recollection of the dream. When Tessie finally emerged in the kitchen, I noticed that she, too, had benefited from a restful night at home. Under the circumstances, neither of us felt like eating a morsel but forced some tea and toast into ourselves, mindful of the difficult day ahead.

St. Joseph's in Kinvara isn't as grand as a Dublin cathedral, nevertheless, the church was filled to capacity. At one point, before Father McLaughlin commenced the memorial service, I stood up from the front pew, where Tessie and I sat, and turned to regard the assemblage gathered in Jodie's honor. I felt comforted seeing so many familiar people, especially the faces of those I hadn't seen in many years. Two rows behind us sat old friends Gerry and Carolyn McBrine and their grown children. Seated beside them were Tom and Angela Casey, who had both taken days off. Their son Padraic, who had drunk a pint with me and Tom at the Quays in Galway City, on the day Tom dropped me at the station, was also there; so was his sister Jacqueline and her husband Phil. Unlike Tessie, Jodie hadn't attended Seamount; even so, several Sisters of Mercy were in attendance, most conspicuous among them Sister Mary Jude Murray and another favorite teacher of Tessie's, Sister Mary Shaun Sevigny. Jodie's fiancé, Terrence, had made the trip across Ireland but wouldn't muster another emotional eulogy. Upon seeing him, I curiously thought of Trish Jennings, who had remained in Dublin to look after Liam McCool, and suddenly I felt hurt that Trish had chosen Liam over me. Further back in the church, I noticed friend Tom Leech, who had closed his Kinvara shop this day, in tribute to Jodie; Frank and Kathleen Hanley, and Michael and Margaret Dolan were there – I longed to hear them play fiddle and accordion again. Michael John O'Rourke and his wife Helen, visiting from America, were still in Ireland and, unbeknownst to me, Father McLaughlin had enlisted Michael John to sing Avé Maria for the service. Even spinster

Francie O'Rourke, who had recovered sufficiently to avoid re-admission at her Gort nursing home, was there. So many good friends alongside Tessie and me – it did our hearts good.

Jodie was laid to rest at Foy's Cemetery in Kinvara in a touching interment ceremony. Following the burial rites, friends were invited for sandwiches and refreshments over to the Pierpoint, as I had arranged.

As Tom Casey, Gerry McBrine, and I stood together sipping pints of Guinness and looking out onto Kinvara Harbor this gray, spring day, Father Jack McLaughlin noticed me looking crestfallen, which I had every right to be, and he crept by just long enough to say, "Life is for the living, Albert, so live it. When you're dead, you're dead."

I must admit that, upon reflection, I found Father's words ironic, coming from a man who was in the business of facilitating eternal life for his flock, and it caused me to wonder if he really believed in a life hereafter. I didn't have an opportunity to immediately respond to Father, because he soon slipped back into the crowd; perhaps, one day, I would query him on his declaration. Instead, I remarked to Tom and Gerry how lonely Kinvara Harbor looked without Angus Wilde's hooker, which had been sold recently at auction to the lad from Westport. Neither man reacted, and I wondered if they, too, might be dwelling on Father McLaughlin's curious remark.

After taking a long draft of stout, Tom Casey belched and said, "I heard on the radio, during the ride over this morning, that Logan McCool is being arraigned on murder charges in Dublin today. He's also being charged with attempted murder and conspiracy to assassinate the British Prime Minister.

"Those things, he did," I only replied.

29

LOGAN MCCOOL COULD'VE EASILY walked into court on his own two feet the day of his Dublin arraignment, but due to the significant amount of blood he lost several days earlier, and a still somewhat weakened state, he was strapped into a wheelchair and wheeled into the courtroom under escort by the Garda. When asked how he intended to plead to the murder of Jodie Doyle, Logan belligerently replied, "Not Guilty. It was an accident. I was trying to kill the friggin' Brit. But if you'd like to charge me with manslaughter, I'll fess up to that." After the judge reminded Logan's barrister that he and his client should practice proper court protocol, Logan said, "By the way, your honor, I'd like to charge the English with trespassing in Ireland... and once we succeed in getting them out of *our* country, perhaps the Scots and the Welch will have the courage to follow suit."

Given the number and character of witnesses in the Long Room on the day my Jodie and Sir Nigel Etherington were shot, I was confident that justice would ultimately be swift; hence, I didn't feel inclined to attend Logan McCool's Dublin trial. As it was, I'd been fighting a mild bout of depression, following Jodie's death, and the idea of again displacing myself for an extended period, in order to relive the horror I had plainly watched through my visual packet, was too unsettling.

Justice *was* swift. After Logan was found guilty on an unreduced murder charge, plus attempted murder, malicious wounding, and conspiracy to assassinate the British Prime Minister, he was sentenced to fifty years to life at Portlaoise Prison, a closed, high security corrections facility in County Laois. Logan would be ninety years old when eligible for parole.

In London, Sir Nigel Etherington was serving a life sentence of a different sort. The former Prime Minister was now a quadriplegic, paralyzed from the neck down, due to the .44 calibre round that severed his spinal column. In spite of advances in the treatment of paralysis in recent years, Sir Nigel's injury was so severe that he would, in all likelihood, spend the rest of his natural life imprisoned in his body; he required permanent use of a ventilator to affect respiration. As a result of Etherington's incapacitation, Lady Greta Hobson assumed leadership as the new British Prime Minister.

Over the succeeding several months, I resumed receiving visual packets but, curiously, the Omniscient One wasn't prompting me into action – at least not immediately. What's more intriguing was that the contents of those packets largely pertained to the lives of Liam McCool and Trish Jennings, neither of whom, presumably, had been returned to clairvoyant service since our lives converged that fateful day at the Pierpoint. Less often, I received packets concerning the affairs of Logan McCool, who now enjoyed rock star-like status among his fellow inmates at Portlaoise Prison, because of the perceived heroics and irreverent nature of his crimes.

Trish Jennings and I exchanged telephone calls about monthly, but I chose not mention that I recurrently observed her on a remote basis at her parents' equestrian centre, because I had yet to discover the purpose of the Omniscient One's ethereal provisions. Trish first called me about a week after Jodie's funeral, to kindly inquire how I was getting on, and it was then I took the opportunity to ask about Liam. Trish responded in a perceptibly vague manner that she and Liam "talked often," since his discharge from Dublin's St. James Hospital, and that he was living off some commissions he had previously earned in commercial real estate in Northern Ireland. She didn't offer any information about communiqués from the Omniscient One, and I didn't probe because I felt I already knew the answer.

Trish worked at the equestrian school on an as-needed basis, helping young people learn how to ride and handle horses, as well as taking tourists on pleasure rides into the short hills. Occasionally, she ventured into downtown Castlebar, to meet with friends and enjoy a bit of the *craic*, but it wasn't until I started regularly viewing Liam McCool driving down from Antrim, to meet with her for pints at a place called The Swingin' Door, that my interest piqued. Those pints inevitably led to dinners, and, given the common denominator of their otherworldly experiences, similar ages, and single statuses, before long, Liam and Trish were holding hands and swapping spit.

I first observed them kissing in a stable at the equestrian centre. Liam had again driven down from Antrim to visit, and was greeted by Mr. and Mrs. Jennings, who were mucking stalls alongside Trish, because the stablehand had called off sick that day. Trish soon interrupted the conversation and succeeded in removing Liam from their company by offering him a tour of the property while adequate daylight remained. After the two were alone, Trish explained that she had elected not to inform her parents of his similar clairvoyant capability, because she didn't want them worrying about her any more than they already did. Liam certainly empathized with her wishes and, suddenly, found her vulnerability attractive. Similarly, Trish had found his vulnerability appealing as Liam hobbled closer, still revealing signs of the injury he sustained in the Dublin crosswalk accident. Liam then moved in for a kiss. At first, Trish behaved demurely, pretending that she hadn't sensed his intentions, and her arms dangled unassumingly at her sides. But soon she subtly elevated her head to receive him, when ready to be taken, and Liam tilted his head and pecked her lips while lightly gripping her biceps. Within seconds, the two were engaged in a passionate, open-mouth kiss, and they embraced.

Trish had actually lied to Liam when explaining why she had ushered him away from her parents. Her real reason was that she hadn't yet thought of a way to break the news to her mother and father that she was currently dating the fraternal twin brother of the man responsible for the recent carnage at Trinity College, which was still making front page news. She wasn't sure if she would *ever* reveal that she had once dated the killer himself.

Mr. and Mrs. Jennings had since sauntered back to their residence, while Trish unpretentiously led Liam down the central aisle of the main stable to an empty stall lined with freshly cut straw. There, their kissing escalated, and they laid down and pawed at each other. Still clothed, Liam mounted Trish and prompted her legs open with his knee; her initial resistance, followed by gentle submission, palpably heightened their mutual arousals, as Liam grinded his manhood against her nether-region and dry-humped her while their tongues wallowed in each other's mouths. Minutes later, the two exited the stable and strolled hand-in-hand back to the one-level, stuccoed cottage that Trish occupied, and enjoyed sexual intercourse for the first time.

I never expected that Trish and Liam would, one day, become an item, even after she had remained in Dublin to continue visiting him in the hospital. Equally as strange, Trish neglected to reference her courtship with Liam during our monthly telephone conversations, despite my explicit questions: "How's Liam doing? Have you spoken with Liam McCool lately? What's new with Liam?"

In the visual packets pertaining to Logan McCool's life at Portlaoise Prison, I deduced that Logan and Liam finally managed to mend the rift between them, which goes to show that the bond between twins is not easily broken. In the beginning, Liam's short missives to Logan, updating him on family matters in Antrim, went unanswered, but, before long, Logan appreciated his brother's efforts and warmed up to him, and he responded to the letters by describing his new life at the prison.

Early on, Logan was faced with having to work in either the prison's kitchen or laundry, and, after contemplating the early wake-up and longer hours associated with kitchen duty, he astutely chose the laundry. He spent most days in the laundry, and was pleased that the prison employee overseeing the section soon entrusted him with learning and performing repairs and alterations on uniforms and related prison wear. However, once it occurred to a fellow inmate that Logan was receiving special treatment and was carrying on like "Betty Homemaker," he attempted to emasculate Logan in front of the prison population by shouting to him across the cafeteria, "Have you made *yerself* a dress yet, Suzie Singer?"

Logan initially said nothing, and considered just walking over and attacking his heckler. In the end, though, he only needed to gaze demonically at the inmates flanking his detractor, who were soon compelled to gang-up and beat the man; corrections officers looked on for more than a minute before interceding. By the next day, the toll of the inmate's insults had manifested, as he limped through the cellblock looking like a human eggplant.

As a matter of procedure, Logan was searched for objects like scissors and sewing needles upon departing the laundry section each afternoon. But his violent days were over with, he reasoned, and there was no need to acquire such weapons, especially considering his celebrity-like status. He also knew that the discovery of any weapons, pilfered for use as prison currency, would ultimately lead back to him, and that he would be stripped of his cushy situation. Logan thusly kept his nose clean while working in the laundry.

Most prisoners incarcerated at Portlaoise are violent offenders with chips on their shoulders, who, in many respects, are beyond reach, which seemed to describe Logan perfectly. However, unlike many inmates, Logan unexpectedly took advantage of the availability of a prison chaplain to talk things out, admittedly doing so, at first, because it was just another way to maintain contact with the outside world.

Among the chaplains frequenting Portlaoise Prison, Logan preferred the counsel of Father Daniel Stewart, a man of like age, who inmates favored because of his non-traditional appearance and liberal demeanor. "Stewie," as Logan liked to call the priest, which soon caught on with other inmates, shaved his head clean, even though his marginal, premature balding didn't warrant it, and wore a Vandyke beard.

During their early sessions at Portlaoise, Father Stewart helped Logan work on anger management issues, and they explored why Logan thought things had gone badly for him in life. Over time, the two focused more so on the important matter of how Logan could presently achieve peace and redemption in his life. And, as each weekly counseling session concluded, more often than not, Logan and Stewie found themselves engaging in healthy, genial debates over the merits of their two favorite football teams, Cavan and Meath, which added real enjoyment to their conversations.

One uncomfortable topic that Logan had avoided discussing with Father Stewart was his relationship with the woman who had spurned him, Trish Jennings. If Logan's brother, Liam, had written about Trish in his letters, perhaps Logan would've made a point of familiarizing Stewie with the "Witch of Castlebar," as he was fond of calling her, but which she certainly didn't deserve. Quite the contrary, Liam had purposely omitted news about Trish in his missives, because he anticipated that the mere mention of her name would incite Logan and inevitably cause another breach between them. What's more, Liam implored his aging parents not discuss his relationship with Trish in their own correspondences to Logan; nevertheless, in the end, Logan still managed to learn about Trish and Liam's growing affection, after their engagement announcement, containing photo of Trish, appeared in the *Irish Times*, which Logan read almost daily in the prison library. Logan, naturally, became infuriated upon noticing the announcement and, as a result, wrote a letter to Liam in which he cursed out his brother and instructed him to never contact him again. Before Logan had an opportunity to mail the letter, though, he received a letter from Liam informing him that he would soon drive down to pay him a visit him at the prison. Consequently, Logan tore up the letter he had written, because he had resolved to deal with his fraternal twin, in person.

30

A NOW BEARDED, SHAGGY-HAIRED LOGAN McCool sat in a chair behind the protective glass in the visitors area, waiting for his brother to enter. Moments earlier, Logan had been summoned from the prison laundry, notifying him that Liam had arrived and was currently being processed through reception.

Liam and Logan's visit would be limited to thirty minutes, according to prison policy: not all Irish prison practices are as stringent as Portlaoise when it comes to visitors and inmates interfacing, but the facility is a high-security prison designed to protect the public from the violent tendencies of its residents.

Logan observed his brother passing into the visitors area and reached for the telephone on his side of the glass, in anticipation of speaking with him. Liam smiled warmly, once vaguely recognizing Logan, and shuffled across the floor before coming to rest in a chair. Logan's failure to reciprocate with a smile momentarily unsettled Liam, but he discounted the omission, giving consideration to Logan's circumstances in life. Liam shifted in his seat and strained to look closer at his brother, finally lifting the handset to his ear.

"I hardly recognize you. What's with the hair... and the beard?"

"I can't explain it, brother. I just felt like letting things grow." Logan scrutinized Liam's face and wondered how long it would take his brother to reveal his engagement to Trish, if at all.

"I have some news for you, Logan. But, it's not exactly happy news."

"Oh?"

"Mother and Dad sold the house in Antrim and have moved to Londonderry."

"But they've lived there happily for thirty-six years. What would prompt such a move?"

"I'm afraid it was an accumulation of hate-mail, mocks, and glares, from townsfolk, after the house was identified on the evening news... as the place where killer and would-be assassin Logan McCool lived for much of the past three decades."

"Good grief. I suppose that's why they've written so seldom."

"Yes, well... mainly because they've been consumed with matters pertaining to selling a home, buying a new one, and moving." Liam changed the subject and focused on Logan. "So, how are ya? You described prison life in your letters, but how're you doing... really? You don't look so good."

"Walk a mile in my shoes." Logan only replied.

"You mentioned that you've got a pretty good deal working in the laundry. You still there?"

"Yes." Logan then decided that Liam wouldn't likely divulge his recent engagement to Trish, and his anger began building.

"How's the food? Any good?"

"Is this why you've come, brother... to recount all the things I've covered in my letters. I thought the reason you drove down from Antrim was because you had special news."

Liam studied Logan through the glass. He knew his twin too well and sensed Logan had something else on his mind.

"Well, I thought the news of Mum and Dad moving *was important*."

"But that's not the real reason you're here, is it, brother?" You made the long journey to Portlaoise because you wanted to tell me, personally, that you're a warlock. Isn't that so?"

"Warlock? What the hell're you talking about? I'm not following."

Logan leaned toward the glass, his eyes bulging and face growing scarlet. His unkempt, long hair and beard further accentuated his menacing look.

"You're not following? Well, do you follow when I say that only a warlock would marry a witch! The Witch of Castlebar!"

Liam didn't immediately respond because he was confounded over how Logan had learned of the engagement news.

"I had planned on eventually telling you about Trish and I marrying, Logan. It's just that... the wedding's a ways off. Any number of things could happen between now and then."

"Liar! You figured that because I'm shut off from the world in this *shithole* that I wouldn't find out! I read more newspapers in a week than you do in a year, you *arse*. When's the wedding?" Logan demanded to know.

"Well, Logan... I don't know why that's important. It's not as if you'll be able to attend."

Logan became more irate once sensing that Liam would refuse to disclose the wedding date. He now stood up behind the glass, and a corrections officer, who had overheard the escalating conversation, rushed toward Liam.

"I want to know the date of the *god-damned* wedding, Liam!" Another corrections officer presently entered the space in which Logan stood.

"July 18th, if you must know. It's a summer wedding."

"A summer wedding, eh? Well, that's just nifty, isn't it?" Logan said sarcastically. "I don't mean to impinge on your splendid summer plans, brother, but if you betray me, by marrying Trish Jennings, I'll string you up by the feckin' gonads and let you hang until dead. You got that, *Judas* ?"

Liam actually laughed at Logan's proposal.

"And how do you plan to pull *that* one off, *brother*," Liam asked, now mimicking the way Logan often addressed him when trying to make a point. "Perhaps some Martians will pick you up in their spaceship, in the prison yard, and deliver you to the destination of your choice? Logan, I'm not going to apologize for accidentally meeting and falling in love with the woman you happened to date a short while. Get over it! What does it matter? Your life, as you knew it, was over the moment you shot those nice people in the Old Library. And you threw *human excrement* down on the Prime Minister before shooting him? What the hell's wrong with you, *brother*," Liam again asked tauntingly. "And, by the way, the woman you killed, Jodie Doyle, was the daughter of a friend of mine."

"Good," shouted Logan, now trembling furiously. "England out of Ireland!"

"She was *from* the Republic, you *arse*! County Galway!" Liam shouted back. "Jodie was a public school teacher and an innocent bystander!"

Only nine of the thirty minutes had elapsed since Liam's arrival and, despite their being separated by a protective glass partition, the brothers were split up due to the disruption they had caused to other visitors. Logan was consequently escorted back to the prison laundry, and Liam left for the visitors reception area, where he checked out and departed Portlaoise Prison.

Eleven weeks following their heated exchange in the prison visitors area, the silence finally broke, and the brothers resumed contact, but it took Logan's initiative to smooth things over. Then again, Logan's motive for re-establishing contact wasn't genuine, so, had their quarrel actually been resolved? I'm here to tell you that it was not, but I have the benefit of hindsight in relating events.

Logan had portrayed himself as contrite in most of his subsequent correspondences to Liam, until persuaded that he had regained his brother's confidence, so that he could continue to hear, from the horse's mouth, as it were, the everyday details of Liam and Trish lives. At first, Liam couldn't understand Logan's eagerness to know such mundane matters, but Logan explained that, as a prisoner shut off from the world, he derived enjoyment from living vicariously through him.

The wedding day now lay only three and a half months ahead. Logan had once fumed when envisioning his Judas of a brother in the arms of the woman who spurned him, but now he delighted. He even delighted after Liam reported, in one of his innocent letters, that he decided to move out from his Antrim flat, because Mr. and Mrs. Jennings had invited him to stay at Jennings Equestrian Centre, where he could live and work during the period leading up to the wedding. According to Liam, Trish had already moved up to the main residence, a quarter-mile away, to live with her parents, so that he could assume occupancy of the white, thatched roof cottage, nearby to the stables. Following the wedding, Liam and Trish intended to live as newlyweds in the cottage while saving money for their future.

Logan had never had the opportunity to visit Trish at the Castlebar equestrian facility during their brief courtship, but, presently, he had fixed in his mind the layout of the property, thanks to Liam's letters.

And so Logan delighted more and more with each letter received; insanely so, it's fair to say, because it aided him in formulating his plan to deliver murder and mayhem into the lives of the happy couple – murder he intended on dispensing personally.

31

I WAS ELATED THAT TESSIE decided to remain in Kinvara following her sister's funeral, because she had once seemed so resolute about moving to Cork City after giving up island life on Great Blasket. In deciding to move back to Kinvara, I think, in part, she felt sorry when imagining me sitting home alone and brooding. The reality, though, was that I had long grown accustomed to living by myself, and if Tessie desired to experience city life then she should do it, I thought and told her so. Instead, she took a job as the purchasing manager at the Londis market in downtown Kinvara.

Occasionally, she journeyed up to Galway City, to stay with a girlfriend for the weekend, and I think we both enjoyed the respites. There, they browsed the shops, ate dinners out, and, I'm certain, enjoyed a bit of the *craic*, in the pubs at night, with the lads. She also traveled once to Great Blasket Island to attend a baby shower, but, despite the joy of seeing her friends and former workmates again, Tessie assured me she had no intentions of returning to live on the island.

As for me, life had returned to normal except for the intermittent visual packets I received concerning the lives of Trish, Liam, and Logan – packets of which I still wasn't induced to act upon by the Omniscient One. When the weather cooperated, I still enjoyed hiking about the Burren, because it made me feel young, and on more than one occasion, while hiking, I encountered my successor, who performed geological fieldwork along the west-central coast of Ireland. Each time I departed the chap's company, I couldn't help but wonder if life might've shaken out differently if I had delayed my retirement. Would the Omniscient One have engaged me a second time? Yes, I decided, because I was the only logical choice to flush out Haimish Devlin from the Canary Islands.

I also stopped in at the Pierpoint about twice weekly, for a pint, and, on the odd occasion, peeked inside Sexton's, when collecting my mail at the adjacent post office, to see whether Gerry McBrine or Tom Casey might be about; in which case, if they were, I always joined them.

In late May of that year, about forty-five days before Trish and Liam's wedding, I received an invitation in the mail. Naturally, I would travel to County Mayo to attend the ceremony, and after dropping my RSVP in the mail, I followed up with a telephone call to Trish, to express my surprise but happiness for her, all the while pleading ignorance about their courtship. Following our conversation, I plodded outside to retrieve the *Irish Independent,* and read the distressing headline, "Sir Nigel Etherington Dead at 58." The subtitle beneath read, "Former British Prime Minister suffocates in sleep due to paralysis."

Apparently, the breathing apparatus that aided Sir Nigel in his respiration had its limitations, and once the medical worker, living at the Etherington residence, finally responded to the alarm in the middle of the night, it was too late to resuscitate him. After reading the article, I noticed a related news piece on the bottom half of the front page, "Etherington's Assailant, Logan McCool, to be Charged with Second Murder."

Subsequent to the articles I had just read, I received a pertinent visual packet while sitting in my living room and, due to its timeliness, wondered what the Omniscient one might be brewing. The packet revealed Logan, sitting quietly in the Portlaoise Prison library, reading the same front-page news I had read minutes earlier. Whether Logan learned from the newspaper, at that moment, that he'd be required to stand trial in connection with Etherington's death, or if he was notified beforehand, by a government official, is still unclear, and, I suppose, a moot point.

Logan's position on England's occupation of northern Ireland hadn't changed since the bloodshed he caused at Trinity College, or during his few short months of incarceration; if anything, those convictions had deepened. Undoubtedly, he felt gratified over the former British Prime Minister's demise, because he accomplished what he set out to do and, therefore, believed it helped advance his political objective. Soon, Logan would learn that he'd eventually be transferred from Portlaoise Prison and housed temporarily at Arbour Hill, a medium security prison, to stand trial in Dublin, commencing July 16th. He now wrestled with the idea of delaying his planned escape (and flight to Castlebar), so that he could exploit the Dublin trial setting as a publicity platform to further promote his cause. But, then, Liam and Trish's wedding would go off as planned, he thought, and the idea of their blissful union gnawed at him even more so.

Logan obviously felt confident about his ability to escape from Portlaoise Prison; otherwise, he wouldn't have begun work on an escape costume in the prison laundry weeks earlier. The prison employee overseeing the laundry section routinely assigned tasks and knew specifically what articles of clothing Logan was supposed to be altering or repairing, and, as a rule, Logan waited until the section-head took his afternoon meal, each day, before resuming work on his get-up. During those lunch periods, the supervising employee was typically replaced by a random corrections officer, who observed prisoners working in the section but wasn't familiar with their assignments.

Many inmates worked rotationally on industrial cleaning projects contracted out to the prison system, and much of that work was performed at Portlaoise. In most instances, the inmates wore black jumpsuits in lieu of their normal prison garb when involved in the grimy work. Upon conceiving his escape scheme, Logan had copped one of the torn jumpsuits, turned in for repair, and began fashioning it into a passable priest's uniform. (He had noticed that Father Stewart generally wore the same short-sleeve, black shirt with Roman collar, black pants, black belt, and black shoes during the fair-weather months, so attempted to replicate the outfit). The jumpsuit material was thicker and more durable than standard priest apparel, but it would take a discerning eye to notice the difference, once Logan finished altering it.

First, he needed to cut the jumpsuit in half so that the garment ceased being a single unit. After styling the shirt (even using excess material to replicate a breast pocket), he produced the pants, which included belt loops, although he would never succeed in procuring a black belt to wear with the pants. He also reproduced cuffs on the trousers and stitched material in such a way to simulate normal pockets. When not working on his costume-in-progress, he concealed the outfit in a stack among other jumpsuits. As for the white material necessary to complete the Roman collar, he tore a strip from a new pair of white boxer shorts, and folded and stitched the cloth until achieving the desired look.

On the morning of July 14th, two days prior to his new trial, and a day before he was to be transported to Arbour Hill Prison in Dublin, Logan McCool shaved his head clean and shaved and trimmed portions of his beard, so that only a Vandyke beard remained. Save for his Kelly-green prison garb, he looked remarkably like Father Stewart, who still came to Portlaoise weekly, and would again provide spiritual guidance to inmates this day. One prisoner, sitting diagonally to Logan in the cafeteria that morning, picked up on Logan's resemblance to the priest, and uttered for Logan's benefit while winking, "I wouldn't have thought Stewie to be *capable* of a capital crime."

Following breakfast, Logan reported to the prison laundry, as normal, and commenced work; most workers, including the supervisor, noticed Logan's changed appearance but said nothing. Logan had finished creating his priest get-up several days earlier and now only needed to don it before his mid-morning meeting with Father Stewart, which would prove a project in itself. The way things stood, Logan needed to furtively remove his costume from a small stack of jumpsuits, inconspicuously stuff it beneath his prison garb, and situate it in a manner so as to not draw attention to himself. He then needed to obtain permission to use the commode, in order to accomplish his first stage of changing.

The lavatory adjacent to the laundry was no different from any other lavatory used by inmates. It was simply smaller and contained fewer toilets and, for security reasons, lacked the privacy of stalls. Conversely, the lavatories on the visitors' side of the prison contained all the features of comfort and privacy one would expect.

About thirty minutes before he anticipated being summoned for his counseling session with Father Stewart, Logan observed the section-head demonstrating a task to a laundry newcomer, so he plodded unassumingly to the stack of jumpsuits, where he knelt and extracted the new priest outfit, immediately stuffing the two items inside his loose-fitting green jumpsuit; he distributed the material around his front, back, and lower abdomen. He then stood and routinely removed a black jumpsuit from the top of a stack, indicating to anyone who observed him that he was about to start work on it. Once returning to his station, he sat down and nonchalantly used his arms to further flatten some concealed material he sensed bulging.

Approximately three minutes had passed, and Logan got the attention of the section-head to request permission to use the commode. The supervisor granted the request and routinely picked up a telephone to notify a corrections officer posted in the abutting corridor. Logan would still be in a secure area, once exiting the laundry, but inmates in this high-security facility are rarely permitted to roam freely, and he would again be escorted to the lavatory.

A familiar corrections officer gestured for Logan to proceed to the commode, where he typically hovered outside the door while Logan, this time, only pretended to relieve himself. Logan used this lavatory at least twice daily and usually felt at-ease, but was presently anxious because he needed to work quickly, and imagined the guard or other inmate entering to discover his charade.

Five toilets sat in a single line, only an arm's length apart. Logan stood before a toilet at the far end of the room, and faced away from the door. He quickly extracted the pseudo-religious apparel, scattered beneath his green jumpsuit, and placed it at his feet. He then stripped and donned the priest outfit, at first only fastening the bottom shirt buttons, because, once dressing in his prison garb again, he needed to fold the exposed Roman collar down under the jumpsuit, in order to cover it.

"Let's move it along in there," Logan heard the corrections officer say in a raised voice through the door that separated them. The guard followed with a couple of raps on the door. Logan had received similar advice in the past but, presently, lost a sense of the elapsed time, and was concerned that the guard might enter on this occasion. Suddenly, the door swung open. Logan panicked and flushed a toilet, for effect, and exclaimed, "Let a man a pull up his drawers, will ya."

The door fell shut. Once persuaded that his costume was adequately concealed, he exited the lavatory without meeting the guard's eyes.

Logan had resumed repairing a jumpsuit in the laundry but was soon notified of Father Stewart's arrival. The section-head again picked up the telephone for a corrections officer to escort Logan to the "Sessions Lounge," to which it was commonly referred. Logan was relieved to see a different escort this time, because he would again request to use a lavatory. The guard currently stood in the doorway leading to the corridor, as Logan made his way across the expansive laundry room.

"This is a new look for you, McCool," the officer said, regarding Logan's shaved head and mustache-goatee unit.

"Yes, I was feeling a bit stagnant," Logan responded.

"You're getting a bit pudgy, too," the officer said, turning sideways to allow Logan to pass. "Three less potatoes and three more hours of exercise each week oughta do the trick."

Logan said nothing.

Unlike the visitors' area, where inmates and guests are separated by protective glass and are required to communicate through telephone handsets, the Sessions Lounge is comprised of a series of small, private offices, each furnished with a desk and four comfortable chairs. The top halves of the office doors feature glass so that the guard, patrolling the corridor, can periodically peer in, to ensure guests' safety, in case an inmate was to go berserk.

Logan glanced through a window into an office on the left and noticed Father Stewart sitting alone with a visitor's pass clipped to his shirt. The priest looked down and was writing attentively on a yellow, lined legal tablet. Logan ambled past the office as if overlooking the priest.

"You missed him. You just walked by Stewie," alerted the officer.

Logan often felt tantalized by the daylight reflecting off the walls of the intersecting corridor, when visiting this wing, because Stewie always exited in that direction, and Logan knew it led to freedom. Forty-five feet away, a young officer, responsible for patrolling the Sessions Lounge, sat at a desk, reading, but hadn't yet acknowledged his coworker or Logan.

"I'd like to use the commode before starting my session," Logan beseeched his escort, almost whispering as if to prevent his voice from projecting down the hall.

"Go ahead," replied the officer, who pushed the door open to inspect the civilian lavatory, which contained stalls. Logan entered the bathroom and gawked uncomfortably at his escort for a moment, as if to convey that he wished to relieve himself with some modicum of privacy.

Although various officers escorted inmates to the Sessions Lounge, Logan had repeated the preceding course of action with all officers, ever since resolving to break out from Portlaoise Prison, because he

wanted to condition the guards to expect him to use the bathroom,
where he'd remain until his escort notified the patrolling officer that
he should assume oversight. If the pattern presently held, the escorting
officer would soon tire of waiting and inform his coworker, at the desk,
of the inmate using the commode. The escort then, typically, departed
and returned to his primary post near the laundry. When Logan would
emerge from the lavatory, the officer responsible for securing the Sessions
Lounge often awaited him.

Logan experienced tremendous relief when plainly hearing his
escort shout down the corridor to his coworker, "I've got a man in the
john. He's set to see the priest."

Still inside a toilet stall, Logan had quickly shed his Kelly-green
prison garb and hung it from view on the back of the stall door. He now
desired to exit the lavatory as soon as possible, appearing as a priest, so
that the awaiting officer would hopefully be confused over "Logan's"
whereabouts, thus giving "the priest" sufficient time to endeavor an
escape. He only took a moment to smooth his self-fashioned religious
shirt and to adjust the Roman collar, before stepping out to determine
the guard's location: the young man was still glued to his magazine but
now stood, hunched over the desktop. Logan's hopes surged. He deemed
any guard not waiting dutifully, outside the lavatory, to be a slacker. The
only thing that could throw a monkey wrench into his operation, now,
was if Stewie were to emerge from the office, curious to know why his
penitent was late for counseling. *Was Stewie still writing officiously on
the yellow tablet?* he wondered.

Logan strolled toward the guard, at the desk, who eventually
glanced up but seemed more interested in returning to his motorcycle
magazine. That was a good sign; nevertheless, Logan grew panicky
again when recalling that he conspicuously lacked a belt, and that his
charcoal-colored sport shoes, with Velcro fasteners, might be a tip-off.
He decided to bypass the officer's location without pausing to engage
him, so that his costume flaws wouldn't be easily revealed.

"Where's your visitor's pass, Father," asked the guard, at first,
without looking up.

"You know *what*, officer, I just received an urgent call, and I'm
sure I became distracted. I must've left it in either the restroom or
the office. Once you find it, would you mind returning it to the nice

folks at reception? I really must go. I need to respond to a very serious matter."

"Wait a minute. What happened to your appointment? Where's the inmate that was..."

Logan interrupted.

"We're going to have to reschedule... or just pick up with it again next week. He's returned with his escort to the laundry."

"When did *this* all occur? What was the prisoner's last name?"

"Just now. O'Malley... Joe O'Malley just returned with that tall, lanky guard to the laundry. I really must go, friend. You don't want to be liable for my tardiness. I'm off to perform Last Rites on a prominent person in Ireland. I'm sure you'll be reading about his passing in the *Independent* tomorrow. Check the obits. Bye, now."

Logan boldly walked away toward the daylight at the end of the corridor. During his progress, he glanced alternately at framed photographs on the walls, pretending to survey them, but his real motive was to gauge, through his peripheral vision, if the officer had vacated his desk to inspect the Sessions Lounge. He had not. And as Logan turned the corner to notice the main reception area, he sneaked one final, fleeting look at the officer, to determine if the young man was yet on the telephone, attempting to verify that an inmate named Joe O'Malley had been escorted back to the laundry. Likewise, he had not.

Logan attempted to walk straight through the main doors of Portlaoise Prison but was soon beckoned by a meek but conscientious receptionist, responsible for the issuance and collection of visitor passes; an armed corrections officer stood abreast, in a relaxed, parade-rest stance. When the kind lady asked for the priest's pass, Logan responded assertively, "You know *what*... I just went through *all this* with the guard, down the hall, who's taking care of it. Moments ago, I received an urgent call. I've got an emergency to attend to, and I got distracted and left my pass in either the Sessions Lounge or the restroom. Couldn't you just coordinate with the guard?" he pleaded. "I really must leave. God Bless." Logan then marched out the door without further resistance.

Once in the parking lot, he casually scanned for security cameras, and spotted three so knew it would be foolish to attempt anything rash like carjacking a visitor's automobile. Ironically, both the command center officer, who monitored the security cameras, and a tower guard, watched the priest half-scamper off the property, and they unwittingly discounted the anomaly. When eventually interviewed concerning Logan's escape, the tower guard admitted that he thought the priest's car might've malfunctioned, and he considered calling down to reception but changed his mind, "Because the priest walked away so purposefully... so resolutely, I figured he had a handle on the situation."

Nobody had been the wiser, in fact, until Father Stewart, who had been constructively writing a letter to an enthusiastic seminarian, while waiting for Logan, finally emerged from the Sessions Lounge and was noticed by the guard still leafing through his magazine.

Once Logan McCool was discovered missing, and prison officials failed to account for him, Portlaoise Prison immediately went into lockdown, and citizens throughout County Laoise heard the infrequent but familiar and ominous, blaring siren that signaled a prisoner had escaped. By then, Logan was already riding on an inter-county bus, and would soon disembark in the town of Tullamore without paying his fare, after the driver swallowed "Father Stewart's" latest cock and bull story – hook, line, and sinker. Other paying passengers openly objected to the priest's free passage, but this was Catholic Ireland, and "If anyone should ride for free it should be a priest or nun," the driver counseled one squawking commuter.

Upon stepping from the bus onto the sidewalk, Logan turned and blessed the driver with the sign of the cross, and said, "I'll say a Mass for your family."

He subsequently ducked into a restaurant bathroom, where he changed out of his priest's costume, folded it, and placed it in a common plastic sack he had scavenged seconds earlier from a public rubbish container. He would make use of the priest costume again within the hour. At the moment, he wore a gray t-shirt and athletic shorts he had strategically worn underneath, plus white socks, and the charcoal-colored sport shoes he exercised in regularly in the prison yard.

32

LOGAN'S APPEARANCE AS A jogger making his way through downtown Tullamore, on a bright summer day, had been nothing remarkable, although he did look a tad unwieldy running with a small sack in his right hand. Noticing a church in the distance, he first slowed and then walked upon nearing the place of worship, finally lingering outside to catch his breath.

Two pensioners had just exited Assumption Church, where they made an early afternoon visit to light candles and say prayers. Logan eyeballed them. He had known all along that he wouldn't get far without money in his pocket but, also, realized that to resort to a desperate, high-profile crime like robbery would swiftly put the Garda on his tail.

He entered Assumption with his sack in-hand, and delayed in the vestibule while considering the church interior. No Mass was being said, but he observed several worshippers sitting or kneeling in the pews before a shrine to St. Joseph at the right transept. A parishioner had arrived moments before and paused in front of the shrine to deposit some Euros into a flimsy metal container. The woman then lit a candle and joined others at the opposite pew. Once espying her activities, Logan mulled over how he might acquire the funds necessary for passage to the west coast of Ireland. He subsequently slipped into the vestibule restroom, changed into his priest costume, again smoothed his shirt with the palms of his hands, and straightened his Roman collar. He scrunched the flimsy plastic sack and concealed it in his sock, underneath a trouser leg. He exited the restroom and immediately went into his role, operating as if he had every right to rummage about the vestibule, which he commenced doing. He soon came across a cardboard box filled with church bulletins left over from last weekend's Masses, and removed the bulletins and folded the box tops inside to neaten it; he intended to place the donations collected at the shrine into the box.

Suddenly, the main door of the church swung open, and an elderly couple entered the dimly lit space to behold the younger, middle-aged priest. The husky woman was no shrinking violet and spoke rather brashly:

"Hello, Father, I don't believe I know you. Are you a new addition to Assumption?" Once querying the priest, her eyes dropped immediately to the floor as she circumspectly crept along, wobbling atop her mid-heel shoes and throwing her arms out to her sides to seemingly maintain her balance on the familiar slate surface, where Logan guessed she had once taken a spill.

Logan smiled. "No, I'm afraid not. I'm just over from Dublin to help out for a week or two," he said, gesturing that he was about enter the nave of the church.

"Well, which is it... one week or two?" the woman insisted on knowing, now looking into his eyes up close.

Logan sensed trouble.

"Just one, unless I'm advised otherwise."

"What's your name, Father," she asked more pleasantly.

"Father Molloy. Father Bernard Molloy." Logan nodded at the couple and made his way down the long body of the church. Still curious, the woman sneaked close behind while her husband trailed.

"What's your home parish, Father," she persisted.

Logan had now grown annoyed, and turned but still managed a smile. "The Pro," he said.

"Oh, my," she reacted, dramatically placing an open hand over her heart. "A priest from St. Mary's Pro-Cathedral to help out at our little church. We're so honored."

"Think nothin' of it," Logan replied, turning about face and quickening his gait to depart her company.

More often than not, the various offertory boxes found in big city churches are kept locked and emptied often, due to past instances of appalling thievery carried out by desperate vagrants and juvenile delinquents who don't fear God. The attitude at a small parish, with steadfast flock, like Assumption, however, was that only someone so callous as to hazard eternal damnation would barefacedly pilfer one of their unsecured offertory boxes.

Logan turned from the nave onto the right transept, and the old woman trailing him thought it peculiar that Father Molloy had neglected to genuflect, in reverence, when passing by the tabernacle containing the Holy Eucharist; he smiled thinly and nodded to acknowledge those present at the shrine. By now, the determined woman had caught up, and proudly introduced the priest, in a loud whisper, to a neighbor she recognized sitting among fellow parishioners.

"Catherine, this is Father Molloy... from St. Mary's Pro-Cathedral in Dublin. He'll be helping out over the next week," she said.

"Hello, Father," said Catherine.

Logan looked over his shoulder at the woman while opening the lid to the offertory receptacle. He smiled and said, "I look forward to meeting and talking with you all after Mass on Sunday." He then removed the contents and placed what amounted to nearly two hundred Euros into the empty box.

"You forgot to put your belt on today, Father," Catherine remarked.

"Oh, goodness, me," responded Father Molloy. "Too many things on my mind, this morning, when getting dressed."

Catherine also glanced down at the priest's charcoal-gray, athletic shoes, with Velcro strips, and thought them inappropriate, but sensed she had already caused the priest enough embarrassment, and decided not to comment further.

Having collected the money, Logan shuffled past the parishioners and nodded cordially in departure. He again failed to genuflect and acknowledge the Holy Eucharist, when turning at the nave, and strode toward the vestibule. While carrying out this latest charade, an attractive woman in her early to mid-twenties had entered the church, and presently sat teary-eyed and distraught in a rear pew. *If there was ever someone looking to share her burden, it's this woman*, he thought. *She's probably single and pregnant, and the father took a powder.* Logan regarded the woman, who clearly gesticulated for him to stop, but he continued on by to the vestibule and again entered the restroom, this time changing out of his mock-priest apparel.

Once stuffing the money inside the plastic sack amidst his costume, he cracked open the lavatory door and peered into the vestibule to check for any loitering worshippers he had encountered at the shrine. Nobody dallied, so he emerged in his athletic wear and opened the main door to depart Assumption Church, only to see Catherine gabbing with an acquaintance from town.

"Goodness, Father, you change clothes faster than Superman," she said pryingly.

"Yes, well... even a priest needs his exercise, ladies."

Logan didn't plan on sticking around for any meaningless smalltalk that might lead to his capture, so he smiled and walked onward before finally jogging.

Catherine peered over her acquaintance's shoulder and studied the sack in Father Molloy's right hand, as he edged away. *Something seemed amiss about the priest,* she decided, but couldn't quite put her finger on it. *Father Molloy had behaved a bit reserved and uncomfortable, but, then again, Assumption was largely unfamiliar territory to him.* She certainly couldn't recall him substituting at their parish before. *Perhaps it was that Father Molloy lacked polish, considering that he had been dispatched from prestigious St. Mary's Pro-Cathedral in Dublin.* Catherine resumed talking with her Tullamore chum but inevitably grew distracted and again looked beyond to Father Molloy, now just a dot in the horizon and still jogging awkwardly with his sack. Father Molloy had just turned a corner and would soon board a bus and disappear from Tullamore forever.

The first bus to stop had been bound for Ennis, County Clare and, while Logan knew that Ennis was far west of his current location, he determined it to be too far south; he thusly waited for an alternate bus. Fifteen minutes later, he boarded a bus traveling to Galway City.

The bus soon passed through a small, unremarkable town, and it was just about teatime that July 14th afternoon, so the streets were virtually barren. Once the bus progressed into more rural parts, he gazed out to appreciate the pacifying, lush, green landscape characteristic of Ireland, but quickly found himself staring into oblivion, when fathoming his latest plight. The forces of good and evil fought turbulently within Logan most days, ever since his inception into the Irish Republican Army. In one sense, he wished his current journey would never end, so that he wouldn't have to disembark in Galway and carry out his evil imperative. But once recalling his motive for breaking out from Portlaoise Prison, the difficulties overcome in accomplishing his escape, and fantasizing over the execution of his vengeful plan, it breathed new life into him.

For the moment, he naturally concentrated on eluding the Garda, because to fail in this area meant returning to prison without completing his mission and likely spending the rest of his earthly days in solitary confinement. He therefore tried to anticipate the repercussions stemming from each action and interaction during his progress to Castlebar, which might lead police to him; all the while, operating urgently on the assumption that the Garda was already on his tail.

As the bus passed through the town of Clara, he noticed a church that resembled the one from Tullamore, and he wondered how long it would take before someone recognized his face on the evening news, which would soon air. Once reaching Galway City, he'd purchase a razor and shave his face clean. A change of clothes was in order, too: he'd buy some inexpensive, casual attire at a low-end retail store or thrift shop, using the Euros he had filched from the offertory box. Then there was the thorny matter of where to sleep. He knew the layout of Galway fairly well, because he had visited the compact city twice, on pub-crawls, with friends. He considered renting a room in one of the many tourist homes along College Road, but thought it too risky. Alternatively, he weighed not staying overnight in Galway at all. Perhaps it would be best to just wait for a connecting bus to Westport, the closest major town to Castlebar. But then he imagined some Garda officer checking the station at night and discovering him as he sat waiting for a bus. Logan ultimately made his decision once arriving in Galway.

33

THAT SAME JULY 14TH afternoon, his brother, Liam McCool, had just
finished lungeing a horse, on his own, for the first time, and led it back
to a stall in the main stable at Jennings Equestrian Centre.

Earlier in the day, Mr. and Mrs. Jennings had assisted Trish, Liam,
and the part-time stablehand, train several children to learn how to
ride. After the children departed, and the Jennings elders returned to
their residence a quarter-mile away, Trish tried coaxing Liam out for
a pleasure ride and lunch; however, Liam wanted to make sure he was
earning his keep, and conscientiously remained behind to work in the
stables. Trish thusly ventured out alone, as she often did, but would
soon emerge from the short hills, north of their Castlebar property,
and return to her fiancé, who still exhibited traces of a limp due to the
motorcade accident several months earlier.

Back at the main residence, Mrs. Jennings busily made last minute
telephone calls to vendors, who would be arriving the following day to
set up for Trish and Liam's wedding and reception, which were to take
place at the picturesque manor on Saturday. After Mrs. Jennings got
off the line, she visited her husband in the den and updated him on
wedding day matters. Mr. Jennings had just finished reading the *Irish
Times* and turned on the television to watch the latest news. Predictably,
the lead story dealt with Logan McCool's escape from Portlaoise Prison,
and it was then Mr. and Mrs. Jennings learned that the man scheduled
to marry their daughter on Saturday was the fraternal twin brother of

the killer responsible for the carnage at Trinity College, the previous year.

It seems that when Logan had shot my Jodie Doyle and Sir Nigel Etherington, despite Liam's relation to the shooter, and reason for being in Dublin that day, Liam's name was not copiously reported by print and television news media. In fact, the only place Liam's name *had* appeared was in articles pertaining to the vehicular accident that occurred as the British Prime Minister proceeded to Trinity College, and that news was naturally overshadowed by the bigger story of the assassination attempt. However, now that Logan had escaped from Portlaoise Prison, Liam's face and relationship to the killer were disseminated throughout Ireland and the United Kingdom, because authorities feared that Logan might seek to obtain assistance from his brother.

Mr. and Mrs. Jennings presently sat benumbed in their Castlebar home while watching news reports of efforts being made to capture "escaped convict Logan McCool." Early footage showed helicopters systematically surveying large expanses of peat bogs in south central Ireland, while K-9 teams combed the fields in a ten-mile radius outside Portlaoise Prison. Before long, Mrs. Jennings scrambled to call Trish, who always carried her cellular phone with her while riding, in case an accident was to occur. Trish had already stabled her horse, however, and returned with Liam to the white, thatched-roof cottage, where they currently made love. Meanwhile, her cellphone vibrated repeatedly in the pocket of her riding pants, which lay across an easy chair adjacent to the bed.

Eventually, Trish would return her mother's calls and subsequently make the long march to her parents' home, where she'd be "on the carpet" edifying them about the McCool brothers, to include the revelation that, prior to Liam, she had formerly dated escaped killer, Logan. Within the hour, Liam was also summoned to the residence to participate in the discussion that carried over to dinner.

Mr. and Mrs. Jennings had grown quite fond of Liam in recent months. They deemed him a hard worker who would be good for their daughter, and they privately speculated that if it hadn't been for Liam, arriving on the scene, that Trish, at age 40, would likely never marry. Hence, despite the heinous actions of Liam's brother, and embarrassing admissions of a cover-up by Trish and Liam, the Jennings elders decided not to stand in the way of the couple getting married. Mr. Jennings did, however, insist that Liam contact the Garda to inform them of his (Liam's) current location, and that he would call the Garda immediately if learning of Logan's whereabouts. Liam agreed, and, within the hour, a plainclothes Garda Inspector, no one other than Inspector Pearse McElwee, who resided in County Mayo, arrived to interview Liam about his brother, Logan.

The Jennings intended on remaining closed-mouth about Liam's relation to Logan with wedding guests, notwithstanding recent news reports, in part, because they, too, were now ill-at-ease with their connection to the killer. The Jennings imagined there would be lots of whispering and talk behind their backs, once word circulated about Liam's identity, but rationalized that it wasn't Logan, the escaped convict, after all, who Trish was marrying – it was Liam.

In Kinvara, my Tessie had just departed on a weeklong visit to Great Blasket Island, where, among other activities, she'd attend a surprise 30th birthday party for her former workmate, Patty Reilly. It was a beautiful time of year to be on the island, and Tessie scarcely needed to reach in her pocket while there, so I encouraged her to take advantage. Meanwhile, I was preparing to journey to Castlebar, in two days, for Trish and Liam's wedding. During my last conversation with Trish, she had invited me to stay overnight at her parents home, and, presently, I wasn't sure if I'd take her up on the offer or just return to Kinvara that night. Well, friends, I must remind you that I'm recounting events with the benefit of hindsight when I tell you that I never made that wedding trip to Castlebar:

In a visual packet that, unsurprisingly, materialized long after Logan McCool made passage to County Mayo, I perceived him sleeping secludedly, adjacent to the third rail of the train track, below the passenger platform inside the Galway City train station. In one respect, this had been a foolish, risky maneuver on Logan's part, because if he had rolled over too far during the night, or woke up disoriented and accidentally made contact with the third rail, he would've been history (which actually would've worked out better for all parties concerned). Then again, if one had been searching for a fugitive without the aid of scent-tracking dogs, the modest cranny where he lay, flanking the third rail, might not have been an obvious place to look.

Logan was first stirred that Friday morning by the sound of echoing voices in the tunnel, as commuters trickled in to wait for an eastbound train to Dublin. He remained motionless in the depression that helped conceal him, until sensing the rumble of an approaching train, which he assumed would attract peoples' eyes. He had been reposing at the far, west end of the tunnel, and, after glimpsing the train's beacon, heard an announcement advising of the train's arrival. Once the train's brakes squealed, he rolled out from the cranny and collected his plastic sack containing priest costume, which he had used as a pillow overnight; he leapt up on the platform as commuters positioned to board the train. One rider caught some movement in his peripheral vision and turned to study Logan, from afar, finally resolving that the man was a vagabond.

Logan soon mixed with commuters disembarking in Galway City, and filed into the station, where bus tickets are sold, and purchased a one-way ticket to Westport for a bus departing ninety minutes later. He then ambled leisurely out of the station and, despite being the only "commuter" in exercise attire, attracted no unwanted attention. Moreover, once recognizing that no Garda officers were posted in the vicinity, he determined that search efforts to locate him were still being concentrated in central Ireland.

Within minutes, he had crossed through Eyre Square and entered a pharmacy, where he purchased a razor, shaving creme, and pair of grooming scissors. He then walked a short distance to a busy fast-food restaurant and bought an egg and cheese sandwich and an orange juice, which he nervously consumed before getting up to use the men's room, where he proceeded to cut off his remaining beard and shave clean, accomplishing most of the work within the confines of a bathroom stall, using toilet water to rinse his razor, because he was too paranoid to shave at the sink. Two patrons eventually entered the restroom and observed him splashing water on his face, after he had relocated to the sink, but neither man gave him a second look; his face and head were now hairless.

On the outer fringes of Eyre Square, he identified a department store and waited twenty-five minutes for an employee to open up; Logan was their first customer. He walked directly to the men's boutique and removed a pair of khaki trousers, his size, and a navy blue, short-sleeve jersey with collar. He also purchased a new belt, some socks, and casual footwear, black in color. His transactions completed, he returned to the now familiar fast-food restaurant and accessed the same bathroom stall, this time changing into his new apparel.

Once exiting the restaurant, he passed by a bookstore but soon doubled back after resolving to replace the paperback book about Michael Collins, which was confiscated from atop the gallery bookcase, along with his other belongings, following his arrest and evacuation to St. James Hospital.

With the new book in his possession, he strode out of the store and crossed back through Eyre Square, all the while scanning for Garda officers patrolling the locale. Thirty-seven minutes later, he boarded a bus for Westport, County Mayo with his priest costume still in tow.

On the grounds of Jennings Equestrian Centre, employees of a company specializing in staging outside parties efficiently erected a grand, white marquee-tent that would cover the dinner tables, dance floor, and platform, where live entertainers were to perform. An eighth of a mile away, other laborers worked alongside a local florist to prepare the site where the happy couple was to exchange vows, which was comprised of an elevated wedding platform, numerous rows of seating, and a trellis-like archway adorned with brightly colored flowers of the season. The next day was forecasted to be beautiful; however, in the event of inclement summer weather, the ceremony was to be moved to under the marquee. The wedding venue would be completed by mid-afternoon, that Friday, at which point a caterer was scheduled to preliminarily set up several steam tables. Father Kevin White, a longtime friend of the Jennings family, who had administered the sacraments of baptism, communion, reconciliation, and confirmation to Trish as a youth, thought he might also drop by to survey the site where he was to officiate the following day.

Meanwhile, news reports of a different Catholic priest were surfacing elsewhere across Ireland, after two parishioners from Assumption Church, in Tullamore, identified "Father Bernard Molloy" as escaped convict Logan McCool. Unfortunately, Mr. and Mrs. Jennings were too absorbed in wedding day preparations to catch any news that Friday, because, soon, an unfamiliar Catholic priest would pay a visit to Jennings Equestrian Centre.

34

As Logan McCool peered out to view the unfamiliar environs at a bus station in Westport, Trish Jennings mounted her favorite Morgan for riding, several miles away, in Castlebar. Trish again tried persuading her fiancé to join her for a ride this day, but Liam was caught up on the telephone with his parents, who were due to depart Londonderry, early the following morning, for the wedding. Trish thusly ventured into the short hills alone.

Readers will recall that after Logan and Liam's earlier blowout at Portlaoise Prison, which caused a temporary breach between the brothers, Logan resumed writing to Liam in order to cunningly warm up to him, so that he could stay apprised of their Castlebar activities, with ambitions of eventually using the information against them. One matter that Logan had overlooked, but which Liam had intentionally omitted from his correspondences, was the identity of his Best Man on wedding day, because, under any other circumstance in life, Logan most certainly would've filled that role, in spite of his reprehensible past. The individual that Liam asked to serve as Best Man was Aidan Drury, a man fifteen years his junior, who had been a great friend to him ever since they met on holiday in the Aran Islands seven years earlier.

When I first learned about Aidan, through a visual packet, his emergence and fateful involvement into this ever-thickening scenario quickly grabbed a hold of me and shook me to the very core of my being, ultimately because of his connection to my own life. It was at that moment I reminded myself that I wasn't merely a remote observer of Logan, Liam, and Trish's affairs but integrally involved in the matters at hand – the reason being that Westport resident Aidan Drury, you see, was the chap who bought Angus Wilde's hooker at auction and sailed it back to the Mayo coast. That's right, I'm referring to the very same hooker that Haimish Devlin fled in to the Canary Islands, after murdering Angus Wilde, and the same hooker I treacherously piloted back from Africa to Ireland. If it hadn't been for me, benevolently returning the hooker to Angus' family in Ireland, Aidan Drury would've been fishing from a different boat over the last several months. I think it's also worth mentioning that, while Logan might've heard Liam mention Aidan's name sometime in the past, apparently Logan and Aidan had never met prior to their inauspicious encounter, which would occur on the eve of wedding day.

Logan McCool disembarked in Westport and slinked over to a kiosk, where he purchased a bus ticket to Castlebar, because he hadn't been able to secure a ticket straight through from Galway City; he waited twenty-three minutes before boarding. Forty-seven minutes later, in Castlebar, he hired a taxi and asked the driver to take him to Jennings Equestrian Centre. The driver was an especially talkative sort, and Logan figured that the man was simply ingratiating himself in expectation of a big tip, so he mostly kept quiet. Upon nearing the Jennings property, Logan plainly saw the equestrian sign posted, and instructed the driver to turn onto the private road leading to the stables in the distance. Seconds later, he abruptly ordered the driver to halt the vehicle, and paid him there after relating that he wished to walk and limber up after his long journey.

He climbed out from the back seat, snatched his plastic sack containing priest costume, and shut the door. The driver executed a three-point turn and departed. Once perceiving the taxi to be safely out of sight, Logan scurried into the woodsy area that served as a buffer between the road and the main residence, and crept toward the fieldstone home, where he knew Trish to live with her parents, according to his brother's innocent letters.

It was just after 2 o'clock that July 17th afternoon, and the Sun still shone high in the sky. Logan prowled along the backside of the home and peeped through windows until beholding Mr. and Mrs. Jennings poring over a seating diagram that lay on the dining room table. He paused to study them, all the while waiting for Trish to appear, whom he couldn't have known to be off riding in the short hills. Logan eventually tired of waiting and resolved that the Witch of Castlebar was probably upstairs in her room spellbound by the wedding gown she anticipated wearing the next day. He had a general idea of how he wanted to carry out his murderous agenda but impulsively decided to visit the cottage and stables, first, to audit the activities there.

Scampering down to the cottage was a risky undertaking because only grass and fence existed in the wide-open area between the main residence and paddocks leading to the stables; thus, Logan had nowhere to camouflage himself during his progress. The cottage was closer to the residence than the stables but still far off, so he made a beeline for the main stable. Fortunately, for him, the part-time stablehand had long departed, having completed his morning routine of watering the horses, turning them out to pasture, and mucking a few stalls. Logan listened carefully for any human activity, once skulking outside the main stable, but had yet to detect any.

On one gable end of the main stable, the roofline extended and served as a shelter for hay. He noticed several bales and a small crescent-shaped tool, pierced into a bale, used to cut the plastic twine that bound them. He extracted the tool and cut the twine on one bale. He then pulled the twine free and snapped it to test its tautness. Satisfied that the twine was strong enough to suit his purposes, he gently inserted the sharp tool in his back pocket. He subsequently crept along the length of the stable while peering into stalls, much in the way he had done at the main residence. All horses were currently out on pasture, and there was no sign of Liam, which caused Logan to wonder if his brother might be resting in the cottage. But before venturing up to the cottage he'd first check the second, smaller stable where, suddenly, he imagined Trish and Liam lying naked in a bed of straw, fucking like two wild horses, because they couldn't control themselves and wait to do it in the cottage. The thought of it made him seethe.

After tramping the thirty or so yards to the smaller stable, he again sneaked along the side while stealing looks into individual stalls. He soon noticed that the last stall featured a faux-door, which prevented outside entry. He turned the corner at the end of the stable and saw the two grand doors, accessing the center aisle, to be wide open, and he faintly heard what he thought was a radio playing. He inched forward and peeked into the wide center aisle but saw nobody. He then leaned in and looked to the stall that was blocked from the outside and noticed it had been converted into an office; and, there sat brother Liam with his back to him and feet up on a desk while watching a small, outdated color television. It seems that Liam had returned to the stables minutes earlier to lovingly receive his bride-to-be, who he expected to canter in on horseback at any time from the short hills.

Logan knew that if he was to open the bottom half of the Dutch-style door, Liam would immediately turn and recognize him. And, while Logan envisioned himself besting his brother in a street fight, he wanted every advantage once making his assault. So, rather than open the bottom gate, he gingerly placed his plastic sack, containing priest costume, on the floor, and vaulted over the gate, with the twine still coiled around his left hand.

Even through the static of the television broadcast, Liam sensed something going on behind him and started to turn as Logan's shoes slapped the concrete. In the course of bounding over the gate, Logan had forgotten about the cutting tool in his back pocket, and the object fell to the floor. Liam now plainly perceived another person in the room, but, in the process of turning, his eyes were first drawn to the familiar cutting tool that just impacted the floor. He now intuited danger because the visitor failed to announce himself in some customary manner and had avoided simply opening the gate. Liam clambered out from his chair and began standing as Logan wrapped the baling twine around his fraternal twin's neck, tightening it with both hands. Liam reflexively reached up to try to free himself and glimpsed his assailant's face for the first time.

"Today's the day the Warlock of Castlebar meets his maker," Logan uttered with obvious satisfaction, his tongue wagging, cinching the twine tighter.

"Logan... Logan," gasped Liam. "Don't do this, brother."

Liam now twisted his body in an attempt to knee Logan in the groin, to disable him. When that didn't work, he tried drawing the twine-cutter closer, using his foot, so that he could dip down and pick it up to use as a weapon. But Logan quickly sensed what Liam was trying to do and pulled him away by his neck. In the process, Liam started to lose consciousness, but before he blacked out, Logan kissed him on the forehead and said, "I'm sorry it had to end this way for you, brother... but you should've chosen a different bride."

The dead weight of Liam's body caused the twine to constrict his trachea further, and he slumped to the floor; Logan remained at his brother's side until confident that Liam had given up the ghost. He seized the crescent-shaped twine cutter off the floor and again inserted it into his back pocket. The last thing he did, before departing the stable, was to remove Liam's wallet, cash, and car keys, and drag the body out of view, to buy time. He left the television running.

He collected his plastic sack, outside the gate, and scurried toward the cottage two hundred yards away. Meanwhile, Trish had presently turned around in the short hills, and was headed back to the stables, but was still several miles out. Logan noticed Liam's car parked to the right of the cottage, and, as he moved closer, his eyes were drawn to an unrecognizable white structure off in the distance, which he hadn't noticed earlier when hiking from the main residence to the stables. Once near the cottage, he gazed down into a modest valley, with leveled basin, where some workers were making final adjustments to the white marquee-tent that they had spent the last two hours erecting. Well to the right, he perceived a floral archway, leading to an uncovered seating area and raised platform, and determined it to be the ceremonial site. He laughed diabolically.

The possibility that Trish might be napping inside the cottage occurred to him while stepping up to the door, so he knocked. Nobody answered, and he turned the knob, which was expectedly unlocked in this otherwise safe locale.

Given the compact size of the cottage, it didn't take long to rifle through the contents, once inside. In short order, he had managed to locate Liam's checkbook, to an account at the Bank of Ireland, and some additional cash concealed in a satchel stowed in a bottom kitchen cabinet.

Logan stripped out of his casual attire and quickly donned his priest outfit. He then folded the clothing neatly and placed the items in the satchel, which he decided to take for his own. He also stole a pair of blue jeans, once belonging to Liam, a densely woven sweater, and a better quality pair of athletic shoes than the prison-issue in his plastic sack. Before exiting the cottage, he removed a bible from a small bookcase adjacent to the fireplace. He subsequently placed all items in the back seat of Liam's car, save for the bible, twine cutter, and the three feet of baling twine he had just used to strangle his brother; for the moment, he balled up the twine and stuffed it in his sock underneath his trouser leg. He then marched up to the fieldstone residence in his priest costume, with the bible concealing the crescent-shaped twine cutter in his left hand.

Mr. and Mrs. Jennings had long resolved the seating discrepancy they discovered earlier and had since adjourned to the den to take tea. Mrs. Jennings had been sitting closer to the hallway leading to the front door, and heard someone employing the brass knocker. It had always annoyed her when someone rapped on the door, when a perfectly functioning knocker stood directly in front of their eyes, and she had just decided, during her stroll to the door, that the caller was an observant, considerate person. She opened the door to behold an unfamiliar Catholic priest.

"Mrs. Jennings, I presume."

"Yes."

"How are ya? I'm Father *John Muldoon*. I've come to scout out the site for tomorrow's wedding. Can you spare a few minutes?"

Mrs. Jennings was not pleased to learn what she just heard from the priest, because their longtime family friend, Father Kevin White, had been requested to officiate at their daughter's wedding.

"We weren't told anything about Father White not being able to make it." Mrs. Jennings then turned, to bellow down the hall, "Sweetheart, did you know anything about this? Father White won't be presiding over Trish's wedding tomorrow."

"What?!" Mr. Jennings could be heard shouting incredulously, then rose from his chair and strode toward the door.

"Would you mind if I came in for a moment, Mrs. Jennings," asked 'Father Muldoon.'

"Of course, Father." Mrs. Jennings stepped aside to allow their visitor to enter, and closed the door behind him.

Logan looked to the right, from whence Mr. Jennings approached, and forced a smile.

"Are Ms. Trish and Mr. Liam about?" Father Muldoon inquired, in order to slyly establish Trish's whereabouts.

"I imagine that Liam is down to the cottage. Trish is still out riding, as far as we know. Why? Do you need to speak with them?"

"Oh, no. It's not necessary. I just thought it would be nice to meet the happy couple before their special day."

Mr. Jennings had now sidled up and was eyeballing young Father Muldoon, with his shaved head, and grew troubled, because he just decided that the man who would officiate at their daughter's wedding looked more like a Nazi skinhead than he did a priest. His perturbation was compounded when looking into Father Muldoon's eyes, which conspicuously lacked a universal feature in men of the cloth: compassion.

Father Muldoon greeted Mr. Jennings, so the elder extended his hand and was about to ask the reason Father White couldn't attend the following day, when Father Muldoon reached beneath his bible, to take hold of the concealed twine-cutter, and raised up his hand to swiftly slice a deep gash in Mr. Jennings' neck. The forceful strike predictably staggered Mr. Jennings backward, and Mrs. Jennings screamed at the sight of it, so Logan lifted his leg high and kicked her in the abdomen, causing the woman to topple to the floor; Logan finally dropped the bible. By now, Mr. Jennings had reached up to assess the extent of his wound and felt warm blood soaking his shirt.

Mr. Jennings yelled to his wife on the floor, "That's no priest! Call the Garda!"

He then attempted to wrestle his assailant to the floor, and Logan joined the battle, which caused blood to gush more profusely from Mr. Jennings' neck, because Logan had severed the elder's carotid artery. Logan soon sensed his seventy-year-old combatant weakening, so he ran to Mrs. Jennings, in the kitchen, who now frantically dialed the telephone. Logan dove for the jack and ripped the cord from the wall, prompting Mrs. Jennings to scream, so he marched over and punched her in the face, collapsing her to the floor. He then removed the baling twine, concealed in his sock, and commenced strangling the sixty-something woman, but quickly grew anxious when detecting some vague activity near the front door. Fearing that Mr. Jennings had recovered enough to access an alternate telephone, the killer dragged Mrs. Jennings by the neck, across the floor, until locating Mr. Jennings: the elder's flailing arms and legs had been the cause for all the ruckus, as Mr. Jennings now experienced some kind of seizure. Meanwhile, blood continued pumping from his neck. Mr. Jennings would die several minutes later without any further assistance from Logan, and Mrs.

Jennings had presently also blacked out, so Logan cinched the twine tighter, until observing no further signs of respiration. Like Liam, Mrs. Jennings would also die from ligature strangulation.

Now, believing it might be some time before Trish returned from riding, Logan darted upstairs and began searching through dressers, bureaus, and closets for money and valuables that would help him live on the run: he stole two pair of diamond earrings from Mrs. Jennings' jewelry box and a thick gold chain with locket from Trish's room. While considering the necklace, he recalled having given Trish a silver set of earrings during their brief courtship and how she thanklessly responded, "I'm afraid it's nothing but *gold* for Ms. Jennings."

Logan opened the gold locket and discovered two tiny pictures of Liam and Trish, and he reacted by tipping his head back and again laughing fiendishly. He also stumbled upon four hundred Euros in cash, secreted in a shoebox in Trish's closet.

Once returning downstairs, he removed the Rolex watch from the late Mr. Jennings' wrist, and stole the hundred fifty-six Euros in his pocket. Within minutes, he had also located Mrs. Jennings' purse, sitting on a sideboard in the dining room, and took the ninety-three Euros contained therein. He then returned to the kitchen and removed a cellophane package of sliced turkey, a half-gallon of milk, and a sack of apples from the refrigerator.

Father Muldoon surveyed his victims one last time before departing the main residence, and walked casually down to the cottage. He loaded his booty into the car and pressed the door shut, because he had just decided to loiter shroudedly until Trish returned so that he could also hasten her entrance into eternity. He gazed down to the marquee and noticed that the laborers had finished erecting the tent and had since been replaced by two catering company employees, currently moving steam tables underneath.

Suddenly, he heard a piercing, womanly scream resounding from near the stables, and concluded that Trish had returned to discover Liam's body. He now cursed himself for failing to turn off the television, because the noise had undoubtedly drawn Trish into the converted office, where she found her fiancé slumped against a filing cabinet. That simple blunder had fortuitously spared Trish her life and would consume Logan the rest of his days.

A worker down at the marquee reacted to Trish's scream and had just summoned his associate, as the two middle-aged men sprinted toward the stables. If Logan hadn't seen the two men for himself, making their way to the stables, he might've raced down to murder Trish, but, now doubtful that he could terminate three lives and escape successfully, he climbed into his late brother's car, containing his spoils, started the engine and drove away.

35

TRISH HAD TELEPHONED FOR an ambulance immediately upon discovering Liam's lifeless body, which also alerted the Garda to respond. In the interim, she desperately tried reviving Liam using CPR. The catering employees assisted her, once arriving, but, sadly, Liam had been deprived oxygen too long and was beyond resuscitation. A grief-stricken Trish rocked back and forth, cradling her dead fiancé's body, her tears dropping to his face.

Once emergency personnel arrived, Trish finally attempted to contact her mother and father at the main residence, because she thought it curious that neither had reacted to the loud sirens pervading the locale. First, she tried the wireless intercom system that connected all stables and domiciles, and, when no one responded, she called her mother's cellular phone. Shortly after, she lumbered up to the home to find her parents dead. Initially, she was too traumatized to notify anyone, as she wailed on the floor beside her mother's body, but eventually used the intercom to summon the Garda at the stable who had arrived minutes earlier and were busy sectioning off the murder scene to preserve evidence.

Inspector Pearse McElwee had also heard the description and location of the crimes over police airways and soon responded. Given the national manhunt already in progress, and connection of the escapee to the victims, McElwee had intuited the killer's identity but wanted to hear it from Trish when querying his longtime collaborator, "Who has such hatred in his heart that he would commit these murders, Trish?"

"Logan McCool," she said without hesitation.

"I suspected as much," he said.

By now, Logan had arrived in the parking lot of a Bank of Ireland branch in Westport. He left his black trousers on but changed out of his priestly top and replaced it with the navy blue jersey he purchased at the department store in Galway City. He subsequently gathered Liam's wallet and checkbook and relaxedly entered the bank.

It was a Friday afternoon, a payday, and two people were in line waiting to be served by one of four tellers currently working with other customers. Considering his dicey circumstances, Logan was eager to just conduct his business and depart. He listened in on a conversation between a man and woman standing before him in line, and surmised that the two weren't together but had discovered, during their smalltalk, that they had some mutual Westport friends. Upon learning that the man was a fisherman, Logan was struck with a notion that might help him avoid capture.

Two customers at respective teller windows had finished their business within seconds of each other and departed the bank. Consequently, the woman and man in front of Logan shuffled over to vacant teller windows while bidding each other farewell. Less than thirty seconds later, a third teller shed her customer, and Logan smiled at the woman while slithering to her window.

"Afternoon to ya," Logan said folksily, still grinning.

"Afternoon, sir. How may I help you?"

"I'm afraid I don't know my current account balance. Do you suppose you could retrieve it before I write the amount on my check?"

"I think we can manage that," she said. "If you'd just let me have your checkbook for a moment, so I can view your account information... and I'll get that straight away."

Logan slid the checkbook under the bulletproof glass, and the woman efficiently punched in some numbers on her computer keyboard. She wrote the account balance on a scrap of paper, but, before sliding it back, said:

"If I could just see some form of identification, before giving you the balance. A picture ID would be *grand*," she said.

"Oh, of course," said Logan, removing Liam's driver's license from the wallet he had ready in his hand. Thank you for being so security conscious."

"You can never be too careful these days," she said, taking hold of the license. She looked at the picture and then up at Logan. "Looks like you've gotten yerself a serious haircut there."

"It's a summer cut," responded Logan, rubbing the top of his head and chuckling. "The ladies don't care for it, but it keeps my melon cool."

The teller merely smiled and slid the piece of paper down into the stainless steel, concave area beneath the protective glass, where Logan took hold of it. € 2,732, it read.

Logan consequently filled in an amount of two-thousand seven-hundred Euros on the check, slid it to the teller, and said," I'm off to play a little roulette in London. I've had pretty good luck in the past but don't want my account to be empty when I come back... just in case.

The woman said nothing, at first, and attentively counted out the paper money. "Would you care for an envelope," she asked.

"That would be *grand*," he replied.

The woman counted out the money a second time, in front of Logan, and pushed it down where he could take possession. She then slid him an envelope.

"Thank you," he said.

Logan inserted the money directly into the envelope, which signaled he wouldn't be counting the money for himself.

"Good luck at the tables," the teller said. "Come back and tell us how you did."

"I'll do just that," said Logan. He smiled and turned to walk away.

Once outside the bank, he noticed the fisherman again talking to the woman from line. The two were laughing. Logan unlocked the car door and climbed in. He didn't care to idle for fear of being spotted by the Garda, or perhaps some citizen who might recognize his mug from news reports. He had also just decided to follow the fisherman home.

Aidan Drury drove contentedly back to his seaside cottage after having just made a substantial deposit in the Bank of Ireland, Westport branch. Fishing had been good to Aidan during the few months he had been at it, so much so that he and his young wife had decided to start a family. Mary Drury was now five months pregnant and could barely fit into the dress she had bought to wear to Liam McCool's wedding. Presently, Mary roasted a chicken and some pan potatoes and carrots, anticipating that her husband would imminently walk through the door of their picturesque, hillside abode that overlooked the inlet where Aidan moored his hooker.

A quarter-mile behind Aidan, Logan McCool followed in his late brother's car, eager to discover where the fisherman resided. Once the Atlantic Ocean was in sight, Logan observed the fisherman's brake lights being applied as the car turned a corner to the right; he guessed the man's place to be further north. But, suddenly, Aidan made an abrupt left turn, and the car dropped from sight. Approaching the same corner, Logan soon noticed the fisherman's car descending a dirt road toward a pale, one-story cottage, not too unlike the one he had ransacked two hours earlier, save for a slate roof. Logan slowed his vehicle, so that he was barely gliding, and watched the fisherman park near the cottage. After emerging from his car, Aidan instinctively sensed someone studying him, and gazed far up on the road to perceive the traveler staring down. Logan waved to the fisherman, and, when Aidan waved back, Logan accelerated to the north, until out of sight, which understandably intrigued Aidan. Meanwhile, Mary Drury rearranged some canned staples inside the pantry while the teakettle whistled melodiously a few feet away; she hadn't heard her husband's car door slam, and was oblivious to his arrival.

Aidan was well acquainted with his neighbors along that coastal stretch but hadn't recognized the car belonging to the man who just waved to him; he felt at a disadvantage. He thought about his black hooker, with furled maroon sails, moored at the modest dock he built with his own hands, and, for a moment, felt uneasy about the way the sailboat was secured. The hooker wasn't secure at all, in fact. It was merely latched using a common nautical loop, and anyone could come along, really, board the boat, and just sail away in it. Aidan even left his fishing equipment in the boat, most fair-weather nights, because he was tired of hauling the gear back and forth to the cottage. He thought about the fishing gear and, then, worse, imagined the stranger in the car, hiking down to the dock, after dark, and sailing away in his boat. He thusly plodded down to the dock to consider how he might deter a would-be thief.

Less than a mile away, Logan McCool had just parked his car, off-road, and emerged from a secluded, bushy divide on the opposite side of the coastal route. The Sun was still two hours from setting this mid-summer night but it was now the dinner hour, and few cars passed along the rural road that Logan would imminently trundle over on foot. In his possession were the meager belongings he had filched, to include the food and clothes, all of which were stuffed into his brother's satchel, save for the trusty twine-cutter protruding from his back pocket.

Aidan Drury had finished removing his fishing gear from the hooker, and placed the equipment on the elevated dock platform. He subsequently climbed back down and re-boarded his sailboat to gain perspective of how he might thwart someone from stealing it. Meanwhile, Logan McCool had since descended the grassy sea-cliff, and approached Aidan and Mary's cottage from the rear. He set down his things and slinked along the perimeter of the home while monitoring for voices. Logan couldn't have known that the fisherman was married, although he assumed he was, or that the fisherman's wife currently sat and drank a cup of tea while scanning the specials in the *Irish Times*, waiting for her husband to arrive.

Logan peered through a side window and saw nobody stirring, and still couldn't ascertain, from his remote inspection of the home's interior, if the fisherman lived alone or not. He figured that the man was probably inside fixing himself a drink or eating leftovers, so he departed the cottage and traipsed down a worn pathway to the ocean, where he imagined a boat waiting for him.

Standing below in his hooker, Aidan Drury noticed a dangerous crack that had developed in a dock support, and he contorted himself to analyze how he might repair the fissure without paying a professional to come in and do the work. Several yards away, Logan hiked up a small ridge and now had the watercraft in plain view; he made his final descent. Before stepping onto the upper dock platform, Logan turned to check and see if anyone had detected his intrusion onto the property. He then faced front again and noticed the fishing gear, obviously belonging to the fisherman.

"Can I help you?" Logan heard a voice but couldn't see the man and didn't answer. The fisherman eventually pushed out from under the dock to receive his unexpected visitor.

"Oh, goodness. I didn't even notice you there," said Logan. "Yes... is this the place where one can rent a boat to do some evening fishing?" Logan placed his things on the dock.

"No, it's not," replied Aidan. "Weren't you behind me in line at the bank?" Aidan grabbed onto the dock-ladder and ascended toward Logan, all the while never taking his eyes off him. The predator, however, instantly recognized the fisherman's vulnerable position and calculated his next move.

"Why, yes, that *was* me in the bank. And that was also me in the car up on the road. I was the one waving to you. Allow me to give you my business card." Logan then reached behind to remove the crescent-shaped twine cutter from his pocket, and tore across the fisherman's neck as Aidan reached the top of the ladder.

Logan had had no intention of murdering anyone, when scheming to steal a boat this night. He had, frankly, experienced enough killing for one day, and now felt remorse over the young man, because he held him no grudge. He didn't even know him – at least he *thought* he didn't know him.

Aidan instinctively reached up with his hands to feel his neck, causing him to fall from the ladder down into the hooker. He writhed in pain as blood oozed from his neck out onto the sailboat's deck. Logan peered down at the fisherman and decided that the gaping wound was far worse than the one he had delivered to Mr. Jennings. Aidan soon recovered from his back pain and rose while covering his neck with his hand, as blood continued gushing. He fixed his eyes on Logan, up on the dock, who now only waited for the fisherman to black out.

"Why?! You mother*fooker*! Why did you cut me?!" Aidan shouted.

"I'm sorry, but you got in the way, friend. Lay down and die now and I'll see that you get a proper burial at sea."

"Help me, you mother*fooker*! I've got a pregnant wife up in that house! I don't want to die!"

Aidan tried climbing the ladder a second time, but Logan kicked him back down, and the fisherman's exertions only accelerated his unconsciousness, as he passed out on the bloody deck. Logan didn't hesitate in grabbing a bucket from the items among the fishing gear on the dock; he descended into the hooker and garnered some seawater in order to wash the blood from the sailboat's deck because he knew the stench would eventually attract pestering gulls. Once out on the ocean, he intended to repeat the process after dumping the fisherman's body.

Logan wouldn't learn until months later that the fisherman he had murdered was, paradoxically, scheduled to serve as his brother's

Best Man the following day. The wedding wouldn't have gone off anyway, even if Aidan Drury had unsuspectingly eluded Logan that fateful Friday evening, because the groom was already dead. But, once remorseful over the fisherman's death, Logan would, one day, twistedly delight upon discovering Aidan's identity.

The Omniscient One was true to form when delaying the visual packet that illustrated Logan McCool's heinous acts after breaking out from Portlaoise Prison. In fact, I first learned about the Castlebar murders while inspecting the suit I was to wear to Trish and Liam's wedding, and innocently eavesdropping on the evening news. I had been standing in my living room, dabbing the suit with masking tape to remove lint and hairs, when a breaking news report detailed the gruesome finds out at Jennings Equestrian Centre. I thusly discontinued my work and returned the suit to a closet. Several hours later, on the 11 o'clock news, a report aired about a missing Westport fisherman, who, despite having fished all day, sold his catch, and deposited the week's earnings into the bank, apparently set sail again in the evening without informing his wife. Mary Drury had complained to the Garda that it was entirely out of character for her reliable husband to return home and re-launch without simply walking inside to notify her of such, especially when he knew that a hot dinner awaited him.

The following morning, a sheep farmer from across the road discovered Liam McCool's car in the bushy divide where Logan attempted to camouflage it, and after the Garda put two and two together, marine patrols were soon combing the high seas for Aidan's hooker as far north as Donnegal Bay and as far south as Slyne Head.

Logan McCool had had no experience as a sailor, but, after freeing the single-masted watercraft from the dock and unfurling the maroon sails, he quickly learned, by necessity, how to guide it. Marine patrols ultimately expanded their search north beyond Donnegal Bay, because they knew the murdering fugitive hailed from Northern Ireland, and thought he might try to obtain assistance from his IRA cohorts. But by then Logan was sailing far to the south, along the 10th longitude, and had already dumped Aidan's corpse. Eventually, his hooker would be nudged to the west by currents attributable to the River Shannon, which deposits into the Atlantic Ocean just north of the Dingle Peninsula.

Aidan Drury's hooker had been austerely equipped but did contain a working compass, which Logan relied on as the primary navigation instrument. He also knew that the Sun rises in the east and sets in the west, so, secondarily, tried plotting his course according to the position of the Sun in the sky, factoring in the time of day and season, all the while verifying his accuracy using the compass. He decided to practice such in the event his compass malfunctioned during his progress. Logan later reflected, and felt gratified over his last second decision to rip the Rolex watch from Mr. Jennings' wrist, after tearing through the elder's throat, because he now deemed his ability to measure time invaluable.

Once he sensed the Shannon river currents pushing his hooker away from the Dingle Peninsula, into more open waters, he didn't resist because he wasn't ready to anchor. However, an hour later, upon settling his eyes on, what he perceived to be, a scarcely inhabited island southwest of the Dingle Peninsula, he curiously felt protected, and elected to moor there to procure supplies for his voyage to the unknown. And, as Logan McCool crashed through the ocean white-caps toward Great Blasket Island, now just a half-mile away, Aidan Drury's ashen, bloated corpse bobbed concurrently in the beach waters off the Aran Islands. Death had, for all intents and purposes, already arrived at the latter, while the specter of death loomed at the shores of Great Blasket.

36

It would be two days before I had any contact with Trish Jennings about the tragic events at the equestrian centre, because I figured she had her hands full with the Garda and undertakers. If truth be told, Trish had been the one to call me, because she cared to know if I had received any communiqués from the Omniscient One that might've presaged the disaster. Naturally, I had not (at least yet) or else I most certainly would have alerted her and the Garda. I think it also goes without saying that if I had known Logan McCool was about to anchor at Great Blasket Island, where my last surviving daughter, Tessie Doyle, presently visited with friends on vacation, I would've taken all the appropriate measures.

There weren't too many people in Ireland or the U.K., with access to a television or radio, who weren't aware of the murders in Castlebar. And, even if one hadn't learned the news through electronic or print media, the sensational story was all the talk in the pubs and shops. The tourist home on the isolated island where Tessie once worked, and currently stayed, features no televisions, however, because the old windmill that powers the inn, despite its breezy seaside locale, doesn't generate the unwavering supply of electricity necessary to keep a television running properly, and employees had long ago tired of replacing batteries in radios. If the wind is stiff and sustained on a given night, perhaps guests will experience an evening without flickering lights, but those power fluctuations are purportedly part of the inn's eerie charm. Moreover,

197

copies of the *Irish Independent* and *Irish Times* are certainly delivered on ferries that service Great Blasket each day, but there's a palpable, apathetic attitude that pervades the island, according to my daughter Tessie's earlier account of life there: "Great Blasket is undeniably part of Ireland, but life on the mainland is viewed differently. We have our *own thing* here and tend to tune out to mainland affairs."

Long story short, it would be three days before word circulated at the tourist home about an escaped convict named Logan McCool murdering three people in faraway Castlebar and allegedly hijacking a sailboat on the Westport coast where a fisherman had also gone missing. Regrettably, Tessie had not been present at the inn during those discussions, and there was a very compelling reason for her absence.

As sailor-nouveau Logan McCool attempted his first-ever mooring near a dilapidated, seldom used pier on the northwest tip of Great Blasket Island, I arrived at Jennings Equestrian Centre, in Castlebar, to attend funeral services for his murder victims. Meanwhile, the waterlogged corpse of Aidan Drury had just washed up on an Aran Island beach.

Trish had decided to make use of the marquee-tent and catering services for which sizeable deposits had been made for the wedding that never went off, and after funeral services were held at Holy Rosary Church in Castlebar, interment was performed at a private cemetery located on the Jennings property. Trish had even persuaded Mr. and Mrs. McCool to allow for Liam to be buried there, where Trish desired to, one day, lay alongside her dead fiancé. Following the interments of Mr. and Mrs. Jennings and Liam, mourners and guests were treated to a lavish meal and some subdued entertainment under the tent.

According to the digital time and date stamp on the telephone answering machine in my Kinvara home, Tessie had called and left a message the day I attended the funeral in Castlebar. I hadn't thought to remotely access my answering machine during that brief trip, and why the Omniscient One couldn't have provided a timely visual packet or streamlined information, to inform me of my daughter's call, considering the dreadful implications, remains another great mystery about Him. When I returned home from Castlebar, two days later, the lone message on the answering machine played something like this:

"Hi Daddy... apparently you're not at home. Sorry to have missed you. Listen, I just wanted you to know that I've been having a grand time down here on Great Blasket with old friend Patty Reilly and the rest of the girls... and that I expect to be back home next Tuesday. I also wanted to tell you about the most wonderful lad I met here on the island. Joe O'Malley is his name. I shouldn't call him a lad really... Joe's ten years older than myself, but he's very strong and youthful. Anyway, he and I are headed out on his hooker later this morning for a little fishing and picnic lunch. He seems equally as smitten with me... I think I've already convinced him to relocate up to Galway (laughing). Hopefully you two will meet one day. I've talked long enough now, Daddy. Know that I love you... and I'll see you soon. Oh, and by the way, don't worry about picking me up at the station in Galway. I've already talked with Jacqueline Casey, who works in the city. I'll just ride back with her to Kinvara after she finishes work. Bye!"

I might've otherwise lightly regarded Tessie's reference to a picnic-date with a fisherman on his hooker, until hearing the name Joe O'Malley. I was well acquainted with "Joe O'Malley," of course, after viewing the visual packets that illustrated his Dublin exploits when he first set up at that seedy rooming house near Gardiner and Railway Streets, under the assumed name, and then went out to acquire a .44 magnum pistol. We all know what happened after that. I had also encountered him, personally, as he was wheeled from surgery at St. James Hospital.

Upon hearing Tessie utter the words: fisherman, Joe O'Malley, picnic, and hooker in the same sentence, it immediately sent my mind reeling, and I began calculating if Logan McCool could've reached Great Blasket in the time that had elapsed since Aidan Drury and his boat went missing. Initially, I thought it impossible for Logan to have sailed so far during such a brief period. *But, what if the winds were in his favor,* I thought. I soon became so distressed that I questioned my ability to think straight, and telephoned my primary Garda contact, Inspector McElwee. McElwee jumped right on it, because the international manhunt in progress had been focused more so in the north of Ireland and southern Scotland, after a marine patrol discovered a wrecked hooker beached just south of Malin Head. There, a disproportionate number of Garda personnel had already converged on the flanking seaside towns and were essentially turning the villages upside down in search of Logan; that is, until it was discovered that the hooker-in-question had been sitting there for several weeks and didn't belong to Aidan Drury.

My call to McElwee eventually succeeded in altering the direction and concentration of search efforts being made; however, by that time, McCool was already sailing far south of Great Blasket, off the coast of the English Isles of Scilly, where I once moored en route home from Africa. Riding alongside "Joe O'Malley" in the sailing vessel was his first mate, turned terrified hostage, my loving daughter, Tessie Doyle.

Logan had accumulated ample supplies during his short stay on Great Blasket Island, making several runs back and forth to his moored hooker, and stocked it with enough food and water to get him to the Iberian Peninsula and beyond. In fact, on the afternoon of his arrival, he and Tessie had first met in "Leary's Pub, Grub, and Other Things You'll Need," a quirky establishment popular among island residents and tourists. Originally, Logan had planned to depart Great Blasket immediately after stocking his boat, but the picnic-date with Tessie riskily delayed him an extra day and he'd remain in the hooker overnight.

In a visual packet the Omniscient One inexplicably provided several days *after* Tessie had gone missing, and after authorities failed to locate Aidan Drury's sailing vessel being piloted by Logan, I sat in my Kinvara living room and watched a vindictive McCool maltreat my daughter in countless ways. Prior to their date, Logan had requested that Tessie fix two meals for their seafaring picnic, "...in case conditions force us to be out longer than expected," he had advised.

At first, all seemed normal on the date, as Logan romanced Tessie by wrapping his arms around her while teaching her how to steer the vessel. Once Tessie got the hang of it, she turned to face Logan, and the two kissed and nibbled at each other; but when it was time to eat lunch, two hours later, a now liquored-up Logan deprived Tessie of food and water and threw her to the deck. He then proceeded to chow down selfishly on a roast lamb sandwich that Tessie had prepared with so much care for him. No good deed goes unpunished, as they say. And when Tessie finally charged Logan, in protest, and started to cry, screaming for him to return her to the island, he kicked my daughter in the midsection, just as he had done Mrs. Jennings in her Castlebar kitchen, causing her to double over and collapse. "That's what you get for forgettin' the *fookin'* mint jelly," he slurred while staggering. "And the fookin' bread is drenched, too. Soggy fookin' sandwiches is what we have here. If I wasn't out on the high seas, this shit would go directly in the trash," he said. "I wouldn't feed this shit to the fookin' dogs. Don't you know that you should always spread the mayonnaise between the slices of meat, so that it doesn't soak into the bread? Use yer fookin' head, woman. And that's assuming I even *wanted* mayonnaise on my lamb sandwich... which I don't... so that gets us back to the fookin' mint jelly, doesn't it."

Logan then hoisted a newly cracked bottle of Jameson's and maneuvered the vessel with his other hand like some unruly pirate from the movies.

He drank well into the night because he believed that, otherwise, he'd fall asleep; in the long run, of course, the alcohol would have the opposite effect on him. Meanwhile, an exhausted Tessie finally managed to relax and slumber in the boat, after Logan convinced her that they were sailing back to Great Blasket. In reality, the compass needle pointed south, and they were situated in the middle of the Bay of Biscay, well off the coasts of France and Spain.

In a cruel twist of fate, I subsequently perceived the hooker bobbing about in the same proximity where I once contemplated my own mortality in the black of night, after deciding not to follow a more coastal route home to Ireland, because to have done so would've added a week or more to my voyage.

The skies had now grown similarly black, but the moon provided sufficient light that I was able to make out Logan abandoning the wheel and stumbling over to poke and prod Tessie with his foot. When my daughter awoke, Logan placed his nearly empty bottle of whiskey down on the deck, and bent over to clutch her by her sweater. He was ossifyingly drunk.

"I'm sorry I was unkind to you," he said.

Tessie pushed his hands off her.

"When are we going to arrive at the island," she asked. "I want to go home."

"We're not goin' feckin' home. We're goin' on vacation," Logan said, his anger still simmering.

Feeling despair, Tessie started to cry.

"What's this all about, Joe? I thought you were a nice man. That's why I went out on a date with you."

"Ha! Joe! Who the feck's Joe? Stand up now. Daddy wants some sugar."

Tessie understood perfectly what he meant, and remained seated on the deck.

"Well, if your name isn't Joe, then what is it? Who are you?"

Logan grew silly for a moment and bowed while speaking in French. "Mademoiselle, je te presente Logan. Je m'appelle Logan McCool, et je suis d' Antrim, Northern Ireland. Et vous?"

Tessie had studied German at Seamount, and her French language skills were suspect, but she clearly understood that the drunkard she currently shared a small sailing vessel with, out in the middle of the Atlantic Ocean, was no one other than Logan McCool, the escaped convict responsible for her sister's death in Dublin, as well as the British Prime Minister. Tessie sobbed uncontrollably.

""*Awww*, don't start with the fookin' cryin', will ya. If there's one thing I can't stand it's a cryin' bitch. Stand up now."

He grabbed Tessie by the sweater, and she resisted, so he slapped her firmly across the face. She then made the mistake of punching him in the testicles, which only served to agitate him, because the volume of alcohol he consumed had basically numbed him from feeling any pain.

"Get away from me, you bastard!" Tessie yelled.

Logan's adrenaline surged, and he lifted her up.

"If you're calling me a bastard then you're insulting *me* Mum and Dad, and I don't like that. They've gone through enough shit of late. It also makes you a liar." He then slapped Tessie across the face again. "Drop yer unmentionables, *Missy*. We're goin' to make a baby."

Logan then proceeded to rape Tessie the first of four times over the next nine hours. Miraculously, he managed to stay awake after committing each abominable act, but he was clearly motivated by self-preservation because, despite his inebriated state, he believed that if he were to fall asleep, Tessie would likely kill him.

After resigning to the fact that she couldn't defend herself against his assaults, Tessie employed a new strategy following Logan's second violation: on the third occasion he forced himself on her, Tessie behaved as if enjoying the intimacy, which eminently pleased Logan, but she had done so only because Logan continued depriving her of food and water, and she hadn't consumed anything since departing Great Blasket almost two days earlier. However, in spite of Tessie's gentle pleas for one of the lamb sandwiches he had deemed substandard, or a small drink of water, Logan still refused her nourishment, and the taxing, unsympathetic maritime conditions left my daughter feeling so weak that she was barely able to stand. Logan was slowly killing her. I knew this when watching events unfold in the visual packet but was exasperatingly powerless to do anything, given the delay of the provision.

After mercilessly raping a limp, poured-out Tessie a fourth and final time, Logan struck her in the back of the head with the blunt end of a harpoon and tossed her unconscious body into the Atlantic Ocean, figuring that she would soon drown. The shock of the water actually revived my daughter, though, and Logan had been witness to that, but he was too drunk and weary to circle around and finish her off. In the end, the murderer didn't fret, though, because he had some sense of Tessie's diluted state and doubted she possessed enough stamina to tread water for a sustained period; and, even if she did manage to swim awhile, the sharks would inevitably detect the floating hors d'oeuvre in their midst.

Less than an hour later, Logan noticed some buoys in the distance and realized that he was nearing the Strait of Gibraltar, which elicited nervous anticipation, as he deliberated over whether to continue sailing south, toward the African coast, or steer east through the Strait into the Mediterranean Sea. It was then the Omniscient One tauntingly diffused my visual packet, and I was left not knowing, at least temporarily, if Tessie had somehow survived her ordeal.

Naturally, I immediately telephoned my Garda contact, Inspector McElwee, to inform him of my latest supernatural perception, with instructions of where I thought my daughter had been left to die in the ocean, in addition to speculating that McCool was strangely following the same nautical course that Haimish Devlin once did. McElwee didn't delay in reaching out to Portuguese and Spanish authorities, to request that searches be initiated, as well as a British contingent currently engaged in military exercises on Gibraltar. Said searches were carried out over the succeeding eighteen hours.

37

INSPECTOR MCELWEE HAD HAD no qualms about urging his Portuguese and Spanish counterparts to concentrate their search efforts in the areas I had specified, because my track record of declarations to him had always been reliable. The British military unit serving on Gibraltar expectedly executed their search with particular fervor, because Logan McCool had shot their Prime Minister, who died months later due to complications arising from his injuries. In retrospect, given the variable ocean currents in the region, where the Atlantic Ocean and Mediterranean Sea converge, I think it also would've been prudent to involve Moroccan officials in the search efforts, because Tessie was ultimately found floating on a piece of driftwood two miles off the coast of Tangier. Tessie had survived more than a day after Logan McCool threw her into the ocean, and it wasn't drowning or sharks that caused my daughter's demise. Dehydration had been the culprit.

Tangier, of course, had been my first stop after launching from that small seaside village south of Safi, en route to Ireland, to return Angus Wilde's hooker to Kinvara. It was also the place where Haimish Devlin had intended to flee, once satisfied with his analysis of the unique Water Clock in Fez. And, now, considering the deaths of both my daughters, with the latter occurring essentially in Tangier, it caused me to wonder if the evil spirit of Haimish Devlin hadn't, somehow, brought a curse down on me. It also prompted reflection on whether the Omniscient One really is omnipotent and capable of rendering the

Prince of Darkness ineffectual, if that be His desire, or if He didn't possess a mean streak of his own, because of the way He seemingly maliciously, and tantalizingly, cut me off from discovering Tessie's disposition after she regained consciousness in the water.

When a Moroccan tugboat operator first noticed Tessie in the waters off Tangier, he was certain my daughter was alive because of the way she lay across the piece of driftwood. However, upon closer examination, the man soon realized that poor Tessie had been dead for some time.

The ordeal that had once taken me to Morocco in pursuit of Haimish Devlin was recent history, really, so, between me and Inspector McElwee, working over telephones, we were quickly able to get the appropriate Moroccan officials involved to satisfy their requirements and expeditiously initiate arrangements for Tessie's body to be transported back to Ireland.

I again enlisted Tom Casey to drive me to the Galway train station, and I flew from Dublin to Madrid, Spain, and Madrid to Tangier to officially identify and take custody of my daughter's body. The following day, Tessie's coffin was loaded onto an Iberia Airlines jet, in which I was also a passenger, and flown to Barcelona. Her coffin was offloaded and placed in a RyanAir jet that delivered us to Shannon International Airport, County Limerick, where we were received by a Galway undertaker and driven home to Kinvara. Meanwhile, the international manhunt for Logan McCool had expectedly intensified off the coast of Africa and nearby Canary Islands. What's more, Interpol had provided a picture of McCool to Moroccan and Canary Islands news stations, which showed the killer's picture in a series of breaking news reports.

Throughout the years that I served at the pleasure of the Omniscient One, I had acted on information conveyed to me through dreams, in one form or another, or, most recently, through visual packets. Those transmissions rarely occurred on a real-time basis, and I often had to gauge my responses while factoring in the estimated passage of time since the transpiration of events. Thus, what I'm leading up to is that, when I alerted Garda Inspector Pearse McElwee to the goings-on aboard the hooker off the coast of Portugal, in my eagerness to affect Logan McCool's capture, following his abhorrent treatment of my daughter, my advice to the Inspector about the murderer's destination had actually been conjecture, based on a pattern that eerily seemed to be replicating Haimish Devlin's former voyage. And, now, as I sit here reflecting on past events, I have reason to believe that the Omniscient One may have taken such exception to my presumptuousness, despite my sufferings at the time, He deemed this aspect of my advice a prideful lie; and that I sought retribution against McCool. And I say that because more than a year would pass before I received my next visual packet, updating me of Logan's affairs. (I suppose I should be grateful for being reactivated at all).

As a footnote, having spent six plus decades on the planet, and taking into consideration all my extraordinary dealings with the Omniscient One, I have some deeply entrenched beliefs about Him. Firstly, among the sins that mankind commits, I believe that sins borne from Pride particularly stick in the Omniscient One's craw. Secondly, when the Omniscient One ostensibly said, "Let vengeance be mine," I think he meant it, so just step aside and don't bother taking matters into your own hands.

38

As I busily made arrangements for Tessie's wake and funeral in Kinvara, Logan McCool had long passed through the Strait of Gibraltar (I would learn the following year) into the Mediterranean Sea. The more tranquil waters of the Mediterranean must've relaxed Logan, because he finally succumbed to his fatigue and drunkenness, and ran his hooker aground on a sandbar north of the Algerian port of Mostagenam, where he slept for six hours before waking to realize what he managed to accomplish.

This blunder presented myriad problems for a now sober, but severely hung-over, Logan. After numerous imaginative but unsuccessful attempts at dislodging the boat from the sand, he stripped out of his clothes, save for his shorts, and swam through the murky waters for a half-mile while clutching a fistful of wet Euros, in order to locate and hire some locals to assist him. Ninety minutes later, he and three young Algerians returned to the hooker in a mid-size cabin-cruiser equipped with two powerful outboard motors. Initially, the four men just tried pushing the sailboat back into the water; however, the mixture of sand and mud had facilitated a suction-like effect when the hull impacted the land. In the end, the Algerian boat owner fastened a sturdy rope to the hooker and eased away in the opposite direction to pull it loose from the sandbar, all the while taking care not to hang up his own boat on an adjoining sandbar. Once the job was completed, Logan paid the men the balance of money he promised in Mostagenam, and untied the rope connected to his hooker. The Algerians, however, now demanded more money and cruised alongside while waving their fists and threatening to board his boat and beat him. But once noticing that they had burned considerable fuel, the Algerians finally aborted their extortion attempts and sped away cursing and making derogatory gestures.

From coastal Algeria, Logan's successive stops included the Italian island of Sardinia and the Greek island, Crete, where he rested and replenished supplies. Both islands beguiled him to the extent that he contemplated settling on a small island near Crete, but, after doing some soul-searching, he knew that his destiny lay in the mountains, not on a Mediterranean isle. From Crete, he set sail toward the Suez Canal and Red Sea.

In Kinvara, old friend Father Jack McLaughlin presided over Tessie's funeral at St. Joseph's Church. Tessie had graduated from Seamount some twelve years earlier, but most of the same nuns were still on staff, and they shut down the school that morning and encouraged students to join them in celebrating my daughter's life.

Similar to Jodie's funeral, several months back, scores of townsfolk attended Tessie's service. All the familiar faces were present, but, others, not so familiar, also came in support, after learning that Tessie was the sister of Jodie, and that I had lost two daughters in the span of a year to the same killer. In the end, Tessie's Kinvara funeral was a bigger affair than Jodie's, with the number of people exceeding the assemblage at Jodie's first memorial service at St. Mary's Pro-Cathedral in Dublin.

Following the funeral Mass at St. Joe's, a customary interment was not carried out at Foy's Cemetery due to Tessie's wishes, which were communicated to me by her former workmate and friend on Great Blasket, Patty Reilly: after learning the horrific circumstances surrounding Tessie's passing, Patty had telephoned to inform me that she would be making the trip to Kinvara, at which point she told me that Tessie had once described her fond childhood memories of playing at Traught Beach in Kinvara. "If anything ever happens to me (while on Great Blasket)," Tessie had prophetically instructed, "I want to be cremated, so that my ashes can be scattered along the tidewaters at Traught Beach."

Patty had admittedly thought my daughter's remarks to be morose at the time but was ultimately glad Tessie had intimated her affections for the place, now for the obvious reason.

At the conclusion of the funeral Mass, attendees were, at first, confused after Father McLaughlin failed to disseminate information about the interment rites. But I soon suspected the priest's omission to be deliberate, because, while cremation is permitted by the Church, (provided it's not intended to demonstrate a denial of the resurrection of the body), the reality is that many within Church hierarchy frown upon the practice.

Father McLaughlin gave his final blessing, and he and his altar boys removed themselves to the sacristy, so I scurried up to the lectern and made a brief announcement that Tessie would not be buried at Foy's Cemetery, and I thanked everyone for their condolences and prayers this day. I left it at that. Some people at the back of the church had already filtered into the vestibule but rushed back in upon hearing my muffled words; the resulting speculation, over Tessie's final resting place, produced a stadium-like buzz inside St. Joe's. I had also elected not to host a reception, with sandwiches and refreshments, at the Pierpoint on this occasion, so I'm sure that also contributed to the prattling.

I noticed one woman waddling toward me, against the stream of exiting mourners, so I stood and waited, anticipating that she wanted a word. It was Trish Jennings, who I'm not sure I would've recognized even if she had been standing alone in the church. Trish had put on considerable weight since our last meeting in Castlebar, and I could only figure that, due to the depressing circumstances she had endured, the unfortunate soul had developed an eating disorder. Trish plainly sensed my shock over her appearance, as I stepped from the platform to embrace her.

"Albert, I'm so sorry for your loss," she said. "I only knew Tessie briefly, but I could tell what a special lady she was. You must be devastated."

"Thanks for driving down from Mayo, Trish. Yes, devastated. I'm not sure what to do next in life."

"Just live, Albert. Do what you always do and eventually you'll start to feel better... even though you'll never get over what's happened."

"You're right. The loss of my two daughters will gnaw at me for the rest of my days. I'm almost glad that my wife died so many years ago so that she wasn't witness to what happened to her girls."

"I *do* feel for you." She then changed the topic. "So, the Omniscient One doesn't seem to be much help these days... or at least He's not aiding in a substantive way. It almost seems as though the Adversary is getting the best of Him. And I'm beginning to think that Logan McCool, himself, might be the spawn of the Adversary."

"My line of thinking isn't far off. I received visual packets of Tessie's ordeal out on the high seas, but the packets consistently materialized too late for me to affect the outcome. I have to wonder why the Omniscient One is so fast to act in some matters, and, in others, moves seemingly with callous indifference. What about you? Have you experienced any dreams... received any communiqués from the Omniscient One lately?"

"Nothing. My last consequential dream being the one of Logan in Switzerland, when spending the night at your home." Trish then began trembling. "Oh, God, how I miss Liam," she said.

"It's terrible what happened to you... and me. Our loved ones didn't deserve those things, and neither did we. I'm worried about you, Trish. You don't look so good, if you don't mind me saying. I know a gentleman isn't supposed to say this to a lady, but... you've really packed it on."

Trish actually started to laugh while wiping her tears aside, and I felt better for a moment.

"That's because I'm eating for two, silly man. I'm pregnant... and well into my first trimester... maybe even the second."

"I'm so embarrassed. I'm sorry. I had no idea. Is it..."

She interrupted.

"Yes, Albert. It's Liam's."

"Have you had an ultrasound? Do you know..."

She laughed again.

"No, I haven't had an ultrasound. I think I prefer not to know the sex of the child."

"Oh, this is wonderful news, Trish." I gently embraced her again. "It does my heart good to know that you've got so much to live for and look forward to."

"Yes, I do. Thanks for the kind words."

"Will you be my guest tonight in Kinvara? You must rest before returning to Castlebar. We'll have dinner over to the Pierpoint."

Trish sensed me taking a fatherly role with her and chortled.

"Oh, thanks, Albert. I'd love to, really, but can't. I need to get back to the equestrian centre. The stablehand is looking after things until I return. I've been trying to run things as normal since the troubles up to our place, because it keeps my mind busy... and off things I don't want to think about."

The Troubles. There they were again. I wondered if Trish would've chosen those words, to describe the tribulations up to Castlebar (and Westport), if Liam hadn't uttered them in my kitchen that morning, almost two years ago, to reference the violent times in Northern Ireland. His brother Logan had certainly contributed plenty to "The Troubles," while tramping about Belfast, Antrim, and Londonderry with his fellow reprobates over the years. And then, unfortunately for us all, he commuted those troubles far beyond the borders of Northern Ireland.

39

LOGAN MCCOOL HAD A major predicament set before him. He had just reached the mouth of the Suez Canal, at Port Said, Egypt, and docked to inquire through a Suez Canal Authority agent what he needed to do to make passage through the canal, so that he could reach the Red Sea. He was consequently informed that he had little chance of presently entering the one-lane canal (albeit with many passing areas) because, while recreational watercraft are permitted access, commercial and military ships retain priority passage rights. After asking *when* he'd be able to enter the canal, he was abruptly told, "Perhaps several weeks from now, perhaps never," due to the schedule of vessels and the disruption his lone boat would cause.

Logan was vexed over this hindrance, because his only alternative to reaching the Indian Ocean, by boat, was to sail back across the Mediterranean Sea, again pass through the Strait of Gibraltar, and circumnavigate the continent of Africa, which might take several months – that's assuming he wasn't snatched up by authorities he imagined searching for him along the Iberian Peninsula and northwest coast of Africa.

He now weighed his options: he considered returning to the small island near Crete and waiting several weeks or months and trying again later in the year; he thought about abandoning his hooker near Port Said and hitching a ride aboard a commercial container ship; lastly, he considered just making his way across the Middle East by train, bus,

212

and whatever other mode of transportation, to reach the destination in south central Asia he had long settled on.

A desperate Logan even attempted bribing the port agent, in order to make passage, but, after it was explained that it was simply a matter of logistics, he dejectedly departed the agent's station-office and returned to his hooker. Once setting sail toward Crete, he noticed several recreational vessels making their way toward the canal, so he steered toward them to monitor their progress, anticipating that they would similarly seek passage. At the outset, there appeared to be only ten or twenty of these sport cruisers, but, after the line of boats extended far into the horizon, Logan began counting them and guessed there to be upwards of one hundred. He also determined, by the names and homeports painted on the sterns of the luxury boats, that they hailed from Lebanon.

Eventually, the rally participants would seek unreserved passage through the canal, which Logan discovered after returning to Port Said and again entering the port agent's office, where the rally leader was busy negotiating with the same man who had refused Logan's request. The wealthy rally leader spoke in English, and Logan easily reckoned the transaction being conducted, including the port agent receiving generous illegal incentives for making the impromptu arrangements.

After the rally leader left the office, Logan agitatedly confronted the port agent on the matter of the recreational boats being admitted into the canal when his similar request had been declined. The agent shrewdly informed Logan that, as a port official, he retained the discretion to authorize or deny the entry of individual vessels or convoys based on guidelines governing a diverse range of circumstances; the current consideration being that, the Port of Said, therefore the Egyptian government, had an opportunity to collect significant revenue by authorizing the current nautical convoy, comprising 112 sport cruisers, to pass. Logan subsequently requested that he be allowed to follow the rally into the canal as the last recreational boat in succession, and, after the agent declined his appeal, now, quite clearly out of spite, Logan threatened to report the man for taking bribes.

In the end, Logan *was* allowed to tag along at the end of the cruiser procession, but had to pay miscellaneous legitimate fees totaling some $650, plus $1000 in bribes between the Port Said and Port Tawfiz agents. Ironically, even if traffic conditions in the canal had been such that his initial entry was permitted, his request ultimately would've been denied due to a lack of valid passport with visa. The way things worked out, it was the threat of bribery he leveraged on the Port Said agent, after overhearing negotiations with the rally leader during his second visit to the office, which persuaded the agent to allow Logan to pass without proper papers.

Logan thought about the money in his pocket and, at first, refused to pay the $1000 in bribes, because he couldn't picture himself parting with that kind of cash, which was his lifeblood on the run. The agent responded by explaining that it would, otherwise, be impossible for him to pass through the canal without the Port Tawfiz agent also being paid off, due to Logan's lack of passport. In reality, Logan was being duped because, once passing into the canal, he wouldn't be required to stop again before entering the Gulf of Suez into the Red Sea, which he wouldn't discover until exiting the canal.

After Logan queried the Port Said agent a second time, as to why he was collecting the whole $1000, instead of Logan paying $500 at both locations, the agent replied, "It's an insurance policy to prevent your head from being shot from your shoulders. If I were you, I'd keep my head down anyway."

Logan thought the man to be bluffing, because the rally of boats in front of him would be witness to any shooting, and the agent didn't want any trouble. The agent also clearly didn't care to ruin a good thing because, when Logan eventually did the math, he figured the agent had collected some $28,000 in bribes for allowing the 112 sport cruisers to pass, while collecting $56,000 in fees for the Egyptian government.

With all the commercial, military, and recreational vessels that needed management that day in the canal, it took Logan fourteen hours to reach Port Tawfiz and pass into the Gulf of Suez. Once in the Red Sea, he sailed to the Sudanese port of Halaib, where he docked and procured some non-perishable food and potable water. He later returned to the hooker and slept in the boat under the stars.

From Halaib, he sailed to the island of Dahlak Kebir, off the coast of Eritrea, and dared to beach the boat. He then paid two local boys to bring him a prostitute, because he wouldn't risk leaving the boat unattended. After sleeping on the beach, he awoke the next morning and paid a pittance to several boys, again hovering curiously, to help him push his vessel back into the Red Sea.

From Dahlak Kebir, he intended to stop in Djibouti, but the occupants of two motorboats, exchanging gunfire on the fringes of the bay, dissuaded him from doing so. He couldn't tell if it was a dispute among fishermen, or if bandits were attacking, so he steered clear of the disturbance and fled the area, lest the evil doers, perhaps more evil than he, recognize the Caucasian prey with potentially full pockets and take aim.

He soon found himself in the Gulf of Aden but wasn't yet prepared to traverse the Arabian Sea, so sailed along the Somali coast, on the Horn of Africa, until stopping at a town he identified as Alula, where he beached his hooker in a nearby unspoiled lagoon, and collapsed in the boat and slept for ten hours. When awakening the following morning, he referred to some maps and figured he had sailed some six hundred miles over twenty consecutive hours. Eventually, he heard some vague activity and popped his head up to view some children playing along the beach on the opposite side of the lagoon.

He had removed the Rolex watch from his wrist the day before, when observing the gunfire near Djibouti, and presently judged the time to be mid-morning. He imagined that someone must've noticed his boat since daybreak, and thought it peculiar that nobody had investigated his arrival; yet, strangely, he felt safe in this country of Somalia, despite not knowing what awaited him on the other side of the lagoon, because he needed a break from sailing and had just decided to venture into Alula.

He had kept most of his cash on his person, during his journey, and just removed the balance of the money concealed in an interior boat cranny. He also accessed the two pairs of diamond earrings and gold necklace he had lifted at the Jennings residence. He did so after resolving that, if someone were to steal the boat while he tramped about Alula, at least he'd be in possession of some resources to carry on. He also considered that there might be an opportunity to pawn off an earring or two, to recoup his losses from the Egyptian port agent's office, although that notion quickly faded once reaching the far side of the lagoon and beholding the prevailing humble means being practiced by locals.

He delayed at the place where the lagoon merged with the beach, until confident that some adults had perceived his emergence, because he wanted to gauge their reaction to him. He hoped they wouldn't deem him a threat and that he'd be able to proceed unmolested to a place where he imagined a worthwhile market. Most of the grownups at the beach were young to middle-aged women, who huddled around individual or group campfires while cooking, and monitoring their children. Logan eventually learned that the people along this stretch of beach were nomads who had little concern for his affairs. Soon, several children raced over to scrutinize the white stranger, and some dared to touch his hand to discover if his skin felt like theirs.

After observing only a few frail, old men in the vicinity, Logan guessed that the husbands of the young women must be fishing or engaging in some other means of commerce. He thusly ambled to a cluster of metal shanties far up off shore. Meanwhile, many of the same children skipped alongside to follow the foreigner, and Logan didn't discourage their attendance because he was mindful of the collective eyes on him and cared to be looked upon favorably.

Once reaching the shanties, which were uniformly open on the side facing the road, he was approached by an affable man, in his early thirties, who spoke minimal English. The man clearly saw a potential sale in the stranger and persisted with trying to give Logan a "giant deal" on some bracelets, anklets, and necklaces made from tiny seashells. Several curious Somali men had now circled, and looked on amusingly as the vendor tried to close the deal. Logan politely declined the offer and, instead, asked where he might buy some bottled water, prompting a younger man, with thin mustache and self-rolled cigarette dangling from his lips, to emerge and motion for Logan to follow him. The man spoke better English and wasn't trying to sell anything, so Logan felt satisfied for the moment that the local was sincere in his offer to help. They departed and, consequently, several Somalis, to include some of the nomadic children from the beach, followed until the escort turned to scold them for their pestering behavior. The man angrily stomped out his cigarette to emphasize his point, causing most of the stragglers to disperse, save for three defiant, pre-adolescent children, who ignored his counsel and resumed a more distant pursuit to discover the intriguing foreigner's destination.

The mustachioed escort had now gesticulated for Logan to follow him down a street that ran perpendicular to the shore road, built up with one-level commercial buildings and residential homes. Logan sensed increasing wealth in this area, albeit most homes were still relatively modest. The white stranger had also accumulated a new following in recent minutes, until the escort again turned to shout a few choice words. During the jaunt, Logan thought about his deserted hooker, back at the lagoon, and imagined locals rifling through his belongings, which swiftly stirred feelings of insecurity in him. However, once resolving to venture into town, there was little he could do to prevent such an intrusion, and he'd be happy just to see his boat upon returning.

Nestled among several bodegas on the street was an apparently newly constructed shop. The sign read: "Nur Water Works," with the subtitle, "Helping to Meet Alula's Clean Water Needs." Logan thought it odd that the sign was advertised in English, and his curiosity grew as they neared the business.

A woman in her late twenties stepped out from the shop and looked down the street as if expecting someone, enabling Logan to glimpse her appearance. The woman was an exotic Nubian beauty whose features plainly evidenced the past Italian, Anglo, and Arabic influences in northeastern Africa. Logan guessed her to be about five-feet seven inches tall, her straight, shoulder-length, black hair momentarily taking on a hypnotizing bluish hue as the Sun's rays refracted within it. The local was well groomed and, unlike her fellow countrywomen, even wore a little make-up. She also had on western-style apparel: a white, oxford-style, button-down shirt and slim-fitting blue jeans. Logan thought her to be the operator of the enterprise.

The striking woman instantly recognized the anomalous appearance of a Caucasian in her neighborhood but soon stepped back inside and thought no more of it. Logan surmised (and hoped) that this was the place where his escort was leading him, and, even if it wasn't, he had decided to visit there just to engage her.

Once arriving at the shop, the escort signaled for Logan to enter first, which indicated to Logan that the man intended to prolong his involvement in his affairs, so he thanked the escort outside and bid him farewell, prompting the man to half-bow but linger in expectation of a tip. Logan thusly removed two Euros and handed it to him; the man shrunk upon seeing the unfamiliar currency, finally demanding that Logan pay him in Somali shillings. Logan then proceeded to edify his escort that he had just sailed from the Mediterranean Sea and didn't possess any shillings, all the while, the striking Somali woman musing over the interaction through the glass.

The escort snatched the two Euros and marched away fuming. Logan now feared that the young man might search out his boat in the lagoon and retaliate by stealing something. But those fears quickly dispelled, once turning and settling his eyes on the distracting water vendor, who elicited a different kind of thirst in him. He entered the shop.

"Hello, I noticed your sign in English..."

The woman seemed annoyed by Logan's choice of words and interrupted:

"If you looked closer you would've noticed that the business is also listed in Somali and Arabic," she stated assertively.

Logan thought he would have his hands full with this one, but that wouldn't discourage him from trying to bed her.

"I'm sorry, but I don't understand those languages. I speak and read a little French... that's about it. *You*, on the other hand, speak English very well. Are you from Somalia?"

"Of course, I'm from Somalia. All one has to do is look at me to know that I'm from here. This is my country. How can I help you?"

"Well, as you might expect, I'm here to purchase some water."

"How much do you need?"

"Ten or fifteen liters should do it."

"Well, which is it... ten or fifteen?"

Logan couldn't understand why this gorgeous woman was behaving so bitchy toward him.

"Fifteen."

"I can't do fifteen. The containers are in increments of ten liters with the minimum being twenty. Twenty, thirty, or forty..."

"Then I also assume that you don't sell bottled water."

"Oh, no. If you only wish to buy a bottle of water then you should try one of the bodegas."

"In what type of container does the water come?"

"Are you familiar with the dispensers used in modern office buildings?"

"Yes."

"Like that."

"Ah, things are now coming into focus. I think I'll be requiring two forty liter containers. But before we conduct business, I have some questions for you, if you don't mind... if you're not in a hurry... because you have me very curious. First of all, allow me to introduce myself. My name's Joe O'Malley?"

"Welcome to Alula, Mr. O'Malley."

Logan was irked that she neglected to divulge her name. It spoke volumes, and he now doubted that he'd ever get her alone.

"What's *your* name?"

"Shadia, if you must know."

Although Shadia hadn't encouraged Logan in any manner, he decided that she deemed his appearance, in her shop, entertaining, because of the way her mouth curled discernibly at the edges. True enough, and she had also found his wiry form attractive, in spite of his scruffy hair and briny smell.

"You're not like the others I've encountered here, Shadia. And your English... it's so good. Where did you learn to speak it?"

"I went to secondary school and college in the United States."

"Really? How interesting. How did that all come about?"

"Quite simple, really. My father was a diplomat."

"In Washington, DC?"

"Yes."

"Is that where you went to school... in Washington?"

"That's correct."

Logan felt frustrated over Shadia's brief answers. She wasn't opening up to him. Then he caught a glimpse of himself, reflected in a glass case behind the woman, and felt foolish. His hair hadn't been shampooed in weeks and was spiked out in different directions; his clothes looked rumpled and soiled, and his skin was redder on the right side of his face, than left, due to constant western sun exposure while sailing south through the Red Sea.

"What college did you graduate from?"

"American University... look, Mr. O'Malley, are you going to buy some water or not?"

"Yes, Shadia, I am... and lots of it. Please be patient, because I'm a man who's been out to sea for a very long time," Logan cleverly interjected, to justify his unkempt appearance, "and I could use your kind advice on a variety of matters while in Somalia. Be a good ambassador for your country... like your father was. Would you do that?"

"Okay, Mr. O'Malley, how can I help you?"

"Call me Joe, please." Logan smiled, and Shadia reacted with a thin, forced smile.

"Okay, Joe. What kind of help do you need?"

"First of all, I could really use a bath."

"It's probably best that you rent a room in town so that you can clean yourself up. I can direct you."

"I also left my razor back at the boat. Is there somewhere I can buy a razor?"

"Naturally. I suppose I can help you with that."

Logan sensed that Shadia was finally warming up to him.

"I feel a little uneasy about having left my boat unattended at the lagoon. Do you suppose it'll still be there when I return?"

"Yes, it should be. The punishment for theft is very severe here. Although, I wouldn't be surprised if you discovered a crowd assembled when returning. I'm sure word has traveled quickly about you."

"Shadia, if you don't mind me asking... what is the well-educated daughter of a diplomat doing out here on the Horn of Africa? I imagine that your parents live far away, in Mogadishu?"

"That's very insightful of you. They do, indeed, live in Mogadishu, but my younger sister lives here with me in Alula. The reason I came to the Horn of Africa is that I wanted to help my people. When I expressed an interest in creating a non-profit company that would help provide a reliable, clean water source for northern Somalia, my father assisted me in getting the business started. The company is not for profit in the sense that I take the proceeds from water sales to businesses and wealthy homeowners, and provide free water to schools and the poor."

Logan recognized that Shadia enjoyed talking about her work, and was now encouraged that he might engage her socially.

"That's very altruistic. What does your company do to the water to make it drinkable?"

"First we treat it and then use reverse osmosis... a high pressure filtration method."

"I'm very impressed with the good work you do. Do you suppose I might break you free from work so that I can..."

Shadia interrupted.

"Yes, I'll help you, but what about the water? Are you going to buy water from us or not?"

"I am, but will you take Euros? I'm afraid I don't have any shillings."

"Yes, but I'm going to have to charge you extra for the inconvenience of exchanging your currency.

Logan secretly objected to the surcharge because he needed to conserve resources, but he also didn't want to discourage Shadia in any way. If this had been a man he was dealing with, he would've tried to work some angle, like he did with the port agent in Egypt. For a moment, he fantasized being alone with Shadia in the run down hotel room he had yet to rent, where he seduced her and she resisted.

"In that case, can you also see to it that the water is delivered to my boat?"

"Yes, but there'll be a fee for that, also."

Logan grimaced, which Shadia plainly perceived.

"Few things in this life are for free, Joe. If I'm going to have to pay a couple of strong, young men to lug two containers of water to your boat, then the cost will be passed on to you."

"Just hire one man, I'll carry the other container."

"Okay, and now that I think of it, there will be one additional charge. You're not a regular customer, and won't be returning the empty plastic containers, so I'm going to have to charge you a deposit."

"I tell you what, Shadia... let's just make it *one*, forty-liter container, and I'll carry it to the boat myself... but I'd still like your assistance around Alula. Will you be charging me for *that?*" Logan asked, trying to mask his annoyance and remain pleasant. Shadia sensed his perturbation, however, and derived some satisfaction from it. She laughed.

"No, Joe. I won't be charging you for *that.*"

She called out to a worker in back who brought out one forty-liter container of water. She instructed the man to load it in the back seat of her compact car, parked in an adjacent alleyway. She then told a young woman to handle the front desk while she was away.

Shadia and "Joe" exited the shop and turned a corner to the left where her car sat in an alley. Logan opened the right front passenger door, but Shadia immediately rebuked him, directing him to sit in the backseat alongside the container of water. She did so because she already received enough attention in Alula as a well-to-do Muslim woman, who owned and drove a car, and she didn't want people gossiping about her and the white stranger.

She soon pulled up before a seaside hotel featuring several bungalows, and told "Joe" to wait while she went inside. When returning, she related that she had some idea of his limited resources and that she had negotiated a fair price for him for a bungalow and that he'd be able to pay in Euros.

"What's your living situation, Shadia? Couldn't I just shower at your place," Logan implored.

"Oh, that's not possible," she said in a manner that implied his request was audacious.

Logan entered the hotel and paid twenty Euros for the accommodations, which he found reasonable even though he knew he wouldn't get his money's worth, because he didn't plan on staying overnight. He was also presently dubious that he was going to be able to bed Shadia, and to risk forcing himself on her, as he had done Tessie out on the boat, might prove an even riskier endeavor, resulting in his execution if failing to flee successfully. At least, he'd get the shower he desperately needed.

Logan returned to the car with his room key, and Shadia requested that he carry the water container to his bungalow, so that he'd have it in his possession when ready to check out. The hike to his boat from the bungalow would be considerable, but he could always stop and rest along the beach. Shadia took the key from him and unlocked the bungalow door. Logan stepped inside, and she suggested that he shower while she went out to buy a razor.

By the time Shadia returned, Logan was sitting in the lone comfortable chair in the room with only a bath towel wrapped around his waist. He had sent his clothes out for laundering and was close to dozing off. "Joe" greeted her with a wide smile but tired eyes. In addition to a package of three disposable razors, Shadia had thoughtfully purchased a travel-sized tube of toothpaste and toothbrush for him. Logan was encouraged upon seeing the toothbrush because it signaled to him that the beautiful woman desired to be kissed.

Shadia then realized that she had failed to collect the money for the water, and told Joe how much he owed for the water, razors, toothbrush, and toothpaste. He didn't delay in paying her and went into the bathroom to shave, and brush his teeth, stepping out once with a mouthful of sudsy toothpaste to demonstrate that his mouth would soon be kissable. He raised his eyebrows mischievously.

Finally emerging from the bathroom, "Joe" approached Shadia while wearing the bath towel only, and she reacted by backing up to the door, where he trapped her and moved in for a kiss; however, Shadia swiftly turned her face, and the kiss landed on her cheek. Logan now had his hands locked behind her back and wouldn't let go while trying to charm her, so Shadia adroitly ducked down and slid free.

"Sit..." Shadia half-shouted, "... and I'll give you a massage."

Logan liked the sound of that. He also liked that things seemed to be progressing, albeit at Shadia's pace not his. Likewise, he preferred that the massage take place on top of the bed, but *the chair is a good starting place*, he thought.

Once he was situated in the chair, Shadia began rubbing his shoulders and neck, and he soon became aroused watching her in a mirror on the wall. He subsequently loosened the towel, suggesting that she might massage his lower back.

"Wait!" Shadia demanded.

Logan was accustomed to being in charge but decided to let things play out. Shadia then reached up to massage his scalp and temples. Several weeks earlier, he hadn't had enough hair to grab onto, but now the gorgeous woman was clutching short tufts of his hair and tugging it firmly yet painlessly, as part of her massage technique, to manipulate his scalp. Logan had never received this kind of massage before and nearly went limp from relaxation. He wondered where she had learned to massage like this – *surely they don't teach this at American University*, he thought.

He continued studying Shadia in the mirror, and she glanced up periodically to recognize his mind working. Despite what might or might not take place between the two in the succeeding minutes, Logan was again scheming to lure the beauty out onto his boat, so that he could work her over like he had done my Tessie. He also considered how inconvenient it would be to sail back and drop her in Alula, and resolved that he'd ultimately need to dispose of Shadia in the same manner, despite the risks.

Presently, the extreme relaxation induced by the scalp massage had quashed his erection. The moment Shadia recognized this, she stepped away from the back of the chair, seized the door open, and Logan would gaze her beauty for one final, fleeting moment.

"What's going on? Where are you going?" he asked.

"Away from you, Joe... or whatever your name is."

"Why are you doing this, Shadia? I thought we were enjoying each other's company. We don't have to do anything you don't want."

"I'm leaving because I can see into your soul, where great evil lurks. May the next woman, who crosses your path, see what I've seen." Shadia turned and slammed the door shut.

40

Logan napped for three hours while his clothes were being laundered, and after checking out he departed the bungalow with his cumbersome water container in tow. It was necessary to pause twice on the way back to the lagoon, and the respites spawned new groups of curious children, some tugging on his shirt and asking for money, others touching the foreigner's reddened skin.

He slogged past the familiar nomads on the beach and again struggled with the container upon reaching the lagoon, where he set it down and laid his eyes thankfully on the boat. And, just as Shadia had predicted, word about him had spread during the day: a horde of men and boys had congregated and were examining the unusual sailing vessel, with some wading to inspect the stern. Logan now only hoped that his belongings were in tact.

Once perceiving the white stranger's attendance, the younger males scurried across the shoreline to unabashedly study him as he advanced with the bulky water container. The older males greeted him, and one man, recognizing the traveler's need for assistance, motioned that he would help him lift the heavy container into the craft. Logan thanked the man and inquired if his things were left undisturbed, but nobody among this group spoke English well and they failed to respond. Logan then took a few minutes to inventory his store of non-perishable food, and everything looked in order so he leaned over the edge of the hooker and smiled. He had never worried about the Euros, diamond earrings, or gold necklace with locket, because those items were concealed on his person.

Once ready to depart, he waved good-bye from the bow and signaled that he wished for the strong men of the group to shove his boat from the muddy shore into the lagoon waters. The men understood perfectly, and nearly everyone joined in helping the white stranger. Once the hooker slid from its entrenchment and floated freely in the water, Logan applauded his helpers, and they laughed and also clapped. He soon unfurled the hooker's maroon sails, which immediately collected some wind, and he maneuvered the vessel into the more open waters of the Gulf of Aden. He turned to wave one last time while edging away.

He knew he had gotten a late start this day, and, when visualizing himself sailing across the unfamiliar Arabian Sea, in the black of night, he derived an uneasy feeling and wished he had stayed overnight at the Alula bungalow. He had, after all, paid for the room and could've remained until morning. But then he decided that he wouldn't have been able to rest easy, knowing that his hooker and its stores lay vulnerable to thieves.

Once emerging from the Gulf of Aden into the vast Arabian Sea, he cracked open his last bottle of Jameson's, which he bought at Leary's on Great Blasket Island, and planned to nurse the jug so that it lasted until reaching India. He sailed due east, and, although plenty of daylight remained, the Sun was setting faster than he would've liked. He soon thought of Shadia, the one who got away, and, with one hand on the wheel, unzipped his trousers and commenced masturbating to the Nubian beauty, with thoughts of what might've been, eventually stepping away from the helm to ejaculate into the ocean.

At dusk, he noticed a prominent landmass on the horizon and was confused because he had only been out on the water for four hours, causing him to fret that he had sailed off course. He checked the boat's compass to see if it had stuck, but, after referring to an atlas, resolved that he was approaching the Yemenese island of Socotra, which boasts no permanent residents; and, considering the potential perils of night sailing, the accommodating full moon notwithstanding, decided to beach the hooker, once beholding the island's favorable coastal plain. He didn't venture far that night, but, the following morning, after eating some canned sardines, hiked up a limestone plateau to better view the island mountains that rise up some 5,000 feet. Eventually he returned to his boat and fished for an hour before landing an unsightly fish that he decided probably wouldn't taste very good, and released it back into the ocean. The forfeiture had been one of his few selfless acts in life over the past decade.

From Socotra, he impulsively altered his course and took a more coastal route toward India, a prudent move, really, for this otherwise reckless operator with perfunctory sailing skills, and sailed for the Muria Kuria islands off the coast of Oman. It took nearly two days to reach the islands, and he collapsed in the boat after anchoring off the eastern most island, Al Qibliyah, which, like Socotra, also lacks residents. When coming to, he swam ashore and idled most of the day on the island, this time exploring minimally, but discovered a fresh water spring so returned to his boat at low tide to retrieve some empty gallon jugs to fortify his water supply. He also killed a reptile he guessed to be an iguana, skinned and roasted it, and ate its flesh, despite his ample store of canned staples.

He considered maintaining a coastal route and anchoring next near Pakistan but thought it too indirect, relative to his destination, and, instead, steered east along the 20th latitude toward Mumbai, India. And once in more open waters he felt good about his decision because his sailboat was being propelled speedily by sustained westerly winds that otherwise weren't too harsh on his body.

Two and a half days later, he perceived an archipelago-like array of small islands in the distance, and approached what he believed to be Mumbai Harbor. He now wondered how long it would take before maritime officials or criminal opportunists discovered the hooker he intended on abandoning, because, although the skilled climber had settled on the faraway interior of this mountainous region as his new home, he pondered whether he might ever again require the sailboat's services. He also, strangely, felt attached to the vessel because of the reliable service it had provided, the considerable time spent aboard it, and the unlikely places "they" had traveled. This line of thinking compelled him to impetuously alter his course and sail for an unknown island that he judged to be less populated. Several minutes later, he fittingly drove his hooker up on the muddy shore of a desolate northern stretch of landmass called Butcher Island.

After sailing for nearly three consecutive days, Logan expectedly conked out within minutes of arriving on Butcher Island. He didn't know it at the time, but eventually would learn, that the island is not inhabited in the sense that it's only used by Indian port authorities as a terminal where crude oil is offloaded from tankers into vast containers and stored temporarily, before being piped to Mumbai, five miles away, for refining.

The clanking noises of pressure changes within metal pipes and containers finally roused him from a long sleep, but he was yet unable to identify the source of the distant, intermittent sounds. Feeling lightheaded but rested he soon emerged from his hooker to explore the locale, and, everywhere he looked, noticed "Restricted Area" signs. Once determining that it was only a matter of time before his presence was detected on the island, and that he'd be arrested, he returned to the boat, intending on pushing it from shore and sailing elsewhere. Unfortunately, he had beached the hooker at high tide, however, and presently it was low tide, so the vessel was glued into the mud, with several yards of earthy shore separating the boat from the sea.

With much time to kill before the next high tide, he resumed hiking, this time prowling like a cat burglar, and made his way to the top of a hill in the middle of the island. From this new vantage point, he noticed how densely the subtropical vegetation overspread the island, and how the flora might aid in camouflaging him, should he be discovered.

Eventually his exertions triggered considerable hunger, and he revisited his sailboat to eat some canned kidney beans and to wait for high tide. He passed the time resting, and leafing through an Irish Sport magazine he had practically memorized after looking at it so many times during his voyage.

Once judging the tide high enough, he hopped from the boat and attempted to push the vessel back into the rushing waters. When that didn't work, he scrambled, in between waves, to dig around the perimeter of the stern, eventually moving to the bow to employ a thick branch as a lever, but to no avail as the hooker remained firmly fixed in the mud and sand. There was always a chance that a random, powerful wave would crash ashore and dislodge the boat, or that the next high tide would be higher; however, now confronted with the reality that he might never free the craft, Logan quickly removed his late brother

Liam's satchel and filled it with some essentials. How and when he would actually make it to Mumbai, he presently had no clue. He soon imagined himself abandoning the satchel in some island undergrowth, swimming to Mumbai, and somehow returning to retrieve it, because, otherwise, he wouldn't be able to swim efficiently while hauling a wet bag. And even if he did manage it all he envisioned the eyes he'd attract once emerging from the polluted harbor waters, in sopping clothes, carrying a dripping satchel. Any official summoned to the scene would immediately discover that he possessed no passport, but he expected to be able to effectively mitigate that situation by explaining, "the passport was in my pocket before the boat sank."

What a blunderous move it had been to run aground on this island, he thought, still leaning against his hooker and contemplating the lies he'd need to arm himself with, if confronted.

Suddenly, an industrial-sized whistle blew in the near distance. Logan trundled through some low growth, in the direction of the sound, and observed a stream of multi-national employees, albeit mostly Indians, disembarking a small ferry onto a ramp that led to the oil terminal; the individuals were arriving for their twelve-hour work shift. Soon, the employees they replaced would exit the terminal and board the same ferry, bound for the quayside near the Gateway to India, at Mumbai Harbor.

He crept through some thicker brush with his satchel, turning aside large boughs of vegetation to hasten his progress, and had just decided to insert himself into the departing group whenever they emerged; he began conjuring, to explain himself, if challenged. At one point, as he slinked along the north side of the terminal, a large beige and black snake, with menacing, triangular-shaped head, sensed the potential predator and raised its head while flickering its tongue as if tasting the salty air. The instant Logan noticed the beautiful but undoubtedly deadly snake he darted in the opposite direction through thinner growth, where he enjoyed better visibility, all the while hoping he hadn't ventured into a nest of snakes.

Within minutes, all those disembarking the ferry entered the facility but nobody had yet exited, causing Logan to consider that the employees being relieved were required to brief their counterparts on the status of work matters before leaving.

Logan felt persuaded that he looked "official" enough, toting his satchel, and, rather than wait on the ramp for the employees, boldly decided to board the vessel. A ferry worker stepped onto the ramp as Logan approached, and they exchanged nods. Logan walked past the man and sat inside, self-consciously taking time to comb his hair with his fingers, once situated.

Three minutes later, the parade of departing employees filed onto the ramp leading to the ferryboat. Everyone, so far, looked to be an Indian national, and they immediately eyeballed Logan, the foreigner, upon boarding. Most were blue-collar workers whose uniforms had become sullied during the shift; they wore hardhats and carried sundry meal containers. Logan soon noticed that even those men who appeared to be middle managers wore hardhats. The last man to board was older, dressed better, and carried a satchel not too unlike Logan's. He also wore a hardhat. The man immediately perceived the unfamiliar white passenger, sitting alone, and decided to join him in order to discover his identity. Logan felt panicked.

"I don't believe we've met." The fifty-something man smiled and extended his hand. "I'm Jeyaseelan Prasanth, Executive Foreman of the dayshift."

The workers had largely settled in, and all eyes were on Logan and Jeyaseelan.

"How do you do, Jeyaseelan... I'm Bernard Molloy." Logan shook the foreman's meaty hand and said nothing more because he was still urgently creating in his mind.

"I'm afraid I don't know you, Mr. Molloy. What business have you with us?"

Logan then remembered an advertisement he had looked at so many times in his *Irish Sport* magazine: a company called Pertamina Oil had placed a recruitment ad for "Able-bodied Seamen" to work on oil transport vessels.

"Oh, please don't be alarmed. I'm here in Mumbai, on business, for Pertamina Oil. I've always been attracted to Indian culture, and when I heard there was an oil facility out on this island I began romanticizing about leaving Pertamina, to live and work in India."

The rumbling ferryboat edged away from the docking station into more open waters.

"I see... but I'm still confused. When did you actually come out to Jawahar Dweep? (Hindi for Butcher Island, Logan would learn). I certainly don't recall you riding out on the ferry with us this morning."

"Oh, I just rode out with the crew who replaced you."

"But, how ever did you get on the ferry? This is a restricted boat used to deliver a workforce to a restricted island."

"Well, I told some nice young man, working at the dock, the same thing I told you... that I was considering applying for a job at the oil installation on this island... and that my time in India was waning. I told him if he could arrange for me to ride on the ferry... so that I could see the island... I would give him a generous gratuity."

"What?!"

Jeyaseelan's subordinates hadn't been able to hear their conversation but surmised that their boss was agitated.

"And I have to tell you, Jeyaseelan, as much as I love India, I don't think I could spend twelve straight hours on this island. There's nothing else going on here."

"It's a restricted area! It's supposed to be desolate! Nevermind that now. I want to know the name of the individual who allowed you on this ferryboat. Is he here now?"

"Oh, no. He's probably still back at the dock."

"I want to know his name!" Jeyaseelan demanded.

"*Shree*, I think he said his name was."

"Sri. Did Sri tell you his last name?"

"No, we didn't get that familiar."

"And what did Sri look like?"

"Well... like every other man in India. Brown-skinned, not too tall... a thin mustache."

"How old?"

"Late twenties, I'd say. But, I'm not too good at guessing ages."

"How much did you pay him to get on this boat, Mr. Molloy?"

"Well, I'm running a little low on rupees, so I..."

Jeyaseelan had grown enraged and yelled at "Bernard."

"How much?!"

"Twenty Euros."

"What do you do for Pertamina, Mr. Molloy?"

"I perform refinery-related work."

"Yes, what, specifically, in refinery?"

Logan again felt panicked because he didn't know enough about the oil industry to bullshit his way through this one.

"Well, Jeyaseelan, I think you can appreciate... seeing that you work in a restricted area... that there are proprietary matters that would be divulged if I described to you the nature of my work."

Jeyaseelan did not care for Mr. Molloy's evasive answer. He now considered that the foreigner might be a corporate spy or, worse, a terrorist who had been sizing up Jawahar Dweep, in consideration of an attack. He scrutinized Mr. Molloy's appearance further and wondered if the intruder was who he claimed to be. Logan's face was grossly red due to sunburn, he badly needed a shave, and his rumpled clothing wasn't suitable for a traveling oilman.

"Mr. Molloy, when we arrive in Mumbai Harbor in a few minutes, I'd like you to, first, point out the dock worker who arranged for you to board this ferry. Then, I'd like for you to join me at our terminal office so I can make some calls to verify your identity and occupation through your employer."

"Nothing would please me more than to help you, Jeyaseelan. I certainly wish to alleviate any concerns you have, because I still haven't ruled out pursuing an oil industry job in India, and I want to remain in your good graces. At the same time, I wouldn't want Pertamina to know that I've been using company time to inquire about employment possibilities here. It could be grounds for dismissal. How do you suppose we might work around that?"

Mr. Molloy's latter utterance had made sense to Jeyaseelan, and, suddenly, Logan managed to gain some credibility with him.

"I'll come up with something."

Ten minutes later, the ferryboat eased into the docking station, and all aboard prepared to disembark.

"Stay close to me," Jeyaseelan instructed Mr. Molloy.

"Will do," Logan only responded.

Jeyaseelan allowed his subordinates to exit the vessel first, and said to Mr. Molloy as they walked off the ramp, "Now, I'd like you to scan the area. Once you notice Sri, I want you to point him out to me."

"I'll do just that," said Logan.

After they reached dry land, Logan said, "I don't see him anywhere. Shall we search inside the terminal?"

"Yes, perhaps we should," said Jeyaseelan.

Once they entered the busy terminal, Logan said, "I didn't have chance to use the lavatory while we talked on the ferry, Jeyaseelan. Excuse me while I relieve myself, would you? I'll return directly."

"Yes, go ahead. I'll be over *here*, inquiring about a dock worker named Sri," Jeyaseelan said, motioning with his hand.

"Splendid," said Mr. Molloy.

Logan moseyed with his bulging satchel into the men's room, where he feverishly changed from civilian attire into his Catholic priest outfit; he tucked the satchel high under his arm, to further alter his appearance, and exited the restroom without delay. What he would do beyond flee, if Jeyaseelan stood there waiting for him, he didn't yet know. He was just glad to be on terra firma again, and had every confidence he'd be able to avoid detention. He soon observed Jeyaseelan engaging a supervisor behind the busy counter and slowed to assess if his challenger detected his emergence. Once reckoning that Jeyaseelan was chastising the supervisor for "Sri's" actions, Logan casually slipped through the lobby, to outside, where he swiftly blended with the mass of commuters and tourists.

41

Satisfied that he was far enough from the terminal that Jeyaseelan had little chance of finding him, Logan slowed his pace within the heavy, city foot traffic.

Most of the women in the streets of Mumbai wore brightly colored saris, such as red, lavender, orange, and indigo, which immediately caught his eye and naturally stimulated him. An old, gray-bearded, deformed beggar, hobbling with a makeshift crutch, distinguished the taller, white foreigner in the sea of amblers, and hopped energetically toward him, with hopes of receiving alms. Everything of consequential value in Logan's possession currently rested in the breast pocket of his black priest outfit: the cash, two pair of diamond earrings, and the gold necklace, containing locket. Logan quickly demonstrated to the beggar that his trouser pockets were not pockets at all but had only been stitched to appear that way. The "priest" then briefly opened his satchel to reveal the contents: clothes, a book, two flat cans of sardines, and some personal hygiene products, as if to justify his imminent vacation from the man. Once the disappointed beggar seemed convinced, Logan contradicted himself by asking where he could find a currency exchange office, which, needless to say, perplexed the man. The beggar annoyingly pointed down and across the thoroughfare, and made one final appeal for a few rupees before Logan abruptly walked away.

He soon noticed two currency exchange offices and delighted when recognizing that one was open 24 hours, because it was nearing 6:30

p.m. and he knew he'd obtain a less competitive rate at a hotel. He plainly detected the smell of turmeric, upon entering the office, and looked across to an employee taking his dinner at his desk. The young man ate curry, and Logan's mouth began watering because it had been too long since he had eaten a proper hot meal. The employee sensed the priest staring at him, and he paused to nod and smile. Seconds later, a turbaned, black-bearded security guard, armed with a compact, semi-automatic shoulder weapon, emerged from a hallway. Logan determined the man to be Sikh and felt uneasy to be in the sinister-looking man's company but understood his reason for being there.

During the course of business, Logan casually asked where he might board a train bound for New Delhi. He soon discovered that, due to the high demand for interstate train accommodations in India, he had little chance of boarding a train this day without a reservation. The employee suggested that Logan reserve a seat over the telephone or at an Internet café and then rent an inexpensive hotel room in the Colaba section of Mumbai until able to make passage.

His transaction completed, Logan stood and counted the money in front of the agent, and wadded and inserted it in his shirt pocket before exiting the office. He then joined a perspiring, heaving mass of Mumbai commuters that swallowed him up as he boarded a double-decker bus bound for the Central Railways Station, so that he could go and tender a cash deposit to reserve a seat. During it all, he wondered why these largely Hindu Indians, whose predilection for recognizing the divinity in their fellow man, brazenly disregarded him in his identifiable priest attire and jostled him about, thereby inducing him to press his satchel against his person to shield the valuables contained in his breast pocket.

Despite the high demand for train accommodations, Logan would wait only one day before traveling to New Delhi. After reserving a train berth, he again subjected himself to a rugby-like scrum at the Central Railways Station, this time boarding a double-decker destined for the main bus depot in Colaba. Once in Colaba, he gleefully only had to part with 975 rupees for a room at an unremarkable hotel in the tourist section, and registered under John Muldoon, the undiscovered alias he used when committing the carnage at Jennings Equestrian Centre in Castlebar.

Although famished, he was presently more inclined to sleep, and napped for three hours before showering and venturing out. When doing so, he again slipped into his Catholic priest uniform, mindful that Jeyaseelan and a search party might be scouring Mumbai's streets for him.

He thought back to the wonderfully savory aroma, in the currency exchange office, and inquired through a hotel clerk where he might find a reasonably priced restaurant that served excellent curry. Minutes later, he entered "Paloma's," a bistro near the Fort section of Mumbai, where he ordered the chicken curry with basmati rice, and gratifyingly washed it down with 750 milliliters of Kingfisher Beer. He left Paloma's an hour later and strolled through Fort to view the British colonial estates and civic buildings, which line the streets of the popular British quarter. Like many tourists, he found the architecture inharmoniously appealing, nonetheless experienced feelings of contempt because these remnants of British colonialism served as yet another reminder of Britain's modern-day occupation of northern Ireland. *At least the city wasn't still called Bombay*, he thought.

He rose at 7 a.m. the following morning and prepared to catch the 8:55 a.m. train bound for New Delhi. He preferred regular civilian attire this day and donned his khaki trousers with navy blue top. Once packing his satchel, he left the room unlocked, as requested, and made his way to the lobby, where a continental breakfast was made available, and he steeped a cup of tea, guzzled a glass of some unidentifiable, sweet, red juice and ate a croissant. The tea was so scaldingly hot, however, that he scarcely sipped it before leaving, mindful of the train he needed to catch. He again grew paranoid that Jeyaseelan might glimpse him upon exiting the hotel, but soon remembered that the executive foreman worked the dayshift and had likely been at Butcher Island since 6 a.m.

Logan arrived at the Central Railways Station at 7:50 a.m. He paid the balance on his reserved seat, and a boarding announcement was made twenty minutes later. He had discovered the day before that it would take roughly sixteen hours to reach New Delhi, so he secured a comfortable sleeping berth in an air-conditioned compartment with a capacity for four travelers. He had envisioned himself rooming with three Indian businessmen.

42

WHEN LOGAN OPENED THE door to his assigned AC2 compartment, containing two tiers of two compact beds on each side, he observed a muscular black man, about six feet tall, in his mid to late twenties, already resting on a bottom bunk.

His satchel in hand, Logan turned sideways to fit through the narrow compartment doorway and watched the cleanly shaven man, with closely cropped hair, relaxedly leafing through a magazine titled *Leatherneck*. Logan noted the traveler's casual western attire and guessed him not to be from Africa. Logan nodded and smiled thinly, and the man regarded him, so Logan introduced himself.

"Hello, I'm John Muldoon... traveling from Ireland."

The man placed his magazine down and sat up to extend his hand.

"Hi, John, I'm Ladell Maples. My friends call me 'Sneed.'" The two men shook hands. "I live in New Delhi. I'm just traveling back home."

Logan quickly recognized the man's accent, or lack thereof, and thought him to be either American or Canadian.

"What line of work are you in, Sneed... that requires you to live in India."

"I work at the American Embassy."

"Ah... I see. Consular Office?"

"No, I'm in the Marines."

"Really, now? World's greatest fighting force. Do tell. I've always been a big admirer of the U.S. Marine Corps. Impressive history you guys have."

"Yes, it's a fine outfit."

"Where are you from in the States, Sneed?"

"Arkansas. It's in the south... sorta south central."

"I know exactly where Arkansas is," John asserted.

"Where are you from in Ireland?"

"Antrim. It's in the north. Why? Have you traveled to Ireland before?"

"No, I know some Marines working at the embassy in Dublin. What about you? What brings you to India?"

"Well, I'm afraid I'm one of those mountain-climbing nuts. I'm headed to Everest. Gonna do it the hard way. I plan to start in the Himalayan foothills of northern India, hike to Nepal, and then on up from there."

Sneed looked at the satchel and then at John.

"Traveling light, aren't ya?"

"Oh, that." Logan laughed. "I figured what it costs to check that kind of baggage these days, or to ship it, and it's better if I just wait and purchase my climbing gear in Katmandu. The convenience is worth a lot to me. I didn't want to be hauling extra equipment before I needed it."

"I see." Sneed studied John with some skepticism but thought him to be nice enough.

A faint knock could be heard on the compartment door, and a Caucasian, silver-haired lady, wearing black habit, subsequently made her way in. She carried a lightweight travel bag and peered down over her spectacles at the two men sitting opposite each other on bottom bunks.

"*Helloooo*," she said humbly, slightly gasping, and baby-stepped her way inside.

Logan recognized that the woman was a Catholic nun and stood to greet her.

"Did they go and put you in a cabin with two men, Sister?"

"Yes, well, I requested a 'ladies-only carriage,' but they obviously couldn't accommodate. As crowded as the trains are in India, I suppose it's not easy to please everyone. I'm sure they do the best they can."

The nun had detected a distinct Ulster accent in Logan's manner of speech but said nothing for the moment. Logan similarly recognized the woman's brogue.

"Sister, I'm John Muldoon, and this is Ladell... or Sneed, as he prefers... from America... but he lives in New Delhi."

Logan acted nervously because it just occurred to him that he had almost worn his Catholic priest costume that morning. He then imagined getting caught up in a web of lies that, in the end, the nun wouldn't have believed anyhow.

Sneed rolled out from his bunk to help the nun with her bag.

"Sister, why don't you take my bottom bunk," he politely suggested.

"Well, if it's not too much..."

John interrupted. "Oh, no, Sister. You take mine. And Sneed... you were here before me, so I'll just take one of the top bunks, when it's time to sleep."

Logan was trying to be courteous but had come across a little overbearing and made both Sneed and the nun feel uncomfortable. The nun took a seat in a small chair at the rear of the cabin to catch her breath.

"By the way, Sister... I didn't catch your name," prompted Sneed.

The nun thought that the two men should just be content to address her as "Sister," however, seeing that Sneed asked, she remained cordial, considering that they'd be occupying the same intimate quarters for the next sixteen hours.

"Sister Mary Shaun Sevigny... from Ireland. It's nice to meet you both." She then looked at John's hand and said, "And I'm confident that John is from the Emerald Isle, also."

John chortled. "You're quite right, Sister. How ever did you guess?" Logan humored the nun because he suspected she had recognized his accent. "Well, you're accent was the first clue, and then I noticed your Claddagh ring."

"Ah, yes," said John, "that would be the other giveaway."

Logan flattened his hand to acknowledge the nun's sighting, and Sneed sat up in his bunk to look at the unusual ring, which visibly entranced him.

"Mind if I take a look, John?" I'm kind of a jewelry buff... African gold, mostly."

Logan held out his hand so that Sneed could examine the ring, which is prevalent in Ireland and features two hands holding a heart with a crown on top."

"*Very* nice... excellent craftsmanship. Are they difficult to come by outside of Ireland?" Sneed asked.

"Not so much, anymore. They can be had easily in the States and elsewhere, I'm sure." John said.

Sister Mary Shaun spoke up and caught Logan off guard:

"Where are you from in Ireland, Mr. Muldoon?"

"Dublin, Sister. Call me John, please."

Logan had forgotten he told Sneed he was from Antrim, when they were alone, but Sneed picked up on it.

Sister Mary Shaun also suspected that something was amiss, because John's accent was exclusive to Northern Ireland.

"Where in Dublin," the nun asked.

"Are you familiar with St. James Hospital, Sister? Right in that area."

"I've heard of the hospital but, thankfully, I've been able to avoid any infirmities while in Dublin. I *have* visited places like Loreto Abbey in Rathfarnham, south of Dublin, though. Like many people, I've been a great follower of the works of the late Mother Teresa of Calcutta. When Teresa was still known as Agnes, she joined the Sisters of Loreto and was sent from her native Albania to Loreto Abbey, in Ireland, to learn English."

"Is that your order in Ireland, Sister," John asked. "The Sisters of Loreto?"

"No, we're the Sisters of Mercy, we are. We run a secondary boarding school called Seamount House in Kinvara, Galway. As for myself, I teach Art History. Art of the Middle Ages is my specialty... so, naturally, I've also made trips to Dublin with students to view the Book of Kells at Trinity College. I know Dublin fairly well."

Logan's eyes bulged, and he swallowed out of stress when her words registered, and Sister Mary Shaun noticed his peculiar reaction to her seemingly innocent utterance.

"Brilliant, Sister," Logan finally responded. "And what brings you to India?"

Before Sister Mary Shaun could respond, the Radjhani Express Sleeper Train nudged forward.

"Well, unless someone enters through that door in the next thirty seconds, I'd say it's just the three of us for the duration," observed Sneed."

"That makes things a little more comfortable, doesn't it," added John. "You were saying... Sister. Your reason for traveling to India."

"Ah, yes. Well, I'm on sabbatical, I guess you could say... and the timing couldn't be better, let me tell you. We've endured a lot in Kinvara over the last year... all of Ireland has, really. Surely you heard about those two beautiful women that were murdered, Mr. Muldoon? The Doyle sisters? Well, I knew them both. In fact, young Tessie was once a bright student of mine at Seamount. I remember her well."

"Yes, Sister. The whole thing was just horrible, wasn't it? All of Ireland mourned, I think."

"Ireland is still mourning, Mr. Muldoon, and will continue to mourn until the vicious murderer, Logan McCool, is brought to justice. The Garda is also blaming him for the death of that nice young fisherman, up in Westport, whose body washed up in the Aran Islands."

Sneed sat up more attentively in his bunk.

"Is that the same guy who shot Nigel Etherington, the British Prime Minister?" Sneed asked, looking back and forth between John and the nun for verification.

"Yes," said John.

"That's the one," confirmed Sister Mary Shaun. "And his twin brother, Liam, he killed!" The elderly nun was now leaning forward in the chair. "His very own flesh and blood... with whom he shared his mother's womb! And the parents of the bride-to-be... he killed them all! What kind of man does that? That's what I want to know!"

"That was some murder spree. I can't believe he got away," Sneed said.

Logan was now sweating.

"I can't believe he managed to escape from Portlaoise Prison to begin with," said Sister. "Portlaoise is among Ireland's most secure prisons. A man would have to be very clever to engineer a break out from Portlaoise... even more clever to evade capture, after the fact."

"Very clever, indeed," John said, casually reaching up with a forefinger to wipe some sweat from his brow.

"You alright, Mr. Muldoon? You don't look so good," noted Sister Mary Shaun.

"Well, the air-conditioner is on, but I think it needs to be a little cooler." Logan wished to deflect attention away from his anxious appearance: "I haven't seen a newspaper from home for a long time, Sister. Where is it that authorities are currently concentrating their searches?"

"Perhaps you're coming down with something, Mr. Muldoon," she said, referring to his uneasy state. "Well, the last I saw... police were satisfied that McCool hadn't moored along the Iberian Peninsula, the Azores, Canary Islands, or Cape Verde Islands. They were still searching along the coast of Morocco and western Mediterranean... and were considering extending their search all the way to South Africa. Maybe a lie down will help you, Mr. Muldoon," she went on.

"It's not warm in here, John," said Sneed. "I'm very comfortable."

"It *is* quite pleasant," agreed the nun.

"No, I'm fine, really, Sister. I may be a little dehydrated. I'll just have a drink of water." Logan was compelled to change the subject. "So, why have you chosen to spend your sabbatical in India, Sister?"

"Well, as I alluded, I'm a great admirer of the ministry of the late Mother Teresa. I wanted to visit and see, firsthand, her legacy in action in Calcutta, as well as go to the Loreto convent in Darjeeling, in the Himalayan foothills... where she began her novitiate. This is the trip of a lifetime for me, and I decided to undertake it whilst I still have my two legs under me."

"But why didn't you just fly to Calcutta, Sister? Mumbai is so far away," noted John.

"After a news story appeared in the local paper that I was traveling to India to retrace Mother Teresa's steps, a kind shop owner donated a pre-purchased, roundtrip ticket to Mumbai, and I could hardly refuse the offering. It took a little doing to get the name changed on the ticket, with all the security requirements airlines have these days, but, all I had left to do was arrange transportation from Mumbai to Calcutta. Also, I heard that long-distance bus travel can be a dreadful experience in India, so here I am... on the Radjhani Express. Never look a gift horse in the mouth, as they say, Mr. Muldoon."

"Indeed, Sister. All things considered, sounds like a marvelous trip... and holy. And Darjeeling... now there's a place one can get a good cup of tea," said John, now chuckling awkwardly because he didn't know what else to say.

"What about you, Mr. Muldoon? Why have you traveled to India?" the nun asked.

"Like yourself, I'm also headed to the Himalayan foothills, Sister. The mountainscape is vast, though, so I doubt we'll bump into each other." John again laughed nervously.

"You're going to Darjeeling, too?"

"No, Sister. I'll be disembarking in New Delhi and will attempt one of those dreadful bus rides you so aptly described. I'm traveling due north."

Logan was reluctant to presently disclose his final destination, fearing that his anxious state would aid in foretelling, to the nun, any lies that might proceed from his mouth.

"I see. And what will you do there?" she asked.

"It's a beautiful area, as one can imagine. My plan is to mostly wander and hike about."

Sneed noticed that John was vague with the nun and had chosen his words carefully, especially when failing to share that he ultimately sought to climb Mount Everest in Nepal. Sister Mary Shaun turned to look at Sneed.

"And what about yerself, Mr. Maples... what is it that you do in New Delhi?" she asked politely, to give Sneed equal attention.

"I work at the American Embassy, Sister."

"That's wonderful. Good for you. Now if you gentlemen don't mind, I need to tend to a few things before situating myself for a lie down."

The nun's words signaled there would be a respite from talking, and Logan welcomed it. In the minutes preceding her pronouncement, Logan had been waiting for an opportune moment to disengage and search out a cup of tea, before the conversation developed into an inquisition, thereby cluing her into his identity.

"I'm headed to the dining car where a cup of tea can be had. Would anyone care for anything?" John asked.

"No, thank you," responded Sister Mary Shaun without looking up.

"I'm good," said Sneed. "But thanks for asking."

Sneed returned to his magazine on the bunk, as Logan exited through the narrow compartment door.

43

After paying the requisite rupees, Logan sipped a cup of hot sweet-tea while standing and making small talk with other New Delhi-bound tourists and citizens. During moments of silence, he reflected on his conversations with Sneed and Sister Mary Shaun, and it finally occurred to him that he had informed the nun he was from Dublin, after telling Sneed his hometown was Antrim. He soon grew concerned that his cabin-mates were talking about him and that the discrepancy might cause Sister to consider that he was the killer for whom everyone searched. He did, after all, fit the description better than anyone.

Logan trod gingerly upon re-entering the compartment and immediately tried gauging his travel companions' expressions. Sister Mary Shaun noted John's shifting, calculating eyes but otherwise still sat in her familiar chair and was now drinking some tea of her own. She chose not to acknowledge his return in any overt manner. Sneed also sipped contentedly from a cup while sitting on his bunk.

"When did *ye* venture out for a *cup*?" John asked in a folksy manner. "I didn't notice ye down near the dining car."

"Oh, they provide a complimentary tea service when you pay for a berth in an air-conditioned compartment," informed Sneed. "I thought you were aware but didn't care to wait, because you said you were a little dehydrated."

Logan was exasperated to hear Sneed's advice because, while the price he paid for the tea was paltry, he preferred not to part with any

244

resources unnecessarily. Logan looked over to Sister Mary Shaun, who faintly raised her cup, finally acknowledging him in a seemingly forced gesture.

"I guess I should've read the fine print on the ticket," John said.

"The chap who served us also took our meal orders, which is included in the price of the ticket. There were only two choices, 'veggie, or meat with veggies,' and I didn't know if you had any dietary restrictions, so I took the liberty of ordering you 'veggie only.' I hope that was okay," Sneed said.

"That'll do just fine," John replied, although he was secretly irked because he remained ravenous for protein most days due to the physical demands his arduous maritime journey had put on his body. As it was, he had become near gaunt in recent weeks, after drawing conservatively from his store of canned staples, for fear of running out while on the high seas, and, presently, only his loose-fitting clothes veiled his shrunken state.

Logan's eyes shifted to reflexively study Sister Mary Shaun, who, at first, appeared satisfied to be sitting quietly and taking her tea, but then her gaze seemingly gradated to moments of aloofness and superior contemplation. Logan hoped she was only praying. One thing he was sure of was that the nun's mind was working overtime: he could see the wheels turning, and now fretted that Sister might've experienced an epiphany concerning his identity.

Logan finally climbed up on his bunk and rested while looking at the ceiling and daydreaming; Sneed read his magazine. After Sister Mary Shaun finished her tea, she stood and rolled laboredly onto her bed, and, despite being fully clothed, covered herself straight away with a thin blanket. Several minutes later, Logan heard Sneed lightly snoring, so he glanced down and across to Sister Mary Shaun, who had turned on her right side and was now looking up at him.

"There's somethin' familiar about you, Mr. *Muldoon*... something very telling, indeed," the nun said softly so as to not disturb Sneed.

"That's because I'm Irish and you're Irish, Sister. I should say that you, also, look familiar." Logan whispered and smiled.

"Oh, I'm Irish to be sure. I grew up in Ireland. But my roots aren't Irish. With a last name like *Sevigny*? No, Mr. Muldoon, or whatever your *real* name is, my parents were both French. So, you see, I don't look Irish in a familiar way at all."

"Now, Sister, why would you take that tone of incredulity with me? If I told you my name is Muldoon, it's because it is. I'm John Muldoon from Dublin, Ireland. I'll show you my passport right now," Logan said, still whispering.

Logan, of course, was bluffing. He possessed no passport and, even if he did, it wouldn't have shown him to be John Muldoon. He now panicked that the nun might take him up on the challenge and ask to see his passport.

"False documents can be had easily, by anyone, for the right price, Mr. *Muldoon*. Oh, *yer* from Ireland, alright, but that's all I can say about you. I *know* people and all their earthly ways, Mr. *Muldoon*, and you concern me. It's something about the life you've led that's forged that perceptibly troubling aspect on your face."

"Don't be ridiculous, Sister. You're merely seeing the face of a weary traveler... who's crossed several time zones and who appears disoriented in a foreign land... that's all."

"I've been studying you throughout... Mr. *Muldoon*, and it's not fatigue or bewilderment I see in your face. Oh, no, it's much more. A malevolent life has shaped your disposition. You exude evil like no one I've ever met."

"Alright, Sister. Enough of that, now. You're becoming senile in your advancing years. I feel awful for saying that but don't know how else to respond."

Sister Mary Shaun threw the blanket from her person and sat up in the bunk.

"I'm getting up to move around, and when I come back I'd rather we didn't speak. And by the way, Mr. *Muldoon*, I sleep with one eye open."

The nun clutched her handbag and moved slowly through the compartment door. Meanwhile, Logan was reminded of Shadia, the Somalian beauty, whose remarks, as she fled from the Alula bungalow, echoed so closely what Sister had just uttered. Logan now pondered whether his past deeds really *had* formed an evil visage on him. But, more importantly, had the nun been insinuating that she recognized him to be the notorious killer, subject of an international manhunt? Logan thought about photographs of himself, which were inescapably published in newspapers across Ireland, following new murder allegations, and what he looked like in those pictures relative to his current appearance. His near-emaciated state had rendered his cheeks hollow, and his skin remained weathered and red due to sustained exposure to the harsh, maritime elements. His changed appearance notwithstanding, he convinced himself, at least temporarily, that the astute nun had recognized him. He soon developed a cold sweat but wondered if the anxiety resulting from his consuming thoughts had merely aided in deluding him. Nevertheless, he now weighed getting up to track the nun's movements inside the train, to discover if she sought to notify authorities.

After Sister Mary Shaun closed the compartment door, the sharp latching noise roused Sneed, and his magazine fell from his chest onto the floor.

"Did you catch any of that?" John asked, contorting himself to look down at Sneed in his bunk.

"Any of what?"

"The old bird went bonkers on me... telling me that, in so many words, because of the expression on my face, she thinks I'm evil. And she did it in the calmest way. Doesn't believe my name is John Muldoon, either."

Sneed subsequently weighed confronting John on the matter of where he was really from in Ireland but presently decided against it. *Perhaps "the old bird" was on to something*, he thought. However, in another thirteen hours, they'd all go their separate ways, so it didn't matter much. Plus, he didn't want to rub John the wrong way because he had just decided to make him an offer for the unusual ring on his hand, which continued to enthrall him.

Sneed sat up groggily on his bunk, and Logan climbed down to sit across from him on the nun's bed. Logan clearly felt the need to talk further about Sister's remarks, but Sneed wasn't particularly interested in involving himself in any disputes between two Irishmen, so to speak. Instead, he focused on John's ring.

"Forget about Sister Mary Black and Decker," Sneed said sarcastically. "Let's have another look at that ring. What'd you call it... Cladder?"

"Claddagh, yes."

"Mind taking it off?"

"Sure," John acquiesced, preferring to keep his other cabin-mate in his favor. "You never mentioned the reason you traveled to Mumbai, Sneed."

"I was visiting my girlfriend." Sneed was now looking up inside the ring to check for a common branding mark that indicates the number of carats. "There it is... twenty-four," he said unconsciously.

"Your girlfriend lives in Mumbai, does she? You must ride the train there often."

"No, this is my first trip, actually. I'm trying to figure out if I want to marry her. I first got to know Hyacinth when she worked in the Commercial Library section of the embassy. We dated a while, and then she was offered a higher paying job in Mumbai, where she also has family... so she jumped at the opportunity."

Sneed took out a roll of hundred dollar bills, and Logan's eyes dilated.

"I'll give you five hundred dollars for this ring right now, John."

Logan chuckled. "I won't lie to you, Sneed. It's worth at least that much. But the ring was a gift from my late grandmother, when I was a teenager, and it holds great sentimental value for me. It's not for sale."

"Come on, now, John. Everything on this earth is for sale. How much do you want for it? Name your price."

Logan suddenly liked the position he was in. He again looked at the roll of hundreds in Sneed's hand and thought about the two pair of diamond earrings and gold necklace in his pocket.

"I should really keep the ring, Sneed."

"Seven fifty? I'll give you seven hundred and fifty bucks right now."

"No, really." Logan could sense how badly Sneed desired to close the deal.

"One thousand. That's my final offer. And it's a helluva good deal for a ring that's worth half that much. Whaddya say?"

"I'll tell you what I'd like to do, Sneed, because you make such an attractive offer..." Logan then reached into his top right pocket and removed one pair of diamond earrings. "...See these earrings? These diamonds are almost two carats each. You give me two thousand dollars, and I'll throw in the Claddagh ring."

"I wasn't really in the market for any diamonds. And how do I know they're genuine? I'm somewhat of a gold aficionado, but I don't know much about diamonds..."

Logan interrupted. "I assure you they're real. I give you my word, Sneed."

Sneed looked closer at the earrings and then again at the unusual Claddagh ring, which Logan knew the American wanted so desperately.

"Buy the earrings for Hyacinth, Sneed. Wouldn't they make a lovely engagement gift, if you two were to get married?"

"I don't know. I'll give you fifteen hundred. Let's do it for fifteen hundred." Sneed was clearly trying to bargain the price down.

"I can't do fifteen, Sneed. My conscience won't allow it. Those earrings are almost two carats each. Let's be fair. I'm willing to throw in the ring at that price."

Sneed studied the earrings while rotating them in his hands. He then held one diamond up to the light, as if verifying that it was real, which he had no expertise in determining. Logan amusingly likened it to kicking a tire on an automobile before buying it.

"Alright, let's do this," Sneed agreed, and set the earrings and ring beside him on the bunk. He then commenced counting out twenty, one-hundred dollar bills.

"Good," Logan said, with imperceptible restraint, mindful that the appearance of too much satisfaction on his part might dissuade the Marine from completing the deal. In his mind, though, Logan was jumping up and down like he had just won the Irish Sweepstakes, because he was ever-conscious of how vital cash-money was to his survival on the run. He even considered introducing the other jewelry in his pocket, to take advantage of the situation, not knowing when a similar opportunity might arise and whether it would prove as fruitful. He thought about Sneed's obvious affinity for gold jewelry and wondered how much the necklace, containing locket, might fetch. But then he thought about the pictures of Trish and Liam inside the locket, and a torrent of emotions churned inside him. For a moment, he fantasized about returning to Ireland, one day, and finishing Trish off, but not before taunting her with the necklace by saying, "Ha! I bet you wondered where *this* has been all these years!" In the end, though, Logan decided not to bring to light the remaining jewelry, after speculating that he'd be able to raise greater cash through a Katmandu dealer.

Sneed handed Logan the two thousand dollars, and Logan counted it out before placing the money in a trouser pocket. Meanwhile, Sneed attempted to slide the Claddagh ring onto a finger of his muscular right hand, but the ring was too small.

"A jeweler is going to have to cut it and add some material to lengthen it," he said.

"That's easy enough," said John.

With the deal consummated, Sneed now judged it timely to query John on the conflicting accounts of his home in Ireland.

"John, I don't mean to pry, but you have me a little curious. Why did you tell the nun you were from Dublin after telling me you were from Antrim?"

"Ah, it's nuthin' really. I had been staying in Dublin in the recent past, that's all. Antrim is where I grew up, though."

That seemed to satisfy Sneed, so Logan let it go, but he still hoped the Marine wouldn't pursue the matter with Sister Mary Shaun, when Logan stepped out to cure a bout of cabin fever, because, as informed as the nun seemed to be about the killer that fled Ireland, the Antrim revelation could prove to be the straw that broke the camel's back. Logan subsequently envisioned himself being wrestled to the floor by train employees and then slithering free just long enough to dash and hurdle from the speeding train, only to tumble painfully in some thorny brush, with the remaining pair of diamond earrings and gold necklace flying from his person and getting lost during it all.

Logan had climbed back up to his bunk, since their post-transaction conversation, and Sneed laid back down on his bed while holding his hand up to admire his new acquisition, which he temporarily wore as a loose-fitting pinky-ring. A short while later, Sister Mary Shaun returned from her tour of the train's interior, purportedly intended to maintain her circulation, and she entered the compartment without making eye contact with Mr. Muldoon. Logan couldn't resist analyzing the nun's countenance and behavior, however, because he still feared she might've reckoned his true identity. Sneed naturally scrutinized her, also, due to John's account of their antagonistic exchange, and was impressed that the nun's jaunt seemed to have invigorated her; she now moved energetically inside the cabin and accessed her travel bag to secure her purse. Sister then sat prissily on the edge of her bunk, ostensibly to smooth some perceived wrinkles on her black religious dress, and finally looked over to her muscular cabin-mate on the corresponding lower bunk. She half-smiled, to acknowledge him, and then laid down, again covering herself urgently with a blanket.

Once Sister was situated, Sneed took the liberty of reaching over to dim the lights, and all parties eventually dozed off to sleep. They had been sleeping for more than two hours, in fact, according to my visual packet, until a knock on the door roused them, which was followed by a steward's muffled advice that a meal service was being provided. Sneed bellowed for the attendant to enter, and a young, mustachioed man in crisp, white attire promptly did so while carrying a stack of three covered meals. The attendant squeezed through to the rear of the compartment, where he lowered a table latched onto the wall and placed the meals in a manner that assumed the occupants would be dining together. The young man then delayed futilely, in hope of a gratuity, and bowed negligibly before departing.

Well, given the precedent hostile discussion between Sister and Logan, it didn't surprise that the nun had other ideas about the dining arrangements. There was no way in heaven or on earth that she'd be breaking bread with a man she'd resolutely deemed fiendish. Instead, Sister sat up, pulled the blanket from herself, stepped over to collect her meal, and returned to her bunk. Once she was seated, Sneed rolled out and shuffled over to look under the remaining two lids to discover which contained meat. He then recalled John's patently disappointed reaction when learning he'd be getting a veggie-only meal.

"John, would you like this meal with the chicken? Why don't you go ahead and take it. You look like you could use a little meat on your bones."

"If you don't mind, that would be *grand*, Sneed. Thanks ever so much," Logan said politely, in part for the nun's benefit.

Logan was so grateful for Sneed's gesture of kindness, in fact, that he decided not to try to rob the Marine of his remaining money, which he had been fantasizing about doing ever since Sneed revealed the wad of hundreds. Halfway through the meal, Sister Mary Shaun noticed the Claddagh ring on Sneed's right hand and then looked over to John, sitting at the small table without his ring, and remarked to Sneed in an uncharacteristic, snide manner, "You fellas get hitched while I was away?"

"Sister?" Sneed looked up. The Marine had no idea what the nun was talking about.

"You're wearing Mr. *Muldoon's* ring."

Logan interpreted by the nun's contemptuous intonation that she still didn't believe who he claimed to be, but said nothing and continued eating.

"Oh, John and I conducted a little business," Sneed replied. "I really like the ring. It's very unusual."

"Yes, I told Sneed that I could just pick up a replacement when returning home to Ireland, where they're plentiful," John chimed in.

Logan had looked directly at the nun when talking, but she stayed true to her word and didn't speak to him. Logan wasn't about to kiss the nun's ass, though. As long as she hadn't experienced an "aha" moment concerning his identity, and notified authorities, he didn't care much. In fact, Logan found himself relaxing, before long, after no train employees sought to enter their compartment under any questionable circumstances.

Soon both Sneed and the nun were again sleeping, and Logan pulled out his replacement paperback book about the life and times of Michael Collins. An hour later, he tired of reading and sensed Sneed stirring, so, in a hushed tone, invited the Marine out for a cold drink and a snack. Sneed thanked "John" but stated he didn't currently require any refreshments; nonetheless, Logan coaxed him out of the compartment after gesticulating that he wished to speak with him privately, away from Sister Mary Shaun. This time, Sneed agreed, and as the two moved cautiously through the cabin door, so as to not disturb the nun, Sister opened her eyes, and she and "Mr. Muldoon" looked directly at one another. The nun kept her eyes fixed on him, in fact, until satisfied that Mr. Muldoon was aware that she knew of his movements, and not until then did she look away.

Logan's reasons for wanting to speak to Sneed privately were simple. He knew that Sneed had resided in India long enough that he likely possessed a breadth of knowledge of the country, and his advice could ultimately influence how and to where Logan proceeded. Logan had already resolved to begin his trek in the Himalayan foothills but needed reliable information about safe, worthwhile destinations in northern India, and preferred to discuss matters away from the nun's earshot, in case Sister was to eventually experience that "aha" moment and reference the places to authorities.

Sneed couldn't have known he was being exploited during their excursion to the refreshment stand, and soon Logan had the Marine describing, in great detail, a bus trip he and Hyacinth had once taken from New Delhi to the Garhwal and Kumaon regions, where they stayed for five days and, among other places, visited a wildlife preserve, Corbett National Park. Cunning Logan behaved intrigued and wanted to hear more about the preserve, but not because he desired to tour the area: he secretly wished to avoid it because of the carnivorous tigers and leopards he imagined encountering. Sneed also described some villages where he and Hyacinth had spent the night, and Logan behaved uninterested in those places, all the while taking careful mental notes. And once Logan was confident that Sneed was persuaded that "John" was determined to visit Corbett National Park and commence hiking toward Everest from that locale, Logan changed the subject, but not before suggesting that he would likely travel there via small aircraft, if not by bus. By now, Logan had talked Sneed into drinking a soda with him, and the two men shared a package of peanut butter crackers that John purchased.

All this lying and deceit had been inconvenient for Logan but was necessary to cover his tracks because of the unlikely emergence of the Irish nun, with the active, intuitive mind, who had once, paradoxically, taught Logan's latest murder victim, my daughter, Tessie Doyle.

Before the two men returned to the compartment to rejoin Sister Mary Shaun, Logan cleverly sought to capitalize on the relationship engendered by their earlier jewelry transaction, by persuading his American companion to never disclose, to the nun, the Himalayan foothill destinations they had discussed. "I fully understand that the old bird's not about to call on me for a cup of tea... but I don't want to satisfy her prying mind about where I'm going in the Himalayas," John had told Sneed.

On the other hand, if Sneed, after disembarking and going about life in New Delhi, was ever to learn John's true identity, then Logan knew that all they had talked about would be out the window, and that Sneed would inevitably report their encounter to authorities. By that time, Logan hoped to be far beyond northern India. But then he recalled he had also foolishly disclosed to Sneed, during their first moments together, that he ultimately sought to climb Mount Everest in Nepal. He now cursed himself, as he often did, for his slip of tongue, and considered using his trusty twine cutter, still tucked away in his satchel, to remedy the situation. But how could he pull it off? Even if not in his current scrawny state, he doubted he could overpower the highly trained, muscular Marine. Alternatively, if he struck Sneed as he slept, Logan would also need to polish off the nun. But then if two passengers were found dead in the cabin, and he was nowhere to be found, it would only be a matter of time before police zeroed in on him. No, Logan would have to roll the dice on this one.

44

LOGAN HAD EARLIER ANTICIPATED wandering out to relieve a bout of cabin fever but, presently, decided against it because he remained paranoid that Sneed might unwittingly disclose critical information to Sister Mary Shaun; by staying in their company, the two wouldn't speculate about him. The three mostly slept and rested during those remaining hours, until interrupted for an in-cabin snack service, followed by another tea service, during which time the little conversation that took place expectedly occurred between either Logan and Sneed, or Sneed and Sister.

Logan experienced great relief once the Radjhani Express slowed and began rocking, which signaled their approach into New Delhi. Presently, he wasn't sure if the train was scheduled to continue on to Calcutta, in which case Sister would likely remain in the compartment, or if she needed to disembark and board a different train; and, if that were the case, he intended to shadow Sneed until they broke far away from the nun.

Once the train halted, Sister sat up in her bunk and removed herself to the chair where she had earlier taken tea. She gawked unabashedly, as Logan and Sneed gathered their belongings, but chose not to speak. Sneed finally bid the nun farewell and conveyed how much he enjoyed talking with her during their journey, to which she responded by simply smiling. As for "Mr. Muldoon," he waited until Sneed was through the door with his bag, before turning and saying, "Sister, I hope you have a safe and holy sabbatical to Calcutta... and Darjeeling," to which the nun nodded faintly.

The Radjhani Express was evidently continuing on to Calcutta, Logan surmised, because Sister was staying put.

At 1 a.m., Sneed, followed by Logan, stepped from the train into a technicolored sea of passengers and receivers. Logan's eyes naturally darted about, searching for police, at the same time feeling liberated to be parting the nun's company. While serpentining their way seemingly conjointly through the crowd toward the terminal, Logan asked Sneed if he cared to join him for a nightcap at the bar of his choice in New Delhi. Logan had really only been testing Sneed, though, after again developing unhealthy notions of killing and robbing the Marine – killing him because of what he knew, robbing him for the valuable resources he possessed. Sneed had slept much during the trip from Mumbai and wouldn't sleep right away upon reaching his New Delhi domicile, nevertheless, declined the nightcap offer. Logan actually felt relieved that he wouldn't be put in a position where he felt obliged to act on his deadly impulses. Moreover, he imagined how Sister Mary Shaun would react if picking up a Calcutta newspaper and reading about her murdered former cabin-mate. *The nun would instantly attribute the death to "John Muldoon,"* he thought, *and contact police immediately.*

In the end, Logan coyly asked Sneed to direct him to where he could make a bus connection north, an inquiry he could've made through any station employee. Sneed pointed to a sign, shook John's hand, and the two parted without otherwise speaking. But once stepping away, Sneed turned to yell to John while smiling, "John, I really like the ring. Thanks for making the deal with me." Logan only grinned and gave the "okay" sign, which, consequently, made him feel like a horrible, defective human being, because of the violence he had contemplated committing on the kind man.

45

As stated, the advice Logan had sought from Sneed concerning a bus connection north had only been a diversion, in case Sneed was to eventually discover Logan's identity and notify authorities. In reality, Logan had already resolved to board a train traveling northeast and thought the red herring might buy him some time if police were to pursue him. In his mind, though, he knew that any police agency worth its salt would cover all modes of transportation into and out of the city.

Logan soon discovered that although he'd be resuming train travel, it was necessary to leave the New Delhi train station, in which he stood, and make his way to the old Delhi railway station to make his connection. He thusly hired a bicycle-rickshaw operator to transport him to the station; during their progress, a full moon aided in revealing some breathtakingly beautiful, intricately ornamented structures in the city, their juxtaposition to abject poverty notwithstanding.

Once inside the Delhi station, he learned that he'd again require a reservation to make passage, but small bribes to a customer service agent and the agent's manager secured him a seat; he slumbered more than two hours before boarding the Rhaniket Express, at 3:55 a.m., bound for Kathgodam in the Kumaon region.

The train was scheduled to arrive at noon and would leave him thirty-five kilometers short of the town of Nainital, where Sneed and Hyacinth had once stayed at a spacious, two-level tourist home.

According to Sneed's earlier description, the proprietors also operated a business, "Foothill Trekkers," which provided guides for hire on climbs of varying degrees of difficulty. While Sneed and Hyacinth hadn't taken advantage of the guide services during their stay, Sneed had enthusiastically explained to "John" how they were able to pick up trails "directly behind Bolington Cottage" and venture out for half-day and day-long hikes. Logan had also etched, in his mind, Sneed's memorable description of the sultry lady of the home, Chandra, who managed cottage affairs while her husband, Ravi, principal guide, escorted climber-guests into the Himalayan foothills, most days. "If I hadn't been going out with Hyacinth, I think I would've traveled up there every weekend to hike... despite Chandra being married," Sneed had said. "I wish I had a picture of this woman to show you, John... very exotic and alluring."

Logan felt incongruously irritable but calm upon arriving at the Kathgodam station. Irritable because he hadn't rested well on the Rhaniket Express, after deciding not to spring for a comfortable AC compartment; calm, because it soon became obvious that this mountainous region was far less populated, a conclusion he drew once observing that the station lacked the same hustle and bustle as those in New Delhi, Delhi, and Mumbai.

He immediately sought out a telephone directory to inquire of any vacancies at Bolington Cottage, so that his impending twenty-plus-mile journey wouldn't be in vain. A friendly woman, with verging on husky voice, yet feminine and youthful, answered the telephone.

"Good afternoon. Bolington Cottage."

"Hello. Yes, my name is Mike Harrington... traveling from England. Would you happen to have any vacancies?"

"Well, that depends. Unless we have an empty house, we usually give priority to guests who intend on utilizing our guide services. How many are you?"

"Sorry?"

"How many in your party, sir?"

"Oh, I got you. Just myself. But I *will* be doing some trekking, I assure you. I'm still unfamiliar with the area, so can say with some certitude that I'll be taking advantage of a guide."

"Okay, well, as it turns out we just had a party of three leave us, which frees up two bedrooms. Do you think you'll be requiring a large room? Because I think I'd like to keep that bedroom available for a couple."

"I'm easy to please, really. The smaller and less expensive, the better."

"When do you expect to arrive, Mr. Harrington?"

"I'm not sure, because I feel like a fish out of water here. One or two hours?"

"Where are you now?"

"I'm talking to you from inside the Kathgodam train station."

"Well, today's your lucky day, isn't it? My husband Ravi is dropping off the party of three, I just referenced, at Kathgodam. They're due to catch an afternoon train. Do you currently see any Caucasians in the passenger waiting area... two men and a woman sitting together?"

"No, I don't."

"Good. That means that Ravi probably hasn't arrived yet. I'll call him on his cellphone to inform him that you'll be staying with us. What do you look like, Mr. Harrington?"

"Call me Mike, please. And how shall I address you?"

"My name's Chandra."

"Nice to meet you, Chandra. Well, I'm taller than six feet, white male on the lean side, light brown hair. I'm middle-aged... forty-one years young."

Chandra laughed. "Goodness, I guess that forces me to think of myself in terms of being middle-aged, which I hadn't done 'til now. I'm just a year younger. Anyhow, Ravi should be pulling up outside the station within the next few minutes. He's driving an American SUV, a dark green Ford Expedition. He's in his early fifties... salt and pepper hair, a beard, and glasses."

"Got it."

"By the way, it'll cost you six-hundred-sixty rupees, per day, for the room, which includes a continental breakfast, plus tea in the afternoon. Some guests join us for dinner also, in which case I require advanced notice... and, naturally, that costs extra. But we can talk about all that after you arrive. For now, you best step outside and keep your eyes peeled for Ravi, who I'll call straight away. Okay?"

"That's *grand*, Chandra. Thanks for your wonderful help. Bye."

"G'bye, Mike. See you soon."

46

LOGAN MCCOOL STOOD LEISURELY outside the Kathgodam station and people-watched while taking in views and waiting patiently for the vehicle Chandra had described. Once beholding the bulky, green SUV, he assumed that Chandra had gotten through to Ravi, to apprise him of their incoming guest, because of the way the bearded, bespectacled man shifted in his seat to regard him through the windshield.

Ravi parked curbside, climbed out urgently to help his passengers with their luggage, and then turned to the lone Caucasian standing nearby.

"Hello, are you Mr. Harrington?"

"Yes, I am. Call me Mike, please. You must be Ravi."

"Please allow me to help our departing guests with their things, and you and I can proceed directly."

"That would be grand, Ravi. Take your time."

Ravi carried two medium-sized duffle bags to just outside the station's main entrance and placed them down, while the three guests collected their remaining belongings from inside the vehicle. All parties shook hands with Ravi, and the young lady embraced him before they entered the station. Ravi then tugged upward on his trousers and ambled over to "Mike Harrington" while adjusting his eyeglasses with his left hand and extending his right hand.

"Ravi Dilwali," he said, more formally.

"Nice to meet you, Ravi. I've heard wonderful things about your beautiful place and how one can pick up a hiking trail right near your home."

"That's true. *Many* trails, in fact. Please, let's get on our way."

Ravi held the passenger side door open for "Mike" who sat in the seat and placed his stuffed satchel at his feet.

"You're very kind. I can manage, really," Mike said.

Ravi paced to the driver's side, climbed in, started the engine, shifted into Drive, and eased forward.

"You're traveling very light, Mike," he noted right away.

"Yes, I am... but I thought if I needed any climbing-related gear, I could just purchase it locally. My plan was to take some daytrips while in the Kumaon region, and I didn't want the inconvenience of hauling a lot of extra bags."

Given his life's journey, Logan didn't frighten easily, but, presently, the narrow hillside roads, lacking guardrails, which demanded Ravi's undivided attention, but which the Indian negotiated so skillfully and calmly, were proving a real source of distress for Logan.

"You mentioned you heard about Bolington Cottage from *someone*. Who, may I ask?"

"Oh, just some chap on the train from Mumbai. I didn't get his name." Logan lied.

"Did he stay with us recently? What did he look like?"

"The impression I got was that he lives in New Delhi and he had stayed with you long ago. He was Indian." Logan lied again because he knew if he disclosed Sneed's identity, and something were to go awry during his visit to Bolington Cottage, that a consultation between the two might hasten police involvement and result in his capture.

"My wife Chandra said you're from England. Where exactly?"

"Cornwall. It's in the south."

"I know where it is. I visited England when my brother was attending Cambridge. I toured Salisbury Cathedral, Stonehenge, among other places, and remember seeing Cornwall on a map. Funny, you don't sound English."

"I'm British, I assure you."

Logan fretted, and hoped that Ravi wouldn't ask anything specific about Cornwall, because he had never traveled there and knew nothing about the place. He then sat benumbed, trying to figure out how he had even come up with Cornwall. He quickly changed the topic.

"Do you think you might be available to guide me on a day-hike sometime this week, Ravi?"

"Oh, I'm sure I can work it in." He then chuckled. "I had *better* be able to work it in. That's what pays the bills... that and the guest revenue."

Logan chortled. "Yeah, right."

Logan managed to relax some once they passed into some of the gentler valleys of Kumaon, where they had a lesser chance of rolling down a roadside and crashing to their fiery deaths. He soon found the landscape welcoming, mainly because of the wide-open, undulating, golden fields that merged gradually with more dramatic hillsides, where several cottages now dotted the landscape. Most of the cottages were well kept; a few had signs posted, advertising vacancies. Logan grew encouraged and thought that if his temporary living arrangements at Bolington Cottage didn't work out, he could always move up the road.

"You've come to the Kumaon region at a very desirable time of year," Ravi said. "We're just finishing with monsoon season. I think you'll find the mornings crisp at times."

"Good sleeping weather," Mike replied.

"Indeed," said Ravi, smiling and turning to look at his passenger. "How long do you plan to stay with us?"

"A few days. Perhaps longer."

"This is our place up on the right," Ravi said.

"Looks very nice."

The Bolington Cottage that they approached was very different from the inn Logan had imagined, after listening to Sneed's description the night before. He expected a modest abode set far off the road, at the base of a small mountain range that gradually integrated with higher ranges to the north or west. The cottage he currently made out looked to be a sizeable, stucco or stone-constructed home, which was situated close to the road, and the land in back dropped off to form a grassy basin before rising again to fuse with a dramatic hillside. There, Logan espied the advent of the worn "Foothill Trekkers" trail network. In the distance behind the range, he plainly noticed some of the more colossal Himalayan Mountains that he knew to stretch up toward Mount Everest in Nepal.

The cottage itself featured a conspicuous albeit pale, red, tin roof and an enclosed porch on the front side, near the road. If not entering the home through the rear door, one needed to pass through the porch in order to gain access to the main floor. Outside the front and sides of the home, a multitude of large, terracotta pots, boasting a variety of colorful flowers, lined the perimeter. What's more, a flourishing English-style garden accentuated the backside of the domicile, where some outdoor furniture was situated on an abutting grassy terrace, so that one could sit out and enjoy the natural ambiance.

Once Ravi pulled the imposing Ford Expedition into the gravel lot adjacent to the home, Chandra heard the engine and emerged from the backyard, where she had been pruning flowers.

Oh my God, Logan thought to himself. *Would you look at this. Sneed was right on the money* (with his description of Chandra). He was too mesmerized to speak. Following an awkward moment of silence, Ravi finally said, "That's my wife, Chandra... who you spoke with over the telephone."

"She looks like a lovely lady," Logan only said.

Chandra was an exotic brown beauty with Aryan features yet with a hint of the Orient in her eyes – eyes so dark that she often appeared sedated, which contributed to her sultriness but contradicted her refreshing sobriety, and high energy, that Logan would soon come to appreciate. She wore a casual white blouse, suitable for gardening, and light blue, Capri-style pants that came down to just below her knees. Logan noticed that the woman hadn't shaved her legs for several days but that didn't put him off. The only thing that detracted from her appearance, he decided, according to his western standards, was the customary red dot in the middle of her forehead. He glimpsed her feet, through her sandals, and saw that she had painted her toenails. He then panned up to her hands, after she removed her gardening gloves in anticipation of shaking his hand, and saw that her fingernails were also painted: a purply, crimson shade that played perfectly off her bronze skin. Her shoulder-length hair had been tied in a girlish ponytail, to keep it from her face while gardening, but she had just pulled on a glittery elastic band to free it, causing the hair to fall to her shoulders and frame her wonderfully symmetrical face. Logan was overcome. *She's doing this for my benefit,* he thought, ogling her through the windshield. For a moment, Chandra's raven black hair reminded him of Shadia, the

Somalian beauty, because of the way her hair similarly took on a bluish hue when sunlight refracted within it.

Ravi shut down the engine, and the two men climbed out from the SUV. Ravi spoke to Chandra in a Hindi dialect, obviously to prevent their guest from understanding, but Chandra sauntered over to Mike without responding or even looking at her husband.

"Welcome to Nainital, Mr. Harrington." She extended her hand, her smile melting Logan.

"I prefer Mike, really. It's nice to meet you in person, Chandra. What a delightful place you and Ravi have here. I just love all the flowers."

Chandra still smiled charmingly, and Logan stood before her looking like he had just arrived at the prime rib station of an upscale buffet, eagerly awaiting a juicy piece of meat.

"Yes, well, I wasn't born with such a green thumb, I assure you," she said.

Chandra then looked over to Ravi and asked him in Hindi to collect Mike's lone bag from the car. When Logan saw him reaching across the inside of the vehicle for his satchel, he reached to snatch it before Ravi could take hold of it.

"I'm just traveling with this one bag, and it's so light. I can manage, really."

"Very well," said Chandra. "Won't you come inside and have some tea. I've been steeping a pot in anticipation of your arrival."

"Oh, that would be *grand*, Chandra. I couldn't imagine anything better."

Ravi again spoke to Chandra in Hindi, to inform her of his plans for the rest of the afternoon, and then said to Mike, "I'll just catch up with you later... after you've had chance to settle in. I have some things to attend to in town."

"That's fine, Ravi," said Mike, "I look forward to consulting with you about a trek... when the time is right."

"Yes, we'll do that. See you later."

Logan waved faintly as Ravi climbed into his vehicle and turned over the ignition. The Indian backed up and sped away.

Logan looked to Chandra and wondered how many opportunities he would have to be alone with this bronze goddess during his stay, and if she would ever respond to him the way he presently yearned.

"Any other guests staying with you?" Mike asked.

"Just one, but he's returning to Punjab tomorrow. The house is emptying in a hurry. It often happens that way. It's either feast or famine, it seems. Come along, now. Let's have that tea."

"Yes, let's," said Mike.

Chandra started to lead the way but then paused to take Logan's arm, to escort him. She had only been trying to be polite at the time, but Logan interpreted it differently and became aroused. When reaching the porch, she let go of his arm to enter first, and Logan glanced from left to right and noticed several padded chaise lounges, comfortable chairs, and a daybed set up for guests' use.

"This is a nice space," he said.

Chandra turned only part way but looked directly into his eyes before saying in her throaty voice, "Yes, it's very pleasant. Guests often read and nap here. I generally take tea here, except during the summer months... because of the strong afternoon sun. If I don't lower the shades in the summer, the passive solar heat turns the porch into a sauna. But it's cloudy enough today that I shouldn't have to bother. Please... come in."

They entered the home and were soon greeted by a young woman who had been dusting the parlor; she did most of the house cleaning and helped with cooking and serving when Bolington Cottage was full.

"This is Lali. If it wasn't for her, I'd have no life at all."

The woman steepled her fingers, first in front of her chest, and subsequently at her forehead, to recognize the divinity in their new guest, and as a means to greet him.

"Hello, Lali. I'm Mike," said Logan.

The young woman grinned demurely and dipped in a curtsy-like gesture, before resuming her dusting.

Chandra asked Mike to sit in the parlor while she retrieved the tea service. When she returned two minutes later, Lali left the room.

"I suppose it wouldn't shock you to hear that I prefer this region of India over the south," Mike said.

Chandra laughed out loud.

"The crowds and chaos can be overwhelming, no? Yes, the population is sparser in these parts, and the pace commensurately slower. Although, if you were to venture out and attend one of our Kumaon festivals, you'd experience similar congestion... only on a smaller scale." Chandra placed a cup and saucer before Logan. "How do you take your tea, Mike?"

"I prefer my tea the way Robert DeNiro likes his women... black."

Chandra's hearty laugh caused her to bend forward.

"That's very funny. I needed to hear a good joke after working so hard over the past few days."

"Is this tea from Darjeeling, by chance?" Mike asked, to demonstrate some knowledge of her country.

"No, it's not. Darjeeling is famous for its excellent teas, but we grow some very fine teas here in the Kumaon region, also... and they cost much less. You should take advantage while here. By the way, how long do you intend on staying with us, Mike?"

"You know, Ravi asked me that same question during the ride over, and I told him 'a few days,' but I could honestly see myself staying longer. Does that pose any problems for you?"

"No, not at all. As I mentioned, the house would've been empty tomorrow if not for you arriving. And as much as I welcome a respite, it's always best to have guests."

Chandra poured tea into two cups for them, and Logan raised his cup.

"Cheers. Thanks for being so hospitable," he said, resting his eyes contemplatively on her.

"Cheers to you," she said and took a sip.

Chandra plainly sensed Mike's lustful eyes, but many male guests had looked at her that way over the years, so she didn't think much of it.

Logan noticed a picture of Chandra, Ravi, and a little girl, on an end table across the room.

"Is that you and Ravi in the picture?"

"Yes, and our beloved daughter, Lakshmi, who's six years old. Lakshmi's visiting with my mother in Bangalore for a month or so. In recent years, I've sent her to stay with her during busy times here, because it lightens the load for Ravi, Lali, and me. Sometimes she ends up staying longer."

"That's nice of your mother. Did you say that Ravi is Lakshmi's father? I'm sorry, I just happened to notice that she's lighter in complexion. I hope that doesn't sound rude."

"Oh, no. That's okay. Ravi's the father, I assure you... although, I was once married to an Australian for one short year. David and I met in Bangalore and married young, but it didn't work out. As far as opposites attracting, I had always had a thing for Caucasian men, but

David turned out to be too immature. A bit of a drinker, also. What about you, Mike? Do you drink?"

"Yes, I've been known to take a taste, but alcohol isn't a problem in my life. You?"

"Yes, I like a drink of rum once or twice a month. What's your poison?"

"I'm a beer and whiskey man, I suppose, but I'd hardly turn down a good rum if that was the drink being offered."

Logan threw Chandra a devilish look, and she laughed.

"Well, we'll look forward to a taste tomorrow, perhaps."

Chandra lifted a small plate of butter cookies and offered one to Mike. He removed a cookie without taking his eyes from her. The beauty smirked and took a cookie for herself but did not discourage his gaze. Their sexual tension magnified.

47

LOGAN HAD AWAKENED BEFORE his hosts due to some ruckus in the neighboring bedroom, caused by the other guest, Magesh, who had risen early to pack for Punjab. Logan opened his bedroom window, to allow some fresh air to circulate, but shut it once experiencing the bracing morning air that Ravi had referenced during their ride from Kathgodam.

The evening before, Logan had joined Ravi, Chandra, and Magesh for a goat curry dinner, during which Chandra saw to it that "Mike" received an ample share of meat, after deciding that her new British friend wouldn't fare very well on some of the more rigorous hikes if he didn't eat well. As hosts, Ravi and Chandra had sat at opposite ends of the dining table while Logan sat across from the bearded, turbaned Sikh, Magesh. Chandra offered more basmati rice to Logan, and he simultaneously felt a bare foot brush against his pant leg. In one sense, Logan delighted, because he assumed that Chandra had done it intentionally and that they were on their way to becoming intimate. But the action also startled him to the extent that he lurched, and it interrupted the engrossing conversation he was having with Magesh about life in Punjab.

"Something wrong, Mike?" Ravi asked.

"Oh, no. Just a spasm of some sort. With the lengthy travel, jet lag, time difference, and all, I haven't felt normal since arriving in India, really. I'm sure I'll be fine, though," Logan lied.

Logan looked across to Magesh, to encourage him to continue with his story, but also glanced at beautiful Chandra, who had just taken a bite of food and smiled impishly while the fork still rested between her teeth. *The brush of her foot had been no accident*, he thought. Logan soon became so aroused that he wouldn't have been able to stand if the house had been on fire. He then wondered, given the volume of guests that stayed at Bolington Cottage each year, if Chandra behaved this way regularly. *Perhaps, she's a nymphomaniac*, he thought.

Due to the intrigue Magesh had instilled in him about Punjab, or perhaps it had been the Indian's skillful storytelling ability, Logan composed himself and reengaged Magesh. He was subsequently interested to learn that, unlike Hindus, who worship multiple gods, Sikhs are monotheistic and non-idolatrous and reject the caste system that's so widely practiced in India. Following dinner, Lali cleared the dishes and returned with the tea service and a tray of tapioca puddings, placing a bowl before each of the four. Ravi scarfed down his pudding, collected his nearly full teacup, and abandoned the saucer. "Sorry, friends, I've got some computer work," he said, excusing himself from the table.

Chandra harrumphed forthrightly to express her dissatisfaction over Ravi's early departure; that, on the heels of her husband acting aloof over dinner.

"Don't mind Ravi," she attempted to explain to newcomer Mike Harrington after her husband vacated, "he's not anti-social. It's just that he sees so many guests coming and going."

Chandra now stood up from the table in a manner that suggested she was about to take Ravi to task for being impolite to their guests and embarrassing her. She then paused to sip some tea, seemingly in deliberation, and marched across the floor. Logan and Magesh had remained speechless during it all, until Logan finally looked across to Magesh and said:

"I think Ravi has it coming."

"I think you do, too, Mike," said Magesh.

Logan then felt a bare foot run across his leg again.

It had been Magesh all along! Here Logan had been fantasizing about beautiful Chandra being a nymphomaniac, and it was this macho bastard sitting across from him, wearing the turban, who had been trying to play footsie. Logan seized his pudding and tea from the table and strutted out to the porch. In any other setting, volatile Logan likely would've punched the man out, but, as a new guest in the home, he elected to resign his position at the table.

Lali had since returned to the dining room to refresh everyone's tea, and, when learning that Mike was out on the porch, she followed with teapot in hand.

"More tea, sir?" Lali offered.

"That would be lovely. Thanks, Lali," said "Mike."

Mike and Lali then experienced an uncomfortable moment as they plainly heard Chandra raising her voice to Ravi, prompting Lali to depart. After a minute or two Chandra emerged on the porch looking flustered, which Logan thought only to enhance her beauty.

"Mind if I join you?" Chandra asked.

"You don't even need to ask. It's your home, first of all... secondly, you grace any room."

Logan's flattering words instantly diffused Chandra's simmering ire and she blushed. She then leaned toward the open doorway and summoned Lali in their native dialect to retrieve her tea and pudding from the dinner table and serve her out on the porch. The young woman did so, and, after vacating, Logan innocently questioned Chandra about Magesh.

"So... Magesh is leaving Nainital tomorrow, is he?"

"That's correct."

"First time here?"

"Pardon?"

"Has Magesh visited with you before, or was this his first time at Bolington Cottage?"

"Oh, he's a regular. Usually twice a year."

"Did you know he's a fancy-boy?"

Chandra laughed out loud. She thought she knew what Mike implied but asked him to clarify.

"How do you mean?"

"He'd prefer a slow dance with me rather than you."

Chandra again laughed gleefully.

"I like your twisted sense of humor, Mike. Actually, I had some idea of Magesh's orientation, after Ravi commented a few years back. He thought that Magesh might be coming on to him."

"In all the years he's been visiting, has Magesh ever made a play for *you?*"

"No," she said, and tisked.

"Well, there you have it. He's a fancy-boy." Logan sipped his tea pensively and looked to Chandra. "I was hoping that the probing foot I felt under the dinner table had been yours, but... not so."

At first, Chandra only smiled and dug into her tapioca pudding.

"So, you enjoy a good game of footsie, do you?" she asked risqué and then licked her spoon slowly while resting her eyes on him.

"Just as much as the next bloke, I suppose," he said, maintaining eye contact. "Lali ever leave you alone in the house when Ravi is off in the foothills?"

Chandra understood perfectly.

"She's not my aunt, you know. Lali works for *me*... and if I want her to do some food shopping tomorrow, then she'll do it." Chandra turned the spoon over in her mouth and again licked it methodically while looking longingly at him. There was no mistaking the provocative imagery.

"But where will Ravi be? He has no clients to guide... except me... and I plan on being here."

"Ravi will revel at the opportunity to break from his normal routine, despite the lack of revenue generating events... which reminds me, Mike. We request that our guests pay in advance, and I neglected to collect the money for your stay when you arrived earlier. It's 660 rupees per day, remember?"

"I do. Will you take U.S. dollars?"

"Yes, I'll take the equivalent. I've certainly accommodated guests that way in the past."

"Good. I appreciate it. I have some rupees, but I'm a tad short." Logan lied because he cared not to get caught short, in case he was forced on the run in India, and preferred to spend dollars before rupees.

Lali had risen first and routinely readied the continental breakfast for guests by arranging some crumpets, orange marmalade, blackberry jam, butter, honey, and hot sweet-tea on the table, where the foursome had dined the night before. The pleasant aroma of the warm, unsweetened flat cakes had since wafted upstairs and caused Logan's mouth to water. He sensed that Magesh was still packing, next door, and he hadn't yet heard Ravi or Chandra stirring, so he slinked down to break his fast. He subsequently detected some feet pressing on the creaky stairs, leading from the second floor to the main floor of the home, and soon perceived Magesh, who set down his lone, hulking travel bag near the door to the porch before joining him in the dining room. Predictably, neither party spoke. Logan was hungry enough that he thought he might like a second crumpet so remained at the perimeter of the room with his plate on his lap. Meanwhile, he studied the queer, Magesh, shifting about the table, and deemed him bad mannered, despite the Sikh's sophisticated monologue the night before, because he had just reached up to make an adjustment to his visibly-soiled turban and then stroked his beard, before considering several crumpet offerings with his hands, as if they were tomatoes on a market stand. Given Magesh's ignorant actions, Logan was grateful he had arrived first at the table and that the man was leaving this day; he would not a fetch a second crumpet from this batch. Instead, Logan entered the kitchen to report Magesh's infraction to Lali, who thankfully, but exasperatingly, retrieved the remaining crumpets from the table, following Magesh's adjournment to the porch to wait for Ravi to drive him to the Kathgodam station. *I might be a killer, but at least I'm not a pig*, rationalized Logan. Due to his simple report, Logan would unknowingly score big points with Chandra, who likely would've eaten one of the tainted flat cakes, after Lali later conveyed his thoughtfulness and consideration.

Logan dallied while Lali prepared and delivered a replacement batch to the table, and he ate a second crumpet slathered with butter and marmalade and drank a second cup of tea. He then returned upstairs to his bedroom and showered in one of the community bathrooms, finally laying down again to resume reading his paperback book about Michael Collins. He couldn't remember feeling so relaxed.

Two hours later, he had tired of reading and sat up in bed. He now weighed venturing outside to explore the grassy basin behind Bolington Cottage, perhaps even hike up into the foothills. He also thought of beautiful Chandra, and what her current occupations might be, but he cared not to be obtrusive on, this, only his second day as a guest. Suddenly, he heard a light tapping of fingernails on his door.

"Yes," he said.

"Mike, it's Chandra. Sorry to disturb you."

"Oh, you're not disturbing me." Logan leapt up to seize open the door, and Chandra recognized his eagerness.

"Are you finding everything you need?" she coyly asked, attempting to mask her underlying reason for being there.

"Yes, thank you."

Logan couldn't avoid noticing how Chandra had made an effort to fix herself up this day. She had shampooed her hair and brushed it back on top in order to poof it; she looked like a princess without her tiara. She wore a soothing, lavender blouse and had left the top two buttons unfastened, which naturally drew his eyes down to her faintly exposed cleavage. At first, he didn't deem the presentation necessarily provocative, until recalling the white blouse she had worn the day before, which had only one button left undone at the top. She also had on rather tight-fitting, white jeans. She wore lipstick this day, which matched the color of her fingernail polish, in addition to smoky eye shadow. Also, the traditional red dot he had plainly noticed on her forehead, the day before, was missing. Logan now wondered if Chandra had waited until Ravi and Lali left the house before making herself up in this manner, so as to not clue them in to her intentions.

"What's your plan today?" she asked innocently, as if having forgotten their conversation on the porch last eve, which was laced with sexual innuendo.

"Well, I thought I might endeavor into the foothills... at some point. But there's no hurry."

"Ravi drove Magesh to Kathgodam this morning... then he's headed over to the lake. We have friends there who own horses, and he'll play polo... probably 'til mid-afternoon."

Logan knew that he and Chandra were thinking along the same lines. He shuffled over to her, so that they now talked face to face.

"What about Lali?" He edged closer, still, and would imminently feel her warm breath as she spoke.

"I sent her to the market thirty minutes ago. She'll be gone for two to three hours."

He leaned toward Chandra and pecked her lips once, and she did not disallow his advance, so he shifted and reached to clasp her shoulders and kiss her more substantially. She responded by wrapping her arms around his waist, which caused him to shudder, once comprehending what he was about to do with the exotic beauty. He then kissed her deeply in a full embrace, while exploring her mouth with his tongue, but soon released in order to prod her forward, so that he could shut the door and lay her down.

"Not here," she said.

He kissed her again, this time more lightly, and reached to open the door, eventually picking her up like a groom carrying his bride over the threshold. They exited into the hallway.

"Where's your bedroom," he asked.

"I won't violate my marital bed," she replied.

"Where, then?"

"Put me down, please."

She took him by the hand and led him downstairs. Once reaching the main level of the home, she opened the door to the porch and let go of his hand.

"Pull the daybed away from the wall," she kindly instructed.

"It's a tad narrow... for two people, don't you think?"

"Yes, well... but you'll be on top of me, won't you."

She sauntered around the inside of the porch and paused to lower the shades on the three exposed sides, even though the position of the Sun didn't warrant it. Once the shades were down, she locked the porch door, to prevent anyone from walking in on them, and swaggered to the daybed while unbuttoning her lavender blouse.

"It's best you undress yourself... in the interest of time," she said with discernible naughtiness.

Logan stripped completely in the time it took her to remove her blouse and bra. She giggled at his eagerness, but he mistakenly perceived it mockingly, due to his ultra-slender body, which was just rebounding, really, due to a calorie deficiency in recent months.

"Everything alright?" he asked.

"Fine," she said, smirking.

She then pried herself out of her white jeans, and her breasts swayed according to her subtle movements while bent over at the waist. Logan loved the way her satiny, powder blue bikini panties contrasted her smooth, brown skin. He stood at the daybed waiting. She then reached down to slide-off her panties.

"Leave them on!" he half-shouted.

Chandra derived some satisfaction from his request; she knew he wished to save that delight for himself. She moved closer, and they embraced, kissed, and fondled for a long moment before Mike tugged her down onto the meager daybed, and there, the two did what men and women do the first of many times over the succeeding months.

"Mike" attempted to entice Chandra into his bedroom on numerous occasions during that same span, so that they could enjoy lovemaking on a more spacious bed, but she steadfastly refused, eventually admitting that, to do so, would make her feel like a whore servicing a client. Curiously, she harbored no misgivings about engaging in coitus with him on the porch, under the same roof, off the main floor of the home. However, in due course, the two *would* enjoy lovemaking on a large bed, when Chandra periodically urged Mike to rent a room in one of the pedestrian yet clean hotels in downtown Nainital, where she met him disguisedly for their trysts. Logan, naturally, excruciated over having to part with funds unnecessarily, when he was generating no income to offset such expenditures, but could hardly refuse the propositions.

After fornicating on the porch that first day, they daringly lingered on the daybed while caressing.

"Why so thin?" Chandra asked.

"Me, you mean? Why am I so thin?"

"Yes."

"Part metabolism, part exercise. I've been training in anticipation of hiking and climbing at higher elevations. I should hope to gain weight soon, though." Logan lied because he preferred not to reveal his grueling maritime voyage, during which he often deprived himself to conserve his food resources, because the admission might later aid in identifying him.

"Let's have that rum we talked about yesterday," Chandra suggested, sitting up.

Logan watched her snatch her bra off the chaise, slip it on, and reach behind to hook it. *You're beautiful,* he thought. *And you loved me today. I could never kill you... no matter what.*

48

FOLLOWING AUTUMN TOURIST SEASON, Chandra's mother, Uma, traveled from Bangalore to Nainital to return Chandra and Ravi's daughter, Lakshmi, to Bolington Cottage, and Logan soon noticed that Lakshmi's presence in the home had transformed Chandra, insofar that the beauty radiated a different kind of love when in the company of her adorable little daughter. Chandra also refused to engage in intercourse on the porch with Logan during that first month following Lakshmi's return, and it was then that the two had commenced meeting in a downtown hotel. It wasn't until Uma departed Bolington, six weeks later, and, Lakshmi, now seven years old, was permitted to join housekeeper Lali on "grown up" shopping adventures, that Chandra and Logan resumed stealing love on the porch, which they exhilaratingly pulled off while Ravi guided trekkers in the nearby foothills.

It's with real regret that I've shared the details of Logan McCool's exploits since arriving in northern India, especially with regard to the killer's intimate escapades at Bolington Cottage, however, I deemed the disclosures necessary, so that readers would be well-acquainted with the personalities, geography, and circumstances eventually revealed to me, in a mercilessly overdue visual packet, which predictably led to the Omniscient One's inducement for me to also make passage in pursuit of the fugitive.

When the packet detailing Logan's afore-described voyage from the Strait of Gibraltar to the Himalayan foothills arrived, I was expectedly sitting in my Kinvara living room, reading the *Irish Independent* and eavesdropping on television. Naturally, I felt horrified, beholding the revelations, because I had known authorities to be, even still, many months later, concentrating their efforts in the port cities and towns along the west coast of Africa and western half of the Mediterranean Sea, when clever Logan had long eclipsed those regions.

Despite being deprived communiqués from the Omniscient One for about a year, I still viewed this latest packet a gift, because at least it provided an updated platform from which to work, so that justice could finally be sought on behalf of my two deceased daughters and McCool's other ill-fated victims. Some disturbing details of Logan's sinister deeds I've withheld, to this point, for purposes of an orderly presentation, but disseminate them henceforth: Logan McCool was running out of money and planned to murder Ravi Dilwali, in order to assume Ravi's role as Chandra's life-partner and principal guide of Foothill Trekkers. He had also abandoned all ambitions of ascending Mount Everest in Nepal.

At first, Logan's depleting money supply had been his foremost concern, when contemplating leaving Nainital, but, after recalling that he possessed a redeemable pair of diamond earrings and gold necklace with locket, he did some soul-searching and determined that he just couldn't give up his beautiful temptress, Chandra.

Logan, as Mike Harrington, had occasionally utilized Ravi's guide services during his many months at Bolington Cottage so that his host remained persuaded that "Mike's" primary reason for dwelling with them was an ardent desire to explore the scenic Kumaon region. On his own, Logan set off almost daily on treks of varying lengths and degrees of difficulty, more often than not after just fornicating with his host's wife, and then inevitably bumped into Ravi and one or more clients while out on trails. After resolving to kill Ravi and make it appear as an accident, Logan expressed, to his host, a wish to engage in a trek sufficiently challenging that it required them to camp for two or more nights. In reality, Logan had had no intentions of sleeping overnight in a tent or under the stars. He planned to murder Ravi once they ascended far into the foothills and then delay shroudedly until manufacturing an accident scene.

Naturally, the moment I perceived this information in my visual packet at home in Kinvara, I immediately sought to contact Inspector Pearse McElwee, in County Mayo, who I had collaborated with in past years, and who had served as a reliable source in linking this clairvoyant with the appropriate law enforcement agencies abroad. Oddly, my mind wasn't sent reeling, as had once occurred when intending to involve the Inspector in Haimish Devlin's apprehension in the Canary Islands, nor did I yet experience one of those awful gagging episodes as I did at Sexton's Pub in the presence of Gerry McBrine and Tom Casey. The reason: Inspector McElwee had recently retired. Consequently, his former underling was kind enough to contact McElwee, who, in turn, directed the individual to call and advise me to contact Inspector Patrick Kerrey, who had interviewed me in Dublin alongside British security agent Edmund Rathbone concerning Logan's assassination fantasies. Long story short: Kerrey was on vacation and, given the urgency of the situation, I insisted that his subordinate have the Inspector call me back. When he finally did, I gagged and coughed incessantly, when attempting to apprise him of Logan McCool's whereabouts. Needless to say, in view of an eerily familiar precedent, I could see where all this was leading, so I hung up the telephone. The Omniscient One clearly didn't want to involve, at least presently, any third party interference. But I didn't mind going it alone, really, because, for me, this one was personal, due to daughters Jodie and Tessie's deaths.

I immediately used the Internet to purchase an airline ticket to New Delhi, India. With that accomplished, I performed a search to see whether a Foothill Trekkers website existed. It did, so I recorded the telephone number and made an international call to Bolington Cottage. The local time in Nainital was just after 8 p.m. A male voice, with discernible Ulster accent, answered the telephone, "Bolington Cottage, may I help you?" The respondent was obviously Logan, so I hung up without saying a word.

Logan had spent enough time at Bolington that he now conducted himself more like a resident than a guest and had impulsively picked up the phone in the upstairs hall when passing by. In retrospect, it might've been better if I had just identified myself, at that moment, and informed him that I knew of his homicidal intentions with regard to Ravi because it would've instantly derailed his plans. On the other hand, the disclosure most likely would've propelled him into flight; and, not knowing when or if I might enjoy new advice from the Omniscient One, concerning Logan's activities and destination, I feared I might not draw close to him again for several months or years. I thusly waited fifteen minutes and telephoned the cottage a second time, hoping that someone other than Logan would answer. A young girl picked up, Lakshmi, no doubt, and I urged her to summon her mother. Upon verifying that the party speaking was Chandra, I identified myself and proceeded to report to her the highlighted version of her houseguest's murderous past. Chandra had picked up the phone in her bedroom, while Ravi read a newspaper downstairs, Logan rested in his bedroom down the hall, and Lali performed some preparatory work in the kitchen. Once my words registered with Chandra, she immediately sat on the bed, put her free hand to her forehead, and wept, which prompted Lakshmi, playing nearby, to return to her mother's side as I easily made out Lakshmi's inquiries into Chandra's melancholy state. The difficult part, subsequently, involved me, a man talking to her from several thousand miles away, who she knew little about, aside from the terrifying knowledge I possessed and had just unloaded on her, compelling Chandra not to do anything revealing or impetuous that might scare Logan off and, therefore, jeopardize his capture.

"It must be business as usual with Mike," I counseled the frightened woman. (Except for the obvious, because I was confident that Chandra would manage to deflect Logan's future sexual advances). Most importantly, I urged Chandra to find a way to postpone Mike and Ravi's challenging trek to the Himalayan wilderness, which was scheduled to go off in two days and would place her husband in grave danger. This latter revelation (about Ravi and Mike's planned journey) seemed to especially solidify my credibility with Chandra.

After we got off the line, Chandra accessed the Internet and performed a *Google* Image search for international fugitive Logan McCool, and the results provided a plethora of photos of the man known to her as "Mike Harrington." Next, she researched Logan's sordid past and clicked on a provided hyperlink, "Albert Doyle," which led her to the story of my daughters' murders, as well as a description of my uncanny extrasensory perceptibility. The article also included a picture of Jodie, Tessie, and me, during happier times, as we stood at the switch near Kinvara Harbor, with Angus Wilde's hooker, curiously, the only distinguishable boat in the background.

It would be eighteen hours before my flight to New Delhi departed, so I tended to affairs at home in anticipation of being away for an extended period. The telephone rang as I did some preliminary packing; it was old friend Trish Jennings calling, from Castlebar, to check on me. Trish had given birth, some four months earlier, to a bouncing baby boy, who she named Liam in tribute to her late fiancé. In light of the infant's late father's infamous and harrowing death, however, Trish had decided to retain "Jennings" as the child's surname. Soon Liam Jennings was called LJ, and later in life would routinely write his name as "Eljay."

Trish informed me that, presently, she often met with Mary Drury, wife of the late Aidan Drury, another of Logan's victims, who had been slated to serve as Liam's Best Man. Trish and Mary had once only been acquainted through their partners but, considering their unfortunate common bond, Trish stated that they now got together often to support each other and to socialize. According to Trish, Mary had also given birth to a baby boy, and named him Aidan after his late father, who Logan brutally killed with the twine cutter as the man climbed his dock ladder. Scarcely older than Eljay, baby Aidan was called "Junior" by Mom, family, and friends. Trish finally related, during her call, that although she still mourned for Liam, life was good, especially since the arrival of Eljay, and that she worked almost full-time at Jennings Equestrian Centre to keep her mind occupied. And I say "finally" because I elected to say goodbye to Trish, that day, without informing her that I had, at long last, received an updated visual packet concerning her late husband's brother and assailant, Logan McCool, or that I was about to travel to India in pursuit of him. Trish seemed so at peace during our chat that I cared not to disrupt her life until certain that we had Logan in custody. I thusly bid her farewell.

Gerry McBrine had agreed to drive me to the bus transfer station in Ennis, County Clare, where I would catch a bus to Shannon Airport, Limerick. It was a Sunday, and Tom Casey also had the day off, so he and his son, Padraic, visiting from Galway City, joined Gerry and me on the ride to Ennis. It was good to catch up with the men, but, as with Trish, I chose not to disclose the purpose of my impending visit to India.

Although, I suppose it would've been an interesting empirical exercise to see whether my efforts resulted in a familiar gagging episode.

From Shannon Airport, I made the short flight to London-Heathrow and then flied direct to New Delhi. Having watched Logan's earlier progression through India, in my visual packet, I had a good idea of how to maneuver efficiently using the train system; however, traveling by train would eat up another eight or nine hours, and time was of the essence, so I paid through the nose to secure a last minute ticket on a puddle-jumper from New Delhi's Palam Airport to the Phool Bagh airport in north central India. I again paid a premium for ground transportation from the airport to Nainital, because I didn't have the benefit of Ravi picking me up – not that I could've stayed at Bolington Cottage anyhow, for fear of being recognized by Logan. (Readers will recall that I first encountered McCool after Trish Jennings and I entered St. James Hospital, in Dublin, to visit my wounded daughter, Jodie. Logan was being wheeled from surgery to a recovery room, at the time, and recognized Trish. It was then I first heard him refer to her as the Witch of Castlebar). Presently, if I was to show up at Bolington Cottage, and Logan was to identify me, after paradoxically sharing an air-conditioned compartment with Sister Mary Shaun on the train from Mumbai, Logan would surely become paranoid and, at minimum, flee Nainital. I, therefore, rented a room at Dutton Cottage, up the road, where my plan was to establish Logan's whereabouts through Chandra and attempt to contact local police, so that we could pounce on him. Whether the Omniscient One required that I still go it alone, vis-à-vis Haimish Devlin in the Canary Islands, remained to be seen. As stated, I had, in a sense, wished to settle this matter with Logan by myself, because of what he did to my daughters; then again, I possessed no weapons to defend myself, and Logan was stronger and even more vicious than my previous foe. But then I recalled, "Let vengeance be mine, saith the Lord," and wondered if McCool's disposition might be as facile as Devlin's atop the Fez Water Clock.

49

KARMA WAS AT WORK, I could feel it, which seemed so apropos in this land where the concept of karma was presumably borne. Conversely, if mistaken, my intuition about Logan's fate would sadly prove only a hopeful delusion.

I had traveled in casual attire throughout my journey, and, after depositing my bag at Dutton Cottage, only took time to change shoes before plodding downstairs to telephone Chandra. Lali, her helper, answered: Chandra had trekked into the foothills with "Mr. Mike" early this morning, according to Lali, who was alone because no other guests currently stayed at Bolington Cottage; Chandra's daughter, Lakshmi, was in school, and Ravi had been off in downtown getting his vehicle serviced. Chandra had not informed anyone in the house about Mike Harrington's true identity and sordid past, per my earlier request, and I surmised from the lack of concern in Lali's voice that Chandra had complied with my wishes. Chandra did, however, inform Lali of a prospective caller to Bolington Cottage, namely me.

"Does Chandra hike often?" I asked Lali over the telephone.

"No, sir. It's the first time I can remember."

"And you're positive that Ravi didn't join Chandra and Mr. Mike?"

"Yes, I'm sure. Ravi departed in his car almost one hour after Chandra and Mr. Mike left the cottage on foot."

"I see."

"Did Ravi know that Chandra and Mr. Mike intended to hike together this day?"

"Of that, I'm not aware, sir. I can only assume."

The night before, Chandra had enticed Mike by telling him that she thought she might derive some pleasure from a change of venue for their love-making, a natural setting in which they'd first enjoy a romantic lunch. Chandra seldom endeavored into the foothills, these days, and hadn't in many years, in fact, due to the responsibilities of motherhood and managing the cottage. She had once hiked often, though, especially when first meeting Ravi and moving north to Nainital, and the network of trails was still mapped out in her mind.

Logan had long been using the lightweight daypack he purchased in a shop in Nainital. Meanwhile, Chandra had accessed one of Ravi's many packs, early that morning, and filled it with delicious foodstuffs and beverages, and the two set off shortly after a breakfast of scones, jam, and black tea, while Ravi still slumbered upstairs.

Chandra was certain Ravi would be troubled to learn from Lali that she had wandered off into the foothills with their longtime guest, but was careful not to lie, because she knew that, to weave a tangled web, would only complicate matters once filing her regrettable police report.

"I'm taking you to one of my favorite places, on my *most* favorite trail," Chandra had informed Mike as they set off across the grassy basin behind the cottage. "Eventually you'll recognize the trail, I'm sure, but I plan to take you off the beaten path."

Logan only smiled but secretly reveled as he watched Chandra's cute bottom shift in the snug-fitting hiking pants she wore. He subsequently envisioned himself mounting the beautiful temptress in a sunbathed field, where they would enjoy intercourse repeatedly throughout the afternoon. Chandra could've led Logan on the road to Hell, that day, and he would've followed; and, in a sense, she was.

Once they ascended a few hundred meters up the familiar central artery that originated at the basin, the pathway split into five separate trails. Ravi commonly referred to this point as "The Hand" – each trail constituting a finger. As one proceeded up any given trail, he or she soon discovered that each successive trail continued branching out, like blood vessels, the total sum comprising the vast Foothill Trekkers network.

Most trails were clearly marked so that hikers could easily find their way back to one of the five fingers, which made for an uncomplicated return to the central artery leading to the basin and Bolington Cottage.

"Ah, so you're taking me up *Hoodwinked*," observed Mike, as they started up the ring finger of The Hand.

Mike had hoodwinked her, so Chandra deemed it ironic that she should bring him up the aptly named trail, which featured a grove of fig trees near the edge of a scenic but secluded canyon, where they would later rest and eat.

"Ravi ever... take you... up to... Banyan Canyon?" Chandra asked, huffing and puffing.

"It's been a while since you've hiked. You're a little winded," Mike noted. "No, I can't ever recall visiting Banyan Canyon. It's kind of a funny name, isn't it?"

"Good. I'm glad... he never... took you there," she gasped. "He and I... frequented there... long ago. But now... it will... belong... to you... and me." Chandra lied. "Near the edge... of the canyon... there's a grove... of Banyan trees. They bear figs. There... we'll picnic."

"Why not take a break, honey. Catch your breath."

"I'm alright, really. Just out... of shape. Continue."

The two hiked for nearly an hour before reaching Banyan Canyon. The dense grove of Banyan trees, Chandra had described, provided ample shade, which they both appreciated after trekking through vast pockets of exposed mountainside. Logan awed audibly once passing through the grove and gazing down to behold the abutting canyon. Soon they shed their backpacks and, upon catching her breath, Chandra removed a flimsy summer blanket on which they could sit and take their lunches. The blanket had just been a prop, though, because after learning Logan's identity, the sum of his crimes, and his intent on killing her innocent husband (from yours truly), she had already resolved to eliminate Logan before another situation arose where sex was implicit, but, more importantly, before Ravi fell victim.

Chandra sidled up to Logan, with her hands on her hips, to share his view into the canyon.

"It's been many years since I've hiked here," she said. "There's been a lot of growth."

"I thought I saw some movement down there," said Mike, pointing toward the sandy canyon basin.

"There're tigers and leopards in these parts, you know. Tourists love to visit Corbett National Park, over in Garhwal, to see the indigenous wildlife, but, while a large concentration of animals roams there, the wildlife isn't exclusive to the park. One needs to be vigilant when hiking anywhere about the Garhwal-Kumaon region. Did Ravi ever discuss that with you?"

"We observed barking deer fairly regularly, but he never mentioned that tigers and leopards were common in these parts. He probably figures that such information might scare off potential clients."

Logan had actually known about the tigers and leopards, due to Sneed's admonition aboard the train from Mumbai.

"Possibly. Although, I've never heard him voice that concern," replied Chandra.

Logan then turned and shifted so that he stood behind lovely Chandra. He slipped his arms around her waist and interlocked his fingers in front of her, and he found it odd that she hadn't reached up to place her hands over his. He rested his head comfortably against hers while continuing to marvel at the natural canyon formation, and then kissed the side of her head. She still failed to reciprocate with any display of affection.

"You want to experience something extraordinary?" Chandra asked.

"What's that?" he said.

"I want you to trust me for a moment, okay?"

"Just for a moment?" He laughed.

Chandra only smiled while looking obliquely, so that he could see her reaction.

"Change places with me. You stand in front," she prompted.

Logan again kissed his temptress on the side of the head before moving in front; Chandra assumed his former position and wrapped her arms disgustedly around his waist.

"So far, so good," Mike said.

"Now... close your eyes. Promise you won't open them 'til I tell you."

"Okay... promise."

Chandra removed her arms from around his waist. Logan subsequently detected the stirring of fabric and imagined the beauty shedding her top; when, in reality, she had been wiping nervous sweat from her palms onto her hiking pants. She then stepped back and rocked forward to forcefully plant her palms at the base of his spine and jar him from the canyon ledge.

In that instant, Logan opened his eyes wide and turned to look at Chandra, because he was incredulous of what she had just done, meanwhile dragging his feet along the ledge, in a desperate attempt to slow his advance, and flailing his arms backward to try to shift his weight. It was too late.

"You were planning to kill my Ravi, *LOGAN MCCOOL!*" Chandra bent over the ledge and shouted, exuding an impassioned, justified aspect, as he plummeted away.

Flipping over like an agile skydiver, Logan glimpsed her one last time.

"But I loved *youuuuu...*"

Understandably curious, Chandra leaned over the ledge to track Logan's descent. First, he impacted the inside of the canyon wall, half way down, and then collided with the bushy part of a tree growing out sideways, which further decelerated his fall, and Chandra grew concerned that he might actually survive. But then she watched as he resumed descending rapidly, until pounding the canyon's sandy basin.

He lay motionless.

She studied him from afar for several minutes until convinced that he would not regain consciousness. She folded up the summer blanket and inserted it in her backpack, which she donned. She checked Logan, remotely, one last time, and fled for home with his backpack in tow.

50

AT BOLINGTON COTTAGE, LALI had been preparing lunch for Ravi, who had called her on his cellphone after leaving the mechanic's shop. Earlier, Ravi had grown disturbed and suspicious when learning from Lali that Chandra had ventured into the foothills with their longtime guest, Mike Harrington, especially considering that Chandra hadn't hiked in many years and failed to notify him of her plans.

Ravi entered the home and immediately questioned Lali if she had yet heard from Chandra. She had not. He thusly dialed Chandra's cellphone number while Lali served him lunch, and he soon became exasperated when hearing it ring upstairs: Chandra had foolishly neglected to take the phone with her. But then Chandra burst through the backdoor of the home.

"Is Ravi here?! she grilled Lali, standing at the kitchen counter. Chandra tossed Logan's backpack to the floor and removed her own, letting it slide off her back.

"He's in the dining room," Lali answered.

"Ravi!" Chandra yelled, storming toward the dining room.

Ravi stood up from the table, sensing the urgency in his wife's voice.

"In here."

Chandra turned the corner into the dining room.

"Mike Harrington fell down into Banyan Canyon! In all likelihood, the poor man has already died, but we need to call for rescue, and you and I need to hike back up there."

"What?! What happened?! And why were you up there with him?"

"We were talking about the trail network last eve, and I asked him if he had ever stumbled upon the canyon. He hadn't, and then he persuaded me to take him there. You were already asleep, so I didn't want to wake you to inform you that I'd be hiking in the morning."

"Then why didn't you just wake me in the *morning*?! *I* could've guided him there. You didn't even leave a note... and why didn't you bring your cellphone along, in case of such an accident... foolish woman!"

"I didn't bother with a note because I had informed Lali. As for my cellphone... I just plain forgot."

"Lali! Get in here!" Ravi shouted.

Lali scurried into the dining room, arms straight at her sides, like a Private reporting to a General.

"Why didn't you inform me, first thing this morning, that Chandra had gone hiking with Mr. Harrington?!"

"I assumed you knew, sir. But you'll recall that we did talk about Chandra and Mr. Mike hiking... just before you left to drop your vehicle with the mechanic."

"Forget about that now!" Chandra shouted, in a brilliant bit of playacting. "We *need* to call for *rescue*!"

Chandra thought it best that she be the one to call authorities, and did so. Meanwhile, Ravi entered a room off the kitchen, where he stored hiking and climbing-related gear, and retrieved some scarcely used equipment that would enable him to scale down the canyon wall, albeit he imagined a rescue team doing such. Ravi had, of course, trekked the foothills extensively over the years and didn't even need to look at a trail marker to aid him. However, scaling a mountainside or canyon wall was something different altogether, because, while he knew the fundamentals and possessed the basic equipment, it was a far more dangerous undertaking for which he had little expertise. While Ravi assembled the gear, Lali informed Chandra that I had arrived in Nainital and had called from Dutton Cottage. Hence, she jotted down the number to Dutton and took it with her, intending on telephoning me from the canyon ledge.

Once Chandra got off the line with the emergency response team in Nainital, she and Ravi agreed that she should get a head start and depart immediately for Banyan Canyon because she was out of shape and it would take her longer to ascend. In the interim, Ravi would wait at the cottage and then guide the team up from there.

Unsurprisingly, Chandra didn't neglect to bring her cellphone on this occasion, and she called Ravi just as he and the response team had maneuvered from the central artery of The Hand onto the Hoodwinked trail.

Mike Harrington's body was missing.

Chandra subsequently related that, prior to his fall, Mike thought he had seen a wild animal at base of the canyon, which is the reason he had moved to the ledge and ended up losing his footing, she lied; the exception being that Logan had noticed something stirring below.

Despite Ravi and the rescue team swiftly ascending Hoodwinked, it would take some thirty minutes before the group arrived at Banyan Canyon. Waiting alone at the ledge, Chandra had telephoned Dutton Cottage to give me the news while still nervously scrutinizing the canyon basin for Logan's body. I had accepted Chandra's words at face value, at the time, but would later learn the actual transpiration of events concerning Logan's "accident." Chandra still didn't believe that Logan had survived his fall, and neither did I, based on her description, and she suggested that I check out from Dutton Cottage and later join she and Ravi over to Bolington. After explaining to her that I had already paid for a night's lodging, she insisted that I check out from Dutton, regardless, because I could stay at Bolington free. She also wished for me to be their dinner guest but asked, for the time being, I not mention to Ravi or authorities that I had telephoned from Ireland with my assertions about Logan. I imagined the questions and confusion that would likely arise from agreeing to Chandra's request, but, considering the woman's courage over the past two days, and my undeniable satisfaction over Logan's disposition, I complied. Much to Ravi's relief, the Emergency Response Team scaled down the canyon wall, without him, to the area Chandra had pointed out, and scoured the basin for more than two hours until losing the trail for Mike Harrington. Once ascending to the ledge where the Dilwalis waited, the group leader reported that the injured party had visibly bled, and that they followed his trail until blood was no longer evident.

Chandra gnashed her teeth in distress. She fretted that Logan had somehow survived his ordeal and would, one day, return to Bolington Cottage to exact vengeance. But then the group leader described a pattern in the soil that suggested the victim's body was probably dragged, which provided Chandra temporary relief, once imagining a tiger or leopard hauling its quarry across the landscape; the rescue team failed to discover any remains, however, that would bear out her hopes.

Before dusk set in, a helicopter was dispatched from Lucknow, so that emergency personnel could search the canyon from a different vantage point, and the crew up on the ledge descended to the basin a second time to investigate new territory. No dead body was ever found, and the official determination, days later, was that wild animals had likely torn Logan's body apart, although the regional police supervisor rebuked the team for the supposition, because not a shred of the victim's clothing could be presented to support their finding.

I had done as Chandra asked and moved up the road from Dutton Cottage, and Lali and I became well acquainted during the hours we waited for Ravi and Chandra to return home from the search effort. Lali had earlier shown me to a room on the second floor, and, after unpacking my bag and washing up, I furtively sought out Logan's quarters, where I rummaged about looking for the remaining pair of diamond earrings and gold necklace, with locket, that I wished to return, one day, to the rightful owner, Trish Jennings. (I wouldn't learn until years later that Logan had taped the jewelry to underneath a bottom dresser drawer.) On the nightstand beside Logan's bed, I saw the killer's paperback book about the Irish revolutionary leader, Michael Collins. Otherwise, Logan had only carried some clothing items with him after abandoning his hooker down at Butcher Island, so I also checked his pockets. I discovered no cash, but, then again, he had little money remaining, hence his plan to kill Ravi and step into his host's shoes.

I then inspected Logan's satchel, and one item at the bottom of a zippered, side pocket immediately gripped me upon discovery: the crescent-shaped twine cutter he had used to kill Mr. Jennings and Aidan Drury. At the time, I had no idea that Logan's backpack, which Chandra brought back with her after pushing him off the canyon ledge, still sat on the kitchen floor, or else I would've sidetracked Lali and examined its contents also. Later, while Ravi, Chandra, and I would dine, Lali thoughtfully returned the backpack to "Mr. Mike's" vacant room, "so that his belongings could be returned to his family in Cornwall, England." Poor Lali was ignorant of the facts. She couldn't be helped.

Ravi and Chandra finally returned at half past eight that evening. The two entered the home through the rear door, and I first perceived Chandra ambling from the kitchen into the dining room while I waited in the parlor. Her frazzled, wearied condition notwithstanding, I immediately came to understand why Logan had been so beguiled by her. And, perhaps, "beguiled" is too modest a descriptor. I had previously only observed the young, middle-aged woman through the detailed visual packet I received two days earlier in my Kinvara home; however, to regard her in the flesh was a wholly different experience – Chandra was a creature, so alluring, that would make any man lovesick.

"You must be Albert." She extended her hand and smiled measuredly.

"I am, indeed. Chandra, I presume. Lovely to meet you." I shook her hand.

"Ravi's washing up in the kitchen. He'll be out before long. So... I trust you had no trouble finding our place."

"None at all." I almost hoped that Chandra wouldn't ask any questions that required too much thought, because I was still hypnotized by her and envisioned myself transforming into a stuttering fool. I think she sensed my nervousness, though. Perhaps mine was a common reaction, I thought.

"Why don't you and I go and sit on the porch, Albert. We should talk. I'll have Lali bring us a drink. Is rum okay?"

I had always despised rum because of its exceedingly sweet taste, but, because this intoxicating beauty was offering it, I seemingly lost all willpower to refuse her."

"Rum would be *grand*," I responded.

"Oh, please don't say *grand* in that manner, Albert." Chandra's face grew glum. "Mike... I mean Logan, used to say 'grand' like that all the time." She then smiled again, albeit more thinly. "Sorry. I hope that didn't sound too harsh. It's been a *helluva* day."

"I understand completely."

"How do you take your rum?"

"With a couple of ice cubes," I said.

"Certainly. Let me inform Lali, and then you and I can mosey out to the porch."

"Thank you," I said, nodding.

Chandra strode toward the kitchen while Ravi finally emerged from the den, which adjoins the kitchen at the opposite end, so husband and wife failed to pass by each other.

"Mr. Doyle?"

"Yes, sir."

"Welcome to Bolington Cottage." Needless to say, Ravi had also endured a difficult day, and he tottered across the floor to shake my hand without managing much of a smile. "I look forward to talking with you over dinner. Lali will be serving us shortly."

Meanwhile, Chandra had relayed the cocktail order to Lali and passed back through the swinging door that separated dining room and kitchen. She immediately observed Ravi and me chatting, and panicked that Ravi had unknowingly gotten to me before she had an opportunity to fine-tune her story.

"Thank you," I said, to acknowledge Ravi's kindness. Before anyone could utter another word, Chandra spoke up:

"Ravi, would you like Lali to fix you a drink?"

"I already told her to serve me my *usual* upstairs. I'm headed in for a quick shower before dinner.

"Yes, you do that... have yourself a shower."

Ravi nodded in departure and trudged upstairs. Lali had, since, finished preparing the cocktails and emerged with a tray containing three drinks.

"Follow me, Albert," prompted Chandra, "although, you already know where the porch is, don't you... having walked through the front door when arriving." Chandra laughed at herself for a moment, which I later found ironic when discovering, for the first time, that she had pushed Logan to his death. A subsequent visual packet helped fill in the blanks for me, which I appreciated, and would later become the basis for a stalwart, trustworthy relationship with the woman because, while she had strayed in her marriage and resorted to killing a man she deemed a serious threat to her family, she would never lie to me in the succeeding years. But, then again, her striking beauty could seemingly mitigate almost any injury she had caused.

Lali served Chandra and me our drinks out on the porch and continued upstairs to deposit Ravi's cocktail on his dresser while he showered. Dusk had rapidly faded, and only a few slivers of daylight remained on the horizon, as Chandra and I now considered the murky outdoor landscape through the porch windows during an awkward moment of silence. Two oriental-looking orange globes, suspended from the ceiling at opposite ends of the porch, illuminated the space and made for an otherwise pleasant ambiance.

Chandra sipped her rum and studied me pensively, as if assessing my trustworthiness. She was about to impart that, based on the information I had conveyed to her from Ireland, coupled with her corroborating Internet research on the killer, she had decided to eliminate McCool as a threat before he could harm any of her loved ones.

"You really put a lot of faith in me... when calling long-distance to notify me of Logan McCool, didn't you Albert? Have you considered that you also put me in a precarious position, when requesting that I do nothing until you arrived? Can you imagine what it was like for me here, in the hours and days that followed? You could've just called police, you know." Chandra put her drink down.

"Well... notifying the police wasn't such a simple matter, but I'll explain that later. Yes, I realize the idea that a mass-murderer was sleeping down the hall was probably a perilous feeling for you."

"Yes, I'd say it was a *tad* riveting," she said blatantly sarcastic, eyeballing me. "Things were much more complicated than you could've known. Logan and I were having an affair. Moreover, if I had told Ravi about your call, and that Mike Harrington was actually Logan McCool, an international fugitive, he likely would've reacted in a hostile way. Ravi often becomes irrational when hotheaded, you see, and I'm sure he would've confronted Logan. And, once Logan realized that his alias had been compromised, and his identity revealed, he might've killed us all. At the very minimum, he would've fled, but not before informing Ravi that he and I had been lovers, I'm sure. The latter I could've dealt with... I probably deserve that. But I don't think I could've lived with myself if he had harmed a hair on anyone's head."

"I understand perfectly where you're..."

Chandra interrupted.

"I killed Logan McCool, Albert." She raised her glass and guzzled the contents, as if self-medicating. "I pushed him from the ledge down into Banyan Canyon. I read all about his past on the Internet... what he did to your daughters, and I *had* to eradicate the threat before he did as *you* said he would... before he killed Ravi," she said justifyingly. "Now, I did some thinking, during all those hours up at the canyon today, and I'm convinced that if you step forward and inform police that *you*, a credible clairvoyant, traveled here because of a vision you had... *then* police will take a closer look at our family and interrogate everyone... and this thing is going to unravel. I'm sure of it. If sweet Lali had been the one carrying on with Logan, I think I would've been able to recognize such, with all my womanly intuition, and while I'm confident that I can trust Lali to never reveal, to Ravi, any suspicions she may harbor relative to Logan and me... if pressured by a skilled criminal investigator, I think she would admit her suspicions. Consequently, I won't be inclined to lie in order to conceal the affair. Then... they'll *really* put me and Ravi under the microscope concerning Logan's plummet into the canyon. You can see where this is all leading."

"My... you *have* thought this through, haven't you?"

"Yes, Albert. And I'd like the matter to rest as simply as this: a man named Mike Harrington accidentally plunged to his death after peering curiously into the depths of Banyan Canyon. That's what I want to read in the newspaper. Do you not feel any sense of deliverance after the way things worked out?" Chandra asked with those beautiful brown eyes resting on me.

"I'd be lying if I said that I didn't experience feelings of relief and satisfaction."

"There. Good. So, you'll let things be?"

"I think that I probably can."

"Think? Probably? Those words aren't reassuring, Albert. Remember, this thing all came about because of *your* telephone call."

"Yes, I can state, sincerely, that I can't foresee, at this time, any reason to pursue this matter further."

"Alright... that's sounds better."

"What's your plan if Logan is located, and his true identity comes to light?" I asked.

"He won't be found. I imagine he's passing through the intestines of several carnivores right about now. But, in the remote chance he's located and it's determined that he's someone other than Mike Harrington, I would *have* to plead ignorance." Chandra picked up her glass. "How 'bout a refill?"

"Do you have any spirits other than rum?"

"We have white wine, Kingfisher Lager, Bass Ale, and Jameson's Whiskey."

"Jameson's Irish Whiskey?! Why didn't you say so? Heavens... that would've been my first choice."

As much as I loathed rum, the first drink had loosened me sufficiently, and Chandra's outlook brightened upon seeing my reaction.

"Silly me. I have an Irishman sitting in my house, and I neglected to offer him Irish Whiskey. One Jameson's coming right up."

51

I DIDN'T PARTICULARLY NEED TO remain at Bolington Cottage, following the swift official determination that Mike Harrington had died as a result of his fall into Banyan Canyon and was devoured by wild animals, but I did, because, for one, I was yet unable to escape the potent spell of Chandra Dilwali's exotic beauty. I was more than two decades her elder, and she was married, yet my heart leapt each time she sashayed into a room. Unlike young Logan, mine had been an infatuation with unrealistic expectations; this, I knew, but allowed myself to be spellbound anyhow, because I doubted that, once departing India, I'd ever set eyes on the likes of her again.

After informing my hosts that I had decided to stay the week in order to more adequately explore the natural splendor of the southern Himalayas, Chandra secretly insisted that I stay at the cottage for free. Chandra was a good and generous person, but I reckoned that she had made the offer as sort of an insurance policy, a bribe, if you prefer, that I keep quiet about the actual transpiration of events. I declined the offer and told her that if I didn't pay my way I wouldn't be able to rest easy.

Bolington had taken on new guests in the preceding days: two honeymooners from Austria, plus two unmarried diplomats from the British Embassy. And despite Chandra's increased workload at the cottage, I persuaded her to break away and guide me on a morning hike up to Banyan Canyon, so that, before returning to Ireland, I could view the place where Logan had plummeted, all the while hoping and believing that I would remotely notice what search parties had failed to see. I soon learned that Ravi, that same morning, had been guiding the Austrian honeymooners up "The Bird," a trail that constitutes the middle finger of The Hand. Banyan Canyon is wedged between Hoodwinked and The Bird and, although the meandering pathway to access the canyon is more rigorous via The Bird side, I wondered if curiosity over Mike Harrington's missing body might've drawn Ravi back there. Periodically, Chandra and I gazed across the canyon, expecting Ravi and the Austrians to emerge from the thicket at any time; meanwhile, Chandra grew sullen, and understandably so, because, there, she had pushed a man off a ledge.

"Is this the spot?" I verified.

She only nodded.

Chandra and I had grown quite close during the week I stayed at Bolington Cottage. We spent many hours together while Ravi guided guests into the foothills, and she and I now shared a common thread in our lives. It thusly pained me to leave Nainital, but when it was time to go, Chandra volunteered to drive me to Phool Bagh airport.

After I removed my travel bag from the vehicle, Chandra retrieved a teak woodcarving, wrapped in newspaper, from the backseat and peeled back the layers to reveal the contents.

"I want you to have this, Albert," she said. "From me to you... so you'll always remember us here in Nainital."

"Oh, thank you, darlin'. You're so sweet. May I ask what it is?"

"This is Lord Ganesh. You'll notice he has the body of a strong man and the head of an elephant. Ganesh is the remover of obstacles, through wisdom and faith."

"It's beautiful. I'll always treasure it," I said, gazing at her lovingly, knowing that I could never have her.

I held out my arms, and she embraced me warmly. She then leaned back and kissed me on both cheeks, which would've been sufficient to induce fantasies for years to come, until she moved closer and caught me off-guard by pecking me on the lips, which rendered me speechless. Sensing this, she said, "Bye," projecting a broad, toothy smile, and then skipped girlishly to the driver's side of the vehicle, where she inserted herself and drove away.

Chandra probably imagined I was flying directly home to Ireland, once my puddle-jumper arrived in New Delhi, but I had other things in mind, which I hadn't shared with her, because to have done so would have caused her to worry needlessly for weeks and months to come: if the late Aidan Drury's hooker still lay beached at Butcher Island, I had decided to return it to his widow, Mary, in Westport, County Mayo.

Now, mind you, I'm no glutton for punishment. I had no intentions of replicating, in reverse, Logan McCool's sailing voyage from Ireland. Even if successfully traversing the Arabian and Red Seas, the Suez Canal, and Mediterranean Sea, I had envisioned how heart-wrenching it would be to pass through the watery locale where my daughter Tessie spent her final hours atop a piece of driftwood, not to mention where she had been repeatedly violated. And, from there, I'd need to repeat my previous journey past the Iberian Peninsula, across the Bay of Biscay, past southern England, eventually sailing near Great Blasket Island, where Tessie had spent so many happy years. No, that would be too tormenting a voyage, I decided, both physically and emotionally.

Once locating the vessel on the same remote Butcher Island beach where Logan had run it aground, I returned to Mumbai and recruited ten able-bodied seamen, who were in limbo waiting for their next commercial fishing expedition, to free up the boat and sail it some five miles to Mumbai Harbor. There, they dismantled the boat and catalogued the parts according to my specifications so that it could be shipped via airfreight. I paid the men the equivalent of almost one thousand five-hundred Euros to accomplish such, and spent another two thousand Euros to transport the hooker, now contained in several long containers, which, astonishingly, already sat in my Kinvara yard when I arrived. The logistics had been an expensive undertaking but, considering the convenience factor, I thought it well worth the cost.

The reason Chandra would've objected to my initiative, I'm sure, is that with the yet unexplained re-emergence of the hooker in my yard, without any explanation of, or allusion to, Logan's whereabouts, investigators would inevitably question me and, in the end, be led to her. Well, I had already thought of a plan to work around that potential debacle. I painstakingly painted each section of wood before reassembly; the hooker would appear beige when completed.

Oh, the hooker received plenty of long looks as it began taking its familiar shape in my yard. Yes, indeed. Tom Casey and his wife Angela stopped by one day as I worked on it, which was a little unsettling, because I was forced to lie to Tom that I had purchased the hooker at a deep discount due to the assembly required. I also told him that I planned on selling it.

"I might be interested in taking it off your hands," Tom said. "How much do you think you'll be asking for it?"

"Oh, the boat is already spoken for, Tom," I said. "A nice lady from Mayo is buying it for her son."

"Is this what you're going to be doing in retirement, now," asked Tom, "assembling boats and selling them?"

"I don't know, Tom. I doubt it. I saw the boat advertised in the classifieds and thought it would be an interesting project."

Tom peered across the yard and studied the detached mast with furled maroon sails resting on its side.

"I haven't seen too many hookers with maroon sails in these parts. "Angus Wilde's boat is the only one that comes to mind," he observed.

I instantly developed a cold sweat because I had forgotten all about the sails when painting the boat sections.

"Yes, I don't really care for the color... although, the brightness does make the boat more visible out on the seas. If the buyer doesn't care for the sails, he can always replace them," I said, and left it at that.

Tom's astute observation actually inspired me to purchase some used white sails, two days later, and discard the maroon sails before anyone else noticed. Nevertheless, I imagined the sails might serve as a hot topic of discussion between Tom and Gerry McBrine the next time they met for pints at Sexton's. Moreover, I'd be lying if I said my oversight didn't result in a loss of sleep, as I pictured the Garda knocking on my door.

The hooker now sat up on blocks, and a few short days before putting the final touches on it, I received an email from Chandra. The news was grim. Despite his superior physical conditioning, from almost daily strenuous hikes over the preceding two decades, guide Ravi Dilwali died unexpectedly of a heart attack. To make matters worse, Chandra blamed herself, because, just days prior to his infirmity, Ravi accused her of having an affair with Mike Harrington, to which she admitted, and Ravi asked for a divorce. Chandra related in her email that she eventually dissuaded Ravi from pursuing the divorce, but, shortly after, he sustained the fatal heart attack. She also described feeling totally spooked in recent weeks, because, since Ravi's death, there appeared to have been some illegal entries into Bolington Cottage. She arrived at the conclusion after she and Lali discovered some canned goods missing from the pantry, as well as a backpack and other climbing gear from the adjacent Pack Room. I reassured Chandra by telling her that if Logan McCool had somehow survived his fall into the canyon, knowing him, his reemergence into her life would not be so subtle. I hoped my words had put Chandra's mind at ease, but, in the back of my mind, I feared the worst.

52

I HAD A VERY GOOD feeling about this day. Even on sunny days in Ireland the clouds often threaten, but, on this day, the skies were flawless.

Since returning to Kinvara from India, I had only ventured into town to collect my mail and do some light grocery shopping, but, today, I had resolved to visit the Pierpoint, because, there, I'd be able to look out onto Kinvara Harbor and satisfyingly behold Aidan Drury's hooker, which I finished reconstructing three days earlier.

The day before, the sailboat was towed from my yard and launched into the harbor waters by Fred Hurley, a longtime Galway acquaintance who I hired to perform the work. I had considered driving down to monitor the launch, but it had been approaching the dinner hour, and Fred made his living doing such, so I had full confidence in him. An hour after securing the hooker at a slip, Fred telephoned to assure me that the operation was a success and that the boat hadn't taken on any seawater. I felt relieved. Following dinner, I called Mary Drury up in Westport to reacquaint her about who I was and to give her the good news that I had acquired, "through charity," a used hooker in remarkable condition that I wished for her to have as a replacement for her late husband's boat. Naturally, I felt guilty over my duplicity but hoped the Omniscient One would overlook the transgression. Mary was overwhelmed by my generosity but thought that someone else could make better use of the boat, citing that it was now just she and baby Junior at home. Mary and I then talked about the vacant dock, down below her lovely coastal cottage, and agreed it was a shame that no boat was moored there.

"Surely, Junior will want to do some sailing and fishing one day," I appealed to Mary.

"Yes, but he can't even walk yet, Albert," she said.

Mary remained non-committal but didn't rule out taking the boat, although I think she was just being polite. We ended our conversation that evening not knowing if or when she might take possession, and I wondered if she would've reacted differently if knowing that the hooker was the same boat once owned and operated by her late husband. The solution to that problem was exasperatingly meted out the following day:

Gerry McBrine and wife Carolyn had been closing up the post office as I drove en route to the switch that leads to the harbor, so I tooted my horn at them. Once parking near the Pierpoint and climbing out, I looked off to the right to search for the hooker before entering the Pierpoint but didn't immediately find it, and thought that Fred Hurley had secured it in an alternate slip at the north end of the harbor.

I never entered the Pierpoint that day.

After pacing back and forth in front of the consortium of harbor boats a half-dozen times, I failed to locate the beige hooker with furled white sails, so accessed my cellular phone to call Fred Hurley. Fred was still "out in the field," according to his wife, who called him on his mobile phone. Fred subsequently returned my call and described where he had docked the boat: the precise location I had requested. The boat was missing from its slip, so I reported the incident to the Garda.

Who is the troubled soul that filched the hooker, I wondered. I wondered, also, if the guilty party would've thought twice about stealing it if he had only known the boat's disastrous history. There were certainly days, as I sat contemplatively at home over the years, that I considered the vessel to be cursed. And by no means was the list of casualties limited to the boat's owners and passengers. Oftentimes, it was death by association, it seemed, as in the cases of Father Ruben Serna in the Canary Islands, the Jennings elders, Liam McCool, British Prime Minister Nigel Etherington, and, of course, my Jodie Doyle. *What was I thinking when I decided to return the boat from India?! What had I been trying to prove? I should've just allowed it to break apart and rot on that muddy, north side beach of Butcher Island.* But, before that would happen, some unwitting Indian fisherman likely would've discovered the unique hooker and took it for himself, after rationalizing that Lord Vishnu had blessed him with the find. Then *his* troubles would begin.

Despite my suspicions, which bordered on belief, I pridefully didn't want my efforts to return the boat from India, and all related hard work to again make it seaworthy, to be in vain, so I commenced checking in with the Garda twice weekly to inquire if any progress was being made in locating it. If I was lucky enough to get an investigator on the telephone, I was usually told in short order, "No, Mr. Doyle, we haven't found your bloody boat!" It soon became clear that the Garda was working on more pressing matters, so, after two months passed, I stopped calling them and wrote the hooker off. *Good riddance*, I thought.

It was a particularly humid afternoon, and I was parched for a cool refreshment so decided to venture out for a pint. I still had a bad taste in my mouth about the hooker being stolen, and would be reminded of such if returning to the Pierpoint and looking out onto the harbor, so thought I'd pay a visit to Sexton's instead. Suddenly, as I removed my car keys from a hook in the kitchen, a visual packet materialized. I thusly returned the keys to the hook and sat down at the breakfast table to view the contents, and soon made out beautiful Chandra Dilwali sitting alone in her English-style garden behind Bolington Cottage. Chandra was visibly distraught and heaved rhythmically in her chair, as if chanting or praying, except that no words were being spoken. "Come to me, Albert. Come to me," I finally heard.

Chandra's utterance had certainly shocked me. In light of our age differences, I didn't consider that she was pining for me by any stretch, but, when reflecting on how her life had changed for the worse, after taking the most recent hooker operator, Logan McCool, as a guest at their cottage, I looked upon Chandra, more so, as a lost sheep in need of shepherding; and, in me, perhaps, she perceived a wise and steady friend. That visual packet had been the most abbreviated conveyance the Omniscient One ever provided over the years, and I wondered what He had up His sleeve.

Once the packet diffused, I telephoned Chandra in India but decided not to reference her apparent moment of despair that I just witnessed remotely. Housekeeper Lali answered, who dispatched Lakshmi into the garden to summon her mother to the telephone.

"Chandra, Albert Doyle here. I know we've been staying current through emails in recent months, but I thought I'd call to hear your lovely voice."

"Oh, Albert, I'm so glad you called. Would you believe it if I told you I was just in the garden thinking about you?"

"If that's what you're telling me, then I believe it."

Chandra laughed.

"What are you doing now in life, Albert?"

"Well, I completed a carpentry project a while back, but, since then, I've grown a tad restless. I think I need more structure," I said.

"A part-time job is what you need. Do you think you'll ever return to northern India?"

"I enjoyed the area so much I was actually considering a move there."

My vision of returning to India, for an extended period, had just been fantasy, really, inspired by the notion of exotic, husbandless Chandra prancing about the countryside, and I had just thrown out the line to gauge her reaction.

"Well, I think you're just trying to tantalize me now," she said coyly, "but, if you're serious, I could give you the structure you're looking for. How'd you like to work part-time as a guide at Bolington, in exchange for free room and board?"

"Some of those trails on the Foothill Trekkers network are quite steep. I think I'd probably disappoint your younger clients."

"Oh, I wouldn't expect you to take on such trails in the beginning. But, after you get in hiking shape, I think you'll surprise yourself and actually look forward to some of the more challenging trails. I've been serving as primary guide ever since Ravi died, and the activity has completely rejuvenated me."

"You make an attractive offer. Will you give me some time to think it over? I'd need to tie up some loose ends before undertaking such a big move. I'd probably look to lease out my home."

"Take all the time you need, Albert. The offer stands."

I then changed the subject. "Any more mysterious occurrences at the cottage?"

"What do you mean?"

"In one of your emails you described how some food items were missing from the pantry, in addition to a backpack and some climbing gear."

"No, nothing further, I'm relieved to say. The police insist that an unscrupulous guest was responsible, which I told them was absurd, seeing that no guests were staying at the cottage at the time of the loss. I still believe that there were one or more illegal entries, but, since then, I've changed the locks on the front and rear doors, and Lali, Lakshmi, and I are now being much more careful."

"Yes, you do that. Be very careful, because the world is a better place with you in it."

I could sense Chandra blushing, even over the telephone.

"Oh, you're so very nice, Albert. I hope you'll come dwell with us."

53

THE LURE OF LOVELY Chandra Dilwali, essentially alone, in the Himalayan foothills had preoccupied my thoughts in the days following our long-distance telephone conversation, and I soon began obsessing over a return trip to India. I thusly advertised my fully furnished home at a considerable discount, and once Tom Casey learned the rent amount he contacted his son, Padraic, in Galway City, who ultimately became the lessee.

The night before departing Ireland, I telephoned Trish Jennings in Castlebar to inform her of my plans, as well as to apologize for not driving up to Jennings Equestrian Centre since returning home from India the first time. Trish, naturally, proceeded to interrogate me about my motivation for moving, and persisted that I was being actively engaged by the Omniscient One while withholding information from her. Consequently, she nearly succeeded in persuading me to divulge the details of Logan McCool's painful departure. Still mindful of how radically the disclosure might complicate mine and Chandra's lives, though, I remained tight-lipped. In the end, Trish and I updated our contact information so that we could continue communicating while I stayed in northern India.

In view of the apparent permanence of my move, I'd travel with considerably more luggage on this occasion. And once my departure from Kinvara loomed, Gerry McBrine insisted on driving me to the airport. This flight would leave from Dublin Airport, however, and I didn't want Gerry to have to drive across country, so I asked him to just drop me at the Galway train station. Gerry's wife Carolyn joined him, as did Tom and Angela Casey, in order to give me a proper bon voyage, not knowing when we might meet again. I had always appreciated their friendship and thought it was very decent of them to see me off.

After saying our good-byes, I lugged my heavy suitcase on wheels, plus carry-on, toward the station entrance, where I soon encountered Sister Mary Shaun Sevigny, who had just disembarked a train originating from Dublin. Sister, of course, had once shared a compartment, unknowingly, with Logan McCool from Mumbai to New Delhi, and the nun was presently on the final leg of her trip home to Kinvara after concluding a lengthy sabbatical in Calcutta and Darjeeling. Sister knew well my track record as a credible clairvoyant in these parts, especially considering that she had once taught my late daughter Tessie at Seamount, not to mention my instigation and resolution of the Angus Wilde murder case, which put Seamount notably on the map. And bearing in mind her disconcerting contact with "John Muldoon," on the train to New Delhi, Sister would've undoubtedly derived satisfaction upon learning that Muldoon, aka Logan McCool, had ostensibly received his comeuppance in life. However, in spite of this, I was again forced to preserve the secret of Logan's disposition, in order to protect Chandra Dilwali, the intoxicating temptress for whom I would again ascend the Himalayan foothills.

"How was your sabbatical to India, Sister?"

Sister Mary Shaun failed to recognize me at first.

"Mr. Doyle? I wouldn't even *know* you. You look so fit and well-rested... and rather youthful, I would say."

"Ah, yes, well, being at home suits me, Sister. And you know how I like to hike about the Burren."

"How did you know I was on sabbatical to India?" she asked.

"Word gets around fast in Kinvara. I heard about the plane ticket to Mumbai that was donated to Seamount, which facilitated your passage. Would you believe it if I told you that I was traveling to India, myself, right now? I'm actually moving there."

"Really now? What's your destination?"

"Northern India. The Himalayan foothills, just west of Nepal. A small town called Nainital."

"Haven't heard of it. I spent some time in the foothills, also... but well east of there... in Darjeeling... which reminds me of the dreadful man I traveled alongside from Mumbai to New Delhi. He was a *jackeen* headed to the same area that you're traveling. His face troubled me greatly... his smile never reached his eyes. John Muldoon was his name. He had been wearing a Claddagh ring, until the black American sitting across from him coaxed him into selling it."

Sister's eyes searched pensively, as if desiring to give me all the information she could about "John Muldoon" so that I would beware of him. Little did Sister know that I had remotely observed Logan's entire voyage, from Ireland to India, in a visual packet. I wished I could've alleviated the nun's concerns about Logan, but, again, just couldn't without compromising Chandra's identity and actions of taking the law into her own hands.

"Well, Sister, I should be on my way. I need to check in early for an international flight. I know you can relate. Bye now."

I resumed wheeling my suitcase, but Sister extended her arm to stop me. She had something on her mind.

"Mr. Doyle, the last time we spoke it was after Tessie's funeral Mass. I know that your faith has been severely tested... with the losses of Jodie and Tessie. Are you still angry with God?"

The nun had struck a nerve when phrasing her words that way, and I responded in a manner not intended to disrespect Sister, but, more so, to remind the Omniscient One of my disgruntlement over, what I considered to be, His unfair dealings with me.

"I'll thank for you for your prayers, Sister," I responded curtly, to reinforce her belief, "and may all your sons grow up to be bishops," I added. I then strutted toward the station without looking back, but I could make out the nun's reflection in the glass door that was propped open. Her mouth was agape.

I had emailed Chandra my itinerary prior to leaving Ireland, and discovered her waiting at Phool Bagh airport when arriving, which delighted me because I thought I might need to arrange alternate transportation to reach Bolington Cottage.

Chandra was as captivating as I remembered. She was also dressed smartly and had clearly taken time to groom herself. I placed my bags down to signal that I intended to embrace her, and she held out her arms to receive me. As I released, she slipped her arms up around my neck and kissed me substantially on the lips. I was decidedly overcome by the beautiful woman's expression of affection but tried not to let it show through, and, in the end, thought she was merely grateful that I had rearranged my life to help she and her family.

Once reaching Bolington Cottage, I lugged my heavy suitcase upstairs while Chandra followed with my smaller bag. In conversation during the ride back from the airport, we had resolved that I would take one of the medium-sized bedrooms, saving the bigger rooms for guests. I then spent a short while doing some preliminary unpacking before joining Chandra, Lakshmi, and a couple of Norwegian hikers for dinner. And after Lali served us a savory entrée that she claimed not to be curry but, similarly, featured a generous amount of turmeric, she, too, sat and ate with us, which she had never done during my initial visit, because Ravi hadn't permitted such.

After dinner, Chandra suggested that she and I adjourn to the porch to discuss, in more detail, the duties I would perform in exchange for room and board. Upon entering the cottage two hours earlier, I noticed the porch furniture had been rearranged since my first stay, and each time I glanced at the daybed, now situated at the opposite end of the space, I couldn't help but visualize she and Logan bumping uglies there.

Soon, Lali brought us tea, and business talk switched to more mundane topics, during which Chandra related that she desired to better acquaint me with downtown Nainital, so that I could venture there alone to take care of personal matters like getting a haircut and doing my banking, because I mentioned I had arranged for my monthly pension to be deposited electronically in the Bank of India. The following day, she and I would enjoy lunch at a cozy bistro in Nainital.

After conducting two weeks of assigned guest hikes in which I served as a guide on treks of easy to moderate difficulty, plus leisurely but more strenuous hikes with Chandra, I had become well-acquainted with the Foothill Trekkers network. I was also now in the best physical condition of my life and felt gratified over my decision to relocate to northern India. During more recent hikes, as we descended from one of the finger trails onto the central artery, Chandra had begun holding my hand, and, while the display of affection never failed to cause my heart to skip a beat, deep down, I was impressed that it was more a cultural practice between close friends. On a couple of occasions, she had also pecked me on the lips at the end of the night, before bed, similar to way she had kissed me at the airport. Admittedly, there were times when I felt like grabbing the beautiful woman and pulling her in close for the kind of kiss that would really test the waters – especially one night after she dared to kiss me while wearing a tantalizing, translucent, summer night shirt – but I cared, more so, not to behave in a manner that made things so uncomfortable that Chandra was compelled to ask me to leave.

Weeks later, we had just finished dropping the last of a houseful of guests at the Kathgodam railway station, and Chandra made an impromptu call to Lali to inform her that she and I would not be returning home for dinner but, instead, dine out in Nainital. In doing so, Chandra was recognizing all the hard work she and I had done in the preceding days, which exceeded the services normally offered at Bolington and included a guided tour of Corbett National Park in Garhwal, as well as escorting a guest up a section of Nanda Devi, a mountain in northern Kumaon. She and I returned to the bistro where we had eaten lunch weeks earlier and, this time, enjoyed dinner outside on the deck, under an ambiant overhang, in a dining area dimly lit by a single oil lantern. When first entering the romantic setting, I asked Chandra:

"Is this where you and Ravi used to dine?"

"Never did," she replied. "We only ate inside."

I thusly asked, "What about Logan?"

Chandra laughed. "No, and I'm *so* glad, because I had once almost taken him here... just days before you first called the cottage."

Chandra ate some chicken dish swimming in an ectoplasmic-looking green sauce that was not visually pleasing, but, which, after sampling, I decided was delicious. I ordered the more safe lamb biriyani, and we shared a bottle of local red wine. We were both too full to fit dessert and agreed we'd just eat a bite of chocolate at home while taking tea.

Bolington had had a prosperous week, and Chandra insisted on paying for the meal, so I took care of the tip. Once we stood up from the table, I noticed her peering over my shoulder, so I turned curiously to assess what she was looking at. I observed nobody, but, apparently, that was the point, because, earlier, another couple had been dining at the opposite end of the deck; they had since departed. Turning back to face Chandra, I sensed that the beautiful woman had shifted closer: she desired to be kissed, and my loins immediately swelled, because I now realized that in all the previous times Chandra had kissed me, she had sought to advance our relationship.

I leaned forward and tilted my head down, and Chandra looked up until our lips met. She soon slipped me the tongue, and we embraced and pawed at each other for a long moment until an adolescent busboy, who wandered out unassumingly to clear the table, interrupted our passion. Chandra and I swiftly separated, and she combed her hair with her fingers while laughing, due to the awkwardness, which prompted me to chuckle also.

We kissed briefly inside the car, and then she drove us to a vacant parking area that abutted a boat landing at the lake, where we again kissed and groped like teenagers in heat, until the windows fogged, and she suggested we get out and walk to the lake. There, we stood silently at the water's edge, under black skies peppered by a few stars and the meager light emanating from a quarter-moon, with our arms around each other.

Things really moved fast that day, I recalled thinking, and I was still incredulous that I actually had my arm wrapped around the youthful goddess beside me. I also wasn't sure if we were yet a couple, but it appeared we were on our way.

Chandra raised her left hand to point at something: the lights inside a prominent residence, across the lake, illuminated several objects on the landscape.

"That's where Ravi used to play polo," she said. "We both spent a lot of time at that house, but I don't go there anymore."

"No? You no longer care to watch the men play?"

"I never watched them much to begin with. Ravi and his mates would play while I mingled inside with one of more of the wives... if I went at all. Usually, I was too busy taking care of things at Bolington. Once the players finished up for the day and we socialized as couples, it made for some interesting times, but I don't feel I have anything in common with them anymore. Plus, only one or two of the bastards even attended his funeral." Chandra turned away in disgust. "Let's go home," she said, taking my hand.

Once arriving at the cottage, we climbed the back steps and entered through the rear door into the kitchen, where Lali was still tidying after having fed herself and young Lakshmi, who had fallen asleep in front of the television upstairs. Lali only nodded and smiled, until Chandra asked her something in their native dialect to which Lali responded negatively in English.

"Good night, Albert," Chandra abruptly announced and strode through the kitchen and dining room to the stairs leading to the second floor. Chandra had distanced herself from me during the few minutes we were home and, despite our romantic dinner and passionate kisses, it appeared we'd resume our familiar roles.

I bid Lali a polite good night and slogged upstairs after deciding to forego taking tea and chocolate. Once opening the door to my dimly lit room, I shockingly beheld Chandra standing before me in bra and panties only. My manhood leapt. I paced to her and dove at her mouth, tongue-first. I then wrapped my arms around her and grappled her inordinately soft skin, finally sliding my hand beneath her panties to stroke her smooth buttocks. It had been decades since I felt this way, I realized. Chandra had since reached down between us and was unfastening my belt buckle and trousers. Once unzipping me, she thrust my skivvies down and grabbed my rock-hard implement. I had lived enough years to know what would happen next so proceeded to unbutton my shirt, and Chandra let go of my organ to help expedite my divestment. I now stood naked while attempting to step out of my rumpled trousers, which lay bunched around my ankles. Meanwhile, Chandra had reached behind to unhook her bra, causing her breasts to flop and bounce before settling. She was beautiful. She seemed intent on taking the lead, or perhaps it was her degree of arousal, so I hardly dissuaded her. She looked upward to be kissed once more, and, after we were both out of breath, she pulled me toward the bed while sitting on the edge. Chandra then commenced performing fellatio on me so avidly that I doubted I'd be able to continue standing, due to the sheer ecstasy, all the while fondling her marvelous breasts and caressing her rigid nipples. I soon thought that I would arrive, as it were, but, first, cared to reciprocate, so gently placed my hands on her lovely brown shoulders and eased myself backward. With my hands still on her shoulders, I guided her down on the bed so that she now lay on her back. As I climbed beside her, she raised her buttocks and reached down to slide off her panties. We then turned on our sides, to face each other, and proceeded to kiss and fondle, naked, on the bed several minutes longer in the most rapturous moment I can ever recall in life, before I performed cunnilingus on her in aching anticipation of our sexual union. Upon finally mounting her, I gazed down at the sublime temptress and knew it wouldn't be long before I exploded into her, which I did, and she did not deter me, instead, spreading her legs wider and pulling me in deeper for maximum penetration while detaining me.

Chandra and I carried on in this manner about twice weekly, mostly in the evening, while Lakshmi and Lali slept. And, when the opportunity presented itself during the day, as Lali grocery shopped and Lakshmi attended school, Chandra invited me into her spacious bed, where we enjoyed relations more comfortably, and I maneuvered enthusiastically about the beautiful creature like she were a gymnastics pommel horse. Three months after I had returned to Nainital, to work as a guide and live in the Himalayan foothills with lovely Chandra Dilwali, I had impregnated her and asked her to be my wife. Her gleeful acceptance of my offer returned a kind of happiness into my life that I would have never again thought possible.

54

CHANDRA AND I WOULD live blissfully together over the succeeding *two decades* at Bolington Cottage during which time I received nary a visual packet or embedded dream from the Omniscient One.

My previous years of hiking the Burren and Cliffs of Moher in western Ireland had, thankfully, aided me in adapting to my new role as primary guide of Foothill Trekkers, which I took over from Chandra, full-time, five months before she gave birth to our twin girls. Chandra's mother, Uma, who was scarcely a decade older than myself, traveled up from Bangalore just prior to the births and stayed with us for six months to help care for infants Saritha and Namitha, a time when I constantly found myself reminded of the ancient adage, "The Lord giveth and The Lord taketh away," which certainly seemed to apply to my late daughters Jodie and Tessie, if vainly putting myself at the center. In this case, I hoped that this latest bestowal served as a restoration, of sorts, which would allow the girls to live long and happy lives. I realized it had been morose to think of things in such terms but, given the traumatic precedent events in my life, these were the thoughts running through my mind.

Those first months after Chandra's mother returned to Bangalore were predictably hectic due to the additional workload, but somehow we made it all come together. Both Chandra and Lali had their hands full between child-care and tending to guests' needs, and, before long, young Lakshmi assisted with babysitting when I was out guiding trekkers on trails.

Trish Jennings and I periodically exchanged emails after I left Ireland, and she was expectedly ecstatic to learn of the unlikely turn of events in my life, and promptly sent gifts along for the twins.

I suppose it's no surprise that Trish never married, following Liam's tragic death, and, while I was certain she would've reveled knowing that her fiancé's killer, Logan, had departed for another dimension, I remained mum in order to protect Chandra, the new love of my life.

Trish dedicated most of her time and energy to raising Eljay and operating Jennings Equestrian Centre, and, in her correspondences also never failed to mention Mary Drury and son Junior, who visited frequently. Trish and Mary had become close friends, since the respective tragedies that brought them together, and their two boys played like cousins, according to Trish. Eljay and Junior typically rode horses for an hour or two while Mary visited with Trish, but, more often than not, the boys returned the horses to the stables so that they could climb and explore the nearby short hills on foot. Years later, during the summer of their eighteenth birthdays, the boys' mutual affinity for climbing took them to the Pyrenees Mountains, bordering France and Spain, where they successfully scaled the highest peak, Pico de Aneto. One day they aspired to climb Mount Everest.

Some twenty years after returning to Nainital, this 82 year-old had been enjoying a late afternoon siesta on the hammock adjacent to Chandra's prolific garden, in back of Bolington Cottage. These days, given our more advancing years, Chandra and I had been alternating when guiding guests on hikes of easy or moderate difficulty, and for those clients wishing to engage in more challenging treks up on The Hand, we had arranged for a spry 38 year-old, Fareed, a neighbor from down the road, to serve as guide.

Suddenly, I derived a feeling of doom as I lay in the hammock. Dazed somewhat, I shifted and looked about trying to reckon if I had experienced a nightmarish dream, which might've spawned the ill-fated feeling. Panning across the immediate landscape, I noticed that those persons I cared about most in the world were safe and secure: lovely Chandra, now 61, her splotches of gray hair notwithstanding, was on her knees, weeding and turning soil in the garden; our 19 year-old twins, Saritha and Namitha, were playing some new board-game that was all the rage in India; Lakshmi was entertaining a lad from Chennai, with whom she attended medical school in Delhi; and Lali could be seen through the kitchen window, standing before the sink. *It must've been a dream*, I thought, and, subsequently, laid back down, trying to drop back to sleep, in hopes of resuming the dream I had forgotten, which, of course, never happens, even though we want so badly for it to work out that way. The ominous feeling again inundated my being and, this time, I recognized it had not been a dream, so I reflexively opened my eyes to behold a familiar conveyance, suspended and vacillating slowly, like a flag flapping gently in the wind. I gasped, and Chandra had heard me and lurched around; the distraction of our eyes meeting caused the visual packet to diffuse – not that she or the other ladies could've perceived the paranormal device intended exclusively for me, anyhow.

"You alright?" my wife asked.

"Yes, honey. I think I'll be going in for some tea, though. Care to join me?" I knew Chandra would decline, because she had just commenced gardening ten minutes earlier, but I made the offer, nonetheless.

"It's too warm for hot tea. How about if I have Lali bring us some iced tea?"

"That's alright, I had planned on going inside anyway." I then rolled out of the hammock onto my feet. Even though two decades had elapsed since I last received a visual packet, I was still versed on the Omniscient One's modus operandi: I knew that the moment I again situated myself, and was free from distraction, He would resume generating the eerie production.

"Suit yourself," said Chandra. "You're *certain* that you're okay?"

"Yes, I am. Thanks for your concern, sweetie."

I stood and sauntered across the grass to the exterior staircase leading to the kitchen door. Once inside, I greeted Lali, fetched a tea bag, placed it in a cup, and poured some boiling water. I then gingerly made my way upstairs to the bedroom Chandra and I shared, where I sat in a comfortable wingchair adjacent to a wooden clothing valet. The tea needed more steeping, but I drew a meager sip before placing the cup and saucer on the table beside me. Once the Omniscient One was sure He had my undivided attention, the visual packet again materialized.

Logan McCool had not died that day in the canyon twenty years earlier.

But this revelation shouldn't surprise. Not if one stayed clued into to my recurrent foreshadows, plus cryptic language when referring to Logan's "painful departure" and (Logan) "departed for another dimension." I realize that this latter delineation was especially misleading, considering that those of us who believe in an afterlife tend to think of it as a different dimension; except, that, in this case, the narrative was worded so that it might be interpreted that the dimension in question was Up, as in Height, as in Altitude, as in Mount Everest.

Even though I experienced real dread upon reckoning the information in this new packet, my ill feeling soon tempered once identifying some time and date indicators in the illustrated device that suggested Logan remained far away in Nepal, where he had resided for two decades. Henceforth, I offer this summary, which details the life of Logan McCool since Chandra Dilwali pushed him from the ledge at Banyan Canyon that memorable day:

The abrading action of Logan's body against the interior canyon wall, during his freefall, had obviously been excruciating, but if Chandra had studied her antagonist more closely, she would've noticed that he never lost his wits, despite his desperate circumstance, and actually steered his way toward the bushy tree growing sideways, which he knew would brake his fall, by agilely pushing off the wall with his feet and hands. I think it's also fair to assume that if the tree had not existed, Logan would not have survived his plummet to the basin; however, the way things worked out, he ended up with a dislocated shoulder, badly bruised hip and leg, and a scraped, bloodied face due to his violent tumble through the raking tree branches. Moreover, I suppose it helped that some intermittent monsoon rains, in the preceding weeks, had softened the earth below, thereby cushioning his fall.

The severe trauma of his impact on the canyon floor had been such that Logan merely lay motionless for a long while, hoping to recover, after sensing that he was hurt badly but not yet knowing the extent of his injuries. And once Chandra determined that Logan had, in all likelihood, died, she collected their gear and vacated the ledge in order to return to Bolington Cottage. Minutes later, oblivious to anything Chandra was currently doing, Logan staggered to his feet, coiled his arm around a sturdy tree branch, and yanked on it unbearably until resetting his dislocated shoulder. His agonizing scream echoed through the canyon, but Chandra had already descended too far on the Hoodwinked trail to perceive his cry. Now fearing that the scent of his blood might attract vicious carnivores, he slogged determinedly to the opposite side of the canyon and, relying only on his strong, dexterous toes and fingers, began a protracted, difficult ascent up the interior wall, which ultimately led him to a major trail, The Bird.

Once recognizing his position up on The Bird, he sought out a water source that he knew to originate from an area of distant waterfalls. He rested after hydrating himself and then perused some bushes until identifying some edible berries that he recalled Ravi pointing out so many times during their treks. When feeling well enough, he returned through the woods to the distant ledge, opposite to where Chandra had pushed him. The rescue effort was well underway, but he failed to pick out Chandra and Ravi from his concealed location, and, once hearing the voices of rescue workers resonating within the canyon walls, he fled through some low-lying vegetation and forest until reconnecting with The Bird trail, where he commenced hiking northward.

Logan's previous months of hiking familiarly about The Hand had unquestionably benefited him, and he would secrete himself remotely in its countless natural margins and mews, over several weeks, before again daring to descend the central artery leading to the grassy basin behind Bolington Cottage – the reason being: he was sure his identity had been disseminated by Chandra, and that a manhunt to capture him was in progress after his body had gone unaccounted for. His other consuming thought was how Chandra had discovered his identity. *Who or what was her source?* He turned the question over endlessly in his mind, and rarely slept in the same location on consecutive nights, often sheltering himself by assembling numerous dead tree branches into a coffin-shaped tent and spreading leaves over the structure before inserting himself in the natural insulation.

During those first nights in dark isolation, he often found it difficult to sleep, and reacted hyper-vigilantly to every twig snap and rustling of brush while imagining carnivorous predators prowling nearby, ready to pounce on him in his vulnerable state. His fears subsided with each passing night, however, and, once sleeping more soundly, he inevitably awakened feeling more refreshed and better healed.

He continued sustaining himself on water and berries in the early days and weeks following his ascent but, eventually, supplemented his diet with more dense, caloric figs after locating an alternate grove of Banyan trees, because he was still too wary of returning to the grove adjacent to the ledge where Chandra had pushed him. After healing sufficiently, and adequate time had passed that he thought authorities had abandoned their searches, Logan ultimately returned to Bolington Cottage, ever-mindful that he had left a valuable pair of diamond earrings and gold necklace with locket taped to the bottom of a dresser drawer. He still had several hundred Euros in his pants pocket, and Mr. Jennings' Rolex watch on his wrist, which still operated perfectly despite the forceful blows it sustained during his fall.

Logan had recalled that Chandra often liked to go out for dinner on Wednesdays, with her family, (if no guests had requested an evening meal), to break up the workweek. She also always invited Lali, her helper, to join them, despite Ravi's annoyance; however, Lali keenly recognized such and, more often than not, declined Chandra's kind offer of inclusion, settling for some quiet time alone at the cottage.

On the Wednesday evening that Logan finally risked returning to Bolington Cottage, he had hoped desperately that all circumstances would work in his favor, so that he could enter the home without incidence: he wished that Chandra, Ravi, and daughter Lakshmi were away at dinner and that Lali had joined them; and, if no guests currently stayed at Bolington, then that would certainly be a bonus, although he could easily work around that one, he rationalized, by conducting himself familiarly within the home, claiming that he, too, was a guest, if noticed or challenged. If that failed, he imagined himself accessing one of the many sharp kitchen knives, carving the guests into unconsciousness, and seizing their valuables. The one factor working in Logan's favor, which he couldn't have foreseen but would expressly benefit from, was that Ravi Dilwali had died of a heart attack three weeks earlier, and Lali unfailingly joined Chandra and Lakshmi for Wednesday dinners out; in fact, Chandra insisted that Lali accompany her so that she could enjoy some adult conversation over dinner.

The Sun had set but the skies were dusky. Logan delighted, once noticing that Ravi's familiar green SUV was missing from the gravel lot, and skulked toward the rear of Bolington Cottage. Upon reaching the home, he crept up the back steps, leading to the kitchen door, but had only made the advance after verifying that Lali wasn't perched familiarly at the kitchen window, inevitably washing something at the sink.

He eased the screen door open and tried turning the knob on the primary door, which was locked, so he spent a moment inspecting the cottage interior through the window in the door. Predictably, there were lights on, so he delayed in an attempt to detect any shadows that would point to people moving about, even if it was just someone flipping a page on a newspaper. Satisfied that the first floor was occupant-free, and that Chandra had only left some lights on so that the house wouldn't be in darkness when they returned from dinner, Logan slinked down the back steps and around to the right front corner of the home, instinctively sinking to his knees and stealing a look at the porch through the maze of potted flowers. The shades were up, and he plainly saw the two suspended orange globes illuminated; he again lingered to see if any motion originated inside. He had now settled on the porch for his break-in, because he knew that the outside door was routinely left unlocked and, once inside, the veil of the windowed structure should obscure his crime. Still crouching and peering over to the porch, he was reminded of the many carnal sessions he had enjoyed with Chandra on the daybed, and, despite the woman having shoved him from the canyon ledge, patently to kill him, he still, curiously, yearned to be near her.

During the few minutes he delayed outside the porch, the skies had surrendered its remaining daylight, and the cloak of night should further abet him in his crime, he thought. He now only hoped that the Dilwalis wouldn't return home from dinner before he had an opportunity to complete his mission. That last notion impelled him to shuffle urgently over to the porch, while still bent over at the waist, to glance in a window; the space was populated only with furniture. He stood erect, paced to the front door, and effortlessly turned the knob to gain access. Once inside the porch, he walked the few steps to the main door of the home and peeped cautiously through the window. He observed no one and tried turning the knob, which was expectedly locked. He didn't dare knock, fearing that a recognizable face, like Lali's, would appear, yet, strangely, he weighed kicking in the door, an action that would similarly draw company.

He impulsively turned around to audit the familiar room's contents, trying to conjure a way into the home without being detected. Suddenly, the light emitted from two powerful high beams washed the inside of the porch. A vehicle had just turned the corner and approached. *Was it Ravi, Chandra, et al., or perhaps some guests who had rented a car?*

Logan panicked. He could've made a break for it, but his emergence outside would definitely aid in identifying him, in spite of his changed appearance: living like a feral creature over the preceding weeks had grown him a new beard, like the one he once wore at Portlaoise Prison, before trimming it down to look like Stewie the priest, except that this beard was particularly unkempt due to his living conditions. The hair on top of his head was long again also, and God knows it needed shampooing, just like the rest of him. Minutes earlier, when standing at the kitchen door, he had caught a glimpse of his bedraggled self in a window reflection, for the first time in two and a half months, and the image looking back reminded him of mass-murderer Charles Manson, save for the swastika tattoo in the middle of Manson's forehead.

He casually sat down on a chaise. He had now resolved to hide inside the porch and attempt to overtake Ravi if the family entered through the front door, which they almost always did. After immobilizing Ravi, he envisioned himself bludgeoning the Dilwalis using random porch objects, except for lovely Chandra, who he irrationally believed would acquiesce to living the rest of her days with him.

In the end, Logan never scrambled within the porch to conceal himself. He remained seated, stupor-like, on the chaise. The car sped on by. It had not been the Dilwalis. He stood back up.

At the far end of the porch, he noticed a thinly constructed cardboard box, the kind a large birthday cake might come in. Inside the box, Chandra had stored a spare set of a gardening tools: a trowel, a claw, a dandelion fork, and some gloves, so that she didn't have to walk out back each time she needed such tools; the items were used exclusively for the flora growing outside the porch. Logan briefly examined the tools and deemed none useful. He then studied the box itself and tore off a flap, finally folding it over. The cardboard exterior was different from the interior in that it was white and relatively slick. He repeatedly ran the crease, formed by the new fold, through his fingers and pressed it hard to give it a firm edge. He then tried inserting the cardboard between the door latch and its catch while pushing on the front door. It took a little doing, but it helped that the device was pliable, and it worked; the door opened. He unlocked the door from the inside and closed it.

The foremost thing presently on his mind was to get in and out of the cottage before anyone could detect his intrusion and identify him;

better for them if he went unseen. He paced to the second floor, two steps at a time, as quietly as possible, and proceeded directly to the room he had occupied for several months; he noticed that no guest currently stayed in the room and that his belongings had long, since, been removed.

He scurried to the dresser and opened the bottom drawer. He felt underneath the central slat and recognized the strip of duct tape he had used to secure the diamond earrings and gold necklace. He tore the tape away, and the jewelries remained stuck to it. He folded the tape and inserted it into his right front pants pocket. He then inspected the dresser drawers and closet. All were empty.

He exited the bedroom and ambled purposefully down the hall to the master bedroom room, and rummaged for cash, which he failed to locate, and then did the same in Lali's room. It had always struck him that the jewelries worn by the women of the house were inexpensive, costume-jewelry, so he passed on stealing it. He bypassed daughter Lakshmi's room altogether. Once taking flight downstairs, it occurred to him that he had seen nothing of Ravi's belongings in the master bedroom, not even clothes in the closet. He stopped in his tracks and weighed returning to investigate; that is, until hearing the rumble of another passing vehicle, which underscored his need to collect some essentials and flee.

He walked from the den into the kitchen and removed a can opener from one drawer and some ordinary plastic sacks from another, where he knew Lali to keep them. He also filched a single set of eating utensils, a scarcely used cleaver that wouldn't be missed, a lone plastic plate, and a plastic cup. He subsequently entered the pantry, to quickly inventory the goods, and pilfered several cans of legumes and a handful of teabags from a box. From there, he scuttled into the adjacent Pack Room, where he knew Ravi to store all hiking and climbing related gear, and burgled a spare set of hiking boots, a large backpack suited for overnight treks, a small, two-man tent, a lightweight sleeping bag, a thick woolen blanket, a compass that clipped onto a zipper, an inflatable pillow, two pair of densely woven socks, a pair of winter gloves, and a winter hat that pulled over his ears. He needed to pass back through the kitchen in order to exit the cottage through the rear door, but paused at the refrigerator and stole four Clementine oranges and two bottles of water.

Now ready to depart, he recognized his torn feelings for Bolington Cottage. In one respect, he wished desperately to wake up from the nightmare he had been living in the wild over the last several weeks, so that he and Chandra were again slumbering intimately on the porch daybed. But that was not to be. With his hand on the doorknob, he peered one last time into the dining room where they had eaten so many delicious meals together, as if he had been one of the family, which thusly reminded him of why he had been scheming to eliminate Ravi. *Ravi didn't deserve to die for loving Chandra,* he thought, during an uncharacteristic compassionate moment. *It's best that things worked out the way they did. I wish Ravi well,* he whispered unconsciously, oblivious to the fact that his affair with Chandra had led to Ravi suffering a fatal heart attack. He then exited the cottage through the rear door and tramped down the back steps, with his varietal haul, and unwittingly stomped Ravi's ashes in the backyard, where the family had performed the Hindu cremation ritual weeks earlier.

Logan returned to The Hand for one night, to organize his gear, and then re-packed in the early morning light. Once departing rural Nainital it would take him several days to traverse north central India into western Nepal. Occasionally, he encountered paupers living under circumstances not too unlike those he had endured while dwelling about The Hand for so many weeks, and he wondered how these men and women managed during the cold winter months. He also met peasant farmers, and asked for directions to vendor stalls where a hot meal could be had, because his supply of staples was rapidly diminishing. The encounters prompted the curious peasants to unfailingly question the unsightly, western stranger about his attendance in their respective remote corners of Nepal, and he generally satisfied their inquiries by lying to them, with compass in hand, that he was circumnavigating the globe.

Logan eventually stumbled into the town of Dondeldhuro, where he recuperated in a ramshackle rooming house, ate ferociously, and had his tattered clothes laundered, which rendered them even more frayed. He emerged from the lodging, two days later, feeling rejuvenated, and converted some Euros to Nepali rupees at a bank before hopping a bus, east to Nuwokot. In downtown Nuwokot, he toured an outdoor market while waiting for a connecting bus to Katmandu.

As the distressed bus, sputtering blue smoke, rolled in to Katmandu, Logan was surprised and disappointed to discover that the city was westernized in many respects, especially with all its fast-food eateries catering to tourists. He disembarked and checked into a middle of the road hotel but soon ventured out to buy some new clothes, after deciding that he probably wouldn't fetch as much money for the jewelry he intended on pawning if appearing desperate and destitute. He also got a haircut and a shave.

Before searching out a pawnshop that afternoon, he impulsively entered an establishment called "Benders," for a pint of ale, in the tourist district, after deciding that he liked the name. It would be his first *taste* in months, and the result was that he wouldn't emerge from Benders for six hours. Ironically, he had nearly turned and walked out of the place after noticing that Bass Ale was served, because he knew it to be a popular English ale, and cursed the "*friggin' Brits for getting their grimy mitts in the first place* (he) *had entered.*" It would've been a mistake to depart Benders based on this bias, however, and if it hadn't been for an attractive, business-minded hostess accosting him and dissuading his flight, Logan might not have overheard an invaluable conversation taking place between two Americans sitting at a booth, adjacent to the bar where he sat.

While throwing down glass after glass of Kingfisher lager, he soon realized that the two Yanks were among the many mountain climbers who had traveled to Nepal that autumn to ascend Mount Everest. And, given his own affinity for climbing, coupled with his current inebriated state, Logan nearly intruded on their conversation, to which, in all likelihood, the tipsy Americans would not have objected; instead, he inched closer and shrewdly monitored them. Before long, he learned that the two had already hiked to Everest's Base Camp but opted not to continue their ascent to the summit due to one climber's discontent over the particular Sherpas they had hired:

"I need someone I can understand when the wind and snow are blowing at 75 miles an hour," one Yank had grumbled to the other. "Communication is critical under such conditions. Safety *must* come first or everything else is meaningless. Those Sherpas' accents were so thick, I could hardly understand anything they said," the man went on.

The American's complaint to his associate had planted an idea in Logan's head, and, while he was tempted to approach the men to try to strike a deal and operate as their paid guide, he knew that he needed better equipment and more climbing experience in this harsh, oxygen-thin, most unforgiving mountain region on Earth.

After the Americans left out of Benders, Logan paid his tab and trailed the men from afar, mostly in curiosity, although he did fantasize about murdering them at their hotel so that he could rip off their climbing gear and money. The Himalayas is someplace he imagined himself dwelling for the rest of his natural life, however, and that violent notion quickly vanished. Once the Americans turned a corner and were out of sight, he sought advice from a street vendor on the location of a reputable pawnbroker and, despite his conspicuous intoxicated state, managed to secure more than 320,000 Nepali rupees for the two diamond earrings, the equivalent of almost 3,000 Euros. He subsequently opened the locket on the gold necklace to view, one last time, the pictures of his late fraternal twin brother, Liam, and The Witch of Castlebar, Trish Jennings, before forfeiting the item. But the love-hate emotions the piece unexpectedly stirred in him were such that he experienced an overriding compulsion to hold on to it, and he would carry it reliably on his person for the rest of his days. Instead, he pulled the late Mr. Jennings' Rolex watch off his wrist and pawned it for some 90,000 rupees; later, replacing it with an inexpensive digital watch.

Over the succeeding *two decades*, Logan would live with a middle-class Nepali family outside Namche, the Sherpa capital of the Himalayas, where he rented a room featuring a private entrance so that he could come and go as he pleased; plus, he had meal privileges. Once acclimating to the higher elevation, and acquiring more suitable climbing gear, he traveled almost daily into nearby Namche to a humble, one room social club, where Sherpas congregated between expeditions, in hopes of engaging one of the many members of the international climbing community seeking guides for hire. In spite of the Sherpas' initial consternation over the business Logan increasingly took away from them, there was little the natives could do to deter his attendance, especially considering that he sought only the prevailing fee from clients; albeit, during the early days, he aimed to engage only those climbers wishing to ascend as far as Everest Base Camp, because those early runs to Base Camp, he knew, would help train and prepare him for, one day, reaching the summit.

His first ascent to the summit nearly killed him, as his attempt was made as neither a guide nor client. (He had learned of the arrival of an extensive French climbing party who brought their own guides, and he intercepted the group at Base Camp, where he tagged along and attempted to blend in). Logan succeeded in making the grueling ascent of Mount Everest on that trek and, what's more, could rightfully lay claim to such to prospective clients, but he lost three fingers and two toes to frostbite in the process. In the end, he ascended to the summit one more time only during his lifetime, after encountering some generous Italian climbers, who, like the Americans in Benders, preferred a guide they could better understand. Logan lost two additional fingers on his left hand to frostbite following that climb, and supported himself financially for the rest of his days by guiding clients to Base Camp only.

Twenty-two years after fleeing Ireland in the hooker he had stolen from his murder victim Aidan Drury, Logan McCool, now 62, was a toothless, mostly fingerless, *feck*, whose leathery, tanned face, from recurrent exposure to the severe elements, scarcely resembled the man from his Portlaoise Prison photo. And I think it's fair to say that any efforts by law enforcement to age-enhance that photo, to approximate his recent appearance, in hopes of finally picking him up, would be dreadfully futile. The transformation had been too extreme; surely his outing would require divine intervention.

Despite his western heritage, Logan eventually gained acceptance among the Sherpas, and, presently, played a friendly game of chess with a retired local guide at the social club, meanwhile, sipping a favorite black tea from India's Kumaon region, where Chandra dwelled, because drinking the tea made him feel close to her, still, after all these years. Suddenly, two young, strapping Caucasian lads entered the club in search of one or more guides, which was always a welcomed sight at this gathering place where locals vied for business. Like many climbers arriving in Namche with plans to ascend Mount Everest, the lads had taken a short flight from Katmandu, the day before, to a mountain airstrip in Lukla and then hiked 2850 meters to Phakding, where they lodged overnight. The next morning they rose and hiked another 3450 meters to Namche, and were further directed to the Sherpa social club, where they serendipitously encountered Logan.

Ten years or so ago, Logan would've leapt up ambitiously to engage the prospects, but now, at 62, he was far less tenacious and wasn't hurting for money. Instead of musing over how much he might be able to overcharge the youths, he seemed content to be sitting quietly and playing chess. He looked away from the lads and gulped some Kumaon tea, which had grown cool but still summoned Chandra to mind: Logan thought of her often, especially when lying on top of a favorite local prostitute and fantasizing it was *she* that he was fucking on the porch daybed at Bolington Cottage.

Logan thought he recognized an Irish brogue being spoken so moved Knight to Bishop-three and excused himself from the table. He took his tea with him and soon refreshed it with some boiling water, meanwhile hovering to listen in on the negotiation taking place. He was now certain that the young men were Irish, and was struck that the one doing most of the talking was naïve.

"I'm helping to put a son through college and will take you to the summit for five hundred less," Logan said forcefully enough to get the boys' attention.

After underpricing his competitor so drastically, his fellow guide cursed at Logan in Nepali, which he knew him to understand.

Logan's skin was so bronze after climbing at high altitudes for two plus decades that the lads thought the toothless man to be a local, and they were surprised to hear him speak English so well.

"How many times have you reached the summit," one lad asked assertively.

"Four times," Logan lied.

"You look rather... mature. When did you last ascend?"

"Less than a year ago," Logan again prevaricated, confident that neither the young men nor the few Sherpas present could possibly verify such.

"What part of the world are you from?" the other lad asked.

"England," he said, and then realized how awful it made him feel to say that because of his revulsion for the English.

"Really? Whereabouts?"

"Cornwall. It's in the south." Logan recalled that he had once told Ravi Dilwali he was from Cornwall, and decided to use it again.

The more self-assured of the two young men extended his hand while introducing himself.

"How do you do, sir. My name's Liam Jennings... from Castlebar, County Mayo, Ireland. My friends call me Eljay. Feel free to do the same."

Logan reached to shake the young man's hand while it felt like his heart was descending into his intestines. He hadn't yet considered that Eljay might be the son of his late twin brother, Liam, and Trish Jennings; he had only reacted, viscerally, to the sound of two names he cared to never hear again in the same sentence: Liam and Jennings. Then he thought about the man's home, Castlebar, and thought, *no, this can't be. I killed my brother. There's no way this kid is his bastard son.* Logan grew weak in the knees, and Eljay again spoke:

"This is my best friend in the world, Junior Drury from Westport, Ireland."

Logan tried smiling while shaking Junior's hand, but, just as Sister Mary Shaun had described Logan (to me) at the Galway train station, as she returned from sabbatical, his smile never reached his eyes. Logan then recalled the research he had once done over the Internet, at Bolington Cottage, about the murders he committed in Ireland, and that's when he first learned through an *Irish Independent* article that his victim, Aidan Drury, had been slated to serve as his brother's Best Man on the wedding day that never came to pass. Now, as he stood and talked with these two lads, he was hearing *Drury* and *Westport*, on the heels of *Liam* and *Jennings* and *Castlebar*.

"Junior? That's kind of an odd first name," Logan prodded.

"It's Aidan, actually. I was named after my late father, and my mother always called me Junior."

"I see. How do you, boys. Now will you be requiring my guide services or not?"

"I can't foresee anything that would stand in the way. What shall we call you, sir?" Eljay asked.

The diminutive Sherpas in the room had always known Logan as Tedi; "Tedi the Yeti" they called him, as in Sasquatch or Bigfoot, because of his relatively tall stature. This is what the natives had come up with after Logan started trekking with them more than two decades earlier and fatefully introduced himself as Teddy Halloran.

"Just call me Teddy," replied Logan, mindful that his fellow guides were within earshot.

"Does Teddy have a last name?" Eljay asked, tongue-in-cheek.

"Halloran. Teddy Halloran," Logan responded with perceptible annoyance, now standing with his hands on his hips.

"Junior and I don't care to idle too long in Namche, Teddy. In fact, we think that we could easily hike to Base Camp and wait for you there. How soon will you be available to climb?"

"I only need one day to get my gear together and to take care of some matters at home. Don't attempt to go it alone to Base Camp, boys. The trek is more demanding than you might imagine. You'll need an experienced guide. We'll depart from here at 6 a.m., the day after tomorrow. Alright? And you should have cash in hand when arriving."

"That sounds agreeable," Eljay said, looking back and forth between Junior and Teddy, to verify that Junior also approved. Junior only nodded. "Very well. 6 a.m., Thursday morning, it is. See you here."

"See you then, boys," Logan said, and picked up his mug to splash more hot water into it.

Eljay and Junior thusly departed the Sherpa social club.

Logan could've easily organized his gear and packed that evening and been ready to commence climbing the following day; however, based on the scam he intended on running he needed to, at least temporarily, move out of the quarters he had rented over the last several years – reason being, all Sherpas knew where he lived, and after Eljay and Junior were swindled and returned to the club to search him out, he knew that the Sherpas would direct the victims to his place of residence.

Logan had offered the men a discount for his guide services to the summit, but, after collecting the money, his scheme was to flee surreptitiously after stopping overnight at Pheriche, Lobuche, or Base Camp, all of which regularly bustled with trekkers during the spring and autumn months. Once running off, he planned to take any number of intersecting paths that split off from the Base Camp trail; he intended to live in the mountains for many days or weeks, just as he had done at The Hand in the foothills near Bolington Cottage, until feeling it was safe to return to his familiar community. He imagined, then, what the reactions would be among the Sherpas at the social club, especially considering that he'd taint the guild's reputation, but he just couldn't resist trying to get one over on, what he perceived to be, two daft greenhorns, knowing it would result in a sizeable payday. Logan would spend the day prior, to their departure, stocking up on food and other supplies, to help sustain him in the austere conditions to which he intended on subjecting himself.

Two days later, at 6 a.m., Eljay Jennings and Junior Drury arrived at the Sherpa social club, which was locked, so they waited outside. Tedi the Yeti was nowhere to be found, but they hadn't yet relinquished any funds to him so didn't fret. Twenty-five minutes passed before an elderly Sherpa appeared, to open up, and invited the young men inside for a hot beverage while they waited. It would take several more minutes for the water to boil, and, in the interim, Tedi finally showed up, riding in the rear compartment of an oversized all-terrain vehicle that was scarcely larger than a golf-cart. Once the driver parked the mini-rig, he stepped out and helped Tedi load the men's gear into the back, which quickly drew Junior outside, because he had been keeping a close eye on their things. Eljay followed Junior.

Logan thought that the lads might complain about his tardiness, and was ready for them.

"Sorry for the delay, boys, but my driver had a little domestic issue to deal with," Logan lied, and didn't seemed concerned that the driver had overheard him.

"Yes, Tedi, we were a little concerned that you were going to be a no-show. Is the delay going to affect our ascent in any way?" Eljay asked while studying the two men loading their gear.

"Not at all," replied Tedi. "Don't you worry. We'll still make it to Base Camp in six days. Get yourselves a cup of coffee or tea, now, before we leave. Soon we'll be on our way.

Neither man cared to return inside for a hot drink, so Logan said, "I'll need to receive payment before we depart."

Logan had long decided that Eljay was the more clever of the two greenhorns, and he looked to him first. Meanwhile, Junior didn't care for Tedi's shifty aspect, and watched as Eljay reached into his pocket for the money.

"This will cover the two of us," said Eljay.

Logan reached for the money, but Eljay pulled it back before Tedi could snatch it with the thumb and pinky remaining on his left hand.

"We're going to do things *properly* on this trek, isn't that so, Tedi?" Eljay ascertained while searching their guide's face for deceit.

"I wouldn't have it any other way, boys. I want to return home safely, too, you know." Tedi smiled thinly, and Junior thought him to be evil.

Eljay handed "Tedi" the money, and Logan tested them and see if they possessed additional funds.

"You don't have to pay me in rupees, you know. I'll take Euros if you prefer."

"That's all there is," Eljay responded warily.

Logan counted the money perfunctorily and inserted the wad in his pocket.

"We should go, now," Tedi said. "Hop in the back with your gear, and I'll ride bitch with Anand."

Both Eljay and Junior laughed at Tedi's last remark, and the cynicism that had prevailed during their exchange seemed to dissipate.

Three days prior, in Katmandu, the young men had called their mothers, respectively in Castlebar and Westport, to talk at length before undertaking their colossal but risky adventure, which they still couldn't be talked out of, and it occurred to Eljay's mother, Trish Jennings, after studying a regional map more closely, that, upon their descent from Mount Everest, they might consider visiting "Uncle Albert" in nearby Nainital, India. If truth be told, at 84 years young, I could only recall having met Eljay once as toddler, and I never would've recognized him, if he were to show up at Bolington Cottage, if it hadn't been for the Omniscient One's advice, which, as aforementioned, arrived in the visual packet I presently disseminate.

As Eljay and Junior shifted in their seats during the bumpy ride in the back of the mini-conveyance, they further discussed the possibility of straying over the border to visit Uncle Albert. And if either lad had mentioned the town of Nainital, during it all, Logan's ears naturally would've pricked, but, currently, he was still in a state of denial that the two young men were the offspring of the parties he had murdered in Ireland some two decades ago. Likewise, Eljay or Junior couldn't have known that the man sitting in the right front passenger seat was the assailant who killed their fathers and Eljay's grandparents.

Before departing the Sherpa social club earlier that morning, Eljay and Junior had imagined themselves trekking on foot, and, as the foursome currently motored past numerous trekkers and Sherpas, lugging full packs and sundry gear, Junior opined to Eljay, under his breath, that Tedi was gypping them, because they were commencing the climb too far up on the trail.

"He'd drive us all the way to Base Camp if he could," Junior complained.

"It's probably due to the late start," said Eljay.

Eighteen minutes later, Anand parked his all-terrain vehicle in an open, craggy area adjacent to a trail that's used as a resting place by Tibetan yak caravans that have crossed over the glacier; the irregular, challenging terrain ahead made it impossible for any wheeled transports to proceed further.

The first leg of their trek was to the village of Tengboche, and the cellular phones they carried would operate until passing just beyond there. Once ascending to a higher altitude, one requires a satellite phone to communicate long distance.

After an hour of hiking with full packs on their backs, plus carrying gear, the two lads wouldn't complain about where they resumed ascending, because of their increasing light-headedness, spawned by the ever-thinning oxygen supply. The foursome paused often during this stage (from Namche to Tengboche), and Junior snapped a picture of Mount Everest once they got their first good look at the peak.

They soon passed through several small villages boasting teahouses, which are popular among trekkers and feature basic lodging and meals, prompting Eljay to express a desire to rest and eat. Logan considered the request but decided they weren't far enough away from Namche for him to pull off his caper, and that Eljay and Junior might track him down and beat him to a pulp. Accordingly, the nefarious guide insisted that they carry on toward Tengboche.

Two and half hours later, they descended a stretch of trail that led to a wide footbridge at a river near Phunki Tenga, another popular place to rest and eat at a teahouse or vendor stall, which they did, each devouring a steaming bowl of buckwheat noodles in hearty broth with scallions and coriander.

Despite the generation gap between "Tedi" and the young men, the trio had now spent enough time together that a certain camaraderie had developed. However, any playfulness was soon tempered due to the stiff demands of the next stretch of steep, irregular trail that ascended toward Tengboche, and Junior requested that they be allowed to rest, once reaching a well-known Buddhist monastery he had read about when researching their prospective trip in Ireland.

The trio arrived at the monastery in late afternoon, and Tedi instructed the lads to shed their packs and leave them on the ground with their other gear, before entering, because, otherwise, it would be disrespectful to unload their cargo inside the temple. In reality, despite the numerous times he had ascended to Base Camp over the years, this was the first time Logan had delayed at the monastery at Tengboche; he now lied to his clients in order to manage their perceptions, after appraising their weariness and deeming it the right time to flee without providing the guide services for which they had paid. After the lads cast their gear, stretched their muscles, and collected themselves, Tedi encouraged them to enter and tour the temple while he remained outside and protected their belongings from mountain thieves he alleged to be prowling opportunistically. What's more, he claimed that he would soon join them, once a monk happened by, because he typically made a small donation to the monastery if a monk agreed to mind their equipment, which, of course, was also double-talk.

The lads concurred and walked inside the temple, prompting Logan to abandon their gear and scramble about trying to locate a Buddhist monk; he knew that once Eljay and Junior emerged to behold the monk that they would wait around for "Tedi" to surface. And after sufficient time had passed that the men sensed that something was amiss, Logan hoped to be long gone. In the end, however, Logan failed to immediately find a monk, and fled impulsively with his unwieldy backpack in tow.

Every dog has his day, so the expression goes, and, for Logan McCool, that day had, at long last, arrived. Both Eljay and Junior had been admiring the ancient yet robust architecture inside, as well as an iconic sculpture of the Buddha and some extraordinary carvings and paintings; and, as Eljay inched deeper into the temple, to consider yet more artistic renderings, Junior instinctively returned to the doorway to check on their things, because Tedi had never quite gained his confidence. "There had always been something about his face," he would later recount to inquisitors.

Junior's and Eljay's gear was still sitting on the ground, but neither Tedi nor a monk stood watch over it, so Junior peered south, in the direction of the trail from whence they had come, and, there, in the distance, he espied the familiar person of Tedi the Yeti waddling down the trail, with his cumbersome backpack toward Phunki Tenga. Junior subsequently alerted Eljay, but took flight without waiting for his lifelong friend, and pursued Tedi while yelling the thief's name and cursing at him. Once realizing that younger, more agile Junior was chasing him, Logan urgently removed his heavy pack and abandoned it; with his pocketful of cash, he'd recover his losses many times over.

Eljay had just exited the monastery and passed by their gear on the ground and apparently wasn't concerned about the thieves Tedi claimed to be lying in wait. Further down the trail, Junior had gained ground on Tedi, so the reprobate halted to collect some throwable rocks and hurl them at his hostile suitor, which only succeeded in slowing Junior, who dodged the projectiles, as Eljay approached from the rear. Tedi soon resumed flight, but both men clearly saw him descending laboredly on the part of the trail leading to the footbridge suspended over the river at Phunki Tenga. Crossing the bridge from the opposite side was a party of twelve American trekkers.

Now, the thing about humans is that we tend to walk on the same side that we drive, when encountering approaching traffic. Thus, in the case of Logan, he rushed past a teahouse onto the footbridge and, upon encountering the Americans, stayed to the left, because he had always driven on the left side of the road in Ireland. As for the Americans, they noticed the hurried person drawing near, and kept to the right while continuing to march. The result, of course, is that something or someone had to give: it was one against twelve.

The moment Logan collided with the two front trekkers, lugging immense stores of equipment, he deflected off the stalwart procession and tumbled beneath the railing that adequately safeguards crossing pedestrians, so long as they're upright. But Logan was no longer on his feet and had rolled to the edge of the pliant bridge, where he clutched at the bottom railing with his left hand while trying to grip the slatted platform with his right. He quickly had three factors working against him: the momentum of his tumbling body, gravity (once he began slipping), and, most importantly, his incomplete set of fingers, especially on his left hand. With ten digits, he might've prevented his fall, but, on his left hand, he operated mainly using his palm.

Logan plunged some thirty feet onto the rocky shoreline below, landing on his head. His fall was considerably less than his trip down Banyan Canyon, some two decades earlier, but this time there was nothing to break his fall. Moreover, it was the way he fell – he had broken his neck.

Junior and Eljay had witnessed the mishap from afar during their descent and immediately clambered down the riverbank once arriving at the footbridge. Meanwhile, the Americans struggled to shed their bulky packs and offered assistance.

Eljay's cellular phone was again in operating range, so he removed it to make an emergency call, but Junior reminded him of the teahouse a few meters away, and yelled up to the Americans, still gaping down from the bridge, to run inside and urge the teahouse owner to call for help.

Logan remained unconscious, and, while he breathed faintly through his nostrils, his chest soon quit heaving. Eljay again checked Logan's pulse. It grew weaker each few seconds.

"He's gone," Eljay finally shouted. Another trekker ran inside the teahouse to request that the owner make a second call, because he knew that emergency service personnel would respond differently.

Eljay pulled "Tedi" away from the water's edge, and, once he was situated, Junior reached inside the deceased guide's pocket to remove his money. Most of the Americans had started loading up again, but one Yank, still looking below, noticed Junior's extraction and protested.

"This guy just ripped us off," explained Junior. "That's why he was running. He was supposed to guide us to Base Camp, but he waited for the right moment and fled. We're just taking the money that's rightfully ours."

Junior's explanation had sounded reasonable, and all present, save for Eljay, Junior, and the decedent, resigned themselves to resume their northward trek. Eljay and Junior subsequently waited fifteen minutes for someone to emerge from the teahouse with news of what would happen next, as far as the disposition of Tedi's body, but when no one came, Junior trudged up the riverbank and walked inside the teahouse.

It seems that due to the difficult terrain and lack of suitable landing space for a helicopter near Phunki Tenga, and the fact that the accident victim was dead, authorities had requested that the teahouse owner arrange for the victim's body to be transported, by a local with a yak, to the Lukla landing strip, and all parties would be compensated. Once Junior learned this, he returned outside and relayed the same to Eljay, who still sat on the rocky shore beside a dead Tedi the Yeti.

Ironically, Eljay felt uncomfortable abandoning Tedi's corpse, despite the swindler's infraction, but he eventually joined Junior back up on the trail. Minutes later, the pair again had the monastery in sight, but first they stopped to collect Tedi's pack, which still lay undisturbed after apparently failing to rouse the curiosities of the twelve passing Americans.

Eljay donned the backpack to carry it up to the monastery. Once arriving, he opened it up to rummage through Tedi's belongings, because they had now decided to hazard ascending to Base Camp without the aid of a guide, and thought they might salvage some food items. The plan was to link up with a new guide at Base Camp rather than return to Namche.

While Eljay sorted through the pack, Junior reached curiously in his own pocket to remove the twisted wad of Nepali rupees he had taken from Tedi at the river. He peeled the cash open, to count it, and a gold necklace with locket fell to the ground.

"Ha. There was a little buried treasure inside," he declared, and picked up the necklace by the locket. Eljay merely glanced at Junior and continued sorting through Tedi's effects, because there was little a piece of jewelry could do for them on their journey, he *thought*.

Junior opened the locket and shockingly beheld a much younger "Aunt Trish," as he had always called her, despite their lack of blood relations, juxtaposed with another tiny picture of a man who looked vaguely familiar. It hadn't yet occurred to Junior that the other party was Eljay's father, Liam McCool, whose portrait still hung over the fireplace in the main residence at Jennings Equestrian Centre, which he had viewed on countless occasions over the years when visiting Eljay and Aunt Trish in Castlebar.

"This can't be," Junior said, stupefied. "Tedi had a picture of your mother in his pocket."

Eljay jumped up and snatched the necklace from Junior's hand.

"That's my father with her. My mother has the same full-size photo of herself in a picture album at home." Eljay was understandably *more* dumbfounded. "Are you sure that you didn't already have this in your possession, and scooped it from your pocket when removing the money?"

"Not a chance. I've never seen this before in my life. And what right would I have to possess it?"

Eljay removed his cellphone and attempted to make a long distance call to Ireland, to speak with his mother, but couldn't presently pick up a signal. He asked that Junior remain with their belongings while he slogged back down to Phunki Tenga to make a call from the teahouse. Once reaching the place, he tried a second time, to complete the call using his cellphone, and this time it went through.

It was still morning in Ireland, and Trish had been down at the stables, so when Eljay received the answering machine he left a brief message. He secondarily called Trish's cellphone, which was clipped to her riding pants and currently vibrated. Trish flipped open the phone and recognized Eljay's number displayed in the Caller ID, causing her heart to sink, because she feared something had gone wrong during her son's ascent to Everest. In a manner of speaking, it had.

"Eljay, is that you?" Trish answered with concern in her voice.

"Yes, Mum."

"Are you alright?"

"Yes, I'm fine. Listen, this call is going to cost a bundle so let me get straight to the point."

"Okay."

"What do you know about a gold necklace with a locket that contains tiny photos of you and Dad?"

"Sacred Heart! I've been missing that for years."

"Well, I'm standing here with it in my hand, right now. The locket was in the pocket of our guide, who died a short while ago."

"What?! How is that so?"

"Let me ask you something. I remember you once mentioning that the man who murdered Dad and grandma and granddad had ransacked our house before running off. What was his name and what did he look like?"

"His name was Logan McCool. He was on the slender side... about six feet one or two and had light brown hair. But aren't you using the Sherpa guides you once described to me?"

"We hired a Caucasian guide because he had lived in the region for many years and apparently had lots of experience climbing to the summit. Plus, he was charging us five hundred less than the Sherpas. His name wasn't Logan McCool, though. Teddy Halloran, he called himself... from Cornwall, England. His hair might've been brown once, but it's gray now. He's definitely taller than six feet... and he's also dead."

"Logan despised the English too much. He never would've claimed to have been from there." Trish grew skeptical for a moment. "But he *was* a mountain climber, Eljay! He once climbed the Matterhorn in Switzerland! Did he speak with an Ulster accent?"

"Well, if it's him, he won't be climbing anymore. He didn't speak with much of an accent at all. He also tried ripping-off Junior and me... he fled with our money... and then collided with an American trekking party on a footbridge, while trying to escape, and rolled off and landed on his head. The poor bloke broke his neck. I'm walking over to the bridge right now to take another look at him." Eljay did so and leaned over to gaze below at the rocky, river shore where he had sat earlier with Tedi as he was dying. "He's gone. After he died, the Nepali government made arrangements for his body to be transported on the back of yak, to a mountainside landing strip in Lukla. From there, I suppose his body will be flown to Katmandu. What they'll do after that, I don't know."

"Eljay, you should try to locate and accompany the party who's delivering the body. If it's truly Logan McCool, there's been a monetary reward outstanding on his head ever since he committed all those murders in Ireland, before you were born. Once you tell your story to police, and the Garda and Interpol are notified, you'll likely receive recompense."

"How much? Because Junior and I wouldn't want to miss out on reaching the summit."

"I don't know how much, but I can try and find out. More importantly, I'm asking you to take responsibility and see this matter through, Eljay. Families have suffered greatly because of Logan McCool's actions. He murdered the father and grandparents you never met. We need to find out if it's Logan on the back of that yak."

"Alright, Mum. Message conveyed. Junior and I can always return to Everest another year."

"Precisely. Call me back when you find something out."

"Will do. Love you."

"I love you, too... and stay safe. Bye."

"Bye."

Eljay scampered off the bridge and over to the teahouse to inquire from the owner how many minutes had elapsed since Tedi was removed. The owner guessed thirty minutes. Eljay then re-ascended the meandering trail that led to the monastery, where Junior presently lounged against the backpacks on the ground.

"Let's go. Unless you've discovered something of interest among Tedi's gear, just leave his shit and let's get outta here. My mother thinks that Tedi might actually be Logan McCool, the bloke who killed your father and mine."

"What?!"

"You heard right. And there was a reward on his head. We're gonna track that yak driver down and stay with the body until it's fingerprinted in Katmandu. We've got a story to tell, and if there's money to be had, we deserve to collect it."

The two men donned their backpacks and descended without looking back at the Buddhist monastery. One day they hoped to return and do it more justice during a second attempt at ascending Mount Everest.

Trekking *down* the trail predictably took less time and, despite their cumbersome packs, they finally caught up with the yak driver about three miles short of the Sherpa capital of Namche. The driver led the yak by a short rope, attached to a crude harness, and Tedi's body was secured, stomach-side down, on the beast; a blanket shrouded his body, in respect. Eljay greeted the driver and identified himself and Junior in relation to the deceased, but the driver acted indifferent. Once they reached Namche, Eljay requested that the driver delay there so that Junior could summon some of Tedi's guide-friends from the Sherpa social club, because he thought the men would be interested to know of Tedi's demise. The driver complied, and several Sherpas were visibly upset to view their longtime associate dead atop the yak, despite the guild's early objections to his imposition. Chief among the mourners was Tedi's frequent chess opponent, who rested his hand on his friend's corpse and wept gently. He then asked if he might take possession of the body so that Tedi could be cremated there. The yak driver responded by disclosing his strict orders to transport the body to the Lukla airstrip.

From Namche, the lads accompanied the yak driver and corpse to Phakding, and the four lodged in cramped quarters overnight at a teahouse, where Junior awakened frequently, because, as much as he had rightfully distrusted Tedi in life, he curiously trusted him less in death. What's more, in spite of the bracing evening air that expectedly carried over to morning, Tedi was rapidly growing foul in decomposition. And once the foursome descended to the mountain airstrip at Lukla, several hours later, and Eljay and Junior identified themselves to the pilot, Junior was forced to sit beside Tedi in the four-seat Cessna aircraft that awaited them, as the pilot routinely belted-in the corpse upright in a seat. This time, Eljay rode bitch to the pilot while Junior sat with dead Tedi, and his crooked neck, who now had an oil-stained rag draped over his head, secured by a bungee cord, because the departing yak driver had snatched the wool blanket that covered the body. Now the lads couldn't help but stare at Tedi's graying hands, missing so many fingers, while they breathed in seemingly noxious fumes of rot and decay that had overtaken the plane's cabin.

After Eljay and Junior recounted their story to police in Katmandu, and included the fantastic find of the locket on Tedi's person (even though the piece was discovered later among the rupees taken from Tedi's pocket), fingerprints were taken from the victim's few remaining fingers, and palms, and digital copies were transmitted electronically to Interpol; the decedent's identity was later confirmed as murderer and long-time fugitive, Logan McCool. Nepalese medical examiners secondarily took dental impressions, and while his incisors were largely missing, his molars and bicuspids were sufficiently in tact that a match was ultimately made with archived dental records at Portlaoise Prison, Ireland. Subsequently, both a Garda Inspector from Ireland and an Interpol agent were dispatched to physically view the body before the case could be officially closed.

Eljay and Junior puttered around Katmandu for a day while waiting for the police representatives to arrive.

After examining the corpse, the officials met with the two Irishmen to interview them, and, once confirming their identities, the Garda Inspector informed them of the longstanding reward money that had been posted for information leading to Logan McCool's apprehension. Astoundingly, the reward amount had only recently been adjusted after remaining fixed for twenty two years: It seems that Logan McCool had been one of the most sought after fugitives in Europe, and Eljay and Junior would split 300,000 Euros.

Logan's parents had died many years earlier in Londonderry, and he had no surviving relatives, and neither the Irish government nor Interpol cared to bear the cost of transporting his body back to Ireland, only to bear yet more costs relative to his final disposition; thus, cremation arrangements were made in Katmandu. Upon learning this, Eljay unexpectedly felt saddened. The brutal murders of his father and grandparents, and Junior's father, among others, notwithstanding, Eljay recalled the poignant scene outside the Sherpa social club when Tedi's body arrived in Namche on the back of the yak, as well as the touching appeal made by Tedi's chess opponent to allow him to be cremated there. Eljay then shocked Junior by paying to have Logan McCool's body flown back up to the mountain airstrip at Lukla and further transported to the Sherpa social club at Namche, along with instructions for cremation.

The following day, Eljay and Junior hopped a bus toward west Nepal in order to cross the border into the Kumaon region of north-central India, where they would seek out a place called Bolington Cottage, in Nainital, because there they knew their "Uncle Albert" to dwell.

My visual packet diffused.

Three days after Eljay and Junior departed Katmandu, Tedi the Yeti was cremated at the edge of the trail leading from Namche to Tengboche on the ascent to Everest Base Camp.

55

I HAD BEEN SLUMBERING IN my familiar backyard hammock at Bolington Cottage when hearing the conspicuous thuds of car doors slamming. I strained to look toward the gravel parking area but noticed no new arrivals; the driver had apparently dropped his passengers at the front porch, which explained why I failed to see anybody.

In light of the advice I received in my recent visual packet, I was eager to receive Eljay and Junior, so rolled from my hammock and crept up the back steps to the kitchen.

Lali had been peeling potatoes at the counter and said, "We have new guests, sir."

"How many?" I asked

"Two males," she said. "But they're arriving without reservations."

"That's alright," I said. "We've got plenty of room."

I ambled through the kitchen into the dining room and noticed the two young men standing in the porch, talking with Chandra. The bags at their feet were ordinary, and oddly didn't include any supplementary climbing paraphernalia. My arrival at the porch stirred Chandra and the lads, and at that moment I recognized that the men were not Eljay and Junior.

"Honey, say hello to Rolf and Sven from Malmo, Sweden. They're just returning from Nanda Devi. Our friends at Dutton Cottage called to ask if we might take some of their overflow, and, except for Magesh, we're basically empty, so I obliged."

I reached over to shake the men's hands.

"How do you do, fellas, I'm Albert Doyle. Will you be doing any trekking while staying with us?"

Rolf did most of the talking, and stated that they only expected to venture into downtown Nainital, which didn't matter much to me, because, at 84, I scarcely endeavored into the foothills anymore. Nowadays, Chandra still accompanied hiker-guests up on some of the less steep trails, but we continued to rely, more so, on our more youthful neighbor, Fareed, to escort guests on challenging treks.

The twins, Namitha and Saritha, had been upstairs in the room they shared, and skipped down to the porch to join us upon hearing the young men's voices. Rolf and Sven were perhaps a year or two older than our beautiful twins, and, curiously, seemed disinterested in them, which plainly disappointed the girls. Everything came into better focus, later, though, when observing Rolf and Sven over dinner in the company of Magesh, the queer, now a much older queer, who still traveled from Punjab twice yearly to stay at Bolington. Like Magesh, Rolf and Sven were also clearly fancy-boys, which accounted for the intimate accommodations they had requested.

After dinner, I had retired to the porch and was sitting alone while sipping a cup of black tea and devouring a real page-turner, *Grave Matters*, when a taxi from town stopped in front of the cottage. Two strapping lads emerged from the rear, while the driver stuffed the fare in his pocket and paced to the boot to remove their luggage. I studied the travelers through the window and soon recognized them, from my visual packet, to be Eljay and Junior, which elated me. I took a mouthful of tea and placed my book down, to rise and greet the men outside.

"Eljay and Junior, I presume... fresh off the trail to Everest Base Camp."

The two youths were at first speechless. Eljay had been holding a bag in each hand but quickly set them down.

"Uncle Albert?"

"Yes." I walked toward the lads while smiling.

"How ever did you know we were ascending Everest? Have you talked with my mother recently?"

I had now reached the lads and shook Eljay's hand first and then clasped his two shoulders warmly.

"No, I haven't talked with Trish in ages. We do exchange emails occasionally... plus Christmas cards. I haven't seen you since you were just a tike, you know." I then extended my hand to Junior.

"How do you do, sir," said Junior.

"How is it that you were aware we were on the trail to Everest Base Camp?"

"Through a visual packet from the Omniscient One," I replied.

Eljay and Junior looked at me like I had three eyes.

"Come again," Eljay said.

I then proceeded to explain, to the men, what a visual packet is, which logically led to a more comprehensive explanation about my service to the Omniscient One, over the years, and who the Omniscient One is. Eljay digested all of this and sat down, astonished, on the larger of his two bags, because he had had no clue of my extrasensory faculties. It soon became clear that, for whatever reason, his mother, Trish, had elected not to edify her son of her own insightful, albeit still dormant, abilities, not to mention my own; and, when Trish had informed Eljay of the circumstances that claimed the lives of his father and grandparents, there had been no discussion of the clairvoyant personalities involved at the periphery. The result was that the lads were demonstrably apprehensive about entering Bolington Cottage, which they now deemed a spooky edifice that might provide additional disturbances into their lives. They remained uneasy, in fact, until Chandra and Lali, followed by our dazzling twins, emerged outside. And once Eljay and Junior beheld Namitha and Saritha, and the twins gazed back, there was no deterring the ensuing natural forces.

Eljay and Junior lodged with us at Bolington Cottage for several days, but by midweek they had already decided to extend their stay in the Kumaon region (in order to trek and explore the foothills more thoroughly, wink,wink) and rented a waterside cabin, at the lake, with an open lease. While still at Bolington, Eljay had telephoned Trish in Ireland, and he passed the phone to me; despite our periodic emails and holiday card exchanges, it was the first time Trish and I had spoken in years, which renewed our warm feelings of friendship.

Chandra and I had first thought that our twins were too young to get involved in serious relationships, but then recognized that we were probably being overprotective and agreed that Eljay and Junior were both fine young men; and, if that be the Omniscient One's will, so be it.

Before long, Eljay and Junior were conducting all aspects of guide services on behalf of Foothill Trekkers, for which they were duly compensated, hence, pushing Fareed out of the picture. And, even on days when there were no clients to escort, it seemed that the lads gravitated to the trail network, more often than not accompanied by the twins. By now, Eljay had paired up with Saritha, and Junior with Namitha, and, after an afternoon of hiking, the foursome typically descended the central artery of The Hand, onto the grassy basin behind the cottage, holding hands as couples.

I suppose the first indication that Eljay and Junior were serious about remaining in Nainital was when Eljay asked for my assistance in helping them access their monies in Ireland, because deposits of their reward compensations had been made by their mothers into their accounts. Once converted into Indian rupees, one hundred fifty thousand Euros would last each man many years, if spent wisely. But long before those monies would deplete, Eljay and Junior remotely collaborated with their mothers to get the all-inclusive stories of Logan McCool's involvement in their lives, so that, coupled with their own Nepal experiences, they could co-author a gripping, non-fiction account that would provide them considerable royalties for years to come.

Ironically, Eljay and Junior had made the decision to travel from Katmandu to Nainital, partly, in curiosity, to meet "Uncle Albert," but, primarily, to satisfy Trish's request. In the end, however, the two friends would dwell in north central India the rest of their earthly days, leaving Nainital only three times during their lifetimes: once to show Trish Jennings and Mary Drury their respective grandchildren; once each to bury their mothers and close down the estates in Ireland; and once as a climbing duo to Nepal, where they returned to Namche and again engaged the Sherpas to finally conquer Mount Everest, which they accomplished and returned with their extremities in tact; these latter doings observed by me, after I had long departed for another dimension, (that had nothing to do with altitude), and exhorted the Omniscient One to activate and utilize a clairvoyant instrument to transliterate the unique circumstances of my mortal life, and of the lives I touched, the product of which is perfectly bound and proffered for review.

Fantastically, the individual to whom He bestowed the gift of second sight was the author of the book *Grave Matters*, which pleased me infinitely, and the selection of this requested favorite author validated to me, that, by and large, the Omniscient One was pleased with my service.

Lakshmi had succeeded in becoming a medical doctor and married her fellow doctor from Chennai, where they remained throughout their lives, save for once to twice yearly visits to Bolington Cottage; she and her husband bore two daughters of their own. Lali, our housekeeper and loyal friend, had outlived Chandra, and after Chandra died, Eljay and Saritha, and Junior and Namitha moved back to Bolington Cottage, and Foothill Trekkers continued to thrive; one day, their offspring would take over the business.

Chandra's ashes were fittingly spread over her beloved garden, of which she is now part, and it flourishes more magnificently than ever, despite lacking her devout maintenance. Once Lali died, she was cremated in the grassy basin that looks up to The Hand, the view of which she loved so much from her familiar kitchen window perch.

Finally, friends, I'm compelled to report, through this second-sighted transliterator, some disturbing news of which I wasn't aware until passing over to the other side. If the reader had keyed in to some specific language used earlier in this narrative, then the disclosure might not surprise:

Back when was I describing Logan McCool's early imposition on the Sherpas at Namche, I stated that he "fatefully" introduced himself as Teddy Halloran. The reason I was careful to include this adverb was that the year before Logan had fled Nainital for Nepal, I had reassembled Aidan Drury's hooker in Ireland, painted it beige, replaced its maroon sails with white, and asked old friend Fred Hurley to secure it at a slip in the Kinvara Harbor waters. That hooker, you'll recall, was subsequently stolen before the widow Mary Drury, or anyone else, could take custody, and I now know the thief, through my eternal perspective, to be a man named Theodore Halloran, who had once gone by "Teddy." What I'm still working on, and I hope to disseminate in a future communiqué through use of this clairvoyant transcriber, is trying to discover if Logan's decision to use the name, in Nepal, was based on a former friendship with the very same Teddy Halloran, or if he had chosen the name randomly. Perhaps things will come into better focus once Teddy Halloran dies, because, at the time of this writing, he still miraculously lives and, according to my calculations, is more than 108 years old.

It seems that like Logan, Teddy Halloran had fancied himself as a bit of a rabble-rouser and rogue as a young man, certainly not on the same scale as Logan McCool, but a rogue, nonetheless. Originally from the Dingle peninsula, the real Teddy worked as a simple deckhand, and he loved that the large commercial fishing vessel he worked on was home-ported in Galway because, once the ship returned to dock, the city was very conducive to pub crawls. His affinity for revelry notwithstanding, drinking had rarely been a problem in Teddy's life; there had only been one or two incidences, over the span of a decade, when his carousing narrowly delayed his fishing vessel's launch. Teddy's problems soon compounded, however, once marrying a Dingle girl named Sylvie, who he unexpectedly met in Galway and forced him to live and behave more responsibly. After the wedding, Sylvie moved from Dingle to Galway so that the two could live together in a flat, as husband and wife, during the periods the vessel was docked. The problem was that, once Teddy returned to port after extended periods at sea, especially without imbibing, he still preferred the company of his shipmates. Quickly able to foresee the kind of married life she would suffer with Teddy, Sylvie walked out on him and returned to Dingle, which soon gnawed at Teddy, and his drinking worsened to the extent that he began sneaking whiskey onto the ship and was often drunk on duty.

Five months after Sylvie had left him, Teddy was sacked from his job, and he persuaded a fellow deckhand, Willie, to join him on the kind of memorable pub-crawl that would help him, at least temporarily, forget his troubles. That crawl started out in the afternoon in Galway, but, before the evening was over, the two found themselves in Kinvara, after driving cock-eyed to a pub called The Old Black Shawl, where Teddy claimed to have once found romance. The action had been slow that night at The Shawl, however, so Teddy enticed Willie to follow him on foot to yet another bar, Sexton's. There, the two continued drinking pints, and waited in hope that a couple of pretty lasses would soon enter. When that didn't pan out, Teddy suggested that they try one last spot, the Pierpoint, before returning to Galway City, where the action was guaranteed.

Now strolling under a quarter-moon, around the switch toward the Pierpoint, the two paused to take in the harbor sights, and wavered at the protective railing while saturating the proximate night air with their profuse alcoholic exhalations. Teddy soon thought of Sylvie and started with the crying jags. He then commenced a depressing monologue about what a shitbum he was for drinking too much, too often, which led to his wife leaving, and costing him his job. All this melancholy talk alienated Willie, who suggested they return to Galway.

During their discourse, the two had been standing before an ordinary hooker that they didn't know to be legendary in many respects. The sailboat was beige and featured white, furled sails.

"Who the *fook* painted this, I wonder," remarked Teddy. "A hooker should always be black... like the boat *me* Daddy had when I was growin' up. I don't care for the white sails, neither. They should be scarlet... even better, maroon."

"Different strokes for different folks," Willie replied.

"It's an abomination, I tell *ye*," said Teddy.

"Who gives a *shite*. It's just a *fookin'* boat."

"Ready to go the Pierpoint?" Teddy asked, gazing across to the pub, where he could make out some merriment going on inside.

"I don't wanna go. Let's just drive back to Galway."

"But you've never been there. I want you to see the place. Besides, both of us are too drunk to drive."

"I'm sure it's a very nice place, but if we're still hopin' to get laid we should leave now for Galway," responded Willie.

"I'm not goin'. You go ahead," Teddy said.

"But how will you get back to Galway? There's no bus service until tomorrow. You gonna get a room at a tourist home?"

"No. I'm goin' home to Dingle... I just decided. I'm gonna try to work things out with Sylvie."

"Tonight?" Willie laughed because he knew it would be even more of a predicament to reach Dingle this late in the evening. "And how do you intend on getting there?"

"You let me worry about that. I'm goin' over to the Pierpoint for a nightcap. Comin'?"

"No, I'm afraid not. I've got a pub in mind near Eyre Square."

"See you," Teddy said.

Willie snickered, and the two men parted ways.

The real Teddy Halloran never entered the Pierpoint that night. Instead, he staggered over to the slip containing the beige hooker with white, furled sails and boarded it. He unknotted the rope that secured the boat to the slip, and used an oar to push it away from the dock.

Once in more open waters he swiftly unfurled the sails, which soon collected some light winds, and skillfully maneuvered the vessel west out of Kinvara Harbor. He continued sailing west for several minutes, until gradually steering south toward the Dingle peninsula.

Part of Teddy's inebriated self had only wanted to borrow the boat so that he could obsessively paint over the beige color and replace the white sails, both of which he had found so objectionable. But, once sailing away, he knew that he would never return the boat, justifying the thievery by convincing himself that anyone who painted the boat beige didn't deserve to keep it anyhow. The foremost reason he had seized the hooker, however, was that he knew it would immediately set him on course to Sylvie, who he deludedly envisioned waiting for him.

Teddy's father had owned a stately seaside home on the southwest tip of the Dingle peninsula, and Teddy beached the hooker in front of the property at about noon the following day. Within the first week, he had painted the hooker black, replaced the white sails with maroon, and commenced fishing for a living.

He never informed Sylvie, upon returning to Dingle, that he had been fired in Galway for drinking on duty, and she was won over that he had quit his job to be near her again. What's more, she was elated that Teddy had apparently given up the drink, his last taste being the pint with Willie that night at Sexton's in Kinvara. Soon, Sylvie moved in with Teddy and his elderly father at the seaside home, and the couple didn't waste any time in producing a son, James. As for the drink, one day Teddy regrettably returned to the bottle, when his troubles grew too immense to bear:

Eighteen months after they parted company, Willie traveled to Dingle to visit Teddy and Sylvie, while his ship was in port for an extended stay for repairs. Within hours of Willie's arrival, Teddy took him out for some deep-sea fishing on the hooker, but never revealed to his unsuspecting friend that it was the same sailboat they had stood before, intoxicated, that night at Kinvara Harbor.

The two rogues sailed southwest past Great Blasket Island, and, three hours later, with no sight of land in any direction, they pulled in the sails and dropped anchor to commence fishing. They landed three worthwhile salmon in no time, but the refreshing winds eerily died and the fish stopped biting, so they reeled in the anchor and unfurled the sails, intending on returning to Dingle.

But, there, far out in the Atlantic Ocean, stillness prevailed, and Teddy and Willie would sit and stand and pace and sleep, as hours turned into days, and days into weeks, because no winds were spawned to propel the hooker. And during that same anomalous period, despite possessing perfectly functioning fishing equipment, and sitting over what is generally considered one of the richest fishing grounds on the planet, the two failed to catch any more fish to sustain themselves; neither did they have drinkable water.

Seventeen days earlier, Teddy had discharged the lone emergency flare on board, to signal their distress, when observing a sizeable commercial cruise ship in the horizon. That ship neglected to respond, and on the occasions he and Willie yelled and flailed their arms urgently at other engine-propelled boats in the distance, the passengers merely waved, as if returning a greeting.

The two men, with all their seafaring experience, were expectedly perplexed over the protracted maritime conditions that led to their miserable circumstance, because they had never experienced such, and Teddy wondered why no official naval boats searched for them, reasoning that Sylvie must've telephoned someone.

Blistered badly after nearly three weeks of sun exposure, and parched to the brink of death, Teddy waited until Willie faced away from him, and desperately struck his friend down with a heavy oar. He then carved him up with a fishing knife and proceeded to cannibalize him over the succeeding two days. Once devouring what he judged to be all of Willie's beneficial body parts, and weary from fighting off scavenging seagulls, Teddy tossed his friend's carcass into the sea, and the winds paradoxically returned. Those winds gradually intensified into hurricane-like gusts, except that there were no accompanying rains, and, consequently, his hooker now moved at the speed of a more powerful cutter toward the Dingle peninsula.

Back at home, a dejected Sylvie had scuttled outside to collect some bed sheets from a backyard clothesline that were flapping furiously due to the same steadfast winds currently propelling Teddy's hooker.

Weeks earlier, Sylvie had notified maritime authorities of Teddy and Willie's failure to return home, and, after two days of ardent searching, using watercraft and aircraft, the mission to locate the missing men was called off. Sylvie had not actually mourned her husband's loss, though, because she remained suspicious that Teddy had lapsed into drinking and again preferred the company of his mates; this time, fleeing with Willie to some exotic port. She never shared her beliefs with authorities.

In the weeks since the men went missing, Teddy's father had died, and one can only assume that the stress and anxiety the elder experienced, concerning his son's apparent premature demise, ultimately contributed to the cardiac arrest that claimed his life. It seems that Teddy and his father were very close.

Intensifying winds were now thrusting Teddy's hooker about so violently that he had all to do to prevent himself from bouncing from behind the boat's wheel into the sea; the same journey that had taken he and Willie three hours to reach their fishing spot would now take Teddy less than an hour to return to Dingle.

Back behind the seaside home, a lashing, whipping bedsheet, that Sylvie attempted to gather in from the clothesline, had just wrapped around her head and face, and the more frantically she tried to remove it, the more disoriented she became. The woman soon dizzied, due to lack of oxygen, and fell and hit her head on the hard ground, which prolonged her unconsciousness, as the sheet still covered her nose and mouth. Tragically, Sylvie would never revive.

And when it finally occurred to baby James that he missed his Mum, the youngster toddled outside to find her asleep in the backyard, so he let her be. Meanwhile, he fascinated over ordinary yard items being picked up by invisible forces and shot across the landscape. He then fought through powerful drafts of air to make his way around the front side of the home, where Daddy often anchored his boat offshore, and he was drawn to the action of huge waves crashing frothily on the beach. James edged as close to the ocean as he could without falling off a concrete retaining wall, but it only took one mighty gust to whisk the boy from his feet and turn him, also, into a projectile, tossing him some twenty-five feet onto the sandy shore.

At first, the tot understandably cried, but he soon collected himself and again stood to marvel at the deafening waves surging up to drench his shoes and socks. Little James was now excited to be on the beach, because his pocketed position between the retaining wall and shore was protecting him from more powerful winds blowing overhead, while gentler winds served to dry his tears.

Presently, Teddy speedily approached the southwest side of the Dingle peninsula, and he imagined how Sylvie and his father would react to his return after being stranded at sea for some three weeks. There were moments, during his progress, that the hooker rode like a catamaran, tipping on its side so that the hull was exposed. The wind force had also pasted his hair back straight, and his scorched red cheeks flapped in unison with the maroon sails above. He looked villainous.

From a distance, he noticed a small child standing on the shore. The toddler was alone, and he could even make out the boy's fluttering gray sweatshirt and blonde hair flying about. *It must be James,* he thought and then panicked, because he wasn't seeing Sylvie or his father to watch over his son. Teddy now estimated his sailboat to be speeding along at more than forty knots, and was grateful, despite the boat's current unwieldiness, because he recognized his need to reach shore before a mammoth wave swallowed James up and dragged him into the ocean. Teddy believed he was now close enough that James could hear him, so he yelled to his son:

"James! Stay back from the water! Get back!"

In spite of his father being away for an extended period, and accepting Mummie's explanation that Daddy had gone to heaven and wasn't returning home, James was sure he recognized his father's black boat with dark red sails, so he staggered through the wind, toward the water.

"Back James! Get back! Away from the water!" Teddy screamed, motioning resolutely with his hand.

Teddy was less than fifty meters from shore, and the winds seemed to increase in intensity. He now considered abandoning the wheel, so that he could attempt to haul in the sails and just glide to shore.

Suddenly, an enormous wave crashed at James' feet, which caused the youngster to fall sideways, and Teddy lost sight of him; he believed the wave had pulled James into the water. Teddy wrestled with the wheel to steer to the left, where he guessed James to be, and visualized himself running the sailboat aground, hopping out and rescuing his son.

Much to his relief, once the wall of water flattened out, he noticed James rolling up on his own. Teddy continued his course to the left and, currently, was a few meters from shore.

James stood and again cried, this time from the trauma of the wave knocking him down. The boy was a sopping wet mess of sand and mud, but Teddy knew that that was all reversible. James' tearful expression instantly transformed into elation, however, once recognizing his father in the approaching boat. He subsequently trundled several feet to his right, directly into the path of the oncoming hooker, as Teddy ran the boat up on the beach and crushed his sweet baby James.

Realizing what had happened, Teddy leapt out of the sailboat and worked like a madman, trying to lift and push the boat off his son, but it took another crashing wall of water, several minutes later, to finally dislodge the hooker. He then performed CPR on James, but the oxygen that had been pressed from the toddler's lungs was the least of his problems; he had already died from massive internal injuries.

After numerous failed attempts at resuscitating James, a teary-eyed Teddy carried his dead son up to the house, only to discover Sylvie's bluing corpse wrapped in a bed sheet in the backyard. Later, he would discover from a neighbor that his father had also died – all this, on the heels of having killed and cannibalized his best friend at sea.

This had just been the inception, really, for Teddy Halloran. Indeed, Teddy would be subjected to countless other calamities and tragedies during his lifetime, after taking possession of the hooker. And I couldn't help but again reflect on how the lives of its past owners and passengers, as well as friends and family in the periphery, were affected in some profound way. It also caused me to wonder how Angus Wilde had first come across the hooker, and what the boat's dubious history was before he acquired it. I must question Angus if ever encountering him in this otherworldly margin. If not, perhaps the Omniscient One will favor me with His enlightenment, not that He's obliged to do so.

Sadly, the *real* Teddy Halloran would never make the connection between his underhanded acquisition and ensuing miseries, and, instead, regularly voiced his assorted grievances into the bottom of a whiskey bottle, while sitting on the porch and looking out toward Great Blasket Island. Yet he endures.

As for Tedi the Yeti, his windblown ashes are stomped almost daily, during spring and autumn months, by trekkers ascending to Everest Base Camp.

About the Author

Born in Boston, Massachusetts, H.J. Walkins is a former plainclothes U.S. Secret Serviceman, who served in every major protective division of the U.S. Secret Service, to include the Presidential and Vice-Presidential Protective Divisions, during the Reagan and Bush (41) administrations. He retired as a Special Agent of the Department of Defense. He also served in the U.S. Marine Corps at the American Embassies in Jakarta, Indonesia and Manila, Philippines. Mr. Walkins received his Bachelor of Science degree, Magna Cum Laude, from Saint Joseph's College, Standish, Maine.

The author lives in the short hills of the Blue Ridge Mountains of Virginia, where he raises cold-weather mountain sheep. He holds dual citizenship with Ireland and has traveled extensively throughout the Emerald Isle.

********Bonus Material********

The following sample story appears in a fiction series soon to be released by H.J. Walkins

Sad Maddie Weller

Maddie Weller wasn't well. Maddie wished she was *weller*, but she wasn't well at all. The last time Luke Holcomb saw Maddie, they literally bumped into each other at a recycling station. Luke had been wobbling with a stack of newspapers, ready to plunk them down, when the early middle-aged woman emerged from the side of a bottles and cans repository.

"Hi, Maddie."

"Hello," Maddie said with distrust in her face.

Luke perceived that Maddie didn't recognize him, even though he was a distant neighbor who happened upon her once or twice yearly over the past thirteen years.

"I'm your neighbor... Luke. I helped you move some firewood that day about five winters ago."

Maddie seemed to exude some recollection in her aspect, but Luke was impressed that she merely recalled the undertaking of having moved the wood and had forgotten her helper.

Luke was actually being kind when referring to it as firewood. Upon encountering Maddie, that bleak winter day, they had been

355

far away from their respective homes, and the wood was long from being burnable. Luke had typically been on a walk with his dog, and Maddie was dragging two dead tree branches, not simultaneously, mind you, because, together, the branches were too unwieldy to manage. First, she dragged one branch for about fifty yards, set it down at the side of the road, and then returned to haul the other sizeable branch, placing it with the first, which she resumed dragging. Once reckoning Maddie's laborious, time-consuming activity, Luke had paused to aid her, by lugging one of the heavy branches to her home, which was in emblematic disrepair.

"I'm the one who's always walking his dog along Harpers Ferry Road," Luke said, shoving the stack of newspapers into the recycle bin.

Maddie finally made the association.

"Oh, *yeah.*"

"How's everything going, Maddie?" Luke asked with some condescension.

Luke had a pretty good indication of how things were going, by the woman's characteristic appearance; however, whether she harbored those same beliefs, about the state of her life, hinged on the words she was about to utter. It was a particularly warm spring morning, which would only draw warmer as the day progressed, yet Maddie wore a floppy, wool winter hat, a turtleneck sweater full of snags and holes and badly stretched out at the neck, a tattered, lined windbreaker, and winter boots. The food-stained, brown pants she wore were ripped on one leg up to her knee, and revealed a conspicuous film of dirt on her shin, which matched the grime on her face and hands. Luke slyly edged backward, once sensing an objectionable odor emanating from the lamentable woman.

"I'm not doing too well," she said.

"Oh, I'm sorry to hear that, Maddie," Luke said in a manner that begged to satisfy his curiosity.

"Yeah, people tell me I'm mentally ill."

Luke wasn't surprised to hear Maddie say that, although, during his first encounters with her more than a decade earlier, he thought she might've sustained a head injury. He arrived at the conclusion because, on the whole, the woman had appeared lucid, and managed to live on her own in a farmhouse on a considerable tract of land. Nevertheless, he now realized that she had declined in recent years.

"There are some good medications out there, Maddie. Are you taking any meds?"

"Uh-huh. But sometimes I forget to take them. Other times people steal 'em."

"Steal them?" Who's stealing your medications?"

"A man and woman break into my house at night. He rapes me while she steals from me."

"Do they steal anything besides your meds?"

"Food and cigarettes."

Given her unmistakable, deteriorating condition, Luke doubted that little of what the woman had to say was true.

"Have you tried calling police?"

"They're *in* on it."

"Oh, they *are*?"

"What about your Dad? Have you called him to help you?"

"He's in on it, too."

"Well, Maddie, I hope you get the help you need, because you've got lots going on in your life. It sounds like you probably need to go back to see the doctor, first... so he can write a new prescription to replace your missing medications."

"I think it'll be easier if I just kill myself. I mean... don't you think?"

"Oh, you don't want to go and do that, Maddie. There are too many people who enjoy you being around. I know I always like running into you in town."

"Yeah, a lot of people *do* enjoy me being around... especially the ones who rape me and steal my food and cigarettes."

"Well, I hope you solve your problems soon, Maddie. But, in the meantime... would you do a favor? Would you please promise that you'll make an appointment to see your doctor... and then remember to keep the appointment?"

"Yeah, I'll do that."

Luke then watched in horror as the deranged woman climbed behind the wheel of her old, scraped up sedan and drove away. His mind reeled while resuming his recycling tasks. He wondered how Maddie supported herself and did simple things like get her vehicle inspected

357

and renew her registration and drivers license. *She must be receiving help in life*, he thought. Luke soon became fixated on learning more about Maddie's sad life, ultimately, in order to help her.

Luke presently began walking his dog in the evening so that he could monitor the activities at Maddie Weller's home. Three nights after altering his walking schedule, he noticed a jalopy, with West Virginia plates, parked next to Maddie's car, so he doubled back and sneaked along the old abandoned chicken farm until passing onto Maddie's property. It was just past 8 p.m., and the revealing sun was rapidly setting. Luke only hoped that some critter didn't dart out from the abutting woods and excite his dog, because the commotion would inevitably attract attention from inside Maddie's house.

Luke, first, peered through the middle window of the small, one-level farmhouse and determined that he was looking into the den. The television was on, but nobody sat nearby to watch it. He slinked three steps to the right, to another window, and observed a heavyset, bleach-blonde woman rifling through some kitchen drawers and cabinets.

"Where'd ya hide the ciggies, this time, *youuu* sneaky bitch?!" the woman yelled down the hall. She stood and waited for a response but heard nothing so sat down at the breakfast bar, from where she could view the television. On the counter, next to her, sat two plastic sacks filled with miscellaneous groceries, which she had hand-selected from the refrigerator and pantry. The woman picked up a lit cigarette from an ashtray on the breakfast bar and took a draw from it. Maddie's voice could finally be heard. She was responding to the woman's query:

"I quit them cancer-sticks, I told, *youuu*" she yelled from the bedroom.

"Liar!" the woman shouted and stood to march toward Maddie. "I smelled cigarette smoke the moment we arrived!"

"That's yer own smoke, yer smellin'," Maddie said.

"Liar! Liar! Liar! she yelled. The woman now looked into the bedroom at her husband lying on top of Maddie, who wore only her brazier.

Outside the home, Luke had since scampered down to the bedroom window, to watch and listen to the same hostile conversation, and he beheld Maddie being raped.

"Ya didn't even take her bra off, ya slouch! Remove her *god-dernt* bra!" she commanded her husband.

"She smells, Momma. I don't wanna lick her."

"*Lordee*," the woman said, and turned about face to return to her smoldering cigarette.

"When are you gonna take a bath, li'l Miss?" the rapist asked.

"Never! Not as long as *you* keep comin' 'round! Don't you know that I remain foul so that you can no longer stand me? But you just keep comin' back for more... because you're a pig... like yer wife!"

"Momma, Maddie's calling us *pigs*," the man turned to shout.

"Just find out where she's hidin' the *god-dang* ciggies, fool!" she yelled back.

After the man finished his business, he collected his clothes and ambled, nude, down the hall to the den. Maddie remained in bed, seemingly numbed, for a long moment, but then rose to shut the door and dress herself. Once the man put on his clothes, his wife ordered him to carry the plastic sacks, containing groceries, out to their car. She then glanced down the hall and noticed that Maddie had closed the bedroom door.

"Watch what happens *next time* if I don't find *no* cigarettes, crazy lady!" she shouted and slammed the door behind her.

Luke crept along the backside of the home until reaching the end, where he could scrutinize their car more closely. He recognized the make and model, but the car had been parked too far away to make out the license plate, beyond the familiar color and font-style that helped identify the state.

Thirty minutes later, Maddie called police to report the crimes committed at her home. Accordingly, the dispatcher relayed the information to two patrol officers riding in the vicinity.

"Mad Maddie's at it again," one officer said to the other, with discernible angst.

They neglected to respond.

Two nights later, Maddie's aging father, Franklin Weller, stopped by after supper to routinely look in on his daughter; he and his late wife had once lived in the old farmhouse where Maddie currently dwelled. Franklin had long known that his daughter wasn't well. That's why he made sure Maddie had a place to live, for free, while he made a modest monthly mortgage payment on a condo unit in a seniors-only complex at the opposite end of town. At least, there, he could enjoy some peace and privacy during his remaining years. In recent years, county property taxes had skyrocketed, and although Franklin was able to deduct the obligation when filing his annual income tax, the mounting tax had, much to his dismay, eroded his purchasing power. He thusly justified filching cigarettes from his daughter, whenever visiting, to help support his smoking habit.

The next evening that Luke Holcomb was out walking his dog, he noticed a police car parked at Maddie Weller's farmhouse, and felt relieved but curious; he knew it would be riskier than ever, with police present, to trespass onto her property and peep through a window to discover what measures were finally being taken to help the sad woman.

Once loitering along the, now familiar, backside of the home, Luke stole a look into the den and perceived a uniformed officer sitting on the couch while enjoying a soft drink, smoking a cigarette, and watching a sitcom rerun.

"Don't wear her out," the officer shouted toward the bedroom. "Save some for me."

Luke traipsed to the bedroom window and peered in to see the other officer still dressed, save for his skivvies and trousers pulled down around his ankles. Plus he still wore his shoes. The officer lay on top of a nude, visibly soiled Maddie while raping her.

"I'm not sure you want any of this, tonight," the officer yelled to his partner in the den. He then looked into Maddie's sad eyes. "When are you going to take a bath, woman?"

"NEVER!" Maddie screamed.

Maddie Weller wasn't well. Maddie wished she was weller, but she wasn't well at all.